For those who find comfort in the melancholy

ALSO BY CAMILLA ANDREW

The Sanguine Sorceress (The Essence of the Equinox 0.5)
When The Stars Alight (The Essence of the Equinox
Book 1)

Book Two Of

THE ESSENCE OF THE EQUINOX

CAMILLA ANDREW

We Will Devour The Night
Copyright © Camilla Andrew 2024

An Inkwell of Nectar Press

Camilla Andrew asserts the moral right to be identified as the author of this work. A catalogue record for this book is available from the British Library.

This novel is entirely a work of fiction. The names, characters and incidents portrayed in it are the work of the author's imagination. Any resemblance to actual persons, living or dead, events or localities is entirely coincidental.

For information contact :
contact@aninkwellofnectar.com
https://www.aninkwellofnectar.com

Edited by Molly Rookwood

Cover art & Illustrations by Eeva Nikunen

Drop caps by Megan Wyreweden

ISBN (paperback) 9781739308926
eISBN 9781739308964

First Edition: September 2024

10 9 8 7 6 5 4 3 2 1

CONTENT WARNING

PRAISE FOR CAMILLA ANDREW

"Just as rich and decadent as the first book in the series, WE WILL DEVOUR THE NIGHT is a brilliant and sensual must-read for fans of yearning, complicated love, nuanced characters, and intricate politics in a fantasy setting."

Morgan Dante, author of *A Flame in the Night*

"WE WILL DEVOUR THE NIGHT lures the reader back into a sensual and deadly world of magic and immortals, putting on display Camilla Andrew's full world-building prowess. The political and the interpersonal dance a tense waltz in this sequel that explores the beautiful and terrible ways that magic can heal or destroy."

Ladz, author of *The Fealty of Monsters*

"In WHEN THE STARS ALIGHT, Camilla Andrew serves up luscious prose to deliver a romantic fantasy that is equal parts delectable dream and decadent nightmare as tensions mount between two compelling leads on opposite sides of the same political coin."

Ladz, author of *The Fealty of Monsters*

"Camilla Andrew's WHEN THE STARS ALIGHT is a dream for fans of the decadent fantasy of ASOIAF, the lush prose of Angela Carter, and the gothic sensibilities of CRIMSON PEAK. Darius and Laila are two of my favorite fantasy characters I've read about in recent years."

Morgan Dante, author of *A Flame In The Night*

"WHEN THE STARS ALIGHT is a must-read for villain x heroine enthusiasts. Luminous Laila and seductively calculating Darius form an aesthetic dream of a pairing, thanks to Camilla Andrew's lush worldbuilding and spellbinding prose. An absolute romantasy gem."

Audrey Rose, author of *Dragonsong*

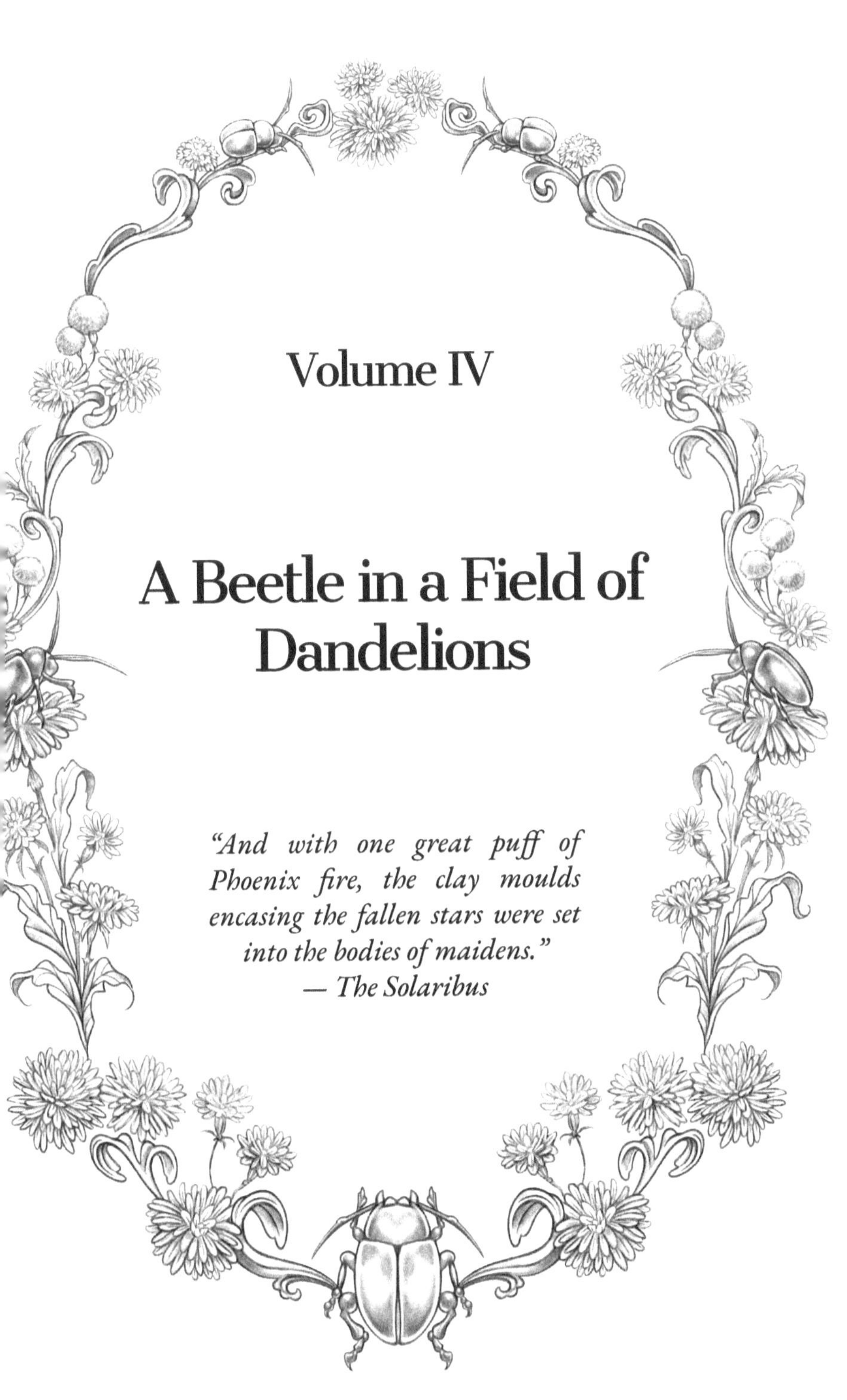

Volume IV

A Beetle in a Field of Dandelions

"And with one great puff of Phoenix fire, the clay moulds encasing the fallen stars were set into the bodies of maidens."
— The Solaribus

I

IT HAPPENED ON NIGHTS LIKE THIS.

On certain nights, when the planets aligned, there would be stars struck with a wanderlust so heavy it ripped them clean from the skies. They fell in a celestial shower towards the cradle of the sea, washing ashore along the sands of Soleterea.

As this occurred so infrequently, it incited a frantic response among the solarites, who had the coasts cleared and consecrated to ritually harvest the souls of their new descendants. They arrived carrying nets of moth-silk gauze and tanks full of plasma which they used to carry the stars to safety.

Though these events rarely wrought more than a few dozen stars in total, those that fell had a finicky habit of rolling up in the most elusive of spots. So the solarites would make a sport of it—splitting off into sets of two or three to scour the beaches, ensuring every star was claimed.

In one of these sets Princess Laila could be found, her net at the ready and her competitive soul in full throttle. She had made a wager between herself and her ladies to see who could amass the most stars, and she was determined not to be outdone.

"Come on, girls!" Laila's voice rang out to her protégées, bouncing across the wet iridescent sand.

Behind her, Oriel and Astrid were attempting to balance the handles of the tank between them to keep from sloshing puddles of plasma onto the shore. Within the glass, eight stars floated in suspension, faint white aureoles surrounding them like dandelion clusters.

Laila turned back to the star in her sights, detected by its kaleidoscopic silhouette. She nudged the star into her net and carried it over to the tank. "And this makes nine." She dropped the star into the plasma with a triumphant smile.

"Should be more than plentiful to claim a win, Your Radiance," Oriel said, hopeful this would spell the end of her labour.

Laila hummed in uncertainty.

"Surely you do not suppose we should find others?" Oriel hopped from one foot to the other in distress, looking across the crowded beach to their fair-headed kin. "Why, the shores have been picked clean!"

"Just one more," Laila said, coyly holding up a finger. "One."

Oriel and Astrid groaned in unison.

"Oh, come on, you spoilsports." Laila chuckled softly as she propped her net on her shoulder and tilted her head. "Ten is a... nice, round number. Respectable." She gave a firm nod. "At ten, I will stop. And as promised, there will be a huge, fattening sundae in it for both of you."

Predictably, that had them perking up in an instant, and on the promise of sundaes they followed close behind their leader like pearls led on a string.

Laila skipped past the vivacious skirts of seafoam, intent on searching the gap between two blue-grey rocks in the distance. Her nape prickled with the sense of aether—the mystical element all those of celestial origin emitted. A pungent odour wafted from the mineral as she neared, and she steadied herself with a hand on the damp, rugged surface to peer around the bend.

And there she found it: a star nestled in a patch of sand. A parade of star-motes danced along the flecks of hidden crystal within the craggy rocks and made a firmament of them.

Laila shook her head to clear the trance of this mesmerising sight, then prepared her net for a catch. But before she could claim her prize she was intercepted by another net—one belonging to the smilingly impudent Hélène Mielette.

"Oh, do forgive me, Your Radiance! Was that meant to have been *your* star? How troublesome." Hélène fixed her face in an expression of feigned sympathy tinged with self-satisfaction.

Laila smoothed out her rage like she would a crease on her skirt. Good sportsmanship would require her to accept the loss with grace— even if impulse would have her swat Hélène's smug mouth with her net.

"It's not a problem, Hélène," Laila said, sticking her net into the sand as a display of surrender. "Finders keepers, and all that."

"Indeed," Hélène agreed with a toss of straightened pearl-blonde hair over her shoulder. She scooped the star into her net and then deposited it into the tank held by her lady. "How many are we at now, Luna?"

"I believe this would make seven stars, madame."

Hélène gasped in faux-surprise. Her lilac eyes radiated with glee.

"Seven stars, well isn't that a feat! I had only managed five last harvest. Still, it was enough to win in any case."

"Seven stars is a most impressive number, Hélène," Laila praised, sweet as apple pie crust. She heard the horn blow in the distance and knew the last of the stars had been swept from the beach. "You are certain to make a grand statement when it comes to rankings."

With that, she turned on her heel and prepared to retreat.

"Say, I can't help but notice you're being rather coy about your own haul," Hélène said in displeasure, resting one hand on her hip. "It's nothing to be ashamed of, I'm sure. What was it? Five? Six?" She paused to wet her lips in thought. "Four?"

The latter provoked a titter from Luna.

"Every star collected is a victory worth celebrating, Hélène. I'd be as proud of four stars as I would of nine," Laila said over her shoulder. She gave her a regal wave. "See you at the podium."

"Why did you lie about your number?" Astrid whispered once they'd made enough distance.

"Let her think she's won this battle." Laila waved her off. "I'm a generous sort, after all. And this war is mine to be won."

A statement, they would all soon see, that pertained to far more than this frivolous affair.

Once the stars had all been collected, the solarites secured their tanks on the ætherald-powered aero-lorry to be delivered to the Nursery—the haven where stars would be stored to await insertion into their new bodies by a prospective solarite mother—for safekeeping.

Laila had been to the Nursery only a handful of times after harvests, as the building was under restricted access most days. She could recall the maze-like formation of rounded glass tanks gurgling with warm fluid, kept under the careful watch of the Holy Phoenix—a statue that symbolised the avatar of Asemani, who blew the flame that set their first bodies from clay into flesh.

The room's molten aroma never failed to remind her of air singed by a strike of lightning, a scent still as potent when she walked in to survey the newest arrivals. She pressed her hand against the hot crystal carapace of a chamber as from within a star twinkled exuberantly in response.

"Preparing to make your own selection?"

Laila swivelled round to see Alia Rose, the Nursery governess and her own aunt, draped in her blue silk mantle embroidered with stars in gold thread, and she clutched her chest with a hearty laugh. "Oh, heavens, no! I'm far from prepared for motherhood." *If ever.*

She tried to envision herself with a portly pink bundle in her arms, feeding her starlight from breast or bottle and keeping her crib by a curtainless window so the sun could toast her skin to the golden brown hue of their kind.

The thought kindled a vague sensation of wrongness, so she tried to reel even further back. To think of each painstakingly precise knead as she sculpted her perfect babe from kaolin and rosewater, painting the golden veins with her ichor before finally inserting the star that would bring her daughter to life.

Neither image did anything more than leave her feeling distinctly out of body, like she was watching someone else do it even when she installed herself in that place. It would not be forced upon her, this she knew with assurance, for it was the refusal of one of her ancestors to create an heiress that led to the electoral college deciding upon future rulers thereafter.

"It's smart of you to consider," Alia said, moving closer to her. "Not every solarite does. My sister included."

Laila snorted in disdain as her aunt's words called to mind a similar conversation they'd had decades prior.

"My role here is simply to assess whether a potential mother has the means to care for a starlet. Whether she has sufficient wealth, support, mental and physical competency—"

"What about love?" Laila asked, her jaw clenching. *"What about nurturance?"*

"These things are impossible to assess from reports alone."

Laila sighed as she turned back to the chamber. She knew it wasn't Alia's fault her mother had been approved for maternity, but it had felt better to offset the burden of blame to an external party. To stop having to root for the fault within herself.

"I can't fathom being responsible for another person."

"Yet if you desire to be impératrice, you will be responsible for many."

"That's different," Laila replied instantly.

"How?"

Though she knew the question would come, she could not yet voice how it was different. She could only return to herself as a child, looking up to her mother with big, pleading eyes.

"More distance," she decided to answer. Then she plastered on a smile. "Well, I can see everything is in order here. So I shall leave you to it."

"Of course," Alia said, lavender eyes tender with warmth. "Just know you are always welcome, Laila. Perhaps not here, but my château is always open to you."

Amira had never been close with her sisters, had always instilled in

Laila the notion that they were weaker branches of the family tree whose influence would rot her budding blossom. For this reason, Laila had never been able to close the broadening gap within their dynasty. She doubted she would be able to start now.

"Thank you, Aunty," Laila said, offering her a lukewarm smile of cordiality that implied she truly did mean to consider her invitation, and then she continued on her path to the exit.

∽

When she reached the courtyard of Château de Rosâtre, the grounds buzzed with activity. Laila rolled down the window of her milk-white aero-limousine and tried, in vain, to stretch her head far enough to see beyond the spring-blooming hedges of gold roses, the cluster of sprites gathered at the gilded gates.

"Cressida, what's going on?" Laila asked the gatekeeper once they'd neared, her elbow propped on the car door.

"A visitor." Cressida could barely keep from rolling her eyes. "From Mortos."

The name seemed to melt the crowd, as if by sheer malediction, bringing the hippogriff-led coach at the centrepiece hurtling into view.

Laila recognised it intimately—this particular model had been stationed in the courtyard many times over the past two decades. Its shape resembled a large black-lacquered armoire with silver six-headed eagles embossed into the metal. The rex's coat of arms.

"Still behind the times, I see." Laila clicked her tongue in disapproval. A light jest in reference to how sentimentally those in Mortos kept to their tradition of hippogriff travel. Most others in Vysterian high society had been making the gradual transition to the aeromobile, a recent invention from Odakan aeromagy. "You'd think receiving the rex's envoy would create less of a spectacle by now."

"You know how it is when a Mortesian visits." Cressida sighed in displeasure. "They can neither arrive nor leave without causing a stir."

"So it would appear." Laila's lips quirked in response as she withdrew into her seat and wound up the window.

Now the aero-limousine was in view, the sprites had begun to scatter, making ample way for her driver to land before a sprite guard opened the door for her.

"Her Luminosity has requested you join her in the audience salon to receive her guest."

Laila took his gloved hand in her own and straightened his silk cravat with the other, offering him a smile in gratitude. "Thank you, Narcisse."

She ascended the steps into the stuccoed hall and pivoted round into the salon, surprised to discover it empty. Laila sighed, realising that her mother's tardiness would be why she had been put to the duty of reception. She wasted little time acquainting herself with the room's refreshments.

She stuffed a blue macaron into her mouth and filled her glass with rosewater. She was rinsing down her macaron with a hefty sip when a knock on the door halted her.

Laila spluttered on her drink before clearing her throat. "Yes, come in." She lowered her glass as the sprite herald opened the door.

"Your Radiance, if I might present—"

"Our awaited guest from Mortos!" Laila declared brightly, turning on her heel. She knew she'd need to launch in quickly with the regrets for her mother's timing. "Yes, you must be positively exh—"

"Hello, princess."

Laila's words tangled in her throat until she released only a shaky, choked sound. Her smile, her voice, and all coherency of speech perished on her lips at the sound of those words. Even after twenty years, they seemed to glide with liquid ease down her spine.

Darius Calantis entered the room, the crawl of a smirk already sprouting on his lips, snuffing any lingering doubt over whether it was truly him she had heard.

Upon seeing him so near and so vividly, Laila barely noticed her glass slipping from her fingers. It burst into sharp confetti against the marble tile and left a puddle at her feet.

II

ARIUS GLANCED DOWN AT THE PIECES OF BROKEN glass at Laila's feet, then trailed his eyes back up to her face with a smile. "I can see I might've caught you off-guard."

Laila suppressed the impulse to scoff as she gestured towards the splinters and made them glow with aether. She knew Amira would have her head if she encountered a mess. "Not at all, Darius Rex. The impératrice should be with you in a moment, if you'd please take a seat."

He didn't move, at first, remaining leaned against the wall to observe her. The decades had treated him well, if sight alone was any indication. His dark hair had retained those loose princely waves. He had altered the Mortesian court fashion—his black velvet kaftan extended well past his knees to the floor, bordered with oak leaf embroidery in gold thread. A matching belt emphasised the slightness of his waist, and a parting in the garb's thigh revealed a black set of form-fitting breeches.

Laila took a furtive peek at his elegant pose before redirecting her concentration to the mending of the glass. "Won't you please sit rather than skulking in that corner? You are unnerving me."

"Forgive me." He chuckled, head cocking to one side. "I was just admiring your handiwork. Rather convenient, your aether magic. I wish chaos provided the same skill."

To this, she said nothing. She took the newly repaired glass in hand and sat down on the settee, pointing towards the other vacant chair.

Darius took the opportunity to refamiliarise himself with the salon. His eyes swept over the sumptuous giltwork panels and heavy green silk curtains, the bronze wall sconces with glass rose-petal lampshades. He took his place on the settee carved in the form of a gilt rose-garden trellis and propped one leg atop the other.

Laila cleared her throat, smoothing out her linen shorts. "So?"

"So," he answered.

Laila laughed airily. "I feel as though one of us ought to say something."

"How about we start with the customary, then?" Darius gave a half-shrug with his elbows. "You look well."

"Well enough, I suppose." Laila tucked a stray curl behind her ear, peeking up at him through demure lashes. She was aware her satin blouse and linen shorts were a simple affair, and she felt uncharacteristically underdressed before his regal attire. "Had I known you were coming, I would've—" She shook her head, realising how puerile the concern for her appearance was. "Why are you here?"

"I was invited, directly, upon the summons of the impératrice herself."

It dawned on Laila that she ought to consider this yet another test from her mother. Amira *wanted* to see how Laila would react in Darius's presence. In light of this, she was determined to keep her true emotions tucked beneath the surface.

"And where is our impératrice this fine spring afternoon?" Darius asked.

"Likely withheld by a prior engagement." Laila poured them both a glass of rosewater. "Hence I am at the helm of your welcome committee."

"Well, I can certainly fathom worse hosts." Darius scooped up the glass and perched it between his sensuous lips, a dimple forming in his razor-boned cheek as he smiled.

The smile alone made her want to fidget, coaxing a warmth to her cheeks that threatened to soften her lacquered veneer. She took a sip of water to neutralise it. After nearly five decades of this, Laila thought she'd been prepared for the sheer levels of spite Amira had in store for her. Yet her mother continued to surpass expectations.

"If the impératrice asked for you directly, then the matter must be grave." She would keep the conversation removed, political. He was just a king, after all, a foreign king of a foreign land. There was no reason to read too much in the way his eyes rested upon her countenance with a lover's fondness. "You haven't been causing *too* much havoc up north in such a short amount of time, surely?"

"Twenty years since we've seen each other, and already you launch into matters of state." He shook his head with a wry chuckle. "That's a fine record. But you can't expect that I would give myself over that easily."

"I fail to see what you mean—"

"If you want a tête-à-tête, then I expect to be asked properly. Trying to extract me for mere dregs minutes before the arrival of your mother isn't befitting of that Soleterean etiquette I so know and love." His smile broadened, along with the depressions in his cheeks. "Ask me to dinner."

She was so startled she almost didn't know what to say. "Excuse me?"

"I was thinking... tonight, perhaps?"

Affront burned on her cheeks. "You have some nerve."

His words had the intended effect, causing her to lose decorum. She ought to have known he'd come prepared to break her most predictable form of defence. He wanted to dismantle her guard, chip away at all that finely-glazed polish to someplace still raw and sensitive and exposed that she had not yet learned to fold away behind prim-laced pleasantries.

"I'm only asking for one meal with you, Laila," Darius said, his eyes as crystalline clear as a blue tarn. Though not nearly as innocuous. "Where's the harm in that?"

It was the first time he used her name, and the effect was immediate. She glanced away to shield her face from him.

He was right in saying that one meal would be a harmless thing— had she been dining with anyone but him. However, Laila had enough self-awareness to question whether she could trust herself. And yet, curiosity overruled...

"Well?" Darius asked, having taken a lengthy sip of water in patience. "What do you say?"

Laila pressed her lips together, eyes roaming over him with scepticism. Could she survive an evening with the serpent without becoming infected by his venom? It took a moment before her resolve depleted, ever so slightly. Then her lips gradually parted in a willingness to accept.

The door opened at that very moment to announce Amira's exceedingly convenient arrival. One would almost think she'd been eavesdropping, preparing for her precise timing to strike.

Laila shot up from the settee in an instant. "Maman!"

Amira entered in a blue striped walking suit appliquéd with flowers, a large feathered hat covering her platinum braids. "Welcome back, Darius Rex. I hope the princess has been tending to you well in my absence."

"Your Luminosity." Darius stood to bow. Here was where he played at being the well-tailored beast, not like the other coarse-mannered brutes of his kind. He had learned to maintain respectability and make play that he was domesticated. Brought to heel. Brought under *her* heel at least. And what a fine one it was this afternoon—white leather with a gilt birdcage frame adorned with flowers.

"Princess Laila has been enchanting. As always."

"Pleased to hear it." Amira narrowed her gaze on her daughter. "You may leave us now, Laila."

"But—" Laila halted, knowing better than to question that imperious stare. She dipped her head coyly. "It was nice to see you again, Darius Rex." She cast another secretive look towards him before making her exit.

Amira invaded the seat she'd vacated, removing her cream lace gloves. "Well, the reapers certainly work fast, but you work faster, it seems."

"I am unsure of what you would expect, dangling her in front of me like that." Darius returned to his catlike repose on the settee.

"Oughtn't you to have taken on a Mortesian bride by now? Rutted her to produce heirs? Or whatever undignified acts you creatures partake in to spawn more of you..." Amira waved a hand in dismissal as she picked up a macaron.

Darius did not rise to the bait.

"I suppose this is beside the point now, isn't it?" Amira took a sharp crunch out of her macaron. "We'll skip to the subject of why you're here, shall we?"

"I do apologise that I didn't sooner answer your call," Darius said without a hint of irony. He kept his head slightly bent, shoulders tractable. He knew Amira would want a show of his humbleness, and so he would give her one. "Mortos has been seeing some difficult times as of late."

"Yes, I have been hearing there have been a number of qarna insurrections in the hinterlands," Amira said, plump lips curving upwards. Having others ingratiate themselves to her was always the most satisfying part of her role. "You haven't been having trouble feeding them again, I'd hope?"

Darius massaged his temples, suppressing a sigh for what would come. Little did he like to expose his vulnerable underbelly to the White Lioness, but he'd found himself out of options. "The summer hasn't been what we'd hoped it would be. And the typical channels I'd turn to for aid have been compromised. My prefects forecast the winter is likely to be abominable and will cause—"

Amira's amethyst eyes lit up with understanding. "A famine."

"Indeed," Darius confirmed. "I've been trying my best to prepare for it, but unless I can tackle this one mitigating factor... the results won't be favourable."

"Yes, I'm sure." Another punctuated bite of her macaron followed. "While we're on the subject of disasters, certain areas of the continent have seen an alarming increase in chaotic magic activity since we opened our doors to your kind. You can understand that—chaos magic being a forbidden art here—it has come to be some cause for concern to see so many new incidents."

Darius chose his words carefully. "I must apologise for any... transgressions you've suffered on behalf of my people. I have made it well known in Mortos that chaotic magic must be limited in Vysteria. And I can assure you we are more than happy to facilitate deportations for any misuse—"

"It isn't your kind that concerns me," Amira interjected. "It's the humans."

Darius's brow arched in bewilderment. "Humans cannot practise chaos magic."

"Not in the way that you use it. But I've certainly seen evidence that they can be infected by it. Especially when in possession of a chaotic artefact."

His expression grew cagier. "What are you suggesting?"

"Someone in your country has been smuggling vast amounts of chaotic magic objects to certain... illicit dealers in Thalistan. I want you to find this person and apprehend them immediately. Or I shall have to rethink our trade arrangements. I'm sure I need not remind you of the infamous Moongrass Debacle—"

"I will look into it at once," Darius said.

"Regarding the matter of your crop problem... I am always open to renegotiating the ætherglass plan we once discussed."

Darius exhaled in disappointment, having expected nothing else. "I appreciate your generosity in this instance, but I must decline. Once again."

"Still?" Amira wiped down her fingers on a napkin. "I must impress that I believe your stubbornness is coming at a detriment to your country as a whole. I'd take some time to think on it... I'm sure you'll come around to see my view in due course."

He suppressed a hmph of amusement at that. There was only one reason Amira would be so persistent and "out of the kindness of her philanthropic heart" would be very far down that list. "I'll manage. Somehow, we always do."

"See that you do. You have done well to keep your menagerie of beasts in order for two decades thus far, Darius Rex. Let us not see all your efforts fall to ruin over a bout of famine and trafficking, shall we?"

Darius nodded in acquiescence and acknowledged the threat behind the words. *Keep your house in order. Or I shall send someone to order it.* He knew Amira did not trust him. She regarded him as something immeasurably crass to her but a necessity nonetheless: her tamed beast that kept all the other beasts from scratching away at the door.

"You are dismissed." Amira picked up another macaron.

Darius stood to bow and take his leave.

"Oh, and I expect you to make your way back to your accommodation without approaching my daughter along your path."

That had him freezing, against himself. But he ought not to have expected anything different.

"As you wish, Your Luminosity." He slinked out of the door without looking back.

Darius stayed in Le Creissant only one night before he was homeward bound again.

His black coach, led by hippogriffs, soared above the cobbled streets of Mortos, rousing the sleepy homes of the capital and its fiendish inhabitants. Darius loomed behind tinted glass, his face chiselled with troubled introspection. Beside him, a gold rose sat on a tufted seat of red velvet. Deep in thought, he slid his fingers across the petals, having plucked it from the pavilion before he'd left.

He should not have gone to Soleterea. He should've followed his instincts in recognising the lure Amira had set and sent someone else in his stead. He'd thought it would be enough to catch a glimpse of Laila after so many years, to hear the sweet timbre of her voice as she said his name. Small things he could commit to memory so that he might swaddle himself in them to keep him warm over a decade, a century.

However long it might be until her absence became tolerable to him. If it ever did.

He'd been foolish to think it'd ever stop there, that the moment he saw her he wouldn't feel the inevitable pull he always did to be in her orbit. He thought of the flash of her gold hair beneath the sunlight when the rigidity of her spine gradually loosened in his presence as though, for once, he could cease to be an object of fear.

It no longer mattered. She would always remain enskied in her world of laughter and light, unpoisoned by his degeneracy, while he would always be shackled to the accursed land of Mortos.

He picked up the rose and fastened it to a buttonhole on his kaftan.

Since the coup on Gravissia, the city had come back sleeker and sharper than ever before. New gargoyle-ridden towers had replaced the ones that had been felled by solarite starships. They stood solemn, edged with silver and gold, fitted with reflective panels of low reliefs and grotesques in the shape of raptors and wolves.

It was a modern eye that Darius had applied to the redesign of his capital, but he never failed to preserve the spirit of its origins for the more nostalgic. This sentiment extended to various other changes he'd made to Mortos during his reign so far, from the court fashion to the redecoration of the Citadel's interior itself—a slow purging of the unfortunate massacre that had occurred there.

The coach lowered to a stop inside the courtyard. A guard arrived to open the door, and Darius stepped out onto gravel still moistened from the last spring storm.

The Citadel panted smoke from a pre-lit fire as he entered. His arrival had been heavily anticipated, and the servants had already put together a tea set for him in the drawing room. There was the customary samovar with its pot of burnt honey, vol-au-vents with mushroom and shrimp filling, stinging nettle blini smothered with lingonberry compote, and lemon tea cakes.

He helped himself to one of the miniature yellow cakes, pouring himself a glass of hot tea with squeezed lemon. Then he retreated to the divan, flinging himself atop the serpentine frame as figured hippogriffs peered at him between the scrolls. His fall was cushioned by tufted seats of carmine velvet, plump and rich to his travel-weary form. He took a sip of tea still piping with steam, a bite of cake still moist, and for a moment allowed himself to entertain this pure moment of perfect peace.

"A visitor awaits you, Your Majesty," his corpse-servant Kirill droned from the shadows.

Darius massaged his temples with a sigh. He knew he would only have one caller at this hour. "Send him through." He took a sip of tea as the shadow of the figure elongated across his Seraji rug. "It's been a long journey, Delanus. You'd best make this quick."

"Forgive the intrusion, Your Majesty," his prime prefect replied, making cautious strides into the room with his cloak draped along one arm. "I am afraid I was too eager to hear what news you would bring from Soleterea."

"As disappointing as you might have predicted." Darius took a bite of lemon cake. "Impératrice Amira has yet another errand for us to run to stay in her good graces, under the threat of embargo."

"Curse it all!" Delanus clenched his fists, approaching an intricately carved armchair that matched the rest of the furniture. Maintaining a careful distance. A few decades prior he might have taken Darius's less than modest sprawl as an invitation to observe. But enough time spent serving under his rule had diluted Delanus's desire into fear—perhaps even more intensely than his predecessor.

"She has tasked me with uncovering some elusive trafficker of chaotic artefacts to humans," Darius said, one arm tucked beneath his head. An artful pose. He was still as beautiful to Delanus as ever, with his long throat, his doe-like yet angular features. But such a pleasing façade only served to disguise the putrid cruelty festering beneath it. A cruelty that, much unlike his father's, was committed by a startlingly lucid mind.

"Peddling artefacts to humans?" Delanus scoffed in disbelief. "Who would partake in such indignity?"

Darius chewed delicately on his lemon cake in thought. "I'd consider the pirates again, much like with the moongrass, but even they would be getting their supply from somewhere. Contact the sea wardens and have them on high alert for suspicious activity on the docks. However these artefacts are getting out, they are likely being boarded with inconspicuous cargo. Anyone with a vast amount of ships ought to be considered a suspect."

"Sounds like a task for your Eagle Eye." Always the play for Delanus. His answer to everything had become a tiresome excuse to thrust his daughter before Darius's eyes.

Darius sighed at the notion that he had not already considered that avenue. "Alas, she is currently still patrolling the forests for the infected. However, I may set her on the task to raid the docks with a convocation."

Delanus made a noncommittal sound, shifting in his seat.

Darius tilted his head in expectancy. "What is it, Delanus?"

"A spy sent me this today. It seemed relevant." Delanus reached within his kaftan to produce the scroll of a canvas tied with ribbon.

Darius snatched it from his grip and unfurled the scroll. His eyes roved over the dense greenery of the canvas, humidity practically seeping through the fabric. It was no land that could be found in Mortos. "The Parvani Rainforest." He tapped his lips in thought. "I suppose it's as good a lead as any. I'll have to get someone to start searching there. Dominus's body has been missing for twenty years now, and for twenty years I have sought, and failed, to locate it. Should he be alive and well by some divine intervention, it will be my foremost goal to ensure I find him before anyone else."

III

OWN IN THE RURAL OUTSKIRTS OF THE RAINFOREST, the earth trembled with the percussion of Thalistan. The music of this country was ancient and earthly, an ancestral magic seeping deep within the soil. It started as a constant seismic bassline, then shimmied up the boles of shaggy-haired treetops until it set to flight screeching flocks of tropical birds.

The rapturous hymnals of the witch-women answered the call of their land. The wind carried their voices, elevating them high into the trees where the spring blossoms matured into the lushest fruit.

The seasonal choir carried from the food forests to the battered dirt trail at the gateway of the wood, where Elina Panja entered the forest like a friend visiting for supper. The trees embraced her arrival, their intricate shadows detailing her skin in foliate patterns. This was a wizened road, natural and unrefined, worn into submission by the many heels and hooves that came before it.

Tonight, she meditated with the earth to renew connection to her aether—emerging fuller and wiser and more whole for the experience. On her back was a sack filled with snacks rolled tight in banana leaf—chunks of arrowroot and dried mango pieces sprinkled with chilli, a glass bottle of mint-infused rosewater in a woven basket cover.

She took a swig from her water bottle before looking up to trace the stars, knowing they would guide her path. She observed that the formation of the sky had shifted—a sign some stars had fallen.

The sight of falling stars always intrigued her as much as it saddened her, for it always led to questions that had been eternally left unanswered. No one truly knew how a star became a solarite, only that as soon as one fell another sprang up in its place. And when a solarite perished, a new star burned into existence. If nothing else, her kin agreed they looked like stars. For their light hair, purple eyes, and shimmering skin were stark opposites to the darker colouring of the Thal.

Elina made a sign of salute towards the mourning heavens before she carried on, the sticky vapour of rainforest heat thickening in her lungs. The palm trees multiplied around her with impassive sentience. They snuffed out what remained of the dwindling moonlight with a stretch of leaves, abandoning Elina to the mercy of a darkness that was not quite so still.

The strangler figs encroached soon after with their snaking venous roots, relentlessly choking the earth for sustenance, and in doing so demonstrated that all that was natural was not good, not kind, not built to nurture. Shrewd faces scrutinised passersby from the bodies of the trunks—their expressions too indecipherable to be mortal.

Elina remained undaunted by this, for this was the part of the country she liked best: when she could be in tune with the earth's natural symphony. The chirp of insects and the whistle of treetops as birds launched themselves from the branches. Her aether felt more elevated here, churning inside her core like a cobra constantly coiling and unfurling again, just waiting for a point of focus to lunge upon.

When Elina was a child, her grandmother taught her every living thing had a soul in it, and that this did not discriminate from trees to rocks to the very houses they lived in. Thus, if one were to listen closely, they might choose to speak with you, imparting special tree knowledge that only those with roots firmly planted in the earth understood. That was how the womenfolk came to wield aether; as Elina learned it, the trees had whispered to an expecting mother, who had passed it to her daughter and then her daughter's daughter and all the lineage since.

The trees barred Elina's way as she travelled, as though in stern warning. Their crooked arms dipped low with gnarled fingers for loose threads of hair or cloth to claim as penance for entry. Elina paused, took off her shoes, and tried to root her feet into the soil like she were a tree herself.

Closing her eyes, she respectfully sought passage into the area, and in response, the trees untangled, boles bending back, a trail of wildflowers yawning awake to welcome her inside. Elina smiled in gratitude as she crossed the threshold, the wildflowers bouncing back to vibrancy even after she stepped on them.

Had Elina followed the careful trail laid out for her, she might never have turned her head towards the malicious strangler fig in the distance. Nor caught a glimpse of what was encased inside. As it happened, fate had chartered a different course, and her mirth vanished when the trees revealed what they hid.

A little off the floral path, there was a fig. And within the clutches of the fig, a body. The fig was white as bone, gaunt as death, its vines having spidered across its unfortunate inhabitant until he was all but entirely webbed.

Perhaps the most telling thing about Elina was that she did not scream. A clinical calm overcame her as she stepped closer to inspect. There was a brief interval between spotting it and stepping closer in which Elina dared to question what she saw. But physician knowledge reinforced the bulge of what was undoubtedly a male body, forcing her to cease her carefree frolicking and commit to her duty of care.

He looked worse up close.

The vines had grafted themselves to his body until his skin split into gleaming pink wounds, his bones shattered beneath.

Elina lifted a hand, slowly at first, before her caution gave way to urgency. She knew the man had to be dead before she even reached him, but her instinct to examine persisted. He smelled foul with infection, his varicose veins ruptured into beetle-black bruises. Where his skin had split, deposits of black blood congealed into lumps.

Closing her eyes, she flattened her palm against the fig and willed it to release him. The fig clenched tighter around him instead. She inquired again. The grip strengthened in spite.

Elina lowered her hand with a frown. Figs could be such hateful things. Fortunately, in this case, she wasn't required to be polite. Not often did she use her aether to exert force over nature. The effects could be exhausting and, if resisted, disastrous. A witch's relationship to her element tended to be one of mutual cooperation. A back and forth, if you would. Where one asked through the tether of aether and the other answered.

Less commonly, said tether could be manoeuvred into a puppet string where a tug of wills commenced with the strongest prevailing. Having now engaged her aether-force, Elina used the strength of her will to splinter the fig until it broke apart into pieces at her feet.

After, she dusted stray shards from the body and put on her shoes. She took out her gloves from her sack next, the motion of putting them on giving her time to think. This wasn't the first time she'd encountered a corpse in the forest. Though it was by far the most unusual circumstance in which she'd found one.

Even buried beneath layers of earth and fungus, he had a swarthy look about him that might belong to her fellow countryman. If not for the height. She'd rarely encountered men taller than her, especially not over seven feet.

"Oh, my Lady... Now what's an occasso like you doing so far out here?" Elina murmured, slightly wary now she'd determined his species. She could see he was not marked like the others and drew her own conclusions.

She decided to check for a pulse, and to her surprise she found one, though it was worryingly faint. While they taught her little of occassi physiology at the academy, she knew enough to understand that unless their hearts were completely removed or destroyed they were impressively hard to kill. From here, she realised she could do terribly little. The healing factor of an occasso far surpassed her skill as a physician, and should she leave him to recover on his own, she could consider her role complete. In spite of this, his compromised condition proceeded to befuddle her. Surely, even at half-strength, an occasso would lay waste to a strangler fig with ease. And would he not wake by now?

Questions mounted until Elina sighed and transferred his large body to the forest floor. His muscle mass had depleted to a point where she wondered how long he had been trapped there. If she could get him breathing, his body was sure to do the rest.

She placed her fingers beneath his bearded chin and tilted it upright, freeing a passage to his lungs. Then she aligned her palms on his chest and compressed them in rhythm. She lost track of how many times she pumped air into before her arms tired. But when she paused for a break, the unthinkable occurred.

A strained, throaty gasp for breath.

Elina flung herself back in alarm, landing on the soft undergrowth.

With a few rapid-fire blinks, his eyes opened, darting analytically over the oval shape of Elina's face and pinpointing the exact spattering of freckles on her thin nose and cheeks.

"You all right now," she said gently, lifting her glove to trace over her healer's tattoo: a strip of eucalyptus leaves creeping from wrist to thumb, as though he might know what it meant. When he didn't respond to it, she spoke on. "I'm a physician. I found your body in the rainforest. You were about dead to the world. I helped revive you."

There was a flex of something indecipherable across his saturnine features. His eyes were green as the forest but the pupils were *round*, not the feline slits Elina would expect. She noticed there were other discrepancies too. His ears were blunted like a human's, and his wounds would not heal.

"You understand me, mister?"

He grunted in response before lifting himself off the ground. He stood with little difficulty, even managing a few steps before he staggered and fell to his knees.

"Oh, I wouldn't be up on your feet just yet," Elina advised, noting his wounds under the moonlight. It was sheer fortune he was not in worse shape.

"I have a lodge not far from here," he said, his face cracking like aged stone with every pain-filled movement he took. He spoke Thal, another unexpected feature. It was perfect but lacked the accent of the rural drawl. "I will rest there."

This surprised Elina, for not many people would make a home so deep into the rainforest. Even those who knew and loved it so well would not dare venture too far north into the territory that had long been claimed by monsters of legend.

The occassi are monsters of legend too, she thought, then remembered she was likely dealing with a fugitive.

"What happened to yer?" she asked without thinking.

He gave a withering look, one that made her muscles feel they were being slowly peeled from the bone.

"I can help… if you tell me." Her offer was a tender olive-branch extended, but the bestial air in his features made her want to retract it.

He moved quickly, not inhumanly quick but swift enough she was not prepared for what he did before he inhaled her. He stored her scent in his olfactory memory so he could track it for later: *gardenia, petitgrain, ylang-ylang, and grapefruit leaf.*

Elina exhaled in terror, her body quivering.

"You saved my life," he acknowledged, a collision of confusion and consideration in his voice, as though he were affirming the information and what to do with it.

Elina shook her head. "No sir, that's Goddess's grace you're bestowing me. You oughta thank her for those healing powers." She swallowed, muted intrigue expressed towards his odd physique. "Well… might not be Goddess in your case… I just sped up what was there."

"Regardless," he pressed on with a casual dismissal of her modesty. "It is customary to repay the services of valour and aid. What is your name, mata?"

She blinked suddenly, his accurate usage of her title catching her off-guard. "Panja."

"Well, Mata Panja." Dominus's lips curled in the faint impression of a smile. "It appears I owe you a debt."

IV

AMIRA PRODDED ONE OF THE STRAWBERRIES crowning her puff pastry with her fork. A light dispersion of berry blood squirted from the fruit, trickling down the tower of whipped cream. She lifted the fruit to her lips and chewed softly, sampling its sweetness. Then she placed her fork to one side.

On the lace-clothed table, melodies emanated from the music box of moonlight serenades she had received from her long-dead sprite lover, Orianna d'Orille, and a bouquet of pearlised musk roses fluctuated with a spectrum of colour in the light.

What caught her attention most, however, was the handheld mirror of ornate gold, which she now turned to face her. "Show me Madhali Azar."

The mirror replaced her silk-sheathed reflection with her magistress.

"Your Luminosity," Madhali said with a courteous nod.

"The sun has struck the first quarter, Magistress. I pray you have good news for me to start my day." Amira's candied tone was warm, yet the undertaste of her inferred threat was tantalisingly sharp.

"I have been looking into the Mielette dynasty as you've requested."

"And what have you found?" Amira squeezed lemon into her butterfly pea flower tea, tinting it from blue to violet.

"As you might have guessed, Lucrèce Mielette has been grooming her niece Hélène for candidacy."

This was just the subject Amira had been hoping to broach. The last quarter of an impératrice's one hundred and twenty–year reign was always a call for the next candidates to begin launching their campaign trails. To keep votes from fragmenting, the reigning impératrice always selected one candidate and the opposition another. This enacted the race course to victory, where runners for the throne would peacock for the favour of the Council of Elders to sway their support.

"Well, don't leave me in suspense." She sipped from her gilt-rimmed teacup. After her own victory against Lucrèce Mielette, Amira had been the first of the Rose dynasty to re-sit the throne after centuries. She refused to let it slip from their grasp. "What is it Lucrèce has up that sleeve of hers?"

"She's been spending a lot of time in Odaka. Mainly on religious missions. She seems to have been stirring up quite a bit of anti-occassi sentiment up north."

"I see," Amira replied, hacking off a chunk of pastry so it sputtered vanilla cream.

The topic of occassi was still divisive among their kind. She had hoped having Darius installed would have settled anxieties, but ever since the incident of occassi pirates flooding the highly addictive moongrass into Thalistan shores, conflict and mistrust between the nations had grown higher than ever.

"If Lucrèce intends to launch Hélène's campaign off the back of anti-occassi sentiment, then she would have a plan of action to offer something in place of our peaceful stance. Dig deeper."

"As you wish, madame," Madhali said. "And there is something else."

"Yes?"

"A few sightings of an occasso matching your description have appeared. Dark hair. Green eyes. Over seven feet."

Amira sipped from her tea in thought. Much like Darius, she had been on the search for Dominus's missing corpse for years, and until now, her search had proved fruitless.

"Where?"

"West Thalistan, madame. The Parvani Rainforest."

Amira drummed her fingers on the table. "I will assemble a team of Lightshields to investigate this further. Do not deploy any of your girls in this instance. We needn't spare any spies to do a soldier's job."

"Of course, madame."

"Cease transmission."

The image of Madhali's stern face scattered into pieces of confetti, rearranging into the shape of Amira. She drummed her fingers again. How Dominus had managed to escape the massacre in the Citadel was beyond her, but she had reason to suspect certain forces were involved. For that reason alone, she would keep his status concealed until she had him in custody.

That aside, there were still Lucrèce's movements to account for. And with her plan of capitalising on anti-occassi sentiment underway, Amira knew she would have to come up with a counterattack.

"Cressida!"

Her sprite guard appeared in her solar at once. "Yes, Your Luminosity?"

"Send for my daughter." Amira fiddled with a platinum blonde braid, the glass beads at the end tinkling. "We have something urgent to discuss."

Cressida bowed her head before setting off in search of Laila.

⚬∞⚬

Across the château grounds, the princess lounged with her feet dipped into a pale green pond flocked with swans and opalescent fish. The heavy perfumery of the rose garden suffused her—blushing pinks and deep reds amorously intermingled with ice blues and summer yellows.

Laila had wasted many afternoons here, pressing rose petals into books and swimming in the pond at night. It was one of the scant few places she knew she could be alone with her thoughts. Thoughts that were formulating around the visit of Darius Rex, who, try as she might, had not vacated her mind since.

While his visit had been brisk, his departure had been ever swifter, and part of her couldn't help but wonder why he did not try to call upon her. Shortly after he'd left she went looking for him in the pavilion, hoping against all hopes he'd be hiding there for her. In spite of everything rational telling her not to expect it, she couldn't keep her chest from sinking a little when she'd found it empty.

It's been twenty years now, Laila, she'd chastised herself at the time. *Of course he doesn't care to chase you anymore.*

If only that had been true for her. Instead, she had spent several years trying to forget him, burying herself in diplomatic missions and fashionable soirées. She'd even taken a series of lovers who were sweeter-natured than the killers she was accustomed to. In the end nothing had worked, for she couldn't escape the haunting of a passion once lost. So she set romance aside and devoted her heart to politics. She never expected she would again experience that feverish heat inflaming her skin. Not until she saw him again.

She kicked her legs back and forth, her toes nudging one of the stray fish swimming up to nip her.

She heard Lyra approaching before she saw her plop down at her side. "Corona for your thoughts?"

Laila snorted in response. "Oh you don't want these."

"Try me," Lyra challenged.

Laila glanced at the mermaid fountain in the distance. "Hélène Mielette is almost certain to be my competitor during the next election."

"And?" Lyra asked. "Surely you can defeat her."

"The Mielettes are a religious-minded dynasty, and we have seen something of a rise in Caelestis as of late." Laila sighed and tossed her curls over her shoulder. "Thanks to Mortos."

"Ah." Lyra propped up one knee and hugged it to her chest. "You think this is your fault?"

"I *know* that it's my fault," Laila corrected with a scoff. "Sometimes I still wish I never funded that accursed voyage."

Thinking of it now only brought to mind the horrors she'd seen, the trials she'd faced, the people she'd lost. And seemingly all for naught.

"Well, I can't say I've always approved of your peaceful stance, and certainly there have been some unexpected drawbacks to our trade union with the country. Still. I wouldn't be too concerned with it hurting your prospects." Lyra nudged her playfully with her shoulder. "We'll find you a campaign cause yet."

"We have twenty-four years of my mother's reign left, and still the clock is ticking." Laila sighed as she withdrew her feet from the pond. "I'm going to need something soon."

"Your Radiance?"

Laila whipped round to see Cressida standing by.

"Her Luminosity most urgently requests your presence."

Laila exhaled sharply through her nose and then glanced at Lyra. "We'll finish this later."

She stood and brushed her hand-painted skirt free from blades of grass, then walked towards Amira's solar. She pondered the topics considered to be of urgency to her mother along the way, estimating it must relate to the matter she and Lyra had been discussing.

Amira had set out a place for her when she arrived, pouring out a cup of butterfly pea flower tea with her aether. "Come in, aurore."

Laila nodded, taking the empty seat with her fingers primly laced in her lap. "Cressida said you needed to see me urgently." She took a sip and found it tart, her hand reaching for her fork to try the pastry set in front of her.

"Yes, it pertains to your campaign."

Laila paused, her forkful of pastry suspended mid-air. "You have a cause for me?"

"As it so happens, yes." Amira twisted her lips into something of a wry smile. "Though whether you'd be up to it is another matter."

"Tell me." Laila folded her hands together, resolute. "Whatever it is, consider it done."

Amira regarded her daughter's firmness with suspicion. "I need you to go Mortos for me."

Laila loathed herself for how instantly her body recoiled without warning, without prevention. How was it that her mother always was able to orchestrate the precise arrangement of words that would do this to her?

"Anything but that."

Amira took a sip of tea, her smile knowing. "I didn't think you'd take too kindly to that one."

Laila's cheeks flushed in annoyance. At herself, but more so with her mother's proficiency at making her feel small. "Why there? Why now?"

"You must understand I have done my absolute best to keep your attention away from the north. I thought perhaps hosting mediations for human-merpeople conflict in Malakia could be your cause instead, but the fact remains that our political fates are irreparably entangled with the fate of that miserable country." Amira gritted her teeth. "Should it implode under my rule, it will be taken as a reflection of our incompetence, and such a stain will be impossible to remove in time for election season."

"What do you expect me to do?" Laila asked, sighing deeply. "Darius Rex—"

"Was your pick, if you recall. His ascendancy made possible through your efforts alone." Amira tittered derisively. "Perhaps you ought to have made your choice with your logic rather than your libido."

"I don't exactly recall being left with many stellar choices in the matter."

"Yet you chose from the very beginning to enact a stance of peace towards these creatures and, by doing so, created a division within our kind in which we are cast as sympathisers to the occassi race. And what, exactly, have you decided to sympathise with? Shall I remind you?"

Laila swallowed in dread. "Maman."

"Shall I remind you what your dear lover Darius has been up to during his reign? Of the Scarlet Supper—"

"Stop it." Laila burst up from her chair and smothered a hand against her mouth. "I know I haven't made the most impeccable of choices with regards to Mortos. But I did what I had to in order to *survive*. If you desire to blame me for trying to protect our country, then please, cite blame. If you want me to feel shame for having extended compassion to a monster, then believe me, I feel shame. None of these decisions can be rescinded now. And if you sending me back there is your way of punishing me—"

Amira's expression turned thunderous. "Sit. Down."

Laila closed her eyes, inhaling tremulously. Then she returned to her chair.

Amira rubbed her temples with her pointer fingers. "Now, before you went off into your petulant little tangent, I had not yet finished what I was trying to say. I need you to go to Mortos as my proxy. The country is unstable, and quite frankly, Darius Rex being arrogant enough to refuse my advice hasn't provided me with the most confidence. Therefore, I want you to go there and straighten the country on my behalf."

"You—" Laila's forehead creased in suspicion.

"I am sure it hasn't helped matters that, every winter, I've had to send copious supplies of famine relief to the country. A decision Parlement continues to hold under scrutiny. I tried interesting Darius in an ætherglass project, but he has stubbornly refused. I need you to go and make him see reason. If we can show the Elders and, indeed, our kind in general some hope that these creatures can be brought into the realm of self-sustenance, then this may be enough to save us and prove your skill at being able to shape a nation in the meantime. You can be known as the one who made that frigid wasteland bloom." Amira paused to take a sip of tea. "Do you believe that to be within your capabilities?"

Doubt clouded her mind, but she knew her mother would want her to show conviction. "Yes, Maman."

"Then I shall make arrangements for you to travel north. And alert Darius Rex of your intentions." She pressed her lips together in thought. "On the subject of Darius Rex—I expect you to keep a clear mind regarding him. Do not, I repeat, do not allow yourself to become vulnerable to his machinations. Am I understood?"

"Trust me, Maman." Laila breathed a bitter laugh. "I know very well how to handle him."

∾

The time leading up to her departure passed in a hazy opaqueness. She checked off a list of affairs she had to see to while her sprite maids wrestled her luggage into submission. By the end, she had seven pastel-coloured trunks arranged into a tower, the smallest one left to her.

Laila slammed her toiletry trunk onto the bed as she pilfered her vanity, arranging hand-blown glass bottles with flower stoppers of moisturiser, hair mousse, and conditioner into plush satin placements. She knew she'd have to keep her hair products well-stocked in the Mortesian climate.

The final thing she reached for was the mother-of-pearl and ormolu perfume bottle holder gifted to her by Lyra, where she had secreted not only small bottles of fragrance, but elixirs of less savoury means. She placed it preciously into the trunk before she closed and snapped it shut, heaving a sigh of relief.

Not long after, Lyra herself appeared, eyeing the tower with an apprehensive grimace. "So you'll be off, then."

Laila spun round in surprise. Then she flew into her guard's arms, tucking her chin on her shoulder.

"If I didn't know any better I'd almost think you were packing up to leave for good," Lyra murmured as she clenched her tight.

Laila took a moment to breathe her in before stepping back. "I wish you could come with me."

"You know I can't do that." Lyra smiled, tracing her cheek with her thumb. "My uncle's blood is the seal keeping Papa Calantis's prison shut. Wouldn't want them getting any ideas of thinking I might be the key to opening it."

Laila swallowed, nodding in understanding.

Twenty years and the sacrifice Léandre made to trap Lanius Rex inside a prison realm was a subject that held them both in a chokehold. Neither dared broach it. Laila always thought, due to the extended lifespans of forest sprites, she might truly have had forever with him and Lyra both. When she thought of her future, she always envisaged it as though flipping a coin into a well with no bottom: a life of endless catered whims and granted desires. As of late, she felt she'd been receiving the opposite.

"Cressida d'Orille is to serve as my guard instead."

Lyra barked in laughter. "Oh, I bet Darius is going to love that. My absence."

Laila's face creased with mirth before she could stop it. It was the first they'd acknowledged the unspoken. "I'm not sure how to face him."

"Well, don't go to dinner with him," Lyra suggested, shoulder lifting blithely. "Unless you want to end up on the table as dessert."

Laila smothered the laughter bubbling in her chest. "I am unsure if this is you being crass or you being concerned."

"With him, I feel safe to bet on both." Lyra stretched her smile wide before it soon faded. "In all honesty..."

"Don't." Laila shook her head. "I know what you're going to say and you need not say it. I am not going to let him get to me."

Lyra tucked her finger beneath the princess's chin. "I'm always a mirror away if you need it. Contact me. Any time." She brought Laila back into her arms and kissed the side of her head. "Be seeing you."

She withdrew with a final smile before turning towards the door.

As much as she loathed the thought of Laila returning to the company of Darius Calantis without her, Lyra knew she could do little to prevent it. She could only have faith her princess would get on well enough without her aid.

With every step she took away from Laila's door, her resolve to part ways with her crumbled. The sprite barely made it through the corridor, however, before she was intercepted by another guard.

"Her Luminosity requests your presence in her boudoir."

Lyra's chest tightened in surprise. It wasn't often the impératrice called on her unless it was concerning her daughter. She rushed to Amira's chambers, hoping against all hopes the impératrice might allow her to serve in Mortos after all.

She was unprepared for what awaited her instead.

Lyra knocked thrice on the door as was custom, waiting for Amira's voice before she entered. "You sent for me, Your Luminosity?"

"Yes, do close the door behind you, Lyra." Amira beckoned her closer with her hand and gestured to a crystal pitcher of rose lemonade. "You may help yourself."

Lyra filled herself a glass, then sat on a chair with one ankle propped on her knee.

"How have you been getting on?" Amira asked, taking a sip from her glass. "I'm sure with my daughter's departure to Mortos on the horizon, you may be starting to feel her loss heavily indeed."

"Well, I—" Lyra shifted uncomfortably in her seat. "I admit a large part of me does feel I ought to be going with her."

"I perfectly understand." Amira had always seen her own dearly parted Lightshield lover in Lyra's relentless loyalty. And her guilelessness. "Your clan's dedication to our dynasty has always gone to exceedingly great lengths. But I am afraid I simply cannot spare you."

"Oh." Lyra's chest deflated.

"Only because I have a far more important assignment for you instead."

"Oh?" Lyra's disappointment shifted to curiosity.

Amira smiled as she picked up a pale blue binder stamped with the royal seal. "Do you remember Dominus Calantis?"

"Laila's first unfortunate error of judgement?" Lyra scoffed into her glass. "How could I forget?"

"What if I told you that he is, by some unforeseen circumstance, alive and well?"

Lyra nearly choked on her lemonade. The last thought she'd had for Dominus Calantis was to lament that it had been Darius, rather than she, who had delivered the so-called killing blow. Now it seemed she had even more reason. "I would say that is a rather grave blunder that ought to be rectified immediately."

"I am glad you see it that way." Amira handed over the binder, crossing one leg over the other. "You shall find the contents of your assignment within. I expect this to be completed discreetly. And ensure the body is disintegrated after. I offer you free rein to assemble a team of your choosing and enact this mission as you see fit. On one condition."

Lyra ceased flipping through the pages of the file to look up.

"Not a word of this to Laila," Amira warned. "Should you be asked, you are to tell her you are on a personal assignment for me in Thalistan, the details of which are to remain classified. Are we clear?"

Lyra glanced down at the images of the Parvani Rainforest before nodding. "When do I start?"

"Immediately."

V

DARIUS SAT IN AN ARMCHAIR OF WINE-COLOURED leather, the arms formed of two watchful hippogriffs cast in bronze with clawfoot legs. The crackle of the roaring fireplace divided his features into warmth and gloom.

He picked up the latest scroll he'd received from one of his enforcers and unfurled it, watching the shadow-ink scrawl across the hidden message: *Found this during our raid on the docks. Should put you on the right path. Your Eagle Eye.*

He regarded it with a slight inching up of the mouth before lifting a box of simple black wood. It had no sheen or polish, utterly pedestrian in design, and yet it exuded such contemptible energy that even the sight of it would cause a mere human to burst several blood vessels.

"A memory box." Darius stroked beneath his chin. That certainly answered Amira's inquiry into Thalistan's recent troubles. Negative emotion was a source of power for occassi. They often extracted it raw from traumatic memories and used it to bolster their own power or to imbue objects with it. If someone was performing this procedure overseas then that could be dire news for the rex.

Darius only knew of one creature who could make boxes like this. A business owner by the name of Sergius Severis. And a colleague for even longer. He'd have to make preparations to pay him a visit.

Darius retrieved a black cherry and cream cheese tart from his tray and nibbled at the fine crust, taking a larger bite to taste the feather-light cream and the tartness of the cherries.

Kirill arrived shortly after, carrying a missive on a silver platter. "A letter has arrived from Soleterea, Your Majesty."

Darius recognised the official stationary and gold wax seal could only come from Rosâtre. He broke the seal with his claw to devour the contents, hoping Amira had suffered a change of heart following his request. He scanned to the end of the letter, stunned to silence at its words. He read through it one more time. And then another.

"Is something amiss, Your Majesty?"

"Laila's coming to Mortos..." His head slowly rose in realisation. He could scarcely believe the words he had read until he had given them voice. A warmth rose in his chest, resting on his lips in a smile. He turned to his servant. "Kirill, I'm going to need you to prepare some rooms in the Regina's Wing."

Kirill bowed. "I will prepare them at once, Your Majesty."

He bit down on his lip, struggling to suppress his glee. As an envoy of importance, he ought to receive her as he would a favoured guest. Though he anticipated Laila would not much enjoy spending her nights in the sepulchral rooms of the Citadel. Perhaps if he lightened it somewhat— introduced some lamps of stained leaded glass, a phonograph to play soft music. Anything to banish from her the dark and silent. He knew it would take time for a maiden of her type to adjust to both.

⁂

Laila pressed her cheek against the window of her carriage, watching slivers of rain slide down the glass. Her arrival to Mortos had been heralded by the profuse showers she'd come to know and loathe of the climate, and the severity of the storm had prevented the hippogriffs from flight. Yet in spite of the ill weather, she had found herself soothed by the petrichor.

Cressida sat across from her, polishing her ivory-stocked sunbeam pistol. The two had not exchanged more than five words since the start of the journey. Laila couldn't help but feel bothered by it. She found herself longing for Léandre's calming presence or Lyra's spitfire, anything other than this professional silence.

"I feel I must deeply apologise for dragging you all the way out here, Ser d'Orille," Laila said when she could no longer take the silence.

"Not at all, madame." Cressida lifted her pistol and inspected the barrel. "It is my duty to keep you safe."

Laila feigned a grateful smile and glanced down at her file. She'd been attempting to prime herself as much as possible on what she'd missed, and it would seem that Mortos had had an eventful two decades in her absence. A civil war had fractured the country over a four-year period, instigated by Darius implementing strict and punitive measures over the distribution of the mystical moongrass—a powder of diluted occassi venom mixed with luneflower leaves.

When it was discovered the residents of Thalistan were becoming severely addicted, her mother had been quick to lock the doors to trade. Darius's subsequent response was thorough. He worked around the clock to execute alchemists and suppliers, dodging several attempts on his life and quelling many rebellions as peddlers clambered to seize what remained of the drug.

Tendrils of mist squirmed in from the trees of the forested trail they drove down as Laila read. Within a blink, the road eclipsed entirely. Another, and a dense white shroud had smothered anything in sight.

Laila lifted her head from the window in alert. The nape of her neck tingled. She knew it was madness, having her stomach sink in dread at the mere sight of a fog, but her nightmares of this country were still too potent to let herself be fooled. When in Mortos, a fog was never merely a fog.

"I can't see a thing out there." She hugged her bright red cape about her shoulders. "Can you?"

"The driver is still going, madame. I wouldn't fret about it."

This assurance did little to settle Laila's nerves. She tried and failed not to fidget in her seat, to think of anything but the blankness surrounding her and what might lurk within. But the fog had stolen her only comfort.

She closed her eyes and tried to focus on timing her breaths like she'd been taught. However, in cutting off her sight, she only focused more on the sound of her blood rushing through her ears. Oh, she missed Léandre. If Léandre were here—

"I need to stop," Laila decided. "I—I need to stop. Tell the driver to stop. I need—"

A shadow smacked against the window too fast for sight, jostling the carriage.

Laila screamed as a face emerged from the mist with a snarl, spraying spittle against the window. The swamp creature's features were rotting away in clumps and being supplanted by toadstools—ghostly white caps sprouted from every orifice.

Before either of the carriage's occupants could react, a hand burst through the window and seized Cressida. The creature took a ravenous bite out her neck, tearing out her artery. She released a blood-filled gurgle of a cry as more infected leikhens feasted upon her warm, ripe flesh, and within two more chomps, her head had been bitten clean off.

"Oh, gods... oh, *gods...*" Laila kicked out her legs and propelled herself to a far off corner as the creatures hauled the remains of Cressida's body out of the window and ripped off bloodied chunks to devour. She knew the meal would only occupy them for a few blessed moments before they hungered for her next.

Her hands readied themselves to summon aether, but it would not come. She was too numbed by fear. "Come on. Come *on.*" She tried again and again, to no avail, striking inside herself for a flame that would not ignite.

You're going to die here, taunted a voice that sounded remarkably like her mother's. *You're going to die here because you're too stupid and worthless and incompetent—*

An arrow punctured one of the creature's flesh-filled mouths and splattered its cranial matter along the carriage seats. More arrows followed. Each abomination was felled, one by one, as wads of toadstool and flesh seeped down the window glass.

There were scarce few moments of silence before another figure approached the door and opened it, revealing a uniformed occassella.

"Everything should be all right now, miss," spoke the husky smoker's voice of a Mortesian Rose, an epithet bestowed upon those with carmine tresses and skin so cadaverously pale it revealed every periwinkle vein. "We've dispensed with the swamp creatures."

Laila shuddered as she wrapped her arms about her.

The occassella looked her over with limpid blue eyes. "You must be the star princess arriving from Soleterea. The rex told us you might come down this road. You'll be safe with us now. I promise." She tipped her fur shako. "I'm Sabina Levitia. One of the rex's enforcers." She wore the distinguished uniform with pride—a black velvet atilla with gold braiding and matching pelisse.

"A... pleasure to meet you." Laila struggled to gain her bearings. "Forgive me, I just..."

"No need to trouble yourself, miss. You've been through quite a shock." Her mouth quirked into a vixen smile that reminded Laila slightly of Lyra. The chiselled crease between her lips became even more emphasised. "But we ought to have you transferred to a new carriage. Please, come with me."

She held out her white-gloved hand to assist Laila out of her carriage. Laila seized it eagerly.

Darius learned of the attack long before he saw her. He had Laila's journey traced through the watchful eyes of his gargoyles until she finally arrived, backlit by pink-orange sun through the gnarled peaks of decrepit treetops.

Darius stood at the bottom of the Citadel steps, watching as her carriage entered the courtyard.

He saw her first as a head of curls teasing against her shoulders, half tied back by pink ribbon. Beneath her red cape was a gown of sheer pink tulle embroidered with flowers, berries, and sequins falling in a continuous cursive.

The sight of her transported him to the first time he'd seen her step onto Mortesian soil, sapping all words and moisture from his lips.

He approached Laila as she closed the space between them, reaching for her hand to press it chastely to his lips. "It's a pleasure to receive you in the Citadel again, Your Radiance."

"Darius Rex." Laila curtseyed, her composure a practised façade tinkered to perfection. "I daresay the country has not changed one bit since I last visited."

"Yes, I am terribly sorry for your rough journey." He held out his arm for her to take. "Please, allow me to escort you to the drawing room so that you may decompress."

She slid her hand into the crook of his elbow. He escorted her up the steps into the Citadel and into the drawing room, candlelit from brass lamps that coddled the room in a balmy glow. A much more primitive counterpart to the ætherald energy humming through the gridlines in Vysteria.

Laila slinked into the room, her fingers skirting the wrought iron frame of the divan before she gripped it.

"Are you all right?" Darius asked, closing the door behind him.

She let him have it the moment she heard the lock click. "No, I am not all right. Not one day I've spent here and already I've been assailed on my journey. A good sprite lost her life today right in front of my eyes."

Darius slumped against the door, head bent in compassion. "My apologies. I've been trying to keep the roads better monitored, but our routes through the wilderness still require... improvement."

"Well, your condolences are insufficient." Laila abandoned the stability offered by the divan in favour of pacing. "It'd be nice if for once I could step foot on this accursed island without a pack of monsters trying to devour me. But no, that's asking for too much, I suppose—"

Darius straightened up by the door. "Laila."

She recognised the intent behind using her name but was too tightly wound to stop now she'd started. "Honestly, what's next? What more does this hovel of horrors have yet in store for me, I ask you? You would think after it had taken *so much* of me to muster the nerve to visit here again that I might, I don't know, be blessed with a slightly less terrifying reception—"

"Laila." He was stepping closer to her now.

She bulled past him. "I know, I am *ranting*. I recognise you likely don't care to hear anything I am saying right now, and that what I may have encountered today may have been another mundane aspect of life for you. But, quite frankly, I have experienced something truly horrid and it would be nice if I could just—"

"Laila." He stepped into her path to take her face in his hands, her body colliding flush against his.

Laila exhaled the last of her frustration in heavy breaths. His body against hers quieted the rabble in her chest, his unhurried pulse calming her own.

"It's all right," he said, bringing her into a tight embrace. He stroked the ends of her hair. She hadn't realised how gratifying it would feel to have her ramblings received with consolation rather than chastisement for once. "You're safe now. I'm sorry that happened to you."

Her eyes fluttered closed as she melted into the embrace. She had not meant to. He was just so much the same as she'd last felt him, last *smelled* him, that she had to angle herself not to get distracted by the sweet musk of his cologne and the memories it stirred.

"I—" She pulled back from him, pivoting to face the other way. "I need to freshen up."

"Of course," he said, pocketing his now empty hands. "Take however long you need. When you're ready, I shall have dinner prepared." He opened the door to call for a servant. "Please escort Princess Laila to the Regina Wing and have her settled comfortably."

"Yes, Your Majesty." The ghoul inclined her head to one side. "If you'd follow me, Princess."

She glanced at Darius one last time before following the servant from the room.

⤞⟗⟞

He'd spared no expense on the preparations, having considered everything from the prism-cut crystal glasses to the ornately patterned flatware. Every dish that arrived was more elegant than the last: figs stuffed with white cheese wrapped in dry-cured ham; raw oysters with strawberry mignonette; saffron rice bejewelled with pomegranate seeds. All were arranged around the steaming main course: a whole roast swan stuffed with oysters and dipped in rose petal sauce, set alongside a boat of pomegranate reduction.

Darius fidgeted absently with his band collar as he waited for Laila to enter, her shoes clacking against the mirrored floors.

"I could smell everything from down the hall. You have outdone yourself." She tucked a loose curl of hair behind her ear, and it sprang free once more as she took in her surroundings. "Oh my."

The room was speckled with tiny crystal formations seeping from the walls and ceiling like dew, embalming them in incandescent heat. Laila took a tentative step forward to press her finger against a crystal.

"I had them harvested from the ores of one of our caves," Darius explained, watching her whimsical delight. A beacon that far outshone any light source the room provided. "I find it reminiscent of the night sky."

At least he could offer her this, an artificial imitation of her past celestial life so that she might become a star again.

Laila traced the formations on the wall like she might attach them together in a constellation. "It's sublime." Her grin unfurled like the petals of a yellow bud in the centre of a pink rose before she stepped away to sit at the table.

He pulled out the chair for her. "I tried to ensure a few things arrived from your home to make you most comfortable." He tucked in her chair once she was seated. "Rose, pomegranates, strawberries. There are a lot of your favourites present."

She surveyed his offering with a critical brow raised that, for a moment, reminded him of Amira.

What to offer the maiden who, from the moment she was brought to air, had been swaddled in silks and spoon-fed with silver? Who traded in sensuality like they were spices? You could placate her, dangle shiny trinkets before her gaze, clasp her long, brown throat in pretty baubles. Mere morsels for her ephemeral appetites; she'd not be cosseted by material gains alone, and he knew it.

Even when he'd come on metaphorical bended knee with his kingdom offered in hand, she'd rejected it an instant. But he wondered if she'd accept him now with his ribs exposed, the pulsing black fruit in the centre of it ripe for the picking. He'd never been able to lay himself bare in such a way before—two centuries of neglect had merely fossilised the worst of his attributes. But he longed to open himself to her.

"Do you… like it?" Uncertainty lengthened each syllable in the sentence.

Still, he couldn't help but feel something crack through the petrification in his chest when she smiled at him and said, "It'll do."

He returned the smile as he watched Laila fill her plate with whatever delicacies happened to be within reach.

"Be sure to try the figs—they're fresh." He helped himself to one. "As is everything you see before you on the table. The swan I hunted myself this morning. Oh, I wish you could've seen it when I picked it out for you. It had such a long and delicate neck… A fine catch it was indeed. As you can see, I'd kill to have you here."

She tried not to read too deeply into the statement as she sipped from her glass of rosé. Her favourite. "I have to ask, why go to all this trouble?"

"We never did get to have that dinner I wanted when I was last in your home." Darius ate his fig with a smile. "Besides, you are a royal guest and I wanted your first official evening here to be perfect."

"Well, disastrous journey here aside"—she sampled one of the figs, enjoying the texture of salted ham—"I must admit this is… rather perfect."

The smile that accompanied her words stripped him back, saturated him with light, and it was all he could do to merely reach for her hand and clasp it like an oyster around a pearl.

Laila looked down at their interlacing fingers, her breath seizing. She pulled away. "I suppose we'd better start on that swan, no?"

"Indeed." Darius hid his frown. Her reaction was not what he'd been expecting. "Though I must ask what it is that brings you to my doorstep. I feel it must be imperative, given how much you loathe it here."

A protestation worked its way up her throat, high and ringing like silver. "I don't *loathe* it here."

Darius raised a brow in response.

"My mother outlined the purpose behind my visit in her correspondence, I am sure." Laila took a sip of wine to steady her nerves. She would need it, if her inkling of where this conversation were to head was correct.

"Yes, she said it was to offer support from Soleterea that she cannot provide me in person. Still, I… thought perhaps there might have been… something else influencing your decision."

Laila traced the rim of her glass. "Something else such as?"

"Perhaps you wanted to see me." His voice had lowered, soft as a bedroom whisper. "Perhaps you... missed me."

"Darius." Laila sighed, having hoped it wouldn't come to this. "It's been twenty years. Surely you don't mean to say you've been living on the hope I'd come back to you all this time?"

"Is that truly so hard to believe?"

"Yes," she replied, exasperated at the very notion. She sucked in a breath. "I'm flattered you feel so strongly about me. Truly, I am. But... the reason I came here, Darius, is strictly political in nature. Nothing more."

"I see." He dropped his hand from the table, his nape burning in embarrassment. How many times would he play the fool for a mere turn of her head? He swiped away his shame and lacquered a veneer of gallantry instead. "I'll serve the swan, then."

He picked up the carving knife and fork, slicing away the meat with ease. If it were only possible, he would excise from their memories the last few moments of conversation as well.

Laila couldn't stomach this impermeable wall of silence rising between them. Of having the screech of cutlery be the only interplay. "I should..." She started to stand from her chair. "I should go."

"Go?" Darius echoed her in disbelief. "Go where?"

"To Drakalyk Castle," she said, whilst edging towards the door.

"Laila, it's late." Darius stabbed his carving knife into the swan, gesturing towards the darkened windows. "The moon is out and there is still an indeterminate number of ravenous monsters who'd love to have you for dinner."

"What does it matter to you?"

"You believe I'd cast you out into the night because you rebuffed my affections?" He couldn't suppress the wound in his voice. "Do you really think so low of me?"

Her clicking heels skidded to a halt before she turned, reluctant to face the sheen of hurt in his eyes. "It'd be easier if I did."

53

VI

OMINUS DROWNED IN HIS DREAMS, sinking through an endless swathe of pale gold. The fluid entered through his eyes, his nose, his mouth. It tasted piquant, like pure electricity. Flashes of light burned his eyelids. His breathing was loud against his ears as he fell and fell. He felt like he was plummeting through space, hurtling down at a velocity forceful enough to set himself on fire. The burn spread through him, setting the inner lining of his blood vessels aflame. Then the heat had reached his chest and sped his heart to acceleration. He resurfaced then, feeling gloved hands and distant, distorted voices—

Apply the sedative. Stabilise the subject.

He sprang upright as the foreign aroma of rainforest sweat chafed his nostrils. It took a few sobering breaths to calm himself from panic, to dull the itch in his gums for fangs that would not descend. He exhaled tremulously as he touched the inside of his mouth, mourning the loss of his creature claws and canines. He'd gone too long without the decoction he used to restore them. This would have to be remedied.

Staggering upwards from his bedroll, he fumbled his way to a kitchen reeking of animal flesh. The scent struck him, close-fisted, and his stomach roiled in response. Dominus traced the decaying miasma to the fly-ridden remains of his last good meal. The numb, fixed eyes of the civet still gazed upon him in judgement.

With a grunt, he rifled through the cupboards and pulled out ingredients. Wolf tallow. Eagle egg. Dogwood root. Asphodel. Sulphur. He combined them all in a cauldron and set them to boil on the stove, watching intently for the broth to turn black.

Strange times had come for him to craft a potion. As a warrior, he'd had it literally and figuratively beaten into him that all injuries were to be healed from within the body alone. That elixirs and brews were feminine playthings. And yet, here he found himself at the mercy of a bubbling cauldron to set himself right. His father would be incensed.

He poured the brew into several vials of crimson leaded glass, hoping his stock would last him until he was able to raid for ingredients again. He lifted the first and swirled it around, not even waiting for it to cool before he consumed it. The potion took immediate effect. His muscles ballooned with strength. His pupils and ear tips narrowed, senses heightened. A sharpness returned to his gums and fingertips to signal his arsenal was at the ready.

He extended his fangs to test the potion's outcome, baring them with triumph. Then he made a forceful gesture at the civet and watched its skeleton contort and fragment to pieces via use of a skeletal hex. He wanted to see something shatter, to dislocate and come apart at the sheer force of his chaotic might.

"Restored at last," he exhaled in relief, though he knew it was not permanent. Without the aid of his decoction, he knew his body was certain to retreat to its insipid state after a week at most. Such had been the case for him since he'd awoken on the riverbanks of the Parvani Rainforest—with little memory of the events before.

The last thing he remembered was receiving the puncture of a dagger at Darius's hand. Then, coldness. Oblivion. He had died, to be certain. And yet, someone had brought him back.

The thought of his death caused his mind to soften and fuzz at the edges until he was swaying heavily on his feet. He caught himself on the edge of the countertop, resolving to think of other things, and gathered up the rest of the vials to attach them to his belt.

As he did so, four figures encroached silently upon his shack.

These were knights of the Iron Clan—forest sprites resolved to rid the world of monsters and those they deemed evil. On the orders of Lyra de Lis, they had been scouring the rainforest for days in search of their occasso fugitive, hoping the retrieval of his head would conclude a successful mission.

It was a chill night, and the sprites were shifting behind the tree trunks with elusive dexterity. Their belts held their two weapons: one sword of a lightning bolt and one pistol full of sunbeams. They advanced cautiously, quietly, their bodies tensing with the thrill of capture and the element of surprise on their side.

They found the shack protruding like a splinter from the earth, all wood and stone and bearded moss. The air around it was dank with moist soil and resin, and a dwindling light from a candle flame signalled its occupancy.

The damp scent continued to suffuse the air once they pushed past the doors, tempered by the distinctive aroma of smoke and burning wood. They discovered the extinguished stove as the source when they moved into his living quarters. With a rudimentary scan, they found it empty.

"Search the area," Verena commanded, having appointed herself the leader. "Caedmon, kitchen. Rainer, bedroom. Leif, with me. I'll check to see if there are any other exits. He can't have gotten far."

The group murmured in agreement as they split off to hunt, ransacking every square inch of the minimal space. Verena did a quick scan of the vicinity with her pistol at the ready, finding no other exits or entrances other than the one they had entered.

"Do you think he skipped out of the window?" Leif offered.

"Large brute that he is?" Verena snorted in derision. "No, I very much doubt that, Leif."

The two others soon reconvened in the main area, their faces saying nothing good.

Verena scoffed in indignation. "Well, he couldn't have vanished, now? Could he—"

Something crucial and utterly bone-chilling entered the forefront of her mind. They had not stopped to account for the shadows.

Dominus materialised into existence as though the darkness birthed him, his claws extended like sickles. He buried his hand into Leif's spine, carving a hole through his chest. A vibrant dispersion of blood splattered across Verena's shocked face before Leif's body skidded off the tips of Dominus's fingers.

The falling of Leif's body unveiled him. He, the predator of predators, the reflective-eyed beast with pupils widened to discs. He flashed a savage grin at them, fangs exposed, provoking them to reach for their swords.

Dominus dissolved once more into the shadows. But they were not so easily fooled, these monster hunters. Verena removed a crystal from her belt, crushing it and tossing it in the direction of where he was last seen.

The powder ignited on his skin with a violent hiss, opening lesions that wheezed with smoke. Dominus let out a pained, bestial sound as the crystal dust dappled him with coruscating light, revealing the hidden outline of his shape to them. Ætherald. The only substance capable of staggering him to such an extent.

The effects waned as soon as they came. For when Verena took a swing at him, he was ready to dodge the slash of her lightning bolt. He narrowly escaped with a scorch to his shoulder, the pain so agonising that his muscles cooked with it. He punched her on the side of the head. She hit the ground. Then Caedmon and Rainer ran in to engage.

He parried them all without tire. They were graceful and acrobatic on their feet as they weaved past his brutish, heavy-handed swipes with ease. Dominus's patience grew thin, and he ejected a tendril of corporeal darkness to wrap around Caedmon's waist. He pulled him near, cleaving his head from his shoulders with one swipe of his claws. The broken seal of tissue in the aftermath soaked his face like a geyser.

A thrust of lightning entered Dominus's back as Caedmon's uncapped neck glugged at his feet. He cried out, going knock-kneed, descending to the floor to clutch for consciousness. The high voltage crackled through his nerve endings, disrupting signals and tarnishing the clarity of his thought.

A line of saliva dangled from Dominus's mouth as Rainer withdrew his sword and nudged him with his foot. A foolish mistake. Dominus responded by murmuring a *fright* curse at him. Rainer crumpled beside him, vomiting blood and entrails until his body deteriorated into an amorphous mass on the ground.

He feasted on Verena's fear and disbelieving horror as she struggled to see him through the coating of blood streaming into her eyes from her scalp.

Dominus rose slowly, taking his time to approach her as she whimpered and struggled to crawl away. He put down his boot on her spine, leering at her. "Last comrade standing, it would seem."

"May Asemani strike you down!" Verena spat at his feet. "Vile creature."

"Not a terribly polite manner to address the one who controls your fate." He applied enough pressure to fracture her spine.

Verena shrieked loud enough to send the birds fleeing.

"That one's to paralyse." Dominus inched up his foot to rest on her head. "This one will kill."

Verena snuffled into the floor, tears and blood obscuring her vision. "Then hurry up and do it."

"Tell me who sent you first."

"I'd sooner die than talk!" Verena vowed, stifling her sobs. *Oh, gods, but I didn't want to die like this.*

Dominus closed his eyes, inhaling deeply in impatience. "You know, it is a shame. Before you'd said that, I might have thought to spare you as the messenger."

He squelched her skull beneath his boot, sending out a spray of cranial matter. An eye popped free of its socket for a few paces, slowing to a halt at Leif's body.

Dominus wiped his foot clean on the rug before making his way out into the night.

Elina awakened to the musical chirping of parakeets. A thin blade of sunlight sliced across her face from a shutter left slightly ajar. She squinted at the assault on her still vulnerable eyes and lazily slung her forearm across her face to shield it. With a reluctant moan, she rose from the cosy haven of her bedsheets and placed her feet on the rough wooden floor.

A chorus of arthritic creaks and groans sounded as she passed through her pastel-yellow bedroom to her bathroom. She knew every nook and cranny of this home. Every weak spot, every squeak of age. For it was her craftsmanship that shaped its character. She who painted the walls, sculpted the ceramic, and upholstered the furniture. It was her paintings that adorned the hallway behind polished sheets of glass.

Her bathtub was a sunken stone pit in the corner of the room with a waterfall spout, mosaic tiles bordering it beneath neatly-spaced sticks of incense. Perched on mossy stone shelves were handcrafted soaps and bath salts, her candy-coloured phials made from diamond glass tied with eggshell-coloured bows.

Elina disrobed and placed her clothes atop one of the many outstretched branches growing out of the crevices in the walls. Her feet grazed a fur throw rug as she made a selection from her phials: powdered goat's milk and olive oil from the orange deserts of Seraj; star anise from mountainous Odaka; rosemary, sage, and lavender plucked from the sun-saturated fields of Soleterea; honey from coastal Malakia.

She filled her bath with the herbal concoction and braved the steps down into the tub. Should she be fortunate, her mother would already have paid tribute to their household deity, providing milk and coconut candies to ensure a comforting temperature. Swirls of lavender and sage stroked against her limbs as she sank. Her night braids swarmed around her as she looked up at the detailed ceiling mural, tracing its vibrant patterns and swirls of floral design. After a significant soak, she emerged from the fragrant steam into her bedroom, pruny as a date. Her forearms pimpled with goosebumps, finding a chill had invaded from the night before, when she had attempted to ward off the jungle-like humidity drifting from the rainforest to her ancestral land.

They'd never tried to erect a more permanent marker between the village and the rainforest, never before presumed the arrogance to do so. For they belonged to the soil and it was to the soil that they would return. Nature was always going to get back what was taken from it, no matter how much one held up their hands in trembling resistance.

She dressed quickly and slid her feet into her slippers, making her way to the kitchen. The saucepan was bubbling on the stove when she got there as her sister, Maithra, sprinkled tea leaves into the water. For a moment Elina stood there, watching her with a smile. The short dark cloud of her ringlets rustled as Maithra added milk and spices to the pan.

Elina tiptoed towards her to encircle her arms around Maithra's waist. The disparity between their heights made it so she could kiss the crown of her younger sister's head with ease. "I didn't hear you come in."

"Ela!" She chuckled in surprise as the attack of affection caused her to jostle the pan. "You sure darn gave me a start! I wanted to surprise you."

"Don't you worry, Maithra. I'm still very surprised." Elina disentangled from her to retrieve her favourite mug, a misshapen product of a child's sickbed project—hardened clay painted over with crooked white flowers by an unsteady hand. The child had died shortly after painting it, and she found that she couldn't let it go. She'd always been predisposed to sentiment. "How long you been back from the docks?"

"Only since this morning. And *hoo wee*—I am ready for a rest." She rolled her sinewed neck. Witches of Thal descent were typically long-limbed and lithe, but Maithra's shape had broadened thick as an ox from years of guiding sails over choppy Malakian waters. "The crew and I been making several round trips to Mortos, and that takes its toll. Though we have the waters on their best behaviour."

Hearing the name of that accursed country, Elina shivered and rubbed her sore eyes. She'd been sleeping rough the past few days since she'd happened upon the occasso in the forest. The encounter still held an eerie unreality, a campfire glisten, like hearing a story that happened to someone else.

"You all right?" Maithra asked, turning the knob of the stove to bring the tea to a simmer.

Elina became intensely aware of how deeply her nails were scraping against the kitchen counter. "I'm fine. A large predator just gave me a bit of a start last night is all."

"Yeah, I seen in the papers what happened to them clan knights." Maithra tutted, her broad nose wrinkling. "You oughta take more care during your nightly hikes, Ela. Perhaps take them a little earlier? I ain't one to henpeck... but times have changed since we've had those creatures coming in from the north."

Maithra strained the tea into their ceramic teapot, moulded into the shape of a green turtle. She lifted it up by its rattan handle and filled Elina's mug.

Elina warmed her hands against her mug, finding herself cold again. She'd also read the article Maithra alluded to, and the story, paired with the knowledge of the occasso she'd seen, caused her to remain silent about her close encounter.

"How about breakfast?" she offered, changing the subject. "I'd better throw some porridge on before Yasmin wakes up for school. Could you fetch her lunch from the cold room?"

"Sure." Her sister flashed a mischievous smirk as she went over to the cold room. Maithra rummaged through the shelves to pick out her ceramic container. Tucked inside were two rice balls made into birds with slices of cheese and carrots. They lay upon a bed of vegetables, a paper cup of soup nestled in the corner. "Now ain't that just *darling*. I don't know how you manage to do this every day."

"Well, it's no trouble, and it keeps her smiling." Elina removed the lace-covered jar of the porridge and added it with almond milk and rosewater to the pan on the stove. "Doesn't take long at all once you've done it enough times."

"You're spoiling her, Elina."

Elina smiled. She brought the porridge to boil until it was creamy and thick, then spooned it into three bowls, adding chopped dates, apricots, a few slices of banana, and some pansy flowers. She never felt more alive than in the process of creation, whether it be food or art or healing. These were the things to nourish and be nourished by.

"Heard from her baba?" Maithra asked, tracing her finger over her first tattoo on her backhand, a rite of passage for every Thal witch who came of age. Maithra's had seven waves of water, in contrast to the spiralling loops of a tree stump Elina had been marked with.

"He lives." Elina acknowledged this with scant emotion as she brought the bowls over to the kitchen table. She set the bowls down and rotated them to sit just right, her shoulders notably tense. "Why you ask?"

"He hollered at me not too long ago. Wanted to know if I'd bring a few things down from the north for him."

Elina froze and turned to face her. "What'd you say?"

"What'd you think?" Maithra arched her brow. "You think I got 'scrote' written on my forehead, Elina? I could sense it ain't nothing I wanted anything to do with. But I thought it best I tell you."

Elina sucked her teeth in annoyance. "And he wonders why I don't let Yasmin see him anymore. That trifling, lowdown—" She rubbed her temples, agitated. She hated the way he was still able to worm his way under her skin after all this time. "Thank you for telling me this. Though I must confess the last thing I want to think about right now is Sadik Yilan. So let's just... sit and eat. I'll go wake Yasmin."

Elina turned towards the stairs as Maithra sat down at the table with a noisy creak of a chair.

The sun leaned intrusively upon the circular formation of little yellow cabins of the Panja residence. The smaller cabins arched into the much larger farmhouse where the matriarch of the clan and her children resided. Thal agricultural families were often large and multigenerational, so the farm work was portioned and shared into slices as easily digestible as mango flesh.

Since Elina and her sister had come of age, they had vacated the main farmhouse in favour of having their own little cabin for privacy. Here, Elina tended to her herb garden. The earth was moist and black as molasses as she dug a hole to put seeds into the planter before tucking them in to rest. She reached for the watering can, a portly floral-painted thing, and fed the earth with the most potent elixir of water and moonblood.

She cupped the buried seeds with her hands and sang to it a fertility chant to coax forth a healthy budding sprout. The first shoot yawned from its subterranean slumber, growing green and thick. Elina trimmed herself a hefty portion and sealed it inside a translucent sachet, placing it inside her basket before slinging the handle into the crook of her elbow.

She exited through the brightly painted turquoise gates to her village. Her clinic sat only a stone's throw away—a quaint little property in pastel green with delicate ironwork coiling like climbing vines over floral stained glass.

The door groaned with rheumatic anguish as she switched the lights on and flipped the sign on the door to signal her opening hours had begun. Before her stood rows upon rows of healing draughts in vivid coloured glass, their labels scribbled in delicate cursive. Each pill, potion, and powder had been hand-blended under the expert tutoring of witch doctors and herbalists, her own home brews added from her ancestors.

Their words and guidance aided her even now, compacted inside the calfskin tomes lined up neatly inside her cherrywood cabinet. These texts that were once sacrosanct to her were soon adorned with her diligent scrawls and absent-minded doodles, revisions to ancient recipes she had improved upon during experimentation, and pressed with sprigs of herb and blossoms she had collected during her travels.

The healer's profession, she soon learned, did not come with the rigid confines found within other elements where *this* happened and then *that* happened and *this* was why. Instead, it was a continuous dialogue fostered between herself and the earth as it found new ways to strengthen and award her—as long as she respected its autonomy.

This strengthened a connection between her and nature, most often made clear by the way birds would sing for her and flowers would blossom in her path. Elina opened up her windows to the silvered lilt of flower birds, and one flitted in from the branch of a tree and came to nestle in her dense curls.

The bird was joined by a neighbour when she sold her first patron an ointment to repair her pelvic damage after childbirth. By the time she had finished recommending a child-preventing potion that induced anejaculation, her head was entirely crowded, and the birds filled the air with their limpid birdsong and the dainty ruffle of feathers.

The sound of the door tinkling dispersed them in a deluge of fragrant petal-feathers. The air grew metallic with their fear. Elina had her back turned to this unexpected visitor, carefully crossing out the appointments she had completed in straight, steady lines before she reached a name that she was not familiar with.

In a community as insular as Parvani, it was uncommon to come across names she did not already have an intimate medical history of, but not impossible. So she gave it no less than a fleeting thought as her next patient prowled towards the counter in her peripheral vision.

"So, what can I do for you to—" A sudden yelp punctuated her question as in the place of the feeble-bodied patient she had been expecting was the occasso she had abandoned in the rainforest.

He pressed a finger to his puckered lips to silence her. "Stay calm."

Elina refused to be soothed, however, and sought comfort in the lengthy space between them. "What are you doing here?"

"I have need of your services," Dominus said, and his voice did not once break from its mechanical monotone. "Common knowledge has it that you are the lover of Sadik Yilan. I must speak with him urgently. I need you to arrange a meeting."

"No." She was offended by the insinuation that she had any form of intermediary privileges between the common person and the slimy underbelly her former lover wallowed in. The clinic was meant to be her sanctuary, her last bastion of defence against the world that knew her only as the crime lord's consort. Now it had been breached, ruined.

Dominus's brow folded like an accordion. "Come again?"

His disbelief was evident and one Elina expected was born of inherent entitlement. This was not a creature who knew rejection often. He assumed militaristic command of the room like it was a territory unattested for and all that lay inside were merely awaiting his unlawful possession.

"I ain't spoken to Sadik in ten years," she told him. "Now please leave my clinic."

An angry flex protruded from Dominus's rectangular jawline as he took a presumptuous step forward and said, "I'm afraid that I must insist."

She realised how different he looked to the sickly figure she'd left behind. His large, stout hands attached to powerful arm muscles swollen as ripe summer fruit, round as mangoes. He could split her open like a watermelon, she realised with startling acuteness. He could scoop out her innards like the ripe vermilion of a pomegranate.

With enough focus, she could commune with her aether to carve a mouth into the floor, allowing the earth to swallow him. Her fingers twitched with the static charge of power.

"And I'm afraid I can't help you," she said. Her voice, soft as dove-feather down, was unsuited for belligerence and yet she steeled herself against the unsteady tremor that threatened to force its way through. "I don't know what you want Sadik for and I don't wanna know. Man's got plenty of joints under his name you can holler at. This ain't one of them. Now leave me be."

Something shifted quickly within his marmoreal façade, a lightning flicker, then his sclera had entirely blackened. He took a step forward, his face further degenerating into something of bestial origin as he parted his thick lips to reveal the point of his fangs—

The floorboard crunched beneath his foot as he walked. A warning. His face changed at the sight of the splinters crawling beneath his feet. Then the ground began to tremble. He looked up at her to see her fist was clenched, her eyes focused, and he understood.

He suppressed the urge to chuckle. As a witch, she had power at her disposal but not enough to be a threat to him. Dominus found Elina almost ludicrously unguarded from him—from the easy reach of her throat to the vulnerable white beaded muslin that sheltered her supple brown skin. He could blur over and snap her neck right now. With something that long and frail it wouldn't take more than a mere flex of his wrist. Perhaps he'd simply tug on that dark halo of hair tangled with feathers from the birds.

"You leave me be," she said, her voice maintaining a calm dignity even in the face of her fear. "I won't tell anyone I saw you. I won't tell a soul. Let me be. You owe me a debt, remember?"

The words vibrated through him, beckoning a memory of where he'd heard them last. A painless death ought to be payment enough. If he moved quickly she wouldn't even have time to scream or to suffer. There was no need to make a macabre scene out of it. But he needed her still.

"You are right, Mata Panja. I do owe you a debt," he said. "And I am a keeper of my word. Which is why I shall spare you when I enter that quaint little farmland you have in the night and rip the throats from your sister and daughter."

Elina swallowed tremulously, tender and fawn-eyed.

Dominus pivoted towards the door in determination. She had no doubt he intended to make good on his threat.

"Wait."

He paused, smiling in triumph. Then he turned back to her. "Well?"

"I'll give you what you want," she said, reaching towards the compact mirror on her desk. "Just... just leave my family out of it. Understand?"

"You have my word."

Elina gulped as she lifted the mirror. If she alerted the authorities he would know of it, and magic or no, she was not prepared to bring an occasso back to her doorstep where he could hurt Yasmin.

She made the call in defeat, deciding Sadik could deal well enough with a monster on his tail.

VII

ARIUS INSISTED LAILA STAY A FEW NIGHTS in the Citadel after her disastrous journey. He cleared a wing of rooms for her, filled with space and light. Mortesian sun blanched the rooms through the gossamer drapes, seeping along the surfaces of curvaceous furniture accented with rusting gilt. Only the leaded glass lanterns remained steadfast in their vibrancy on either bedside table, still dwindling with a flame from when Laila had last lit them.

She peeled back the soft fur throw on her bed, her body toasted warm beneath it. It had been ripped from a sabre-toothed beast with shaggy hair as rich as bonfire smoke. The throw was one of the many provisions Darius had made to ensure her comfort, each one as intimate to her as if he had traced his lips down her neck. Even now he had managed to maintain his impeccable attunement to her tastes, and she couldn't help but feel herself thaw, if only by an increment, when met with his thoughtfulness.

Laila unravelled the silk tignon from her hair and shook her curls free of her pineapple bun. Then she opened up the curtains to banish darkness to the furthest corners.

She decided to go over her mental checklist whilst taking a bath. When she entered the washroom she caught a glimpse of herself in the mirror—her wan face and bruised eyes from lack of sleep. She touched them with a sigh. Terror from her journey had held her in a throttle throughout her first night in Mortos. She'd tossed and turned, hypersensitive to sound, each breath feeling like a match struck against her lungs.

Even now she could feel her aether, buzzing in an angry hive beneath her skin. It itched at her, making her want to shred through filmy skin tissue to free it. In these times, she would think of the meditation lessons she used to take with Léandre in the Dream Realm. The way he would circle a crystal against her temple, commanding her to breathe in time with the gesture. The thought of him made her loneliness feel even more conspicuous, and she resolved to contact Lyra after her bath.

The maids made quick work of helping her wash and dress, though when it came to her hair it was discovered they knew little of what to do with texture like hers.

"I'll take over from here," Laila assured them, picking up the other gift adorning her vanity table—a delicate hair comb of chiselled ivory, elaborately carved and fretted with a background of flowers and birds and foliage. Darius had had the ivory wrenched from the same sabre-toothed beast as her blanket. She wondered if wearing it would give him the wrong impression before deciding not to dwell on it, inserting it into her bun.

She picked up her handheld mirror and called for Lyra, watching the light fluctuate before she answered.

"Missing me already?" Lyra's lips curled into a self-satisfactory grin that Laila couldn't help but share.

"Terribly," she admitted. She decided not to mention what happened to Cressida. "Especially now there's no one there to hold me at night."

"Ah, so you didn't cave and crawl into Darius's bed first thing? I commend you."

Laila scoffed. "You hold me in such low regard."

"Absolutely untrue!" Lyra protested. "I won't hear such slander of my good name."

Laila smothered a hand against her lips, muting her giggle. "How is home?"

"Ah." Lyra swallowed, the verve in her opal eyes dimmed. "I've had to take some leave from Soleterea for a short while. There's been some trouble in Thalistan your mother has asked me to look into."

Laila hummed in interest. "Well, at least you'll be keeping busy. Won't have time to miss me."

"We'll see about that." Lyra twiddled the end of her winter-blonde sprite braid. "And you?"

"My first order of business ought to be to immerse myself in the political landscape. Maman has all but thrown me to the sharks with no life raft. So I shall have to start from scratch."

"You know I have every faith in you," Lyra said, then a sound of interference caused her to look distracted.

"Interloper?" Laila guessed.

"I'll have to see this one, I'm afraid. We'll talk later."

"All right, g—"

The glass faded before she could finish. She set down the mirror with a sigh. Then a knock on the door caused her head to whip around. "Come in."

It was Sabina, leaning casually against the doorway with a lopsided smile. "Darius Rex wishes for me to offer my services to escort you around Mortos."

"Oh... that's..." Laila tried to resist the affectionate flutter that gave her. "Very kind of you."

Sabina nodded. "Shouldn't be too much disturbance if we stick to the safer roads and away from the wilderness. Where would you like to go first?"

∞

Laila's first excursion out of Gravissia led her to the hinterlands. Sabina knew exactly which roads to take to steer them away from the worst of the wild beasts; she only had to fell a few stragglers here or there to get them to their destination safely.

According to Amira's notes, these were the deepest areas of deprivation and where shipments of famine relief were needed the most. As Laila neared the entrance of the qarna village she couldn't help but feel even the smallest atmospheric noise had been snuffed into a graveyard silence. Even breathing too quickly or too loud was a disturbance.

Her primary aim was to investigate how agriculture was handled here, upfront and on the ground. In Vysteria, they'd long enjoyed the prosperity offered by ætherglass houses. The impenetrable domes of crystal treated by solarite magic would drink in sunlight by the gallon and use it to warm and nourish the crops inside their spheres. Miniaturised versions of those same domes would be used to keep crops from withering during their journeys north.

The comparison to Mortos was stark. Instead of glass houses, farmers toiled through a serpentine maze of brick walls heated by pipes of volcanic hot water. From there it appeared crops were funnelled into storehouses and kept prevented from decomposition through the use of chaos magic. They couldn't generate life with their craft, but they could extend what was dead.

Unfortunately, this didn't seem to be enough. The crops were still exposed, still vulnerable to the elements here besides frost alone. As Laila wandered the outskirts of one wall she took a record of the fruits growing and their maturation, jotting down notes in her journal.

A sudden gasp snatched Laila from her thoughts, and she turned to see a small qarnina carrying a basket of apples. When their eyes met, the qarnina paled, legs wobbling in panic.

Laila lifted her hand. "Oh no, don't be afraid—" But the sound of her voice only startled her.

The qarnina dropped her basket and ran, leaving the green apples toppling out onto the brown grass.

Laila drew in a breath as she watched her go before making her way to pick up the scattered fruit and return them to the basket. As she did so, more qarna skulked to observe with their antlers peeking from the sides and over the top of the walls.

"Please, I do not come here to punish you." Laila used a gentle tone. "I have peaceful intentions."

Eventually, an elderly qarnina approached with a shaky tapping of her cane. Her antlers had become spider-webbed with age. "You must forgive their suspicion." Her eyes were twinkling inside their hollow and sunken sockets. "Someone of your standing would typically have little time to spare us unless it is to amuse yourself with our misfortune for sport."

Laila's eyes softened, her chest giving a little hitch of sympathy. "Well, I can safely say today is when that pattern breaks."

The qarnina hummed in response, far from convinced. "My name is Anya. I speak for the qarna here. If you'd follow me, princess, we can speak more comfortably."

Laila allowed them to lead her to the church where they gathered for meetings. She noted the qarna lived rather simply in comparison to the imposing estates of their landmasters erected in black stone. Wood lodges if they were fortunate, mud huts if they were not. Always engulfed by the leafy foliage of lichen and a sprouting of wax-polished fungi—similar to their antlers. They beautified them with intricate floral art and wooden lace, adorning the walls, doors, and windows in vibrant colours. As if they were painting a brave face over their adversity.

Their church seemed, from the outside, a stoic counterpart to the marble-clad temples resplendent in mosaic tiles, crystal chandeliers, and altars inlaid with mother-of-pearl back in Soleterea. However, the rustic exterior gave way to true inner beauty—as the frescoed walls and ceiling could more than attest to. Depictions of the ungodly trio—Calante, his wife Anara the Dea Matrona, and their son Callus splayed across the walls.

Laila's footsteps echoed on the marble floor of the aisle as she took in Anara's canonised visage. Her sleek raven hair, alabaster skin, and pert red lips. She was known to many as the first creation of Calante—a bride to bear his child and give life to the royal bloodline of House Calantis. Her torturous beauty had been immortalised onto pendants and paintings and other such religious memorabilia for millennia. Well, before her Fall, at least.

Laila walked down the aisle towards the altar where a bronze relief of the six-headed eagle leered above, identical to the one in the Citadel's portrait hall. She was met with the same sense of discomfort at its nearness. Tiny serrations of dread scraped inside her chest.

"Thank you for accepting my presence," Laila said, receiving the cup of mushroom tisane offered.

Anya's aged bones creaked as she sat down on a tree stump. "Do tell us why you're here, princess."

"Denizens of Mursk, I bid you good morning." Laila glanced across the morose faces on the pews. "I am Laila Rose, Crown Princess of Soleterea and Espriterre, and I have travelled far to learn more about your country's agriculture."

Murmurs of scepticism erupted.

"I recognise that the best way to learn about something is to gather information from those with the most expertise. And my research has led me to you. So, please, tell me everything."

The murmurs grew louder, more nervous.

Then a young qarnina stood up. She had large round eyes and a delicate build. Most of her height was in her moss-covered antlers. "M-my name is Olga, Your Radiance. And—" She paused with a swallow, tugging on her loop braid. "Since the Culling began, my family has not known a moment's peace."

She told Laila of how the qarna were indigenous to the land before it was cursed and overrun by monsters. Herbivorous by nature, they saw famine worse than any other on the island, and the occassi frequently withheld food and manufactured starvation to keep them complacent, feeding livestock more than them. They'd later adapted to dandelion weeds, nettles, and wild berries, but occassi would demand sacrifices be provided every five years—the Culling—to bolster their undead workforce, and many qarna would sell themselves or their children as indentures just to stave off their perpetually empty stomachs.

After Olga's brave testimony, more were emboldened. They burdened Laila with their grievances of starvation, pestilence, poverty, and foul weather.

"Those bloody corpses have been stealing our livelihood for too long!" cried a farmhand named Rurik. "How's one supposed to compete with something that does not pause to sleep, eat, or piss? Seems there's shit all to do in Mortos other than to scrounge for the scraps our lord tosses us to breed, then wait for the alms we receive for participating in the Culling."

"You receive *compensation* for the Culling?" Laila asked.

"Indeed, Your Radiance," Rurik said. "Every year running up to the grand event we're given a decent supply of essentials to keep us from knocking on death's door. In exchange, we give our bodies to them. And if we cede a Culling we sacrifice alms for a lustrum."

"If the Culling were to be banished," Laila said, "then you would lose these alms?"

"Oh, almost certainly, Your Radiance!" exclaimed Agata, bouncing a baby on her hip. "Why, without that support many of us would lose what little the occassi already deign to provide. A more recent opportunity has arisen with the instatement of the new rex, but even that is in short supply."

"What opportunity do you speak of?"

"The rex offers work in his research facility of Darkwater Towers. It requires residence overseas in the Towers themselves, but it pays a handsome fee to one's family. A far sight better than anything else around here."

It surprised Laila to hear this of Darius. Against herself, her fury waned.

"I want to thank you all for sharing this. I will be sure to mention everything I have heard here in my next meeting with the rex."

The Memory Palace was located in the more affluent underground of Gravissia. There, occassi of certain distinguished stock would venture to sample and critique a variety of traumas distilled as liquid from unwilling participants for clarity, ambience, potency, flavour, and finish and ingest them as though they were fine spirits. There were grisly recollections of many types, the most potent forms of spiritual suffering you could ever imagine—shaken, stirred, and mixed into cocktails to be served alongside dainty morsels and fat cigars.

Darius exited from the carriage and lifted a hood over his features before making his way towards the roped entrance.

"Name and booking?" inquired the doorkeeper.

"I'm here to see Daggerfinger," he said, brandishing his signet ring with the royal seal.

The doorkeeper's eyes widened in realisation. "O-oh, Your Majesty, I didn't recognise you!" he spluttered as he unclipped the rope. "Step through to the bar counter and Sergius Severis will arrive to collect you."

He did so gladly, swerving through the enclosed booths of plush leather and lacquered walnut, the trivial badinage taking place between the patrons, and the waiters carrying trays of delicate appetisers before, finally, he reached the bar. The countertop was obsidian, with carvings of mythological beasts chiselled into the wooden base.

"Your Majesty, it is an honour." The bartender immediately bristled with the acknowledgement of his presence. "May I offer you the usual?"

"Actually, Antonius, I was wondering if you happened to have any non-suffering spirits in stock?"

Antonius blinked in confusion. Ah, but how serious young occassi were. All that hypersensitive pride brimming beneath a delicate seal of stoicism.

"Ease up, soldier, it was a joke," Darius said with a wink. "I'm here to see Daggerfinger."

"I'm afraid that won't be possible now, sire, he is quite…" A muffled shriek perforated the otherwise dignified atmosphere of the lubricating elite. Not even a ripple did they make in response. For them, it may as well have been ambient music. "… busy."

"You mean to say he should refuse a rex's audience?"

The bartender's eyes flitted with discomfort. "Wait here."

Darius watched him shuffle off to meet his master. His hip pressed against the bar and his elbow rested atop the counter. To be truthful, he was rather thirsty, but Mortesian alcohol had a potency that was almost hallucinogenic, and he needed to keep his wits about him.

The bartender returned with a stern resolve in his step. "Sergius Severis will see you now."

He escorted Darius towards the backroom, where another bodyguard obstructed his entrance. He stepped aside to let Darius through to a room where satin ran red as molten lava. Darius felt as though he had stepped into the throbbing walls of a ventricle with all its volcanic humidity.

Velvet blinds smothered out the sunlight, relegating all sources of brightness in the room to the oil lamps. Silhouetted by the glow of the flames was Daggerfinger, ankles crossed over the expanse of his desk.

"Well, well, if it isn't the Great Leviathan himself." Daggerfinger dropped one foot with a softened thud onto the carpeted floor, followed by the other. "To what do I owe the pleasure?"

"I'm here to procure that favour you owe me." Darius unhooded himself and slinked over to the desk to lean against it. "I think it's about time you paid."

Sergius reclined in his chair, fingers locked over his chest. "And what favour would that be?"

"You've benefited immensely through my aid in helping you discover how to extract negative emotion into pure essence"—Darius made a quick sweeping gesture around the vicinity—"so now I'm here to collect."

"And what could the Rex of Mortos possibly need from me?" Sergius asked. "You don't exactly appear to be hurting for much, tucked away in that little castle of yours. Would you have me serve you for free, Your Majesty? I've noticed you like coming here, and yet after all this time, so many decades, you've not once come barging in here asking me for nought. So, what's changed?"

"Tell me why you've been dealing memory boxes to Vysteria."

"Why, I have been doing no such thing, Your Majesty!" Sergius flattened a hand over his chest in feigned hurt. "Surely you are aware that chaos magic is strictly prohibited."

"Don't try my patience, Sergius." Darius's blue-green eyes lit up. "You did well to be one of the few who avoided having their heart on a pike after that witless moongrass affair."

"I see you continue to misdirect the source of your ire." Sergius smothered a low burbling chuckle. "That 'witless affair' was merely the act of a few enterprising merchants trying to restore our country's dignity after a few robber baronesses tried to strip our silver mines for spices. Though I'm sure the Citadel coffers were enjoying its cut before the solarites locked the doors on trade. Who was to know their precious little mortals couldn't handle a bit of powder? Certainly never did us any harm—"

"Enough," Darius responded sharply. "Those who produced moongrass knew precisely the effect it can have on the feeble-bodied. Just like *you* know the danger that could be wrought from allowing desperate mortals access to untapped chaos. My time is paramount, Sergius. We can either have this conversation in the comfort of your office or inside the Citadel dungeons. Your choice."

"Look at you!" Sergius's lips peeled back into a lupine smile. "Get a crown on your head and already you think yourself entitled to start riding my cock like this." His voice dropped to a deep and guttural sound, more akin to a quaking rumble. "Though you do that rather well, if I recall."

Darius suppressed the flex in his jaw. "We are not in university anymore, Sergius. And I am not your mentee. You will show me some respect."

"Did that lunatic father of yours teach you nothing through those beatings, Dara?" Sergius reached over for his decanter of whisky, removing the lid with a hollow pop. "You don't ask for respect." He poured himself a glass. "You earn it."

Darius smoothed a hand through his pomaded hair, soothing his temper along with it. "You are quite right, Sergius." He plucked the tumbler from the occasso's fingers before he could sip. Then he reached around the back of Sergius's head, stroking it. "It seems I am going to have to do this my father's way."

He jerked Sergius's head back at a quick enough speed to fracture his neck.

The dungeon was said to be the oldest part of the Citadel, and the one most resistant to refurbishment. Once, when the occassi were still new and impetuous and full of foolish hubris, the House of Calantis carved a niche for themselves on top of a lava lake. They continued to keep it as a reservoir to extract thermal heating and provide an excruciating torment for their enemies.

Now only the former was meant to be true, at least officially. Though the cacophony of cries, shouts, and guttural grunts could more than attest to the latter. But the atrocities that took place in this noxious pit of corrosive heat would never see the stamp of the official seal.

Delanus remained on the furthermost floor of the dungeon, away from most of the waxing heat of the lava lake that begged to strip the meat from his bones. Even so the humidity lingered, sticky and distracting; it fused his clothes to the silhouette of his muscles.

He knew Darius meant to question Severis down here, and he wanted to wait for the interrogation to be complete, flipping through the ledger of Severis' accounts.

By the time Darius came back, the screaming had finally ceased. He emerged up the steps with sleeves rolled back, a few buttons on his rubakha loosened and his wavy hair slightly dishevelled. He instinctively slicked back his hair with blood-stained fingers, pasting inky smears through the impeccable locks.

"Had a productive conversation with Severis?" Delanus asked.

"Yes, I became very intimate with his inner workings," Darius said with scintillating clearness.

Seeing the predatory gleam in Darius's eye, Delanus asked, "Is he alive?"

Darius tilted his head sideways. "Mostly, minus a few inessential organs. I set the vultures on him."

Delanus gulped at the thought of a horde of ravenous vultures shredding at Sergius's innards.

"It fascinates me how well we can keep going as long as our heart remains fully intact."

His blue eyes had the deadening chill of midwinter; Delanus felt frostbitten when they met his. "So what did he tell you?"

"Unfortunately, I extracted little more than what I already knew," Darius said, a brittle edge waning his otherwise cordial tone. "He sends primarily to Thalistan, receiving a hefty sum in return. Yet he will not tell me to whom and he will not tell me why."

"Do the *whos* and the *whys* matter?"

"If there are factions of humans stocking up on chaotic magic items, then I want to know about it. Preferably before Amira." He ran his fingers down his jawline. "The only two reasons I can fathom for wanting this in large supply is to study it or weaponise it. Both of which I consider to be cause for concern."

Delanus grunted in response, flipping through the ledger again. "Let him cook for a few days and we'll see if that doesn't soften him up."

Darius sighed arduously. "Well, I don't know about you but I think some tea is in order." He lightly skirted past Delanus's shoulder with his own before resting his hand atop it. "Let me get cleaned up and we'll discuss this later." With that, he sauntered up the steps with a jaunty whistle.

Back in the royal antechamber, Laila helped herself to milk and honey while she waited for Darius to arrive. She sipped sparingly at her beverage, finding it to be a much needed comfort. She longed to discuss her recent findings with him and yet, she had not had the bravery to face him since the dinner on her first night.

She told herself this was a fleeting thing, that whatever had led him to say those things at dinner was simply to test the waters for rekindlement. That he couldn't possibly have wanted and pined for her all those years.

His final words to her before he left Soleterea echoed in her mind. *Perhaps one day, a decade or so down the line...*

He had not meant it. She couldn't possibly fathom he could have. And yet, the pain and dejection he had displayed at dinner had been real enough. Her urge to reach out to him and stuff the words back into her mouth had been too.

She took another sip of milk to calm her nerves, then put the drink down in preparation. She could hear his footfalls and decided to act casual, propping her elbow atop the divan with her legs extended.

Meanwhile Darius, desperate for a shower, had not been anticipating to experience any diversions. Hence, when he finally did turn the corner to see Laila sitting in wait, he froze in alarm.

"Oh, good, you're here. I've been waiting for—" Her words died on her lips when she saw him. She sprang up from the chair in shock. "What happened to you?"

He deliberated on many excuses but realised it mattered not what she thought. "Nothing."

He closed the door behind him and smoothed the now drying blood on his hair.

"You're... covered in blood."

"It's not mine," he said, breezing past her.

She swivelled round to face him. "Is that supposed to be of comfort to me?"

Darius sighed, cupping his hands over his face. He turned around to meet the full extent of her judgement. "Why are you here, Laila?"

Laila scoffed in disbelief. *So, this was how it was to be, then.* "I came to tell you that I've held a meeting with some qarna citizens."

"You spoke to the *qarna*?" Darius couldn't believe his ears.

"Well, they are as much a part of the country as the rest of you." Laila steeled herself for what came next. "Have you ever perhaps considered alternative systems to the one you have in place with your ghouls? The benefits of having an empowered workforce can be immense. Vysteria wouldn't be half what it is today without them."

"Let me guess." Darius leaned back against his desk, iron-cast in his conviction, the rigid core found at the root of all things. He would not bend easily to her. "This is about your mother's ætherglass initiative? I've already given her my answer on that."

"Why do you refuse our aid?" Her tone soured into lemon tartness. "With ætherglass, you could help provide every race of this land a far better chance at avoiding starvation."

"Convenient how this would come of great benefit to you, I'm sure. That electoral competition is starting to intensify, is it?" He was unable to stop the splinter of amusement cracking his face. "Laila, qarna are prey, that is simply how they are made. They herd themselves in their little tight flocks and sprout themselves like weeds, praying to see another morning. To slaughter them is the natural order. I see no reason to delay the inevitable, not when I can better extend their usefulness as corpses."

She frowned at him, a delicate crease appearing in her brow. "Yet what is the point of having all this power if we do nothing to make the world a little better, more fair, more survivable? Why continue to simply take and give nothing back? What kind of existence is that? What kind of leader are you—"

"You are still young, princess; you have not yet reached your first century." Darius made an insouciant gesture with his hand. "Soon you will see an entire generation lay itself to rest and never rise again, only to take up valuable land to rot and feed worms. Where does the benefit come from *extending* my hand to my lessers? Sentiment? The perception of benevolence? How hollow must your gestures be if it is all under the guise of *seeming* good enough to be a desirable and electable candidate, rather than out of pragmatic efficiency?"

"That's not. I—" Laila grew flustered. "Stop acting as though my compassion is a pretence, Darius. As though it is not the reason I am here before you now rather than at the side of my mother agreeing that you are beyond reach."

"Your *compassion*?" He spat the word as though it disgusted him. "You made it clear it was anything but compassion that brought you here. Rather, cold, hard ambition." He stood up to make his way towards her. "Let us be truthful. I am not a dog for you to pet and pacify and send away with a scold when I displease you, Laila. How supercilious you are, standing here as though you act purely in the interest of saving us from ourselves. As though we are all wild, savage things from the north infiltrating the poor, victimised south and leaving a taint upon your otherwise unblemished region. If that is truly what you think, then you are better off returning home to Soleterea. You knew what we were, what I am, when you first stepped foot here."

Her breath hitched in anger as he neared. He was too close to her, but she refused to give up her pride and relent. She didn't understand why she let him disarm her with such glib displays of flattery and snake-tongued words, when beneath that amiable exterior was another cold-blooded predator like the rest.

"Perhaps I thought you were capable of being more than this." She gave him a scathing once-over, her voice soft yet scornful. "I see I was mistaken."

He recoiled in spite of himself. Frustration tensed in his muscles from the blood still hardening on his skin as he turned from her and loosened the buttons to his rubakha.

"What are you doing?" Laila asked, sounding breathless. Her hand clutched the frame of an armchair.

"I am going to rinse this blood off of myself, as it has now dried over the course of this riveting conversation." He undid the last button and slipped off his rubakha. "I'd suggest you leave now, unless you are intent on joining me."

Her heart skipped at the sight of his physique, and she hoped he did not hear it. She knew what his intent was. He wanted to unsteady her, ignite a battle between her repulsion and her inextinguishable desire that was so encompassing it made her legs go weak.

When Darius turned to see her still standing there, he gave her an expectant look and popped the button to his trousers next. "Well? Are you coming or going?"

She could've electrocuted him on the spot, but she knew any transmission of emotion, whether it be rage or lust, would be giving him precisely what he wanted. So instead she maintained a prideful dignity and left the room as if he were nothing worth noting.

Darius flinched at the sound of the door closing before stripping nude and staggering into the balneum, too weighed beneath the mounting stressors of the day to do anything but stand underneath the chimera stone tap.

He released a deep sigh of relief when it spewed ice-cold water on his back, already feeling his muscles tense and unclench. A shiver trickled down his spine as rivulets of blood puddled around his feet, rinsed away by sterile water.

He had done that. He had pioneered the filtration systems built by chaos magic to disintegrate all the impurities held within water, providing it fresher and cleaner to all. And yet, she took one look at him and couldn't see beyond the blood still clinging to him from the occasso he had tortured. As if there were nothing else to him but that.

How long would he keep leaving himself open to be wounded by her kicks—to hope he might one day be risen in her esteem to become the noble suitor he so wanted to be for her hand?

Darius bowed his head and flattened his palm against the wall, eager to forget the altercation entirely. Without thinking, he put his hand on his cock and built himself up to erection. He closed his eyes and tried to focus on the sensation of pleasuring himself alone but his mind was too crowded, too full of noise. He needed something to clear him out.

His brow furrowed as he tried to focus on something arousing. A torrid fantasy. Or a patchwork of traits and attributes he had a proclivity towards. Yet nothing seemed to work. Not until he imagined the familiar slide of hands along his chest, helping him to wipe away the blood before they encased him, a warm cheek pressed against his back.

No, no, not this. He couldn't allow himself to think of this. But he couldn't stop the way his body responded to it. A bolt of lightning crackled through him, restoring life and vitality to his weary muscles. His cock stiffened, rigid with alertness, and blood thrummed through his veins in rapid pulsations.

Just the mere thought of her did this. Awoke him from the depths of his lassitude and erased the weight from his shoulders. So he let it play out in his mind. He imagined Laila putting her lips to the space between his shoulder blades and proclaiming she didn't mean what she said. That she did think him worthy. Kind, soothing words of honeyed affection drizzling in his ears.

I miss you. I want you. I love you.

His yearning fuelled his wild lust as the pace of his hand quickened. The whimpers he made grew more feeble until finally he reached climax.

She evaporated instantly after, leaving him behind with his cock in hand and an overwhelming sense of hollowness. He panted a few times and allowed the water to cleanse him of all his sweat and spend.

How pathetic he had become, allowing himself to indulge in these wistful fantasies just to coast him through an evening.

VIII

HE GOLDEN HOUR OF MORNING BLED THROUGH the windows, weakening the ætherald lamps Lyra had been using all night. She rolled her neck to alleviate some of the tension that had been mounting during her sleepless investigation.

She took a swig of violet gin straight from the bottle before glancing over the heliographic reconstruction of the carnage. The dismembered bodies of clan knights were strewn about her in jigsaw pieces. She took another deep swig before dragging over one of the heliographs of interest. Rainer's body stared at her open-eyed, his fire-opal irises now clouded with milk. Along his neck and face were the striations of black veins, a common side effect of chaotic magic exposure.

Since her first mission to eliminate Dominus had gone awry, she had been scanning night and day for any lead she could use to pick the trail back up. He'd been careful enough with his movements, travelling mainly at night and concealing himself within shadows. But he would have to slip up soon. Lyra was sure of it. And once he did, she would gladly drive a bolt sword through his heart.

She corked her gin bottle and put it on the table, picking up the results sheet she'd received from the potion specialist detailing all of the ingredients Dominus had used for his decoction. She didn't recognise the recipe, but it was undoubtedly chaotic in origin, with reagents he couldn't have scavenged easily in the wild. He had to be getting it from somewhere. But from whom?

Occassi would never speak to sprites, that much she knew. Not even if she came under the guise of a polite inquiry. However, there was one demoness she'd been intending to pay a visit to.

She picked up her pistol and slotted it into her holster and then exited onto the forested trails, alive with the ruckus of beasts and humans alike, but it was past the aromatic heart of the wood Lyra wished to travel to. Down the lichen-carpeted steps to where a colony of occassi had festered.

One could tell how much closer they were getting to it by the way the surroundings shifted. The trees that once dominated this natural stairwell crumbled away to give space for this urban enclave. The botanical odours native to the country had been smothered by cigar smog. Even the creatures who'd once called it home had fled, sensing the naked danger in their midst. It was the lair of decomposers now.

Lyra cringed when she accidentally crunched a snail underfoot and scraped off its remains on the kerb, stiffening when she saw the glowing eyes of ravenous rats blinking in and out of the gutters. Her neck prickled with dormant huntress instincts as she kept her focus on the task ahead—the rows of dilapidated stone houses falling prey to foul weeds, moss, and waxen brown mushroom heads.

She meant to breach one den in particular. Whisperings through the sprite network had alerted her to what hid inside, but she needed to see it to believe it.

She didn't bother knocking before she entered, throwing open the door on the tawdry conclave that had gathered. Its members consisted mainly of men. Human men. Scantily clad in fur loincloths and slicked with oil.

A cloud of moongrass smoke veiled the air as it flowed from brass pipes passing between their lips. They converged around the occassella at the centrepiece who sprawled leisurely in a fur-edged cape with a man feeding her grapes coated with his own blood. She hummed in pleasure as she traced her sharpened claws down his face with faint affection before bidding him on his way.

When she noticed the intrusion, she sat up with a coiled smirk on her lips and revealed a tight gown that left little to the imagination. "Well, well, boys. It appears we have company."

Lyra realised she'd not often seen an occassella this close, and the experience was like encountering a rare, exotic beast in the wild. She felt bewilderment, terror, and a little admiration. "Are you Vesperia?"

"Guilty." She cocked her head to one side. "Have to say, I don't get spritemaids knocking on my door too often. To what do I owe the pleasure?"

"I think it might be best if you tell me what all this business is." Lyra placed her hands on her hips, keeping one finger perched on the handle of her pistol.

"Them?" Vesperia's lips broadened to a toothy grin and a hint of fang. "Why, these fine specimens are merely keeping me company. No law against that, is there?"

A vein pulsed in Lyra's temple. "As long as they're all here by choice."

Vesperia's chuckle was thick as syrup as she snapped her fingers.

Immediately, a man rushed forward to offer her a moongrass pipe. "Quite willing, I'd say." She touched her palm against his cheek. "This one became mine after I rearranged his skeleton to cure his humpback. That one over there." She pointed in the near distance. "I extracted a virus from him that would have claimed him long ago otherwise. And that one." She flung her hand in another direction. "I ate his woe and despair and he fell to his knees for me at once. These were lost and discarded lambs when I came here. Wanted by no one. I give them a place to stay."

"And it just happens to be a coincidence that terrible misfortune befalls those surrounding these men shortly after they came to your service?"

"I've already had a lengthy discourse regarding this with your fine uniformed ladies at the Iron Clan." Vesperia handled the pipe with cultivated precision, betraying the ancient aristocracy in her blood. She perched it between her berry-red lips, her dark lashes sweeping low. "If someone's cruel lover has her hair fall out in stress? A domineering employer loses her fortune? A neglectful mother develops a bout of boils? What is it to do with me?"

It was on the tip of Lyra's tongue to command she cease with her smug obfuscations. Preferably with her fist around her throat.

"Yet I imagine that isn't what you are here for?" Vesperia swivelled the pipe in her fingers. Her lips had left a dark red imprint from her lustrous rouge.

"Quite right." Lyra unrolled the sheet she'd been keeping up her sleeve. "I've come to inquire about this."

Vesperia plucked the sheet with her claws and gave it a quick scan with a bemused look and wrinkled nose. "What's this? An ingredient list for a potion? Well. I can't say I understand what you'd want to do with this."

"Why?" Lyra asked. "What does it do?"

"I'm afraid I'm going to have to disappoint you. I don't quite know. It's a recipe far more ancient than my years." Vesperia shrugged one shoulder. "I'd seek someone more senior from the motherland to answer that."

"I don't believe you." Lyra advanced upon her, jaw tightened. Her hand went to her pistol. Then stopped when she realised the men were gathering to protect their eldritch mistress.

Vesperia cocked her head to one side, curiosity sparked at the challenge.

They would be no match for Lyra alone, but harming mortal men would be anathema, and she didn't doubt Vesperia's lack of scruples to use them as shields.

"You've asked your questions, and I've been quite candid." Vesperia handed out the sheet to a man, who offered it back to Lyra. "And I don't appreciate my honour being called into question. I can scent your lust for my blood, huntress, and if I'm honest it's starting to tarnish the ambience. I bid you good evening."

"Evening," Lyra replied through gritted teeth before turning to leave the den. She paused to take a deep breath of air. All that moongrass was beginning to make her feel faint, but not enough to diminish the murderous rage battering at the doors of her ribs to be released.

Dominus arrived in a sherwani suit of all black, as though it were night itself that clothed him. The colourful verve which marked all Thal cities had now long been muted, much to the delight of his senses. Part of his reasoning for seeking refuge so deep within the rainforest was not simply its ease of obscurity but to escape the irrepressible exuberance of Thalistan's lifestyle. The smells were stronger here, the talking more frequent, too much skin and sweat and scent to distract him.

Tonight he would attend an exclusive event at The Blue Lobster, a supper club frequented by the fashionable of Thalistan. One of Sadik's legitimate fronts for his notorious alchemy chain. He'd received the invitation directly from Elina and had snorted in amusement at the brief notice declaring evening attire only. He'd thus mugged and murdered a mortal to facilitate this, helping himself to the contents of her purse.

The body he had left in an alleyway after contorting her skeleton to form the shape of a star. While there were many arts with which he was intimately familiar, from sketching to sculpting to the more abstract of disciplines, the most potent medium for him of all was blood and bone. Taking apart a creature's physical form and refashioning it into a tapestry of carnal imaginings—mosaics pieced together from different shades of bruising, patchwork hides, and splattered murals of viscera.

Now he waited patiently in another alleyway for Elina to arrive. He had insisted upon her accompanying him to the supper club as an incentive for Sadik to meet with him. In the past decades of hiding, Dominus had watched in real time the birth of the mogul and his unprecedented rise to success.

Mundane citizens rarely came into wealth so miraculously, not without there being some unsavoury means involved behind it. Dominus knew it to be true here, in the so-called idyllic continent of Vysteria, as it was back home. He was thankful Yilan didn't disappoint in that assumption. Beneath the guise of zany potions and spell reagents was an interconnected network of smuggling and selling chaotic magic wares on the market.

Suffice it to say, the mortal had money and means, two things Dominus was in dire need of, and a common crook would be a far more easily exploitable mark and far less likely to turn to the aid of sprites.

He heard the faint tapping of Elina's shoes on the pavement as he remained concealed in the alleyway. He emerged behind her with a smile, delighting in her nervous start before him.

"You're on time," he said, glancing over her shawl in celadon silk.

Elina narrowed eyes tinted with a palette of greens and golds in perception of him; her brow and temple were encircled by flower petals. "Let's get this over with."

He held out his arm to her, and she rebuffed him. So he took her arm more forcefully and rested it into the crook of his elbow. "Act natural."

"The disgust I feel around you is all instinct, you'd best believe." Her sable curls were adorned with a gold chain headpiece, and with each birdlike pivot of her head, the dropped-emerald ornament that dangled in the bridge between her eyes frolicked. "What do you want with Sadik anyhow?"

"I need not explain myself to you."

His dismissal riled Elina but she kept it contained. The sooner she could be rid of this ogre the better.

The doors to The Blue Lobster were shrouded by a canopy of cursive iron and coloured glass, fronted by a sculpted façade of its animal namesake that leaned with unsettling verisimilitude over the rim. When they neared the entrance, the door attendant held up a hand to halt them.

"Ah, Ms Elina!" The Thal smiled in recognition. "It's been quite a while."

"That it has, Jagjit." Elina handed him the invitation with a plus one attached. Sadik always sent them in the hopes she would come. She never did.

"Who's the friend?" Jagjit asked, scarcely glancing at the invite.

Dominus lightly tightened his grip on her elbow in warning. He could crumble her mortal bones like chalk if she wasn't mindful.

"He's an acquaintance of your boss." Elina smiled, her doe eyes betraying no untruth. "We're getting them reintroduced."

Jagjit hummed, giving him a onceover. He pocketed the invitation. "Well in that case, enjoy your evening."

With that, they entered through the antechamber to the sound of calypso. The coat area stood to one side, with the lavatories at the other. Brass double doors etched with the relief of peacocks led to the thick of the music and merriment. The club was an elegant palette of dark coffee and gold, several sculptures of the snake-goddess of life, Naya, interspersed throughout in gilt-bronze.

Dominus watched witches and men alike dine at elegant tables with beige leather chairs, with more private alcoves flanked by twisting pillars silhouetted behind sheer drapes of silk. His lip curled in distaste when he saw snake-hipped men wining on raised circular platforms, inciting jovial cheers and hoots of encouragement. *How degrading.*

"Which one is Sadik?" Dominus leaned down to murmur in Elina's ear.

"He won't be down here." Elina glanced upwards at the balcony area where a room was concealed behind tinted glass.

"Get me up there, then."

Elina led him past the servers to another guarded door. "I'm here to see your boss. He should be expecting me."

"Yes, Ms Elina." One of the guards stepped aside while the other appraised Dominus. "The occasso?"

"He is with me." Elina strained what she called her Grim Reaper smile, the one she always used before declaring a grave diagnosis. "Please, Sadik has been waiting a long time for this. He wouldn't want me to be held up."

The two soon relented and opened the door for her. Elina ascended the stairs with Dominus in tow, conscious that her act was beginning to wear thin. It was enough that she would be thrust before Sadik's presence for the first time in ten years, let alone also having to lie to get to him.

At the final door, her nerves had risen to sizzle in her stomach. Sadik would not be so easy to fool as his guards, and yet, at the same time, she would be glad to drop her performance around him. She exchanged the customary words to let them inside.

A man leaned against his desk in wait. His white tunic embroidered with gold was stark against his ebony skin, his long hair bound in gold-cuffed twists. "Well, well, if it isn't my honeybee, come to visit my hive. It's good to see you here, Ela."

"Don't start." These were the first words she had properly spoken to him in a decade, and yet, as always, his expression remained adoring. He was permanently frozen within the first throes of carefree summer love that had sprouted the moment they'd met.

"Now, Elina, is that any way to greet the love of your life?" He straightened with the aid of his cane—a gold-plated staff shaped like a firedrake adorned with obsidian orbs. "The least I could receive is a bit of sugar after you dragged a monster straight through my security measures."

"Sadik Yilan." Dominus savoured the name on his tongue as, at long last, he stood before him. "You're a difficult man to reach."

"For good reason, in your case, though it's not every day I'm blessed with the presence of visiting royalty." His eyes twinkled at Dominus's surprise—he had one black eye and one blue, the latter indelible proof of his bartered soul to chaos. "What might I do for you?"

"I have a proposition for you, one I feel will be quite... piquant."

"Well, I'm certainly all ears," Sadik said, before pointing his staff at Elina. "If you wouldn't mind letting her go first, that is. We don't need her being privy to this business."

"I'm afraid I can't do that." Dominus pulled Elina closer and brandished his claws at her neck. "You see, Elina here happens to be my insurance. Either you give me what I want or I slit her throat."

Sadik bowed his head in acknowledgement. "Your negotiating skills could use some work, monster." His hand slid up the expanse of the staff. "Let me tell you something."

He aimed the staff towards him and shot. A needle-like projectile embedded itself within Dominus's neck, and he accepted it with a smile, knowing whatever effect it might hold would be useless against him.

That was, until it took hold.

Then, slowly, his blood congealed and stiffened in his veins until he could feel every strain of his circulation attempting to wiggle through to his rapidly waning heart.

"What have you—" He could only stop to glance at the webbing black veins in his forearms before lack of oxygen forced him to yield consciousness.

Dominus drowned in his dreams again, his head surfacing as though he were held underwater. He felt lightweight, drifting, and then slowly tethered once more to the lawful bind of gravity. He was hyper-conscious of every frantic lurch of his chest as his bloated heart worked to drum circulation back through his arteries.

A moon-white face met him when he surfaced, her eyes unkind. *Welcome back to the land of the living, Dominus Calantis.*

When he awakened he realised he'd been chained. He could hear the ceaseless chatter of his bindings with every half-inch movement of his wrists. Though his pulse had triumphantly resumed, his veins were still stiffened and sore in black calligraphic patterns. He gave a perfunctory tug of his chains, testing. They didn't budge an inch, but a sudden oscillating stream of light irradiated the metal.

"Wouldn't fancy your chances of slipping free of those bracelets, monster." The sonorous vocals of Sadik rebounded against the metal walls.

Dominus's eyes darted rapidly to locate the source.

He found him seated in a raised booth of reinforced glass. When his eyes eventually met Sadik's, his captor smiled and raised a cocktail glass, complete with slices of lime and an umbrella, in salute. A miniature ocean swirled in glowing aqua liquor.

"Now, those chains are made from genuine meteorite, the cosmic metal of the solarites. The perfect bane for an occasso such as yourself."

Dominus clenched his fists, willpower warring against the futility that confirmed the incessantly blathering mortal was correct. He tried his best to summon a curse to shatter the window and was rewarded with a sharp wasp-sting of pain from his shackles.

"Stubborn, aren't you? Not used to being bested, I gather. Especially from someone barren like me. A harmless little magic-free mundane." Sadik spread his arms in a neutral shrug. "But you know what? That's what I love about chaos magic. And I mean, the real chaos magic. The potent kind. None of this watered-down, back-alley-brew-stirred-in-a-cauldron type shit. No. Real chaos magic. *True* chaos. Well, it favours us all."

Dominus had recognised the potent signature of chaotic magic the moment it had been used upon him. The staff had been imbued with *heartbreak*, likely with the aid of a memory box. What he could not fathom was how Sadik had come to acquire such power.

"If this is your idea of torture, then I must commend you... for I'd rather suffer a miserable death than be forced to endure another second of your drivelling."

"Well, well, it speaks." Sadik was delighted by this development. "But contrary to what you might be used to down in Mortos, I don't believe in torture. Never had the right incentive. Nah, I'm just keeping your ass put long enough for the Iron Clan to come and take you off my hands."

Dominus couldn't allow his journey to come to such a snivelling defeat as this. Not after all he had suffered. He scraped his mind for any figment of an idea that might lead him out of this predicament. But bound in chains with his magic impotent, Dominus found himself swiftly out of options. He didn't know the first thing to say that might sway a mortal of this nature.

Darius had always been the talker, the one with the throat full of sonnets, the silver tongue with its serrated edge. Dominus used to watch him make fine work of his victims—smoothly piercing through raised guards and inhibitions, burrowing through skull and cranial tissue. His weapons were words, and he never needed to pause to reload.

"Turning me over to Soleterea so easily"—his voice crackled before he moistened his lips—"seems foolish... when I could be so much more useful to you free."

Sadik stirred his glass with the cocktail stick and took a sip. "I don't see how that adds up. I let you loose and you might snap my neck the moment you're handy, or go after Elina. I have little use for loose cannons like you, monster. It's detrimental in the realm of business."

"You and I... We can help each other... You have money, connections, influence..." Dominus swallowed thickly. "All things I require... and I assure you... the rewards shall be immense."

Sadik's eyes narrowed in consideration, his interest piqued. "What kind of rewards are we talking here?"

"Soleterea... destroyed my life... ruined my family... corrupted my brother… You help me enact revenge… I shall give you anything you desire."

Sadik steepled his fingers and tapped them idly against his mouth for a few moments. "I'll think it over, monster." He drained his glass and shuffled across to the exit. "I may have a task for you yet."

IX

ABINA SCOOPED A SPOONFUL OF CAVIAR INTO HER mouth, chased by a crunch of gravlax-topped black bread. She gorged herself, unmoved to the disapproving sounds of her father indicating his distaste for her gluttony. "Aren't you going to eat today, Father? You've touched nothing but your water."

Delanus glimpsed his nettle-infused beverage with disinterest. "I was wondering if you were going to leave anything for me but scraps."

Sabina paused mid-munch before quietly resuming.

Delanus spooned a lump of caviar into his mouth for the sake of having something fill it. "How have your patrols been?"

"Good." Sabina took a bite out of black bread. "Still quite a bit of illicit dark objects dealing. Random spouts of occasselle migration. The usual."

She never went into much detail, for she knew her father didn't truly care. Perhaps if she'd been a son rather than this disappointing hybrid of a daughter... but such things were not meant to be.

"We really ought to have stricter regulations in place for those migrants," Delanus grumbled. "After your mother ran off... Well. I kept trying to tell Darius. Clearly his priorities differ from mine."

Sabina dipped her bread into some bat soup. "I'll request it be looked into." That was a lie; in truth, she was glad the caged birds had begun to flee. She'd let go of any notion of her mother when the occassella had abandoned her at her most tender and vital age—the eve of what should've been her first blood. Ever since then she hadn't wanted, hadn't *needed*, to think of her excerpt to curse her name.

But she knew better than to broach the topic, lest she provoke the rage Delanus could unleash upon her at a moment's turn ever since she has been discovered to be barren and no longer fit into his machinations to become the future heir-bringer to Mortos. It was the first time she understood what had led her mother to flee.

Delanus leaned back in his squeaking chair and laced his fingers together. "Good girl."

She sensed his belief was marginal at best but it bothered her not as long as he abstained from asking questions. "I'd better start making my way." She withdrew from her chair and picked up her pelisse. "It was... nice having breakfast with you."

Delanus snorted while keeping his eyes firmly planted on an official parchment.

Sabina lifted a shoulder, knowing it was the best she could hope for, and quietly left the room.

For the upcoming meeting with the prefects, Laila had received a black gift box tied with a bright red ribbon. Inside it was a Mortesian court gown of white satin finished with draped tulle and garlands of miniature white roses, along with a panel of pink velvet at the front clasped with pearl buttons. A kokoshnik of pink velvet adorned with pearls sat on top.

The card left had been unsigned: *First impressions are everything, I hear.*

She decided to heed the message and wear it, noticing that a few of the little buds along her hanging sleeves were beginning to crisp and brown until she rejuvenated them with her life-giving powers. She had her golden hair braided into two canerows laced with pink ribbon in the form of a corset, the kokoshnik fastened on top.

Then she was off to the Eyrie, where the members of the Council sat with Darius at the apex of the ironwood table. When he stood, so too did his prefects, as though he were a puppeteer and they were the marionettes tied to the end of his strings.

"Your Radiance." Darius bowed to her before he turned to his prefects. "Princess Laila has arrived from Soleterea to act as a proxy on behalf of Impératrice Amira. She has, therefore, requested that I call this meeting so we may talk. I trust you will welcome her warmly."

Rather than heed their ruler's request, the prefects appraised her with serpent pupils and cold gazes. Their veneer of ice was a mere cap to suppress the simmering animosity poised to erupt. She'd never been presented before the company of so many male participants in political affairs, and the change in atmosphere was stark.

Still, she blossomed in spite of the frostbitten chill of their reception, and she allowed Darius to take her arm to escort her to a chair before assuming his own position at the head of the table.

"My purpose here today," she said, "is to discuss the relationship between our nations. I therefore encourage you all to speak candidly about how you consider our trade union to be progressing." Even as a peripheral object of the room, Laila siphoned attention in the way a hummingbird drained nectar from a flower. "All commentary, both positive and negative, will be a vital contribution to this report."

The prefects exchanged looks before their gazes drifted towards Darius, almost in inquisition.

"You may speak freely." He sipped from his goblet of polugar.

Delanus was the first to break the fast of silence. "If I may address the primary concern? The immigration policies implemented in Vysteria for occassi: Many of us find them supremely invasive. Not to mention dangerous when mishandled. Enforcing us to acquire permits to practise chaos magic is one thing, but is it truly necessary to draw our blood to track our movements? To brand us for identification like common cattle? Occassi have only ever used marking as a symbol of marriage. You can, therefore, understand the intimacy of it."

Laila had feared this topic would be the first to be broached.

"With respect to you, Prime Delanus, we do allow a measure of autonomy to our member states within the commonwealth. The witches are only taking the actions they feel are necessary to preserve their safety. In Thalistan, tattooing is a staple of Thal culture, and the marking of occassi is merely a reflection of that practice. As for the registry, that is mostly a safety measure. The influx of occassi immigrants has seen a wave of chaotic magic activity to an extent that we have never before been forced to deal with."

"Chaos magic is no more or less harmful than the capabilities of your aether," Delanus replied impatiently. "Why then must we be treated as walking threats while the average solarite gets to run amuck?"

Laila stared at him with the impassive sentience of an alabaster effigy. "I wouldn't put it in those terms, but I am more than happy to be an advocate on your behalf. I feel that a dissenting voice is needed in Parlement when it comes to the status of occassi in our nation. I should like to provide it."

"And what benefit do you happen to derive from supporting us, Your Radiance?" Delanus asked, his golden eyes demanding. "Am I supposed to invest in the idea of your unwavering benevolence towards our kind? A gentle hand extended in the face of ignorance and suspicion? Forgive me if I am not so quick to believe it."

Laila tilted her head, keeping her eyes kind but her mind alert. She would have to work harder to coax this one, she imagined, but every creature had their preferred bait. "I respect your suspicion of me, Prime Delanus, but I only wish for us to move forward into the future with more peace on the horizon. I feel that cannot be accomplished until we truly put aside past grievances. As of now, the witches of Vysteria fear you. Your ways are foreign to us and thus quite unnerving. But this can be mitigated."

"Mitigated?" Prefect Augustus had lit up a cigar, sneering at her through a screen of smoke. "In what sense?"

Darius did not miss the chance to interject. "After consulting with Princess Laila, I have decided to abolish the Culling."

This caused an uproar of outrage and shock. Laila whipped round to face Darius, her violet eyes bewildered.

Darius lifted a hand to silence the room. "In truth, I have been considering implementing this for a while. Looking to Vysteria as an example, I have come to see how far our great nation has stalled in terms of progress. If we are to continue being a formidable threat on the world stage, Mortos must be allowed to advance. Perhaps through empowering our subjects, we will come to empower ourselves.."

"Your Majesty, I implore you!" Augustus said. "The corpse trade has been one of the more lucrative means of generating business ever since we migrated away from being creatures of war. To do away with it now may well ruin our landowners!"

Darius trailed his fingers along his steep jawline. "I am not suggesting we demand every occasso throw their ghouls upon the pyre. Only that we impose a sanction to forbid hunting qarna and implement a decreasing cap for corpse workers." He downed his goblet in one gulp. "Those who transition to using live workers will receive a subsidy for enticement."

"No amount of money will make hiring a qarnun over a corpse desirable," Delanus scoffed, helping himself to a goblet of polugar.

"I recognise that this may be a difficult transition, and thus I only request a trial. In the meantime, any qarna who commit crimes or perish of natural causes would be deemed fair game."

"And what shall replace the Culling in our calendars, then?" Delanus was growing flustered, his pointed ears ink-tipped as he grappled for any excuse he could. "The Culling isn't merely a matter of garnering workers, Your Majesty. It is... an event! A spectacle! A matter of national pride! You could not demand us to sacrifice it..."

"I may have a solution for that," Darius said, tracing the rim of his goblet. "In times past, we had fighting pits where warriors could challenge beasts in combat. It fell out of fashion, but I suggest we bring back the practice. I would be more than happy to lend out my chimeras for such an event. They grow weary in cages and could do with a little roam."

At the mention of chimeras, Delanus's throat bobbled in fear. He had not forgotten the way Darius had made him sit and watch as his father's loyalists were devoured in their seats, too paralysed by poison to escape their fate. The canary-eating grin Darius had given him after had told him more than enough. This was to be his fate, should he not relinquish fealty to Lanius.

"How soon do you propose we enforce these orders?" Delanus asked.

"Effective immediately," Darius replied. "I intend to call a Great Council at the earliest convenience: Anyone who is caught hunting qarna from that day forth will have a fine imposed on them, with potential for more punitive action taken if they continue."

Laila was stunned, and completely unprepared. She had all but counted Darius as being among the ranks she must battle, but, as always, he had swooped to the fore to protect her.

Darius glanced over at her for the first time in a while, his expression inscrutable. "I should think we have covered more than enough during this session, Your Radiance. Wouldn't you agree?"

"Yes," she said instantly, breaking free of her stunned silence to give a vigorous nod. "Yes, certainly. This will do for now."

"Well then." Darius placed down his goblet and tented his hands. "If that is all, my good fellows, consider this meeting concluded."

The prefects excused themselves with a noisy groan of seats as they retreated through the door.

Laila remained, hoping she might talk to Darius in the aftermath. Her feet bobbed impatiently as the last of the footsteps diminished and the only sound left was the drawing of her breath. Seizing the chance, she parted her lips to speak, but then Darius rose up from the table and vacated the room in silence.

When she searched for him later, she found Darius in the Portrait Hall, observing the short line of his dead relations and the spot where his portrait now hung among the rest.

She wondered sometimes if he still saw a forgery in himself, a lingering sense of mis-belonging from how he had achieved his placement. Not in blood and bone as his father had wanted of him, but in subterfuge and foreign intervention.

She understood little of the nobility of combat that so plagued the creatures here. To her, blood was blood; what did it matter how it spilled? Whether at the end of a blade or coughed up as a result of poison, the wickedness done was the same in essence. Perhaps it shook them a little, that for all their strength, speed, and smarts they could still end up laid out at the mercy of someone who lacked for all those things.

Darius turned slightly in Laila's direction, as though he were about to look at her. She hid immediately, pressing against a large pillar and hoping he wouldn't sniff her out. A pause strained for unbearable length and left her heart thundering and her stomach swarmed with butterflies.

"I know you're there," Darius said, wry and playful. "Come on out."

Laila stiffened, going over excuses in her head. She was surprised when a red-haired occassella appeared from a shadow instead.

"You're improving," Darius said.

"Well, I learned from the best." Sabina crossed her arms and leaned against the wall. "Did your meeting go well?"

"I think you know the answer to that," Darius said. "Like a tide meeting much resistance as it eats away at the shore. So goes the way of progress."

"I have every faith in you."

Darius Calantis was known to be many things—a bastard, a blood-traitor and usurper. Rumours had long circulated of his rapacious sexual appetites, that he took occasso and occassella alike to bed. Sometimes both at once. Shame and scornful ambition were said to have been sewn into the seams of his conception.

But Sabina saw nothing except a visionary she was happy to kneel before.

"That means a lot to me, Sabina."

She bent her head in response and turned to the portraits. The paintings were titanic in their brass frames. Sometimes she still expected one of them to wander free. She focused on the porcelain visage of Vasilisa, as doomed as she was lovely. At least, those were the tales that were woven about her before her untimely death at the hands of her husband.

Prior to her fate, she was everything a regina was meant to be—the physical embodiment of Dea Matrona Anara before her almighty Fall. Vasilisa was beautiful. Vasilisa was a mother. And then she died.

There were several more tales like that about reginas. These hollow painted husks who, like vases, were meant to sit pretty for things to be planted inside of them. Sabina preferred other tales, like the one of Narcissa who warded off the siege of lupari troops upon Gravissia with her other ladies. Even when she was caught and tortured, she never once broke, and that was what elevated her in the minds of many when they dared revere her name. Not that she was strong but that she was durable, made even more resilient by the fact that she suffered.

"Why don't you and I have a drink?" Darius rested a hand on Sabina's shoulder. "We haven't had a proper reunion since your travels."

"Lead the way."

Laila watched them go, her heart swelling with tenderness. A smile blossomed on her lips as she decided her confrontation with Darius could wait for later.

That evening, inspiration struck, and Darius retreated to his room. He opened his journal at the drawing desk to sketch his latest chimera. It was little more than a rough interpretation, nothing exceptional. Of the two of them, Dominus had always been the artist, but he made up for it by being a warrior in all other matters. Darius was the inventor, the scholar, the one with the decidedly effeminate pursuits of figure skating and fashion.

Lanius had tried, quite literally, to hammer off his smoother edges, to malign and mistreat him back into order. But even when Darius struggled to embody what his father desired in the hopes he would look at him with something other than thinly veiled contempt, it never stuck. He was too genteel to be a monster yet too pernicious to be anything other than what he was.

He'd had his heart, at least. After Darius had taken control of the Citadel, he had every dust-clogged corner of the grounds scoured for the one thing that remained of Lanius when he was banished to another realm. It had taken a lustrum, but they eventually discovered it wedged inside the taxidermied carcass of a cockatrice.

After a victory in combat, it was tradition to consume the heart of one's enemy. To ingest an occasso's heart was to consume his essence and therefore become him, master him, surpass him. Darius had his father's heart stuffed with herbs and garlic and allowed it to marinate in a fine brandy. He ate him in small, determined forkfuls, chewing him to a pulp, swallowing indulgently. With each bite he wondered if his father could sense him in the confines of his dimensional prison, holding his heart between his teeth. He hoped that he did.

He caught a faint whiff of scent as he sketched—juniper, iris, and lily-of-the-valley. He set down his charcoal. "I didn't think you were coming, Katya."

Katerina emerged from the shadows with a smirk and unclipped her cape. Her dark green robes differed from the court dress of other occasselle, signifying her rank as a blood sorceress of the Vidua Nocte. She wore a velvet overdress with a panelled shirtfront, adorned with gilt pairs of plate-like buckles. On her sleeves were pendants in the shape of overlapping ouroboros.

"Kirill let me in." She draped her cape over the top of a tufted velvet seat and then sprawled across it.

"If you're here on account of my mother, you can tell her my answer remains the same."

"Now Dara, don't be so hard," Katerina said, her voice low and saccharine like something sweetly forbidden. "She only desires to help."

"If by help she means undermining me by trying to control me from the shadows like she did my father, she can keep her aid." Darius inhaled sharply as he continued with his sketch.

His mother had been trying to worm her way into court since his ascension. She'd tried subtle methods at first, sending envoys and missives that he'd repeatedly turned away. Now she was being uncooperative when it came to matters of aiding the yearly crop yield for the summer. She did hate to be ignored.

"You would rather risk a famine than have her at court?" Katerina gasped. Her hazel eyes lit up from amber to green. "You are spiteful."

"A trait that we share, it seems."

Darius knew if he let that venomous viper into the Citadel he would never again be rid of her. He refused to acquiesce to her games. If his mother desired to toy with him, then he would toy back.

Katerina rested her chin on her fist, glancing at his desk. "What are you drawing?"

"I'm sketching my latest chimera," he said before returning to his task. He liked to keep a record of them, making entries of their abilities and attributes and how he might best utilise them. Not all of his chimeras would be employed for warfare; some of them he liked to use for construction or patrol support.

"You have developed a taste for crafting those little pets, haven't you?" Katerina rose up from the seat and stalked towards him, a tigress on the prowl, heavy hips languid in their motion.

"They keep the others in line," Darius said. "There are many who would seek to undermine me if they do not fear me. And the only way I am to be feared in a room full of monsters is if I am the one who bears the biggest fangs."

"Ooh." She slid a milk-white hand along his shoulder. "Sounds rather sensual."

Darius reached up to seize her wrist, pulling her into his lap. He tucked a strand of sable-dark hair behind her ear. She kept it loose and lascivious, as did all blood sorceresses.

Katerina pressed her lips against his in a kiss, then a nibble. Her fangs lightly pierced his bottom lip, and she lapped the ichor with her tongue. Affection often devolved into a feral, ravenous act with her, but Darius relished her hunger. It felt nice to touch and be touched after the sting of rejection. To feel the warm embrace of a lover's desire. Even though there was a part of him he couldn't quite silence that longed for more than this—sex with Katerina would fulfil him mechanically but in the end lacked emotional nourishment.

"Katenka," he murmured in a rich velvet voice, cupping her face to ghost his words over her lips. "Let's go to bed."

"That's a tempting proposition, Your Majesty." Katerina wrapped her arms around his neck. "But I want something in return."

"What's that?"

She tilted up his chin to peck his lips. "Allow your mother at court."

How quickly the flame of lust fizzled at her words.

"Is that all you came here for?" His expression was inked with a smattering of disbelief and indignation, both things he used to mask the faint undertone of upset.

"You know how we play by now, Dara." Katerina chortled at his affront. "We give to gain." She traced her gilt filigree claw guard down his chest. "Mutual satisfaction." Her expression turned mocking. "Did you really expect me to come here for love?"

His cheeks flushed. "Get off me."

Katerina cackled, but she didn't withdraw from his lap. "Now, what's gotten into you? You're usually far better behaved for me than this." She slid her hand along his groin to massage him to stiffness. "I see I've touched a nerve. Shall I stroke it better?"

Darius tensed at her touch, struggling against the moan that threatened to escape him. His sound mind would have him cast her out of the room, but the more brazen her caresses, the more arousal pulsed in his blood and drowned all rational thought.

"Good boy," she whispered, grazing her claws along the inside of his thigh through his trousers until he was throbbing.

"Katya..."

She had his button popped to go further when a knock on the door halted them.

Darius immediately came to his senses as he sped to answer it. "What is it?" he demanded.

Kirill cleared his throat. "Her Radiance requests an audience, sire."

Darius pinched the bridge of his nose, sighing. "Give me a moment." He closed the door and fixed his clothing, taking a moment to calm himself before turning to Katerina. "You stay there."

He opened up to his antechamber to see Laila straightening one of the roses on her hanging sleeve. She folded her hands primly when she saw him.

"How may I help you, Your Radiance?"

Laila frowned somewhat at his propriety. "I wanted to thank you for the support you showed me at the meeting today. It meant a lot to have you on my side." She paused before adding, "I much prefer it when you and I are working in tandem."

"I much prefer having you on my side too." His cold veneer thawed somewhat. "You were right." He paused to appreciate her bewildered expression. "When I have a conviction I have a tendency to become... impervious to voices of dissent. I appreciate you for always being willing to sing a different tune in my ear."

Her face brightened at this, scintillating as a newborn star. "I was thinking perhaps we could further discuss a plan of action. If you're not busy."

"Not at all, I—"

The door opened briskly behind him.

Then out slinked Katerina with an alleycat smile adorned, draping her arms around his shoulders. "Forgive the intrusion, Your Majesty. I was wondering what kept you." Her gleaming eyes wandered over to Laila, warm as a fine whisky with a much too familiar burn. "Ah, you must be the star princess I hear so much about!"

Something plummeted within Laila's chest at the sight of her. The occassella was a voluptuous beauty with sable hair that had a reddish sheen in certain lights. It made her sly, vixen features seem more severe.

"I am indeed." With each word, her throat became a little more swollen. She smoothed out the skirt of her dress. "And you are?"

"Princess Laila, this is Katerina Blackwood of the Vidua Nocte." Darius rubbed at his neck as though he'd been caught doing something shameful, though he did not know why. He couldn't understand the look of betrayal in Laila's gaze. What's more, he couldn't understand why he felt culpable before it. "We were just—"

"Having a private discussion, you see," Katerina interjected, then bit the tip of Darius's pointed ear, freckle-dappled button nose wrinkling with amusement when he lightly nudged her off. "Which we had not yet finished."

Laila did not need them to elaborate on what sort of conversation had likely taken place. "Well, don't let me keep you." She summoned and adorned her best smile. Then she turned on her heel. "Have a good evening, Darius Rex."

"Princess—"

She ignored him. She could feel an invigorating surge of aether coursing through her veins, her body practically *singing* with it, that if she stopped now and looked at him she didn't think she would be able to stop herself from detonating.

She kept walking until she found herself inside her room, then she slumped against the wall. She closed her eyes, trying to think of anything but the images permeating her mind at that moment. She thought of Darius kissing Katerina, his hands on her body, murmuring sweet nothings in her ear, and it made her wrathful.

She approached her vanity mirror and used it to summon Lyra. "Tell me about your day, please."

"What about it?"

"Anything." Laila's voice cracked with a laugh. "How's the weather down in Thalistan? Any interesting developments on this very secret mission of yours?"

"The situation is... more complicated than I thought. I've been tracing some chaos-related murders of sprites, as of late."

"Oh." Laila's face fell.

"I won't burden you with the details—"

"No, it's..." She did her best to keep her reactions measured, still trying even now, to tame her emotions into something more pleasing. "That must be very difficult for you to go through."

"Yes, well, it's... hard to see good sprites die." Lyra's expression hardened. "All for some tenuous grasp at a peace I doubt we even fully attained."

"I wish I could say I knew we made the right choices. All I can think is that there might have been a version of events where we were much worse off than before. And that terrifies me."

"It terrifies me, too."

"If only I were there with you now... It would be better than being here, for certain." Laila tucked a curl behind her ear, and sighed. The thought magnified the sense of isolation she'd sought to lessen.

"Are you all right?"

She knew better than to answer but sensed Lyra would not relent. "I think Darius has taken a lover. He's not married, of course. But he has someone."

"That's good, isn't it? You won't have to worry about him relentlessly pursuing you."

Laila swallowed. "I..."

"Oh, Laila."

"No, you're right. This is a good thing. It's wonderful. It's *brilliant*, even." She sucked in a shuddery breath and forced a smile. "He just... said all of these things when I first came here, and now I feel like a fool for believing them."

"Well, you know better now. Don't you?"

The words pierced between her ribs, though they were said with the best of intentions. Not for the first time, Laila wished Lyra could be softer with her tongue. "I do." She took it with nothing but a smile. But while she'd kept the extent of her wound concealed, that didn't keep it from filling her chest until she had to step away. To remove the dagger and let everything it held at bay spill forth. "I'll have to call you back."

Laila wrapped her arms around her middle as soon as the transmission ended, coaxing herself to calm. As her throat clogged, though, even the faint rocking motion as she embraced herself couldn't soothe her. What she needed was another pair of arms, a tender voice in her ear to smooth away the harshness. Léandre would've done it for her, had he been here with her now. She tried to replicate the feel of Léandre's arms around her, the cradle of his palm on the side of her head as he ghosted *It's all right, princess* into her ear, light as a feathered whisper.

But it wasn't his voice she heard. This one was deeper. Smooth and rich as chenille velvet. It stoked desire in the pit of her stomach, as well as comfort.

"No." Laila clutched her hair and shook her head. "No, no, no, no."

Why did she keep doing this to herself? Why did she keep imagining him back with her? Why was it that his voice, his touch, had become the only one to bring her any solace?

X

THE MEDICINAL SCENT OF FRAGRANT HERBS had a palliative effect on Elina's fraying nerves as she updated her medical journal. She'd recently added some Seraji patients to her roster after they'd moved to the village. It was always fascinating to learn how much whatever element one became predisposed towards seemed to alter their genetic structure.

Fire elementals, for instance, became more highly resistant to heat and burning but it tended to manifest in how their bodies reacted to illness as well. It was why so many had high levels of inflammatory disorders such as rashes, heartburn, and ulcers, whereas elementals who possessed the power of water were more prone to congestion of the arteries and sinuses.

Even psychological illnesses had detectable patterns of occurrence corresponding to whatever element the witch happened to be. All very stimulating to an inquisitive mind like Elina's, as it reminded her of the immense joy she derived from her study of physiology. Once she'd finished with her journal, she drifted over to her neatly compiled bookcase to put it back on the shelf. Then she heard a tinkling noise from the door.

She swivelled round to see a sprite. She looked official, wearing a navy floral-embroidered velvet coat and a lace jabot. A rank or two higher than a simple clan knight, were Elina to guess.

"Ah, hello there. Welcome." Elina moved back behind the counter and huffed some shine on her accent to keep it polished up for rich folk. She didn't often see sprites, for their healing factor was beyond her capabilities, but occasionally they'd come seeking herbs for potions.

"Evening, mata. My name is Ser de Lis." Lyra propped her arm on the counter, one ankle crossed over the other. "I was wondering if you might help me with something."

"Of course." Elina beamed with a genial warmth like a furnace in midwinter. "How can I be of service?"

"I've been making some inquiries at the local clinics." Lyra reached into her coat and produced a sheet. "I was wondering if you could shed some light on this decoction for me."

Elina plucked it to read, stifling a yawn. "Beg your pardon, ser. It's been a busy few days."

"No problem at all."

Elina hadn't slept properly since her hike in the rainforest. She'd been unable to find an optimal position to ward away the night terrors that had been inflicted upon her since those clan knights and then later at The Blue Lobster. If only she hadn't been so merciful. Then the families of those fallen knights would not be arriving to collect the dismantled remains of their loved ones.

Elina looked towards Lyra and realised these were likely her comrades, her brothers and sisters, and she'd aided their murderer in escaping justice. She couldn't be more ashamed. Since then she had been awaiting his return, and no amount of reasoning with her fear could deflate the swelling sickness in her stomach that flared every time the bell at the door rang.

She glanced down at the page, her brow crinkling. "'Fraid I can't make sense of this either."

"I hadn't thought so." Lyra smiled grimly. "However, I was also wondering if perhaps you'd seen any strange clients making odd requests for ingredients like this?"

"It ain't... It's not unheard of for patients to make requests for chaotic treatments. They're quick and effective at quelling infection and removing pain even though the side effects can be... unpredictable. But nothing like what's on this list." Elina handed back the page. "May I ask what this is regarding?"

"I must assert that this is official business, mata." Lyra folded the page and placed it back into her pocket. Then she produced a calling card between her fingers. "If something comes to mind later, do feel free to contact me. Thank you for your time."

Elina swallowed all the unspoken confessions of her remorse and reached for the lightly steaming glass teapot. "Please, take some tea with you before you go." She didn't even wait for Lyra to answer before she poured a sample into a paper cup. "It's freshly made, and I've added some echinacea, which is excellent for the skin."

Lyra took the tea and lifted it towards her in a saluting gesture before she walked out of the clinic.

Elina watched her leave. Since news of the occasso reached the press, a steady increase of sprite presence had collected in the sleepy, bucolic village of Parvani. As Elina closed up shop for the conclusion of another full day's work, she pondered whether or not it might be helpful to reach out with her admittedly limited insight. She knew he was with Sadik, after all. Perhaps if she was forthcoming with her information, they wouldn't think less of her for fulfilling her duty of care.

However, it wasn't her own skin she sought to preserve, but that of her family. Knowing this creature was dangerous and still at large made all the blood in her veins freeze, and not even exposure to the meat-grilling heat of Thalistan could hope to thaw her again.

She pondered it during her short walk home, but after turning the corner Elina was forced to halt, as waiting on the road before the turquoise gates of her farmland was a vehicle that did not belong to her.

The silhouette of the aeromobile was almost jarringly conspicuous, the make and model easily distinguishable from the modest tangas and bicycles she'd come to anticipate from the village transport. She knew immediately who it belonged to. No one else would ever think to ride in something so visibly ostentatious as an aeromobile with mint green paintwork and serpentine ornamentation.

Her suspicions were confirmed the moment she approached her brightly painted door and unlocked it to find that Maithra had arranged a tea setting in anticipation of her arrival. Only she already had company.

Sadik's gold-cuffed twists shifted as he turned around in his seat to look at her. "Ela, about time you arrived!"

Elina did not once budge her gaze from Maithra's, her jaw setting firm in anger.

"He darned tailgated me and insisted I let him through," her sister explained, hands raised in defence. "He told me you knew he was coming."

Elina watched her daughter, now perched on Sadik's lap, nibbling a cookie. She was still in school uniform, and one of the deep blue ribbons in her hair had come loose before Sadik gently straightened it. She was showing him one of the latest hand-drawn storybooks Elina had made, inserted into painted pressboard covers and bound with colourful yarn.

"Come along and sit with us, Ela, we've been keeping the tea warm for you." Sadik raised his porcelain cup in salute before he plucked the pressed flower cookie nestled on the corner of the saucer and took a small bite. "Mmph, these sunflower cookies you made are *delicious*."

Elina observed him with increasing irritation, for it didn't take long for Sadik to capture Yasmin within his thrall. Once she'd loved that about him, the way he needed only to speak a word, make a gesture, to draw anyone into the irresistible field of his magnetic allure.

"Yasmin, love, could you go on upstairs? I need to speak with your baba about something very important."

Yasmin blinked her hazel-green eyes in bewilderment and clutched her father's hand. "I ain't finished showing him my story!"

"We'll only be a moment, baby girl." Sadik kissed the top of her head and stroked her long, dark hair. "Then you can tell me all about it."

"You go on up them stairs, girl!" Maithra snapped at her. She stood up from her chair, intent on marching her up herself. "Ain't you hear what your mama said?"

Yasmin relented with a sulk and tugged her storybook upstairs with her, rapping it against the bannister with every step as Maithra followed close behind her.

Elina waited until the door closed before her hands came to rest upon her hips in indignation. "What are you doing here?"

He looked so sheepish then, munching at his biscuit. She'd always wondered what would become of him when all the pages of his finely inked vocabulary finally ran blank. "I have to speak with you, Ela. It's urgent."

Such a vestige of the man she knew barely anyone refused. Who, upon his arrival into a room, drew every head with his name upon their tongue like a truffle. And yet, here he was stuttering with fear before a past love.

"About what?" she asked, feeling the tightness in her shoulders soften as she moved towards her favourite armchair. She slid her hands over the handwoven silk that Sadik imported from Odaka.

"It's about the friend you brought to the club the other night."

She was not prepared for what that revelation did to her stomach. But of course, she'd known Sadik to have kept unscrupulous company. The occasso must have found a way to obtain what he sought after all. Sadik seemed unharmed, however, and that made her relax. If anyone could slither out of the jaws of a beast looking no worse for wear it would be Sadik Yilan.

Elina took Sadik's shoulder in hand to pivot him into one of the other rooms, closing the door behind them. "What is it?"

Sadik's face cracked into a shaky smile. "I may have done something foolish, Elina, and I need you to see me through it."

Whatever neutrality she may have been feigning before gave way to anger. "What have you done now?"

"When that monster came barrelling into my club looking for me, I thought, perhaps, I'd sell him out to the clan and be done with the whole thing, but"—his face crumpled, and, for the briefest moment, he turned from her—"he started babbling on about how he had a proposition for me and how the rewards would be huge if I let him out—"

Her breath became very, very shallow. "Please tell me you didn't let him out."

"Of course not! I still have him chained up nice and tight at my beach house. But his words got me thinking, and I figured, well, since he's claiming to be indebted to me and all, I might as well exploit it."

"What do you mean?" she asked, wariness encroaching upon her.

"There's a potion, a ritual, that requires the use of a potent form of occassi blood. If I can create it, then those who imbibe it will be granted with untold power."

"So you thought you'd come to me and start talking your slick city talk and what? I'd be putty?" she sputtered, and had Maithra not been in the other room, she would've yelled. "What in Naya's name is wrong with you? Do you have any idea what happens to people who get caught doing chaos magic? The solarites could take away my aether."

"I am asking you to help me change lives here!" Sadik said. "Do you know how many men would kill for the opportunity to wield magic? If this works, we could finally be equals."

"This again." Elina clutched her temple with a sigh. "When are you going to realise that your obsession with proving your worth to me through chaos magic is why I left you? I can't have that around Yasmin, and you know it. And you showing up here unannounced is only going to break her heart. Did you ever even think of that?"

"Ela—" Sadik stepped forward to reach for her.

"No." Elina shook her head. "I loved you with everything I had, Sadik. I never once thought you lesser to me because you cannot wield aether. When are you going to understand that?"

"Easy for you to make empty platitudes when never having to confront real change, ain't it?" He huffed, hands sheathed in his pockets as he scuffed the rug with his foot. Then he withdrew one and reached to take her hand. "I wouldn't have come to you if I wasn't desperate, Ela—"

"And if you didn't think I'd go weak-kneed at the sight of your puppy eyes."

"I'm not here to manipulate you, Ela. I came to you because you are the most capable healer I know. And I know if I can trust anyone with such an immense task, it's you."

This is too much, she thought, rubbing her temples. Then another question popped into her head. "And what are you gonna do with the occasso once you've taken what you need from him?"

"I told him if he helps me then he can have whatever he wants from me," he said, then he held up his hands in defence. "Creature only wants to get back home to his people. Far be it from me to stop him. But he's strong and he's powerful and that is something I sorely need right now."

She glanced away from him, exhaling softly.

"Just the once," he pleaded. "Just to see if it works. And from then on I promise you I will not involve you in it any further."

Her throat thickened as she swallowed away her unshed tears. "All this time and you're still exactly the same."

He had the grace to look away from her. "This isn't about me, Elina, nor is it about my gain. This is about evening the scales. You don't know what it's like to live in a world that was not built for people like you. I have worked so hard, for so many years, to get to where I am now. I watched many in my place try and fail. If making things more fair means I have to make a deal with a demon, then I will do it. But you say the word, I walk away. Your choice."

She knew then, as she had ten years before, that she had lost him. To see him so willing to once more dive into the putrid mire of chaos magic, even in spite of all it had cost them before, was much too far. She raked her fingernails against her tattooed forearm until a crimson welt appeared on her brown skin.

"Get out of my house," she said, voice hollow and fragmented. "Right now. Do not contact me regarding this again. If you so much as darken my doorstep, I'll alert the highest authority in the land to your dealings. Be grateful that Yasmin loves you enough for me to not want to harm her this way." A tear streaked down her cheek. She wiped it away.

"Elina, please," Sadik whispered, his arms moving to embrace her in concern.

"No." She held up a finger to halt him in his path. "My part in this is over."

Sadik's throat bobbled as he dropped his hands. Then he turned and left.

❧

Sadik had his driver escort him to his private beach house by the coast bordering Malakia. He remembered the first time he had brought Elina here, having gifted it to her as a token of his love so she could come to join his insatiable affair with the seaside.

It is due to the sea in my veins, Sadik had once told her. For though his name and hometown were of the Seraji woman who had taken him in, his features spoke to his Malakian lineage—a lineage that always remained an enigma to him due to his early orphaning. He didn't much like to speak of it, and Elina never pried too hard, but he knew she always wondered about the missing branches in Yasmin's family tree and who might have hung there. To break the ice at family events, he would often joke about belonging a little bit of everywhere and thus, ultimately, belonging nowhere.

Sadik stepped out and swallowed a mouthful of briny air, watching as the sun sank beneath the soft lapping waves of turquoise and bled it blood orange. There were moments of perfect stillness that could only be accomplished in secluded havens like this. Where it was just one's hushed breaths in tandem with the tide rolling over the shoreline. The thought of the nights he and Elina had spent entangled on the beach was enough to make him press his teeth into his knuckles, biting back a sob.

He should've known better than to go to her with his plea. But part of him kept hoping she would understand what it meant to live as he did. Yet how could she? She had been shielded from the marginalisation that came with mundanity; all the doors that swung shut for him would graciously open to receive her. How could she possibly fathom the allure of that shadowed stranger two decades ago with his slitted snake eyes, so much like their goddess Naya, promising him wealth and prosperity if only he'd pledge his soul to him?

That one deal had taken the meagre corner shop he'd been clinging to by the edge of his teeth and transformed it into an empire. From the dead-end store clerk she had brushed over with her eyes to a businessman with promise in his future. Something he could offer her. Without it, how could he ever hope to have been worthy of her? To stand under the same sun and breathe the same air?

Sadik sniffled and swept the tears from his closed eyes with his thumb and forefinger, opening them to reveal their mismatched irises. He approached the cerulean façade of the villa, shouldered on twisted pillars. A protruding lip of a veranda patterned with terracotta roof tiles offered shade, and a foliate iron balcony bulged over the first storey.

He climbed the few steps to the hooded archway, where he unlocked the front door. The heavy salted air was replaced with the domestic aromas of a well-kept home. Sadik took off his shoes at the porch and took one tentative barefoot step onto the priceless Seraji rug on the landing. With a deep, sobering breath, Sadik entered the lounge, surprised to find that Dominus was painting.

He had neatly assembled himself a little artist's nook in the corner of the room and had it barricaded with glass jars of mismatching heights, all stained at the rim with paints. His fingers were also stained with paints he had pilfered from Elina's art supplies.

He filled in the outlines with tender, precise strokes that Sadik never would've thought possible for hands of his size. This was a creature who had slaughtered indiscriminately for centuries, but looking at him now, Sadik couldn't see it in him.

When Dominus looked at him, he looked unblemished by all the centuries that had tainted him. Wrists and neck still shackled with cosmic metal. Inhibitors to keep him docile. "You've returned without your lover. I assume she did not respond well to your request."

"You assume well." Sadik inched forward. "What are you painting?"

"My home." Dominus showed him the bleak, fog-stained landscape of pitch-black sand and a sea as pale as mist. "It may not seem much like it to you, but there is beauty in Mortos. Never in my time on this earth have I ever seen anything like it. Rivers and skylines that run red as the blood in your veins. Forests where the trees are so mangled they almost resemble people. And beaches like these, black as midnight, with ice shards that glitter like diamonds beneath the moonlight and a sea that is white as milk."

It was the most Sadik had ever heard him speak in those baritone vocals of his, and the harsh inflections of a Mortesian accent covertly imposed themselves into his articulation.

"You seem to miss it," Sadik said, then claimed a seat at the table a safe distance away from him.

Dominus's jaw gave a visible twitch. "I do, but I will be returning there soon." He set down his paintbrushes, which, up until that moment, he had been dual-wielding against the canvas to paint from both directions.

Not knowing what else to say, Sadik chose the route of diplomacy. "Sure you... want to go back?"

Dominus swivelled on his seat so the full potency of his gaze was upon Sadik. There was something frightfully angular and feline about his eyes, green like the grass grown over burial grounds.

Sadik swallowed. "I just—I mean, a lot would've changed, you know. In the twenty years you were away. Your brother being the rex now and all—"

"If you are under the impression I desire to assert my claim, you would be mistaken. Let Darius don his paper hat and play his chess games." His teeth scraped together in agitation. "He was always better at it than me."

"Then if it's not the throne you want"—Sadik tilted his head to one side—"why go back?"

Dominus smiled, but there was nothing savage in it. "As I said, Mortos is my home. It's where I belong. There is no other place in the world for me."

"Well, that's certainly fair." Sadik tapped his hands idly on his lap. "But you've got an indefinite invitation to stay here should you need it."

"I thank you for your hospitality." Dominus inclined his head in a regal stance befitting of his title. "And in return, I can assure you that occassi keep their oaths. I will therefore do my best to serve your people."

"Trust me." Sadik gave a dull laugh. "I know all about you occassi and your oaths."

"I can see that." Dominus's gaze rooted on Sadik's one blue eye. "You've pledged your soul to one of my kin already. I presume you are aware of the penalties for such a barter?"

"What? Eternal suffering? My soul doomed to become twisted and juiced into pulp to power chaos?" Sadik threw back his head in a louder laugh that could've echoed for an eternity, it was that hollow. "I don't intend on dying for a very long time. As far as I'm concerned, it's the living well that matters. What happens after... It's a necessary sacrifice. Not as if Goddess wanted me anyway." He knew his soul was damned, that the moment the ice-cold hue had claimed his eye he would be spiralling down a stairwell to the netherworld.

Why quit while he was ahead?

XI

ILK CLOUDS BILLOWED IN HER BLACK TEA AS Sabina stirred her dainty painted cup with her ornamental teaspoon. An invitation to the tea room of Domitia Orlovia was a sacred occasion, as chastely guarded as one's underskirts. The decorous ladies' lounge was intended as a sanctuary, a place of refuge, where one could loosen her lips as well as her guard amongst the safety of her fellow occasselle. For no male would be granted entry past the threshold.

As a high-ranking matriarch of seven (once eight) sons, Domitia enjoyed access to many privileges, such as her imposing estate, which had been built and rebuilt with every maternal contribution. She managed multiple properties, received grants for higher education, and was considered first in line for many prestigious roles in judicial and political matters and education of the youth.

Such preferential treatment was one that occasselle still unranked could only dream of attaining, and Domitia wore the gold medal fastened to her breast with pride in the knowledge that she would be forever heralded as the pinnacle of occasselle achievement—pampered, wealthy, and fertile. As triumphant in childbed as an occasso was in battle.

Today's topic of interest pertained to the betrothal of Domitia's grandson, Caius, to Elvira Snegia. Always eager for the opportunity to expand her brood, Domitia had Elvira brandish her engagement carcanet for scrutiny—a strand of glimmering emeralds with one large square-cut gem bordered in a setting of diamonds.

The practice of engagement carcanets started as a warning to other occasso, a show of wealth and dominance: *This one is now currently under the suitor's eye.* An occassella would thus be expected to flaunt her carcanet before others, and the less extravagant and ornamental, the less satisfying the suitor was perceived to be.

Sabina couldn't possibly have found it more degrading. "It's a beautiful collar, Elvira. Caius has done you well."

"You see how large the emerald is?" Elvira protruded her chest to draw attention to the large gem. "Why, when I saw it first I feared I'd have to drag it across the floor!"

"He certainly knows how to choose a gem, my Caius," Domitia said in approval, stirring her tea.

Thankfully, talk of wedding plans were soon disturbed when a servant announced a new arrival. "Her Radiance Princess Laila Rose, ma'am."

Laila entered in a pink and white court dress overgrown with silver foliate embroidery. She looked like a daydream come to flesh. "Good day to you, ladies. Hope you don't mind if I join."

"Ah, princess!" Domitia smiled widely upon beholding her, her bright yellow eyes gleaming. "Please sit and make yourself comfortable. You are more than welcome."

Laila bobbed her head in gratitude, gliding with swanlike grace to the table.

The occasselle regarded her with a gaze nothing short of carnivorous. To them, she was but a prime cut of meat in silk stockings, and they were eager to devour.

"I must say, I have been most eager to find myself among fairer company," Laila said, waiting for her tea to be served before she took a sip. "I find the boy's club in the Citadel to be rather, well... brusque, for my liking."

"Certainly." Domitia rolled her eyes in understanding. "Spend enough time in the company of our coarser counterparts and you'll find everything to be a competition with them."

"Well, I don't mind a little friendly sportsmanship. Emphasis on *friendly*." Laila chuckled, helping herself to a slice of hazelnut and chocolate torte. "Though that brings me to why I'm here: I intend to put together a welcoming committee for occassi relations in each country of Vysteria so that they may dedicate themselves to the specific struggles your race may encounter there. I have noticed that the largest represented group of immigrants happens to be adult females, so I thought, perhaps, some of you would be interested in signing up."

This garnered an unexpected silence, broken only by a burst of laughter from Sabina.

"Don't hope for too many hands, princess. I fear the occassi couldn't bear to release another one of their precious wives for the cause."

"Sabina!" Domitia hissed at her. She turned back to the princess with a smile. "I don't see why some of our higher-ranked medallists can't be considered. If anything, it might be good for them to talk, see how they're... getting on." Her smile tightened. "In any case, we shall certainly broach the topic with our husbands."

Laila's brow raised at this. Marriage was not a common practice in Vysteria at large. A couple would have unions at most, but not the authoritative institution spoken of here. "Well, it is a position that would require travel. I can imagine this is something a couple would wish to discuss."

Sabina snorted dismissively and then grimaced in defence when another pointed gaze was aimed her way. "Oh, I'm sure we all know *discussion* is the furthest thing from what was being alluded to here."

"Sabina!" Domitia's nostrils flared in rage. "Honestly, your tongue hasn't half roughened since you've been mingling with the enforcers. It's a wonder I even accept you here. You won't even dress properly for the event. Would it have pained you to look a lady for once?" Her yellow eyes roamed derisively over Sabina's choice of ensemble, which consisted of a plum kaftan and tight breeches.

Laila could hardly understand the issue. The attire complemented Sabina's powerfully built physique and the deep carmine of her hair.

"A dress would restrict my movements, ma'am," Sabina murmured, eyes downcast. "I need to be prepared for action."

"Yes, well, you ought to be thankful that the rex managed to find you an alternate purpose, considering your unfortunate disposition," Domitia responded as she helped herself to a sip of poppy milk. "In my youth, the best a barren girl could hope for was the convent or becoming a midwife, neither of which would suit someone of your temperament. You always were wilful, and we all know what happens to wilful girls don't we, Sabina?"

The occasselle understood well enough, a subliminal message transmitted through shared glances. Delanus had shown Sabina once what the penalty had been for being deemed too unruly. The gap-toothed smiles and raw finger stumps that blemished the bodies of some in this very room, though they subconsciously sought to conceal them. Their existence remained a breathing relic of a reluctantly forbidden punishment.

Only good wives and daughters got to keep the use of their claws and fangs, their predacious arsenal. So keep them nice and sheathed, and don't talk out of turn to the one who fills your bowl and tightens your leash, lest you find yourself disarmed too.

Sabina recalled another time, in the tea room before this one, when she had snuck in some polugar to spike her tea and became even more generous with her audacious outbursts: *Sometimes I wonder why it is we never keep any pets. And then it occurred to me. We're the pets.*

"Speaking of dresses," Laila asserted, eager to fragment the stiff barricade of silence encasing them. "I have also come to present to you an invitation to my bal masqué, which, with Darius Rex's permission, I have chosen to host in the Citadel so that we might have an event of cultural sharing, of lowering the barriers a bit. Mortos has so much to offer that isn't gloom and bad weather, and I feel the rest of Vysteria is missing it. Hopefully, this ball can be an opportunity to show the world how rich and full of history and art your country is." She gestured for a server to come over with a silver platter, which presented, of all things, an oyster shell.

Domitia handled it with scrutiny, while her fellow occasselle began to hover with increased interest. She cracked open the shell to reveal a fine pink pearl seated on a tiny cushion of velvet. Scrawled in elegant script on the interior of the shell was a message: *Drop pearl in water.*

Domitia allowed herself a curious pause before she did as commanded, dropping the pearl in a nearby glass. The occasselle observed with a coo as the pearl dissolved in the liquid, ejecting a gaseous pink vapour that squiggled the details for the upcoming event in ornate script before it dispersed and embroidered itself onto the cushion.

"I have chosen an underwater theme to coincide with your national holiday of the Hexacost," Laila said. It had come to her in a fever-induced delirium after she had awoken from a vivid dream. She couldn't think of a better way to unite the carefree tropics of midsummer with the dark depths of occassi origins. "I will also be hosting a charity auction."

"Well, I assume we are all going," announced Domitia in the graceful, stately way she often did when making proclamations rather than requests. "A prime opportunity to present oneself at court, I'm sure. The rex keeps himself so secluded even in public events, one would think him a spectre."

"Let's also hope all the rumours circulating about his preference for male company are just hearsay," Elvira said, causing Sabina to suppress a laugh. "It would be a shame. He is a handsome fellow, our rex. He should share his beauty plentifully with his children."

The mention of marriage and children in reference to another caused Laila's chest to flare. Finding Katerina practically in his bed had been insulting enough, but now to be faced with discussions of his hypothetical bride brought another sting of envy into Laila's veins—a potent venom for how foreign to her it was.

"Well, my father won't be content until he has one of us labouring to produce the next heir to the kingdom." Sabina shook her head in scorn and, with a touch too much force, clenched her teacup. "At least the rex is merciful enough not to wear his bride to death for a son." The porcelain crackled.

"Sabina!" Domitia snapped, and like a curse, she turned all the occupants in the room to stone. No one dared move or breathe, least of all the culprit who broke the tentatively held assurance—refuge from the world of the occassi so long as you submitted to Domitia's dominion instead.

Before the younger of the two had the chance to atone for her misgivings, the matriarch had already peeled off her delicate lace gloves. "You know the penalty, Sabina." And it was with such a sad little sigh that she moved towards her. "Fingers."

Sabina grit her teeth so hard her jaw flexed, but submit her hand she did. Every long, lithe digit with its short oval nail filed.

It always hurt her more than it hurts them—that was what Domitia always insisted. She curled one digit around Sabina's own and bent it until it broke.

The dry crunch and the pained hiss that followed were sounds Laila would never forget. Her eyes and ears became enthralled to it, and she was unable to turn away. With each methodical fracture, Laila's own fingers curled into the tablecloth until she realised her nails were audibly grazing the fabric.

By the end of it, Sabina's digits had curved so backwards they were practically touching her wrist. She repaired them with a skeletal hex, choking back gasps.

Domitia tutted as she returned to her seat, rolling her lace gloves all the way down to the frilled hem at the wrist. "You know I don't like having to do that to you girls. But remember, all that I do to you I do with love. This is a cursed world, and we are demons. If you can't learn to take a lashing or two from me, you can forget about ever making it through your marriages."

With a noisy scuffle of her chair across the floorboards, Sabina fled the room.

Laila dash her napkin across the table, then pursued Sabina. "Are you all right?"

Sabina had already transformed to her usual unblemished arrogance as she held up her hand to reveal her freshly healed fingers.

"All better," Sabina said with a grin that was more teeth than mirth.

Seeing how blasé she was in the face of Domitia's violence only served to enlarge Laila's concern. She recognised it too easily in herself. This was not the first time Sabina had suffered at Domitia's hand, nor would it likely be the last.

"She shouldn't have done that to you," Laila said. "It's not right."

Sabina merely sniffed in derision. "Domina Orlovia can do what she pleases. This is her stage, and we're her puppets. She's always had it out for me from the beginning, and everyone knows it."

"Then why come here?" Laila asked, aggrieved. "You are an enforcer, are you not? Surely—"

"That's the thing." Sabina released a harsh bark of laughter. "I don't belong here, but I don't belong there either. Not truly."

Laila's heart sank. "Perhaps you and I can not belong together."

Sabina sniggered, but she found herself appreciating the sentiment. "Perhaps."

Laila smiled at her in affirmation. "I have to go now. They'll be expecting me." But still, she couldn't bring herself to turn until she asked, "Are you sure you'll be all right?"

"Always am, dear," Sabina assured her, lips slightly crooked into that ever-poised smirk.

Laila tossed and turned that night in yet another fitful sleep. Her mind was churning away with all she'd seen and heard at the tea rooms, the implications held within. The cacophony in her mind was soon joined by spectres. She could hear them in the walls, screeching against the glass with jagged nails that couldn't be explained by branches.

She accepted defeat on her quest for sleep and rose, her pink silk chiffon nightgown falling to her ankles. She rang the bell for a maid and requested a glass of warm goat's milk and honey to soothe her.

Straightening her silk ribbon sash, she decided to comb her hair and oil her scalp at the vanity to give herself something to do. She opened her vanity kit and picked up her ornate silver comb from the silk-covered case, then her bottle of gardenia-infused coconut oil. She let her hair down from its pineapple bun and was detangling the knots from her curls when her milk arrived. She accepted it with a smile and took a lavish swallow, then returned to the task of her hair.

She didn't make it long undisturbed before Sabina entered.

"You have a visitor."

Laila frowned into the mirror, wondering who would call at this hour. "Who is it?"

"Darius Rex."

Her hand halted, just briefly. Then she resumed.

"I can send him away if you'd like," Sabina said.

Tempting as the offer might be, Laila was far too curious to do so.

"Let him through." Laila grimaced as she encountered a stubborn knot caught in the comb's ivory teeth.

Darius entered the room, gazing at her through the mirror. He had his head slightly bent in contrition, running his fingers down his aquiline nose.

"Rather unfashionable hour to call upon me," Laila said, still wrestling with the comb.

"Caught one of the maids with a glass of milk and figured you must be having trouble sleeping too." He leaned to one side with a hand on his hip, thigh showing through the slit in his kaftan. "About the other night—"

"You need not explain yourself to me, Darius Rex," Laila interrupted before he could continue. "Who you choose to keep you company in your bedchambers is hardly my business." She dragged her comb through until the knot came free, and she muttered a sound of pain under her breath.

"Let me help you with that." Darius moved towards her, hand outstretched for the comb.

Her eyes met his through the vanity mirror. There were a fair few she would trust with her hair in this manner, but seeing him so desperate to be back in her good graces made her want to make full use of it. She removed the clumps of hair from the comb and handed it to him.

Darius accepted the comb and continued where she left off, his touch firm yet gentle. "In any case, there's nothing going on between Katerina and me, if that's what you thought. There might have been at one point... but that's long over now."

Laila had to wonder how someone he was 'long over' ended up in his bed. Unwilling to concede her agitation, she gestured towards her hair. "You can part my hair into four sections. You'll need to lubricate from scalp to end." She demonstrated first with her fingers and left him to do the rest. "Why does it matter to you what I think?"

"Because I haven't seen you at all since the encounter and I didn't want you to be left with the wrong impression." Darius parted her hair and oiled his fingers, gliding them along her scalp to the ends. His touch made her feel languid, arching her towards him like a cat.

Laila found herself wanting to close her eyes, but she resisted. "Well, it matters not to me whose company you keep. As I've said."

"Of course." He ran the comb through her hair with more ease due to the oil, her curls glistening and slick. A silence fell between them that was only disturbed by each rhythmic scrape of the comb's teeth.

"The first night I came here you were pouring sweet words in my ear like wine, saying you'd been waiting for me. Longing for me." She took an affected husky tone in mockery of his speech. "Was that true or an attempt to lower my guard?"

"Why do you suppose it was a lie?"

"Because you know full well that if my judgement is clouded by you I'm a lot easier for you to manoeuvre."

Darius hmphed in amusement. "I wasn't lying, Laila."

She hated the way he could say her name like it was melting on his tongue.

Laila looked in the mirror and saw his eyes on her. She wanted to not believe him. And yet with a few words, a look, she knew she already halfway did. "Stop looking at me like that."

"Like what?"

With such sheer adoration she had to wonder if she'd never left the sky.

"I visited the tearoom of Domitia Orlovia today," Laila said, needing something, anything, to change the subject.

Darius's mouth inched up wryly. "And how did that go?"

"I have to wonder if there's any section of your society that doesn't resolve conflicts with violence."

He chuckled, smooth as cream to her ears. It felt good to hear him laugh again. "You let me know if you find one."

She smothered her smile in her glass of milk. "I've also met your Eagle Eye."

"Ah, yes. Sabina. Delanus's child." Darius shook his head in amusement. "She showed great promise when she was young and so I took her under my wing. Most unusual, considering her sex, but I believe there should be no barriers to achieving excellence."

"I never thought you'd be one to have a soft spot for children," Laila said, a tender smile blossoming on her lips.

"Well, I never imagined myself as one to care for a child until I met Sabina. She's a truly remarkable creature. In truth, I saw myself in her. She'd been overlooked, barred from fulfilling her duty, and abandoned by her mother. But there was a potential there I saw fit to nurture. I'm very glad I did."

Hearing the fondness in his voice only made her heart hurt. She wished he could've received better in his own youth than he'd gotten.

"I realised I... never asked about your mother," Laila said hesitantly.

Darius flinched before he could stop it. Then he kept combing. What was there to say about her other than that she'd disposed of him? Not that Laila wouldn't understand what it meant to crawl on the floor for the crumbs of an indifferent mother's affections. Some things, however, were better left undisturbed.

"She was a non-presence. Better for me to describe her as a ghost."

"You mean she died?" she assumed, sensing this was a topic of soreness.

He smiled. "Something like that."

She stared at him in that tender, unfathomable way she often did. "You really didn't have anyone, did you?"

Sometimes her words could cut him in the way no blade ever had. "You come to learn just how truly transient things are as an immortal. You become the still point at the turn of an axis and, in the end, you find that nothing matters. Family. Friendships. Love. It all fades."

Laila couldn't help but frown, wondering if perhaps one day what he felt for her would fade too. She took another drink of milk, finishing it.

He put down the comb and rested his hands upon her shoulders. "I believe you're done."

Laila ran her fingers through her oil-slicked hair before turning towards him. "I should probably try heading back to sleep."

"Any reason you're having trouble?"

"I'm still not used to the atmosphere of this place." She fiddled with her fingers. "Before, when Lyra was here, I'd at least have someone to sleep with. That eased it somewhat."

"I think I have something that might help you settle."

"Oh?" Laila eyed him warily.

"You don't trust me?" His lips bent into a playful curve.

"Not when you look at me with those eyes."

"What eyes?" He feigned innocence, but the crevices in his cheeks seemed to deepen. "Just relax... I think you'll like it."

Laila exhaled petulantly in response before she did as he commanded.

Darius murmured a curse that dwindled the candles until they were hooded in lambency.

"What is it that requires us to be in dark lighting, Darius?" Her eyes became slits in suspicion.

"This." Darius raised a hand towards the wall. A shadow rendered from it, growing animate and contorting into shapes that looked nothing like what it stemmed from. With expert puppeteering, he turned his shadows into the form of a princess inside a tower, locked away at the whims of a monster.

Laila stifled a squeal of delight, clapping as a play unfolded before her in cascading figures of darkness, not only in movement, but emitting sound too. There was something so innocent and unguarded about her enthusiasm that it made Darius take pleasure in entertaining her, too.

The story panned away from the tower to the trumpeting fanfare of the kingdom she'd been stolen from. There, a decree to rescue the princess was uttered by a knight, who mounted his braying horse, and rode through several trials of certain death to reach her.

When he did arrive, he waited patiently for three sunrises and three sunsets for the monster to go on a hunt for food, before silently tiptoeing his way into the tower to wake the slumbering princess. He took her hand, urging her to rise from the bed, but as he took her into his arms the princess screamed, cried, and struggled. She didn't want to be saved.

Upon hearing her pleas, the monster returned and slaughtered the knight on the spot, spraying blood and viscera from his felled body. The extent of the violence made Laila clutch her arms with a gasp as the monster hacked off the head of the knight to mount on his wall, along with many others, before returning to the tower to make a meal of his remains with the princess, where they lived forevermore.

"Rather gruesome end," Laila couldn't help but note.

"A horrifying love, to be certain, but it seemed to satisfy them regardless." Darius turned to look at her, and she looked back. Their eyes locked for a moment. A lifetime. Enough for a wordless acknowledgement to transmit between their gazes.

"If I didn't know any better I would think you were trying to give me nightmares," Laila teased, a much needed slice through the tension.

"Well, if you want, I could... stay."

Her breath hitched at the offer, lips parting wordlessly.

Darius sensed the hesitation and dove to salvage it. "We wouldn't have to... I mean. I wouldn't touch you. We could just lie there..."

Laila couldn't suppress her amusement at his flustered cheeks. How rare it was, to see the unshakeable shaken. "You expect me to believe you wouldn't touch me?"

"Maybe I'd rest my arm around your waist." He ran one of her curls between his fingers until it was straight and let it coil again. His thumb traced her shoulder.

"And what else would you do?"

"Maybe press my lips against here." He brushed her hair to one side and touched the prominent knob of bone at the base of her neck. "Stroke my hand along your thigh."

Laila got up from the chair to face him, lingering dangerously near. She was teetering far too close to the edge of the abyss and she knew it. She wanted to fall. She closed her eyes when he touched her hair, brushing it away from her cheek before he leaned near enough to tickle her lips with his breath.

"You can't kiss me."

She hated herself for saying it the moment the words were uttered. She opened her eyes to see Darius was still close, his lips mere inches from hers.

"Why not?" he asked.

"You know why not."

He kept his lips hovering just out of reach as he spoke. "There's only so many times you can turn me away before I stop coming back."

Whether it was an empty threat was anyone's guess, but it provoked the desired result when her throat shifted with a thick swallow.

"You need to go now, Darius." She had brought up her wall of composure now and kept her gaze steady. "Don't make me ask again."

It was the last thing he wanted to do. Darius ached to close the distance between them, but her cold look melted his resolve and, reluctantly, he turned on his heel to leave.

Laila watched him go before throwing herself dramatically onto the bed. She picked up one of the pillows and smothered it over her face. It was going to be a long and painfully frustrating night.

The next morning, Laila travelled once more to the hinterlands with the aim of bringing news of the Culling's abolishment. Upon entering the rural town, she went straight to the village of the qarna and requested a meeting with the village elder.

"You've returned, I see," Anya said. "What is it this time?"

"First, I'd like to impart the news that the rex has decided to abolish the Culling."

A ripple of gasps resounded at that.

"Your doing, I presume?" Anya asked. "That will be both a blessing and a curse to our kind."

"I also have a countermeasure to your harvest issue. It is my intention to introduce a way to shelter crops from poor conditions and increase their survival."

Whispers of awe and disbelief soon followed the declaration.

"How?" Anya asked, eyes narrowed.

"The method is called ætherglass." Laila uncloaked her miniature terrarium, where, inside, a small cutting of strawberries bloomed. "It attracts sunlight and seals it within, allowing for crops to be grown year round without the aid of blood magic."

"But this is—" Anya moistened her lips in uncertainty. "Your Radiance, if what you say is true, the blood sorceresses shall surely revolt! And if you anger Serafina Blackwood..."

A violent hush spread over the gathering the instant the name was uttered. As if they feared in speaking it she would be summoned.

"You allow me to worry about that." Laila's mouth set with determination. "This is a gift I wish to share with you. As creatures of chaos, occassi cannot craft this kind of object. Therefore, they cannot control it." She stood up from the log and placed her hand beneath a golden ray of sunlight. "Aether can be found everywhere, even here in Mortos." She used her power to enhance the tiny dancing particles of charged energy, making them visible to the naked eye. "To attract it requires the glass to be heated a certain way, formed a certain way, coated a certain way. I will oversee the creation of the glass houses and ensure every qarna village has access to a communal garden. With more crops available, we can allow food to be doled out more fairly. For everyone."

The words caused the qarna to glance amongst one another with a wary fear in their eyes. The unanswered question poised between their lips was clear—what would she want in return?

"All I ask is that you sign this petition." Laila pulled out a parchment addressed to the Council. "With enough backing and noise from the common folk, the Council shall have to consider it."

Anya scoffed. "I confess I have some trouble investing in your fanciful whims, princess, particularly when it comes to what the rex stands to gain from agreeing with such a plan. But if it puts food in the bellies of my kind, I care not what you celestials and monsters get up to in your castles."

"You are the soul of the nation." A smile spread across Laila's lips, far more radiant than the streams of solar light surrounding them. "Without you, Mortos crumbles. Remember that. So, do I have your support?"

The qarna glanced among themselves before slowly, one by one, the fungus on their antlers spewed fragrant spores signalling their agreement.

Laila drew in a breath, enchanted by the sight, before exhaling a short delighted laugh.

However, her appreciation was cut mournfully short when the clomp of hippogriff hooves came bounding past the village gates. These were Darius's enforcers coming in for a quick patrol, and they were antsy for conflict upon news of the Culling's demise.

The qarna scattered the moment they heard them arrive, making themselves busy with their typical peasant fare of tending the fields and sweeping the doorsteps. They wouldn't dare raise their heads to look at the uniformed brutes, even their antlers looked downcast in reverence.

"Well, well," crooned one of the mounted soldiers. "Quite the gathering. What are you all up to? Getting ready to celebrate the extension of your miserable lives?"

"There is no celebration to be found here, sir." Anya slowly unfurled her limbs to stand. "Nothing but a friendly gathering."

"That's not what it looks like to me."

"Then check your eyes," muttered a qarnun under his breath while he carried a bag of grain on his back.

The enforcer snapped his head instantly at the insult. "What was that, you ingrate?"

The qarnun staggered backwards, forgetting the occassi had keen hearing. "N-nothing..."

"I'll teach you to watch that tongue of yours." The enforcer shaped a length of shadow into a whip and raised it to strike.

"Stop!" Laila launched in his path before the whip could slash the qarnun's mouth, and she took the blow full-on. It tore a clean cut through her cheek to her temple, spilling a rivulet of ichor. She stifled a cry of pain as her fingers went to touch the wound. "That's quite enough!"

The enforcer's eyes bulged. "Princess! I didn't notice you were among them..."

"Now what is going on here?" Sabina swooped low on her hippogriff and landed with a thud. She took one glimpse of the scene and deduced what had unfolded with acuity. "Tut, tut, Maximus. I'd make yourself scarce for a while. That's the rex's honoured guest, and you've gone and marked up her pretty face."

"I didn't—" Maximus sputtered, the sinews in his neck protruding. "Fly home, Sabina. This isn't ladies' business."

"I'll lop off your bollocks, then, shall I? And then we can talk on equal footing."

His comrades chortled, albeit nervously and quietly. It was clear Sabina outranked them, and it was even more clear they held her in contempt for it.

Laila added, "It is *you* who are out of bounds here, Maximus. Leave peacefully now. Or the rex will hear of this, for certain."

To be dismissed so out of turn would, undoubtedly, cause him to lose face with the qarna. But he knew well he could not contest the princess. The solarites were the only creatures they had not conquered.

He bowed his head in surrender. "As you wish, Your Radiance."

Laila could feel the imprint of his glare long after he left, but she suppressed her disquiet. She would let them see her as something superior and therefore untouchable—an entity of celestial perfection raised under the strict tutelage of the stars themselves. There was little she knew better than how to perform, after all.

With that, she turned her attention to Sabina. "Seems you always appear just in the nick of time to save me." She smiled just enough to keep from wincing in pain.

⌥

Darius observed from the window as Sabina escorted Laila back to the courtyard on the back of her hippogriff.

His stare deepened when he saw the splotches of blood on her face and the gash that still had some ways to heal in spite of her supernatural gifts. It took every ounce of willpower not to storm out to her at once, wary as he was that she might not be receptive to his demonstration of protectiveness.

So he withheld, watching enviously as Laila embraced Sabina, fixated on the length with which she held her. How leisurely they draped their arms around each other. It was too intimate a scene, speaking loudly of an ease she no longer shared with him. To see her offer affection to another so brazenly in front of him struck deep.

At last, they separated, and Laila pattered up the steps into the castle, leaving Sabina behind to see to her hippogriff.

That was when Darius made his move down to the paddocks, approaching behind her and casting a long, black shadow. "Was that the princess you were just with?"

Sabina fed a mouse to her hippogriff. "Yes, she wanted me to escort her to the hinterlands. Why do you ask?"

"Her face." Darius gestured to his cheek. "Who did that?"

Sabina hesitated before realisation dawned. "Oh, right." She rolled her eyes. "Maximus decided to get a little boisterous with the qarna today. They're all on edge due to the Culling ending, I suppose. There was a brief altercation, which your lovely princess decided to get in the middle of."

"Maximus." Darius filed the name away into his mental bank, discarding anything else but that. "Thank you." Satisfied with the knowledge, he turned on his heel to retreat.

"Why the interest?" Sabina called after him.

Darius clasped his hands behind his back. "Needed a name to enter into the chimera pits."

XII

BLINDING LIGHTS ASSAULTED DOMINUS'S EYES FROM overhead. His vision doubled, quadrupled, as trays of medical utensils and hypodermic needles blurred into indistinct shapes. Pinpricks of perspiration swelled into beads on his forehead, and a tube nestled against the inner wall of his throat, taunting him to cough it up. There were hands, gloved hands, and warped voices.

"...Quite fascinating, isn't it? The way a quick dip in the Rejuvenation Spring all but stripped him of his occassi features..."

"...Indeed. He still has the height. But the claws, fangs, eyes, and ears? The decrease in musculature? You'd almost mistake him for a human..."

"...Mm, not quite mortal. His healing factor is still

*rather impressive. A leftover from the spring, I presume.
Still, we ought to run more tests..."*

Dominus groaned as he arched his neck, cool fingers poking and prodding at him with clinical intent. Then a needle burrowed into skin, drawing a slick trail of blood in a curve beneath his elbow, and his eyes rotated into his skull.

He sat up with a start.

His fangs dropped and his claws protruded as he slashed his arm through the empty air within reach. He did not settle even when the nightmare slowly retracted its grip from his mind. Instead, he rose from the uncomfortable patch on the floor he had slept on and paced a few perfect circles in the ground. Tightening a fist, he pummelled a hole through the wall from plaster to brick before he stepped back and clutched his head.

"What in oblivion is wrong with me?" He tugged his hair with intent to tear his cranium apart, so that he might reform the contents to resemble normal function.

A throb in his hand made him realise the punch had caused him pain. After flexing his fingers, he retrieved a decoction from his belt and drank it.

He could not *break*. Not now. He must be solid, immovable oak. But it was so difficult being the whittled wood soldier his father made of him when he wasn't there to wind his key and watch him go. Who was Dominus to direct all this infinite capacity to inflict violence without a firm hand to take him by the shoulder and guide his way?

His chest trembled as he steadied his breaths and, eventually, he returned to that blank slate of numbness he so desired. Now that he was calm, he bumbled into the passageway towards the bathroom until porcelain tiles cooled his calloused feet. A shower would do him good. Water cleansed, purified the mind.

He turned on the tap, switched the thermostat to high temperature, and allowed the condensation to carpet the room like the forest mists during glistening winter mornings. Something that almost brought him close to home.

He thought of the steam baths and hot springs of the Citadel. How they boiled with a volcanic heat that always left him feeling clean and stripped. A tightness in his chest returned again. He couldn't think of it. Of home. He couldn't allow his mind to unmoor itself through excess of wanting.

So he stepped into the shower and let the first needles of scalding water slither through the jungly mane of his hair and beard. Dry, brittle strands rustled against his fingers as he rinsed beneath his chin. He needed a trim. Badly. His hair had gotten similarly unruly when it wasn't lazily half-knotted at his head.

He wondered what his mother would have thought of it. Vasilisa with her immaculate curls carefully arranged beneath her kokoshnik, her carmine lips that were always prettily parted in unspoken disapproval when he trekked mud in from the stables. He remembered the last time he'd seen those lips—desiccated and withered, oozing streaks of black blood around the chin. Stiff, never to move again.

Vasilisa was best known for her vivid autumnal locks, which she liked to wear loose in their natural ringlets down to her waist in intimate settings, like rivulets of fresh blood. This had earned her the moniker of Bleeding Heart among nobility. Not only for her hair colour, but also for her tender and true nature which almost felt unfitting for an occassella.

To Dominus she had been unfitting, perhaps the only one of the Calantis clan to know what it meant to have hands that were spotless.

And the solarites, they had driven his father to murder her. That he could not forgive.

He peeled back the shower curtain and reached for a gaudily patterned towel, which he tied into a knot around his waist. A jellied layer of water still puddled atop his hair, too dense for it to seep through. He squeezed it dry in the sink and tamed it with a comb before returning back to the hallway.

The first door he pushed through ended up being a pastel-coloured child's room with a mahogany cradle shaped like the hull of a ship. An army of stuffed animals with beady button eyes stood guard.

A sculpted mermaid crowned with pearls reached upwards with clasped hands from the front of the cradle. The sides were decorated in coral, fish, and seashells reliefs. The interior was cream silk with silver braiding, and two muslin drapes were fixed to the tail of the mermaid with rings.

On the other end of the room was a polished wood and glass cabinet full of animal figurines still smooth with resin. Dominus could view the steady progression of skill and dexterity in the crafter's fingers as the shelves evolved upwards in detail and complexity from the clumsier carvings of before. He recognised the craftsmanship of Elina's woodwork in both the cradle and the figurines and realised this must have been her daughter's room when she and Sadik were still together. A hand-painted wall mural of an underwater paradise stencilled with the name *Yasmin* soon confirmed his theory.

He approached the desk by the cabinet, drawn in by the handmade helio frame that was a tiny bit crooked to eyes as superior as his own. There, he saw a younger Elina and a baby, their faces creased in mirth as they knelt before a melting sandcastle.

Dominus slipped the heliograph from the frame and pressed his thumb against it, as though he might become absorbed into it. He could envision them so clearly, padding barefoot in the shallows of the sea. Elina sculpting a citadel out of wet sand, and Yasmin's shrill toddler laughter dampening the air as the tide rolled in to demolish it, while Sadik hurriedly snapped his camera to immortalise this moment. He found himself in envy of these mortals and their untainted child's play, how this sepia-toned film was roseate with the warmth of a father's love that he offered them without penalty.

When he was a boy-cub, his rex father would force him to hex his own skeleton to contort it and repair it until he was able to do it without so much as a whimper. That was love in the way of the occassi, that was *family*. It wasn't soft ice-cream summers and building wet sandcastles by the beach. It was allowing someone close enough to decimate you and only hoping that, by the strength of their mercy or your own resolve, they wouldn't.

A door slammed in the distance and, with tense fingers, Dominus slid the photo back into the frame and sped into the spare bedroom. The bed had been far too small to hold him, and he hadn't wanted to risk collapsing the frame. So instead, he had stripped it of its sheets and covers and made himself a makeshift bedroll on the carpet.

Sadik's footsteps were loud and forceful on the staircase as he entered with a monogrammed tote slung over the crook of his elbow.

"I brought you a fresh set of clothes," he declared as he flung the bag onto the bed. "Don't fancy your chances of fitting inside any of mine, and you could do with a new set."

Dominus took a quick glance at Sadik, a dainty-looking man of middling height, and concluded his assumption as correct. Dominus eclipsed him by at least twelve inches. He was also slim where Dominus was broad and elephantine—a magnified presence in this little anthill room.

Sadik tipped the bag on the bed and emptied it to reveal a black silk kurta with Thal embroidery and cream trousers. There were even underclothes and velvet slippers that were similarly decorous. Dominus had noticed how the people here favoured bold, vivacious embellishments and saturated colours that screamed in his face when he saw them.

Dominus shrugged off his towel, uncaring of his modesty, then slid on the loose cotton drawers and trousers and shimmied the long silk kurta past his shoulders. It reached his knees once he tugged it down enough. Judging by the relative ease of how they fit, he guessed they had been custom made, and he wondered where Sadik might have gone to procure them.

"If you'd like I can take you somewhere to get that beard of yours a trim, maybe even sort out that rat's nest you call hair," Sadik mentioned idly, having now made himself comfortable in an armchair. His gold-cuffed twists were perpetually lustrous and tidy. He was heavy in ostentation with his many-ringed fingers, his double-pierced helix, and his ill-matched eyes immaculately shaped by gold pencil.

Dominus grunted uncharitably. "What's wrong with how I look?"

Sadik raised a groomed brow at him and for a moment he saw Darius in his place, fingers tented, always appraising his unconventional technique at lacing his kaftan. *The clothes maketh the creature, Dominus.* But he was no prince any longer; he needn't laud his superior birth over his lessers.

"It's simpler to evade detection whilst I remain ungroomed."

"Perhaps out in the jungle, but here you blend by giving no one any reason to doubt your belonging in the first place," Sadik told him. "You might be a touch lighter than the people here, but you are certainly not as pale as a light-skinned Mortesian. So, keep those ears and eyes discreet and stop brutalising people. You'd be surprised how inconspicuous you can seem."

Dominus's throat rumbled as he sat on the bed and formed a concave in the mattress. "If you are finished mocking me, I would like to know of my next orders."

"Your orders are to join me for breakfast. Then we'll meet a contact of mine who will aid your task."

He stood and tapped Dominus on the side of his arm, almost fatherly, but all his muscles could remember was the threat of harm. So he tensed and curved his fingers into a position to strike before he let the impulse pass.

"I see," Sadik said, having noticed his reaction. Then he raised his hands. "No touching, then. Come along, monster."

He walked out of the room. Dominus followed.

In the kitchen, Sadik served himself rice and black lentil pancakes stuffed with spiced potatoes on plates of banana leaf. He paired this with little silver bowls of chutney and a tall glass of spiced chai. Sadik sipped from the chai first before carefully tearing portions from his pancake and dipping it in chutney.

Dominus devoured his lamb chops with the appetite of a monster. He never realised how hard a real meal would hit him after years of squealing carcasses and carrion. When he finished his first serving, he demanded another.

"You can eat, can't you?" Sadik observed in wary amusement.

Dominus nodded vigorously and took a sip of Seraji coffee. The flavour was smooth, with traces of cardamom and tobacco.

"When exactly do we meet this contact?" he asked as he slurped at the last dregs of the beverage and licked the sludge that remained.

"In due time, don't you worry," Sadik promised. "Just thought you might want something to build your strength up first."

Dominus grunted at the irony of his words and lifted his shackles. "How long must you make me suffer this indignity?"

"Just until I know that I can trust you, monster." Sadik presented his commercial-ready smile. His teeth were near offensively white against his mahogany skin. "The person we intend to meet is willing to pick up where Elina has left us off, so I expect you to be on your best behaviour. All right?"

He grunted again. "To what end do you seek this gambit of making elixirs with my blood? Do you intend to become the first great mortal magician of chaos magic? To amass an army? To conquer this land?"

Sadik leaned back into his chair. "I want to give men the opportunity to know power that has been denied by them by a mere consequence of birth."

"What does the fate of all these mundane men matter to you?"

"Other than being mundane myself, I am probably one of their largest employers on the continent. Before me, the best a man could ever hope for was to lease a shop, become a servant, or, if they were smart, become a secretary or assistant. I worked very hard to avoid such a mediocre fate, but I'm one of the lucky ones. I, therefore, have a vested interest in helping men like me thrive in a world that is slanted in favour of witches."

Dominus couldn't believe it, nor see the use of such foolhardy altruism. Never in his two centuries had he understood what was advantageous about social reform, for it had never elevated a creature beyond his rank or resources. There was no enrichment in wealth, no expansion of power. Perhaps this was why he couldn't blame Darius in the end. He was only acting on his true nature as much as Dominus could only act upon his.

"Honestly, I ought to be thanking you," Sadik said. "The only reason I made my fortune is because of Mortos. The wildlife of your country presented new and interesting opportunities in the field of alchemy and especially medicine." He took a long sip of chai. "However, after the moongrass scandal, the strict regulations on your exports left a market wide open for me to slot into. Peddling all sorts of products that more reputable companies wouldn't dare consider touching."

Dominus nodded, remembering his home at the Citadel—the furry blankets of black moss and asphyxiating vines that, in summers, became stiflingly overgrown. In Mortos, even the flora could be treacherous to those unaware. Dominus remembered vividly the nights when he had been tucked into bed with his mother citing the dangers that befell those who succumbed to the moist lustre of berries or the mystical glow of mushrooms without realising that the former tranquilised and the latter induced delirium. The tales the animals wrought were not much gentler. The potential for the pursuits of magic, however, were innumerable. And there was nothing that generated demand quicker than the allure of the forbidden.

"Even met that brother of yours. Interesting mind, he has."

Dominus went rigid at the mention of Darius.

"The kinds of weapons he's inventing now have Soleterea all up in a stir." Sadik made a fearful gesture with his hands for flourish. "Originally I wanted to lend my backing to him for a chance to invest in his inventions but... no dice."

"It is likely he saw you as an opportunist and a snake," Dominus said with a derisive snort. "After all, it would take one to know one."

Sadik chuckled. "Things seem to still be a little sore between you and your brother, huh?"

"An understatement," Dominus replied cagily. "He betrayed our country, ruined our family, and caused my..." He could not finish the final sentence. "I don't blame him. I know he was being manipulated."

"This have to do with your vendetta against the solarites?" Sadik asked, lowering his voice. "Never cared for the yellow-bloods myself, though it ain't something one goes talking about in public. You see."

"I took one as a lover once," Dominus said, a disbelieving smile still coming to his lips at the thought of her. He shook his head. "She was... Simply to be around her was to be immersed in pure sunlight. She was the most exquisite being I ever had the fortune to know, and the worst mistake I ever committed. I should've killed her. First chance I got."

Sadik's eyes shifted up and down in alarm. "So I'm assuming this... must've been a difficult breakup?"

"Her actions led directly to my ruin. I see that now. I was too blinded by her back then to notice." Dominus picked up a glass of water and lifted it to his lips. "It's because of her that I lost the person I hold most dear. I think I ought to repay the favour."

"Well, I can't say I could be of much help in that regard, but I would be happy to lend my support to your efforts provided you offer me what I need in return." Sadik rose from his chair. "Now, on to our next stop."

Sadik crooked his finger for Dominus to follow and departed from the house with a jaunty spring in his step.

"The Morose Cursesmith" beckoned in a dulled bronze stencil, the shop shunned to an undesirable corner of the city. The sign, nailed to the chipping red door, pointed them up to the second floor.

Sadik pushed past the rainmaker curtains as though it were his own homecoming. Dominus followed as they took to the stairs, knocking on the fissured wooden door.

When there was no answer, Sadik knocked more urgently.

"Yes, yes, I'm *coming*—"

There was the sound of metal scratching and jangling as several locks were unlatched. For a moment, Dominus considered the irony of a proclaimed cursesmith having a fascination with locks and bolts.

The door opened to reveal none other than an occassella, her prodigious silhouette practically filling up the doorway. Her ice blue eyes surveyed them with careful scrutiny.

It was the eyes that had Dominus skidding to a sudden pause as he absorbed more of her—the sculpted planes of her face and ghostly colouring framed by wind-tousled carmine curls. The last he'd seen of those curls, they'd been pinned back obediently into a kokoshnik and that face had been half-obscured as she smiled demurely into a wine goblet.

He had lost so much time.

"Are you Tanya Moroz?" Sadik asked. "We're looking for a cursesmith—we have a job."

Tanya inclined her head but her gaze was a watchful one, the honed scan of a predator. "You'd better come inside."

She barely welcomed them in before the door swooped to a sudden close behind them with a quiet click. The interior of the apartment had as little to say for itself as the outside, but there were small touches here and there (the glass case of pipe-smoking stuffed squirrels, the nesting dolls, the painted figurine of Matrona Anara with her head bowed in maidenly grace) that were like filial nudgings of being welcomed home.

Sadik took his shoes off in the passageway at the corner of the ornate floral rug, and Dominus decided to imitate.

"I have some water heating in the samovar if you'd like tea," Tanya mentioned idly, though for Dominus it was a flicker of familiarity in this dark and unknowable continent. To partake in a ritual that was so entrenched into his domiciliary habits after so long—

"Please," he said, and he tried to sound less parched as he did so. The rug was warm beneath his bare foot before he grazed a cool mosaic.

Tanya poured piping hot water into a glass filled with black tea, then opened a labelled jar of sugar.

"You do not have burnt honey?" Dominus asked, the frown implicit in his voice.

She shrugged and scooped a mountain cap of white crystal—he could turn it to snow if he dreamed enough. "I like the sugar better. I mostly keep the samovar for nostalgia." She let the sugar avalanche into the black gulf of tea and stirred. "It's been a while since I've heard the mention of burnt honey. Though from the look of you, I can tell you are an occasso. What brings you to Thalistan?"

He realised at once it was a mistake to speak, for he had nothing to say in answer to her question.

Sadik dove to his rescue and declined the offer when Tanya gestured to the samovar. "We met on a trip I took to Gravissia some time ago. He is an immigrant like yourself, come to seek new opportunities by aiding me in my business. And on the subject of business…"

Tanya clinked her teaspoon at the rim of her cup and scooped another cap to sweeten Dominus's. "Yes, what can I help you with? As the note on the door says, I can either cast a limited number of curses or break them."

Dominus took his tea without milk and let it warm his hands.

"We're looking more on the casting side. There's this elixir I would like for you to create for me in bulk," Sadik explained. "You'd be heavily compensated."

Tanya tapped her finger against the glass. "Anything that requires me to do something more than once is going to cost you extra. And I want you to know I am not an alchemist, so don't expect to foist all of your potion crafting needs onto me." She lifted her glass to her lips, and the sleeves of her kurta rolled back enough to show the indelible ink of an eternal bond.

"You live alone?" Dominus asked without thinking, without being able to help it.

Her almond-shaped eyes narrowed perceptibly. "Is that relevant?" Her tone sank menacingly low as she put down her glass. "I haven't had sprites come by in a long while, but your fidgety friend here is starting to give me pause for alarm."

"We're not spies for the Iron Clan, I can assure you of that," Sadik said, raising his hands in a show of neutrality.

It was now she came to look at Dominus, *earnestly* examine him, and the ever so faint impression that all was not as he presented. "Perhaps not, but I am not typically one to forget a face, and I certainly know yours—" Then she stopped, her breath withdrawn as her eyes enlarged to the size of coins. She looked like she'd seen the face of a ghost, for that was precisely what he was. "You're—"

Dominus affirmed himself in the silence given by her fear, all the reverent dread of being stood before royalty. "Do you forget yourself, Tatiana Levitia?"

"Do not call me that!" It was a violent hiss with fangs drawn. "I hold no fealty towards that name. My knees bend to a new sovereign."

He was infuriated by her words, squeezing the glass in his hands until it was webbed in fissures. "You would swear fealty to the solarite throne?"

"Sooner than I would to the throne that chained me to my father and then my husband, forcing me to bear thirty-two pregnancies in the hopes I might spawn warriors!"

Dominus's throat clogged like he was suffocated. "Those warriors would've guaranteed your safety. They guarantee *all* our safety."

"They guarantee our *bloodlust*," she seethed, "and I no longer desire safety if it means forsaking my freedom. Here I have my livelihood and I have my autonomy."

His hand snapped around her neck as he jerked it harshly to reveal the mark etched in her skin to declare her race. "Do you call this *free*?"

She punched him so hard he went stumbling against the table. The tea toppled and spilled a brown wave across the surface.

"Your people already laid their mark upon me!" She shoved back her sleeve to reveal the marriage mark on her wrist; the inked emblem of the Levitis house with Delanus's initials. "You may see yourself out now, *Your Mightiness.*"

"Wait—" Sadik called out and threw himself in their path like a dwarf before giants, making himself a barrier between these two hulking monsters squaring to fight. "Wait! We still need your help, Tanya. I'll offer you triple the pay—pluck a number out of thin air if you please. Just don't turn us away."

Tanya was the first to re-civilise herself, tucking away the canines and draining all the blackness from her eyes as she paused to consider. "Triple the pay." Her chin jutted out towards Dominus. "But keep him away from me."

Dominus released a low warning snarl in response.

"Stop," Sadik told him sternly. Then he glanced politely to Tanya. "We're leaving." He marched Dominus outside of the shop onto the ground floor before flapping his arms at him in disbelief. "What was that back there? Huh?"

Dominus's throat rolled menacingly but he said nothing in response.

"Hey!" Sadik took a few brazen steps towards him. "You can't go treating her like that. Not in this country. That might have flown where and when you came from, but things are different now."

So Dominus had seen, and yet he himself was caught like a fly in a vat of amber, watching the world converge around him whilst he remained unchanged. He could not break free of it.

"What in oblivion are you so angry about anyway?"

If nothing else the question made him pause to consider, absorbing his fury in the process. "I don't—" He hung his head in defeat. "I don't know."

XIII

THE SINGING BELLS OF THE TOWER CRIED THE HOUR of gloaming as Lyra approached the temple, and her boots echoed on the floral-painted mosaics leading up to the clover-shaped arches. The dulcet melodies of the choral hymnals both soothed and chilled her, like receiving an embrace from someone who had come in from the cold.

She knelt down in deference before the altar of Oqyanus, god of the ocean and the abyss. The carved effigy displaying his likeness radiated tender warmth and benevolence as Lyra set down tributes of sunflower bread, dandelion wine, and flowers to aid her relatives in the Astral Realm.

Her fingers tentatively encircled the jade leaf–shaped handle of the dagger on her thigh. A gift from Léandre on her birthday. Or perhaps it had been a gift for the Fête. The complete tale eluded her now. She decided against parting with it, for even the living required tribute from the dead to aid them through their realm, and slowly she rose to her feet.

The burial grounds were a long, untamed sprawl of trees carefully maintained by the groundskeepers. Lyra had always found a soft comfort in that, in the thought that in the event of her death her body might be used to nurture something else to life. Most graves were distinguished by a brass plaque and she found his gently laid with sunflowers. The blossoms seemed to be a recent addition and Lyra couldn't help but wonder from whom.

Here Lies Léandre de Lis, read the inscription. She pressed her back against the trunk of his tree and slid down between the roots. She was tired of losing people to monsters. Ever since the death of her mother, she had dedicated herself to the cause of ridding the world of their scourge. And yet, they continued to fester. Seemingly stronger than ever before. Leaving the bodies of good sprites strewn in their wake.

"I know you'll be upset with me for saying this," Lyra said towards the tree, smiling bitterly, "but ever since I learned that Dominus was alive, I just... can't stop thinking how pointless it all was. Everything you did." She cupped her face in her hands and dragged them down. "You told me you gave up your life so I wouldn't have to keep fighting them anymore, and yet... here I am." She closed her eyes, inhaling shakily. "And I am *so* tired."

Her search for Dominus had been endless since the massacre in the Parvani Rainforest. Still, she felt no closer to having caught him than she did the moment she'd been given the mission. All her leads on the clinics had run dry, and the occasso seemed to be taunting her with the latest body they'd uncovered with a skeleton shaped like a star. It was as though he were planning something and taunting her with mere hints to solve his riddle before it was complete.

"I just wish you were here to give me some advice." She touched two fingers to her lips, pressing them tenderly to the trunk, then she lay down on the grass and allowed his branches to offer her shelter. Above her, the sun sank westward to rest its weary head upon the horizon, the last dregs of light squeezing through the spaces in the leaves to dapple her face in flecks of gold.

When she opened her eyes again she realised that she must have slept, for the sky had become a rich blue velvet to signal the coming of night. She rose up from the makeshift pillow she'd made from her arms to find her compact mirror was buzzing in her pocket.

After she rubbed her eyes with a sleepy groan she answered it and saw the face of Madhali Azar. "I hope I didn't disturb your rest, Ser de Lis."

"Not at all." Lyra was already alert. "What is it?"

"I was able to get one of the cursesmiths to talk about the decoction you found. It's an old recipe from the grimoire that was lost ten years ago during the Chamber of Chaos burglary."

"Calante's grimoire?" Lyra asked. "*The* grimoire?"

"The very same." Madhali nodded. "That's not all. The decoction is meant to be a... how shall I put this? It's a serum of sorts. Rather like the purges we use against those infected with chaos magic. But in reverse."

"So you're telling me Dominus is trying to inoculate himself. Against... *aether*?" Her mind scanned for an explanation, finding none. "*Why?*"

"My theory is it might have something to do with the fact that he is, seemingly, back from the dead."

"If you mean to imply someone with aether resurrected him, well... that makes even less sense." Lyra pressed her thumb against her lips in thought. The pieces of the puzzle were there before her, waiting to be assembled. But she couldn't help but feel something was still missing.

Then she remembered something. The body that had been discovered in the shape of a star... could a solarite be behind this?

Lyra couldn't force herself to think it, let alone say it. "If he's immunising, that means he may be weak. We can exploit this."

"There's something else."

"What?"

"We've received testimony from a guard that Dominus has been seen again in Thalistan. And you'll never guess where."

Lyra sighed in disgruntlement. "Please don't tell me Sadik Yilan." She rubbed at her temples. He was well-known for his association with occassi crowds. "That man is a headache and a half."

"I know." Madhali smiled wryly. "It's certainly a lead worth pursuing."

Lyra dug a strand of grass from her hair. "Back to Thalistan I go."

The mint green sign of The Salt Ring was backed by fluorescent light—the emblematic pestle and mortar encircled by the name, written twice, and flanked by the date of establishment. By far the most lucrative seller of alchemy ingredients, Sadik had made history by taking up the middling business of the childless witch who'd raised him and expanding it to a household name. Few could escape his smiling visage on animated billboards beckoning for sales or that incessant jingle on the radio:

> *When you need something to make your cauldron sing,*
> *Head on down to The Salt Ring!*
> *Snake tongue, frog legs, and eye of newt,*
> *All you need to give your potion a boot.*
> *So hop on your broom or give this mirror a ping*
> *To get all you need from The Salt Ring!*

Lurking beneath it was a well-known secret that he stood at the centre of the interconnected web of black market wares, though he kept such a thing far from his legitimate stores.

Lyra never much liked the fact that the Iron Clan didn't simply arrest him. But to their logic he was a necessary evil and was best left monitored rather than eliminated. If not him, then someone else would wriggle in to keep filling the pockets of the Thal officials he had on payroll. Such was the reason why Lyra never became more involved in politics.

She glanced up at the sign signalling the head office before she entered. The reception was of extravagant taste, with a high-domed ceiling of stained glass filtering kaleidoscopic patterns onto the polished floors. The purl of the sculptural fountain was soft on Lyra's ears as she approached the man behind the desk.

"I need to meet with Sadik Yilan." Lyra propped her arm up on the lacquered ebony. "It's a most urgent matter of official capacity."

The receptionist rifled through the visitor's ledger. "I am afraid that Mr Sadik is most booked up for the foreseeable fu—"

"It's all right, Isaías."

Lyra glanced up towards the voice. Upon the stairwell, Sadik Yilan stood in a peach net tunic and satin trousers embroidered with zari and diamanté.

"You can let the spritemaid through."

Lyra nodded towards the desk before approaching Sadik on the stairs. He led the way up towards his office while Lyra scanned her surroundings, mapping the landscape.

He opened the door to let her through before tapping his cobra cane on the floor. "To what do I owe the pleasure of this visit, Ser—"

"de Lis," Lyra finished for him.

Sadik, smiling, gestured for her to sit before taking his own seat on the tufted leather chair. "Could I procure you any refreshment? Tea? Rosewater?"

"That won't be necessary," Lyra said, taking a seat at the desk. She propped her ankle on her knee. "I've come regarding a recent patron you may have received at The Blue Lobster."

"Well, I receive plenty of those, you understand," Sadik said wryly, tenting his fingers together.

"This one is... quite distinctive. An occasso with dark hair, green eyes." Lyra raised her hand above her head. "About over seven feet."

Sadik hummed in acknowledgement. "You are right, that is distinctive. Fortunately, I happen to know of the fellow you speak of."

"You met with him then?"

"Briefly, yes."

Lyra narrowed her eyes. "And what did he want?"

"Creature claimed he happened to have a proposition for me. I heard him out. Didn't much care for what he had to say. He left."

"What sort of proposition?" Lyra lowered her ankle and leaned forward, wrists on her knees.

"He thought I might be interested in performing some chaotic ritual in exchange for money—" Sadik blew his lips in amusement, shrugging with his elbows. "You receive a lot of these opportunistic types when you come into great wealth, as you can imagine. My guess is he's been struggling a bit since coming from the north to our great continent and was hoping I'd take pity on him."

"So then you spoke. And then he left." Lyra gritted her teeth. "That's it?"

"'Fraid so."

Lyra didn't believe him in the slightest. "Any idea where he might have gone?"

"He didn't seem too eager to share his business." Sadik's face was the picture of sympathy. "Sorry I couldn't be of more help to you, ser."

Lyra could feel her fingers flexing into fists but resisted. She had no way of countering the narrative he'd woven so seamlessly, not unless she found another opening. Her eyes darted about the room and then towards the framed heliographs on his desk. In one Sadik had his arms wrapped around a Thal woman, likely his beloved. In the other was an infant smiling towards the camera, the familial resemblance striking.

"This your daughter, then?" Lyra inquired as she casually handled the heliograph on the desk, bringing it closer into view.

A brief glimmer of discomfort appeared in Sadik's dark eyes as he hesitated to take the heliograph from her. "Yes, that's my girl, Yasmin."

Lyra noted the fondness with which he spoke and suppressed the discomfort it brought to her. She glanced closer at the pictures and discovered, with some surprise, that she recognised the Thal woman. "Seems like an old picture."

"About ten years ago." Sadik took the frame from her and adjusted it back in its rightful place. "Reminds me I'll need to badger my old lady for another."

"I see." Lyra rose up from her chair. "That'll be all for now, Mr Sadik. Thank you for your cooperation."

"It was my pleasure."

They regarded each other with daggers concealed behind their civil gazes.

Elina sighed as she exited the gate of her house, and she pursed her lips in thought. Ever since her confrontation with Sadik, she'd been wracked with guilt and worry over the thought that he'd gone and done something foolish. Something irreversible. Worse than when he'd bartered his soul for wealth and bankrupted himself of any virtue in the process.

That moment alone should've removed any kernel of affection she still held for him. Yet here she was with a handwoven basket of kokis in the shape of honeybees, hoping the gesture might re-awaken the first time she'd done this after an altercation between them. How Sadik had gone on to call her *his* honeybee ever since.

She clutched the basket handle tighter as she approached the lone train station to the city. Butterflies suffused her stomach. Her legs twitched with the instinct to turn, to walk away, to sever whatever remaining thread that still bound her heart to his.

Before she could work up the nerve, her path was obstructed by a sudden call.

"Hello again, Mata Panja."

Elina started in the direction of the spritemaid leaning against the wall adjoining an alleyway. "Ser de Lis? I—"

"Hadn't anticipated such a coincidence?" Lyra's lips broadened into a smile. "I'd agree if I hadn't been staking out the house in the hopes I might see you."

"*Me?*" Elina's voice dwindled to a mousy timbre. Never in her life had she brushed shoulders with the wrong side of the law, her tangential relations notwithstanding. "I don't understand—"

Lyra stepped towards Elina from the shadows to further eclipse her way. Though they held the same height, her presence made her seem overpowering. She was statuesque, a legendary figure cut from Soleterean marble. Elina couldn't help but shrink before such majesty.

"Please, ser." Elina kept her tone calm and even from years of medical practice. "I promise you I have done nothing wrong."

"Oh, it's not you I'm after, mata." Lyra helped herself to a warm kokis from Elina's basket. "Let me reassure you of that."

"Then what—"

"You happen to be the ex-lover of Sadik Yilan," Lyra said, accentuating it with a crunch of dessert. "Common word has it that he is a magnet for illicit occassi activity. I was wondering if you were aware of any contact he's had with one hulking behemoth of seven feet?"

Elina's chest hiccupped, her mouth barely forming the words to ask. "Has he—has Sadik been harmed?"

"Not yet," Lyra replied. "However, I feel confident asserting he may well end up dead if you do not cooperate."

Elina's face fell ashen. "Ser, I beg you. I know little."

"But you do know something." Lyra noted this with an even livelier bite of kokis. She was a hound with a scent now. "Go on."

"I know he's been in contact with the occasso of whom you speak, but that's all! He... I... we don't talk."

Elina swallowed as Lyra narrowed her eyes. It made her feel rotten to be dishonest, but she couldn't bear the thought of turning him over to the authorities before she had a chance to reach him herself.

"Hmph. Very well." Lyra consumed what was left of her treat. "I believe you for now, Mata Panja. However, should you happen to run into Sadik or this occasso again, I want you to alert me. Understood?"

Elina wavered in uncertainty.

"Am I understood?"

"Yes, ser." Elina lowered her gaze.

"Outstanding. Now, before we part ways, I would like to bestow something upon you." Lyra slipped her hand into her jacket and produced a finely carved wooden stake etched with archaic symbols.

Elina's lips parted in awe and fear. "Is that—?"

"One of the few ways to murder occassi." Lyra placed the weapon in her hands. "For protection. Should you need it. One pierce straight through the heart should do it. Then twist it." She mimed the gesture. "So the wound won't close."

Elina reluctantly accepted it. The bark was rough on her palm in ways she was not used to from wood.

Finally, Lyra stepped to one side to grant her passage. "Have a pleasant day, mata."

⌾

"Ela! What a pleasant surprise." Sadik closed the door to his office behind him as Elina stepped inside with a quick glance over her shoulder.

She unravelled her shawl to drape it across her forearm. "I don't intend to stay long, I just..." She held up the basket in her hands. "I brought you some kokis."

He recognised immediately the significance of the shape. "Oh, Ela, you..." His throat contracted in fondness. "You shouldn't have."

"I felt that I must." Elina placed the basket on his desk and smoothed her palms down her tunic. "Sadik—" A heavy exhale followed it. "I haven't been able to stop thinking about what you said the other day, and—"

"You've changed your mind?"

Elina shook her head at once. "No, Sadik, I've come to ask that you stop this. What you've done. What you're doing now... It's going to get you killed or worse. I thought I could stand back. Watch it happen to you. But I can't." Tears welled in her eyes and drizzled down her cheeks. "I can't."

"Oh, Elina." Sadik closed the distance between them to encircle her willow waist, resting his chin on her shoulder. She had always been taller than him, always beyond his reach. It never kept him from trying to grasp her all the same. "The last thing I ever wanted to do was hurt you like this."

"Then promise me." She pulled back with watery doe eyes to stare into his. "Promise me you will not accept whatever bargain that creature has offered. If you promise, I—I'll let you see Yasmin again. All she's done is ask for you since you came to visit. But I can only allow it on that condition, Sadik. You *must* stay mundane."

Sadik closed his eyes, drawing in a breath. "Elina, I can't." He stepped away from her.

"Why not?" A flicker of anger crossed her expression. Her face was gilded from the soft-toned light of dusk; it brought out the gold in her brown eyes. "Does our daughter matter so little? Do *I* matter so little?"

"Elina, you are everything to me!"

"Then prove it!" Elina's voice had risen to an uncharacteristic volume. A tender turtledove she was no longer. But she was too impassioned to control herself now.

"All right." He sighed in relent. "I'll stay mundane. I can promise you that much."

She hadn't realised how much she needed those words until she heard them said. Until all the tension uncoiled from her stomach and left her winded. "Thank you, Sadik." More tears fell, but these were from relief rather than anger. She threw her arms around him, burrowing her face into his neck. "You have no idea what this means to me."

Sadik let himself embrace her in the hopes that having her weeping with joy in his arms would be enough. But over the curve of her shoulder, his eyes were deadened.

XIV

AILA SMOOTHED HER FLIMSY GARB OF SPUN-GOLD silk, a pattern of padparadscha sapphires embroidered into the shoulders. The fabric clung to her skin like it was poured onto her, rippling languidly with every movement.

"Do you like it, Your Radiance?" asked Marta.

"Yes, it's... beautiful." She frowned, almost sullen over it. Another one of Darius's gowns she'd received as a gift. She resented him for how impeccable his taste was.

Tonight would be the grand opening of the fighting pits, and the Citadel had been in a tizzy over preparations, as a feast would be taking place in the main hall after the event. Hence Laila was preparing herself to impress, knowing the event would be a momentous occasion in Mortesian history.

She let Marta attach the matching golden cloak around her shoulders before she gave her two indulgent puffs of cloying perfume, causing her to wheeze.

Trouble couldn't come sooner in the form of a knock on the door.

Darius entered with a dramatic flip of his black velvet coat, sprayed with lily motifs in red thread. He filled his clothing with a sleek but plentiful musculature that strained enticingly when he moved.

"You're wearing it," he said, sucking in a breath. "Of all the ones I'd commissioned, that was my favourite. I had hoped you'd take a liking to it."

Laila flushed as his eyes roved over the rippling fabric with lustful appreciation. "Yes, well." She stifled her urge to tug her cape over her. "I feel I should be alarmed that you know my measurements."

"It was mostly guesswork," Darius said, "and memory. Your body has not altered much since I last saw it."

Laila swallowed at the words and the implication therein. She averted from his gaze. "Is there something I might help you with?"

"I was hoping you'd do me the honour of accompanying me in my carriage tonight." His head tilted almost endearingly for his nefarious intent. "Plenty of room for two."

She wondered if that was a dig in reference to her being everywhere he wasn't for days. "Actually, I was intending to make my own way."

"Come now, we can discuss that petition you have travelling through the qarna." He raised his hands up in a display of peace. "Hands to myself, I promise."

Laila couldn't help but laugh lightly. "You've heard about it, then."

"Yes, quite a sneaky thing you did getting them all excited for the ætherglass before I'd even agreed. Can hardly refuse to comment on it now, can I?"

"I thought you could do with a little..." Laila playfully lifted a shoulder. "Nudge in the right direction."

"Your obstinance is irksomely refreshing. I am certainly in need of outsider perspectives." He slid a hand through his hair. "There are times when I fear I'm... turning into him."

"Who?"

"My father."

"You're not." Laila's face softened. "Darius, I've said a lot of things against your behaviour but I've never believed you were him."

"I sense him over my shoulder, sometimes, when I encounter obstacles during my rule. Telling me not to be weak. Telling me to obliterate my opponent at any cost. And it would be unanimous among the prefects. The only voice that gave me some reprieve... was yours. I would think of things you might say in his stead, and it would help me. That's why I need you, Laila. To be the voice that leads me from his."

He never failed to ply her with heart-fluttering sentiments. However, she knew she alone could not be entrusted to have so much rule over him. "I cannot promise to always be that voice, Darius. But I can help... until it leads you to your own." Laila sighed, knowing she was being won over. "I suppose it wouldn't hurt if I accompanied you this evening." Her gaze flitted towards Darius's look of triumph, hardening minutely. *You win this time, you bastard.*

Laila and Darius sat a mere six inches apart, but it might as well have been six seas. Their close encounter in her chambers left the air between them thickened with unresolved desire. This near, he could scent her perfume as the carriage jostled—mimosa, narcissus, and orange blossom with accompanying notes of almond and vanilla. He looked at the few loose curls from the chignon she'd pinned back with a sapphire butterfly comb and imagined running them through his fingers again.

"I realise I've heard all this fuss about these chimeras and yet know very little about them." Laila opened her hand-painted fan to flutter it lightly. "Won't you tell me about them, Darius Rex?"

"Certainly." Darius folded one leg over the other. "In the past I spent years travelling and researching in the field of monstrology with funding granted by my father. Mortos has always been home to a variety of dangerous species, and I've performed many dissections to better understand how they work. It was through this research that I branched out into the field of creating organic matter based on existing biological templates."

"Combining existing templates." Laila's forehead creased in thought. "Do you mean by cross-breeding them?"

"Not exactly. More like... redistributing matter. Reducing something to nothing and building it into something new."

"That sounds horrific."

"Well, that's how I've always understood chaos magic to work. And what is chaos but disorder? Our magic functions on much the same principle. As a solarite you can manipulate matter, yes? Cast illusions and warp reality to your liking. Let's take, for example, that window over there." He held out his hand towards it with a gesture until the glass fragmented. "I could cast a curse on an individual to make the window fracture the moment they look upon it. Or any appliance of my choosing. When left to their own devices, without maintenance, things tend to decay. I can accelerate the process. The same with bodies. I could make you sick, cause your pretty hair to fall out in clumps, morph you into a creature beyond recognition—"

"Are you capable of anything but death and destruction?" Laila asked, before gesturing to the window to repair what he broke.

"Well." He shrugged. "I could as easily kill a fever as soon as I could provoke it, repair a bone as soon as I could break it. I suppose the matter lies less with destruction as a concept and more with what it's used for."

"Why chimeras of all things?" Laila asked, his words having given her something to ruminate on.

"I suppose that was to do with my upbringing," Darius admitted, a coldness glazing his blue eyes. "In spite of my illegitimate birth, my father desired to make a warrior out of me, as is expected of us all. I, however, always had more of a head for books. After I passed my first rites in the wilderness when I came of age, I participated as little as I could in active battle. Due to our natures, we are primed to find satisfaction in barbarity. I was no exception. But I couldn't help thinking that all the bloodshed was a waste in light of our numbers and our poor birth rate."

"I remember. You were to serve seventy-five years." Laila tried to suppress the memory of their time in Soleterea. "Was your turn to artificery immediately after your service?"

"Partially," Darius said. "Mostly it was due to finally conquering the qarnun and lupari races. One of the few useful things my father ever did. This reign of... well, I suppose you could say peace, it allowed us time to evolve a bit. I was ageing in a newer time filled with newer schools of thought—but the old guard still remained prominent."

Darius Rex was a relic of the Old World, where war was their religion and bloodshed their worship. Of the final generation born before conquest ended their undying strife with neighbouring territories. Few occassi had seen active battle since.

"We're here," he said, once the carriage drew to a stop.

The once ineffable stillness of the amphitheatre was ruptured by a noisy assemblage of pumpkin-shaped carriages in the square. Music and the sour aroma of mulled wine spilled abundantly from the toothless maw of the archway.

After Darius had descended he turned to Laila, holding out his hand. She took it after a momentary hesitation and let him aid her, trying not to react too stiffly to his palm on the small of her back.

He led them both past the ticket booths, where qarna and occassi alike had gathered to pay their fees and place their bets. The turnout for qarna, in particular, took Laila by surprise, but it seemed they'd travelled far and wide to observe the outcome of mutant versus monster.

Laila made herself comfortable in the royal seating booth, recalling another time she had sat in these seats beside Darius to watch his brother perform at Callemas. Such an event seemed unfathomably far away from her now, a relic from another era.

Before the procession began, a vendor wheeled up the ramp to serve them hot spiced cider and candied apples. Laila helped herself to both, the caramel warm and gooey on her tongue.

The umpire arrived to the sound of deafening ovation and descended from his bronze chariot to announce the first match. The crowd was thunderous as the oil-sheened occasso warrior stepped forward onto the arena floor.

Laila straightened when she recognised him as Maximus, the one who had assaulted her that day in the village. He strode with confidence, striking poses to emphasise his large physique and pulsating musculature.

Darius rolled his eyes in disdain.

His opponent arrived with a rumble from the floor as burrowing up from underground was the first of Darius's chimeras—an enlarged insectoid with pincers strong enough to dismember a body in one bite.

The creature was massive. Larger than any Laila had seen before. It landed forcefully enough to tremble the earth, causing a seismic rumbling in her chest.

Beneath her the occassi were hollering for blood, their features crooked and grotesque.

Laila shifted uncomfortably in her seat as she observed the creature. The way it writhed with the fluidity of a snake, an eerie sapience to the maw and head surrounding its pincers.

The match did not last long. Within minutes the chimera had the occasso in its grip, slicing him in half with a quick chomp that sent his innards splattering.

Laila sat upright, her breathing shallow.

The crowd hooted in amusement. The umpire most of all. The qarna seemed to be especially gleeful at the demise of their tormentor, but she herself could only feel slightly sickened.

After that, a series of other matches took place in which occasso seemed to be paraded out like lambs greased for slaughter. Even those who managed to best their first opponent soon saw themselves brutalised by the next. They were led up against a mass of sentient moss that stripped flesh clean from bone. A humanoid with writhing tentacles for a head that tore a heart clean from a chest. A catlike creature with icicles for claws that made sliced meat of muscle.

All soon became clear—this was a warning on behalf of Darius. A show of the hidden arsenal he had at this disposal. A menagerie of monsters capable of subduing his own peers, completely under his thrall.

He watched every match with a small flicker of triumph, tallying up each win and marking weaknesses to improve upon for next time. A sprout of a smirk took weed and grew larger with every progressive kill by his inventions.

He sensed Laila flinch away from a particularly gruesome dismemberment as the tentacle-headed creature wrapped himself around every limb of a warrior and slowly pried him apart. He took her hand and stroked his thumb over the smooth beige skin of her backhand, rotating his fingers so they could connect with hers.

Laila's heart skipped as she looked down at their interlocked fingers and then into the bright blue of his eyes, brimming with tenderness. She shouldn't have felt comforted by that. By him. And yet, odds against all odds, her pulse began to settle.

⤫

The banquet took place within the lacquered obsidian walls of the Grand Hall, smooth and lustrous as the unfiltered ink of a cephalopod hollow, suckering in all the light from the lambent chandeliers.

Darius had a series of his favourite dishes served on long tables of white linen. They feasted on blood clams, ox tongue, and salted cucumber. Then on ukha made from mussels, eel, spider crab, and scorpionfish; on coulibiac and lobster thermidor. The dessert was a lemon pound cake four tiers high, glazed with vanilla icing.

Laila struggled to swallow her food as Darius's table was continually flocked by occasselle approaching him with a sensuous slink of hips. The rex steered the reins with ease, composed, charming, and affably fiendish as he sparred verbally with the whetted blade of his tongue against his opponents.

Laila knew it shouldn't have bothered her. Knew how many times she'd rebuffed him by now. But seeing the female attention he drew so magnetically only made her clench her fork until it bent within her hand.

"Oof! Careful now." Katerina plopped into the seat next to her and plucked the fork from Laila's hand. "I hear that happens to be his best silver." She straightened it back into shape before neatly laying it down.

Laila gave her a searing look out of the corner of her eye. "What do you want?"

"To give you some much needed advice: Fuck him or fuck off." Katerina bared her teeth in a feral grin. "And I'd make that choice quickly, as I hear our rex is on the lookout for a bride. So, if you don't wish to be known as the Citadel whore for the foreseeable future, I would get while the getting is good."

Sparks of fury danced along Laila's skin at the sheer audacity of the occassella's words. But she was too used to ironing her temper to let something like this get the better of her now. Thus, she chose the second option: rising up from her seat and making her way back to her room.

Darius caught the glow of her vacating the hall before she left, excusing himself with a smile. He blurred next to Katerina in an instant. "What did you say to her?"

"Who?" Katerina laid her chin on her fist, eyes wide and affectedly innocent. "Me?"

"Don't play games with me, Katerina," Darius warned, his vocals charred rough from the blaze of his temper.

"I see what this is about." A predatory gleam crossed her lips as she sank her teeth into this delectable revelation. "You're in love with her, aren't you? That's what all this charade of playing the tamed beast is really for. Now that's truly pathetic."

His jaw twitched but he didn't dignify her with a response.

"Oh, please. You can't tell me that little firefly could possibly satisfy you for long." Katerina snorted in derision. "She's something you keep trapped in a jar for the night to admire how pretty it looks only for it to expire in the morning. A fleeting fancy. She could never brave the depths of you, Darius." She traced a filigreed claw down the front of his shirt. "Not the way I can."

He swatted her hand away. "You know nothing of me. You and I haven't had any semblance of tenderness between us for decades. Now? We're finished. The only reason I'd dare entertain you is during a moment of boredom."

She snatched his chin and brought them close enough for their lips to be mere shadow inches from each other. "You and I will never be finished."

He broke off from her grip to walk away without another word, without so much as even a glance in her direction.

"You will ruin her, Darius." Her poisonous words spilled into his ears from afar. "You might think you can love her to salvation, but that's a lie. She's better off fluttering home to the south, and you and I both know it."

Laila slammed the door to her room, slumping against it in relief. She didn't realise how suffocating the main hall had become until she was free of it. Pacing about the chamber, she wondered what to do next. Whom she could talk to.

Not a moment later did she hear a firm knock on the door.

"Laila, I know you're in there."

Laila grunted at the sound of his voice. "Go *away*."

"Just let me talk to you," Darius insisted, his voice growing a touch softer. "Please."

It was the softness that did it, weakening her resolve even now. She smothered her face in her hands with a muted sigh. She should let him in. To let him know this was it for them. That she had chosen to extract herself from this continuous cycle of cat and mouse.

She clenched her fists in determination and marched towards the door. Darius, once she opened it, looked so pitiful standing before her at that moment, his shoulders hunched and head slightly down-tilted, blue eyes peering up at her beneath his lashes. She almost feared she wouldn't have the heart to say what she needed to.

She turned her back to him.

Darius entered and closed the door behind him. "What has gotten into you?"

"Nothing." Laila folded her arms across her chest. "I just... wasn't in a partying mood."

"It's more than that." He took a step closer and took her arm. "Look at me."

She hesitated a moment, then slowly pivoted towards him.

"What did Katerina say to you?" he asked, cupping her face in his hand.

"Nothing I hadn't already been starkly aware of." Laila cupped her hand over his, then she lowered it. "Go back to your banquet, Darius. Your guests await."

"I don't care about the banquet."

Laila made a disgruntled sound. "You make this so... difficult." She slid her hands into her hair and paced a few steps away. "You need to give this up."

Darius shook his head in confusion. "Give what up?"

"This." Laila made a broad gesture. "Me." She sighed heavily. "You need to let me go."

His face fell in realisation. Then there was a hitch, a soft shift in his throat. "I can't."

"Why?" Laila asked. "How could I possibly be so significant to you that you couldn't just find someone else?"

"Laila." He moved towards her again, tilting her chin up with his finger. "Do you really think so low of yourself?"

Tears clouded her vision and she glanced away, shoving his hand. "This cannot happen."

"Why can't it?"

"Because you are the rex of Mortos! You are supposed to seek an occassella bride and sire heirs from her. And I am supposed to campaign towards being the next impératrice. None of this factors into us being together. None of it."

His hurt only deepened at the severity of her words, hardening into anger. "You think that's what I want?"

"It doesn't matter what we want," Laila said quietly, "because you know I cannot be that for you. I cannot be the foundation that you lie upon to build your legacy. I have my own to further. And you know I can never bear you sons."

He glanced away from her, throat thick and eyes burning.

She walked past him in dismissal, content for that to be the end of the conversation.

Darius couldn't understand why in this moment of all moments he couldn't let her go. Why seeing the rebuffing swish of her golden curls stirred in him such unbridled ire. Regardless of any such reasoning, he barely let her make it to the door before he snatched her arm, pivoting her into a sudden kiss.

Laila muffled a sound of shock into his mouth as it moved along hers, coaxing her lips open to slide his tongue inside. She closed her eyes, her body responding to him with immediacy as she realised how long it had been since she'd last been kissed like this. She hadn't meant to fold and knew it was even more wrong to pull him closer, but Darius knew exactly how to kiss her, all the little nuances of teasing and touch that she liked, that she found herself not even resisting when he began to unbutton her dress.

"What are you doing?" she asked after she'd broken the kiss, each word ghosting her lips against his.

"Giving us both what we want."

He peeled her dress down to her waist, his lips roaming down the supple arc of her throat with a surge of longing, until he found himself leaving a trail of kisses along her breasts.

Laila shivered in response, her touch-starved body arching towards him the way a flower bent for sunlight. The feel of his lips inflamed her skin. She knew she should put a stop to it, *could*. But the moment she pulled him up to kiss her again, she couldn't keep herself from unbuttoning his black satin shirt and shoving it off him.

She splayed her hands along his chest, her breath suspended as she slid her palms down the ample pectoral muscles to the taut abdomen. She'd forgotten it was possible to yearn like this, to feel a passion so magnetising that each touch only begot more touches. She leaned in and kissed along his breastbone, looking up at him with her gaze heavy.

Darius wasted little time tugging her dress down to her ankles, letting his hands rest on her hips.

Now down to her undergarments, a tiny bit of rationality bled back into her senses.

"Wait." She put her hands on his chest. "This is wrong. We shouldn't—"

Darius kissed her hard enough to turn her next words into a whine before he broke their lips apart. "Get on the bed," he ordered, his voice a low rasp as he walked her back towards the mattress, shoving her atop it.

He removed her shift, kissing from sternum to stomach as he cast the garment to one side. Then he took off her shoes, turning his attention next to her stockings. They were sheer white silk, hemmed with a long stretch of intricate lace that teasingly obscured her beige skin.

Darius stroked his hand along her sculpted calf as he thought of how long he'd wanted to do this. He hiked her leg up to rest on his shoulder and unlaced the ribbon garter keeping the stocking in place. He rolled the first one down with careful movements, stripping it off at the ankle, then he hooked the other leg on his opposing shoulder to do the same.

Laila kept eyes on him all the while, her teeth having left a dimple in her plump bottom lip. Their gazes aligned for a pause as Darius eased his hand back and forth along her leg, pressing his lips to it, before slowly inching along until he was to the inside of her knee.

"Are you going to be taking much longer?" she asked him, head tilted in that haughty, imperious manner she often took when she expected something.

"Oh no, you don't get to rush this." Darius pressed another lingering kiss to her thigh. "You've made me wait on you a long time, Laila. And now I am going to make you wait."

She expelled a short breath of laughter, her expression crossed with disbelief. "You're a bastard."

He chuckled in response, molasses thick. "I'm just getting started."

He flipped her over onto her stomach with disorienting speed, keeping her pinned beneath his hand. She writhed like a bird beneath him, and it stirred something bestial inside, forcing him to apply more pressure. The mere thought of having his passions realised was enough to make him strain against his breeches. He soon unbuttoned them and removed his drawers, pulling Laila's bloomers off and depositing them to the floor.

He climbed further atop her, eclipsing her body with his own. Then he pushed her thighs apart with his knee, slipping a hand between them to find she was already slick with anticipation.

Laila clenched the sheets with her hands, the silk scraping beneath her fingernails as her back craned into Darius's chest. She had to keep herself from crying out in relief from how badly she'd wanted this. He played her like a harp with his lean musician fingers, causing a symphony of moans to expel from her lips and expand throughout the eerie draft of the room.

Darius was throbbing at the sound of her, not helped by the way her movements caused her to rub against him. She was so warm and wet for him, her muscles powerfully clenched around his fingers, that he could only imagine how much better she would feel when he took her. He slid his free hand under her and palmed her breast to mimic the gesture along her nipple. He could tell this was going too slow for her, that this was maddening, and he savoured every minute of it.

Laila bit her next moan into the sheets, not giving him the satisfaction of letting him hear. She wouldn't admit the many nights she'd sought the ghost of his touch along or inside her. Though her treacherous body did most of the work for him. Her legs slackened as her muscles flexed around his fingers, and it wasn't until Darius perched a pillow beneath her that her knees could stay firm.

Now she had the support she felt confident enough to push back against him, trying to increase the depth. The way his fingers pried her open felt too good for words and she wanted more of it, more of *him*, than she was willing or able to vocalise. Predictably, he withdrew his fingers, provoking a whine of frustration.

Darius chuckled faintly in response, finding the sound so petulant and yet so endearingly vulnerable it reached even a petrified heart like his. "Stop trying to take control." He used a hand to pin down both her wrists, the other holding her stomach to keep her in place.

When he pressed his tip against her it caused her to squirm, and he gripped her stomach tighter, guiding her down the length of his cock.

Laila drew in sharply. "Darius—"

Darius shushed her in response. "Let's take it slow."

He made her feel every inch of him going inside her, reminding her of what she'd been missing all these years. It seemed this was the opiate he needed to unravel the tension in his body, and he moaned when she engulfed him, drawing a shaky sound from her as well.

"That's it, you're doing so well," Darius murmured soothingly. "I'm almost there."

She'd forgotten just how much of him there was, and being

reacquainted with the sheer potency of his girth made her breath hitch. She felt like a glutton being fed an excess of dessert, and her stomach clenched from the intensity of it.

"Darius, *please*," she whimpered as her body hung in suspended limbo of release. She knew if she could get her hand between her legs, or move her hips freely, she could find the release he so cruelly denied her. A relief, she realised, she'd been delaying between them since the moment she stepped foot inside the Citadel. "I need—"

He sniped her demand with a hum in refusal. Then he kissed her shoulder. "I want it like this." The emanation of a smirk was radiating off of him in waves.

She hated herself for begging him, knowing he was only enjoying it, but while she couldn't come like this, the current of sparks that surged through her abdomen and spread a tingle in her palms and soles was enough to leave her a shivering mess. She was hovering on the edge, a lit fuse with no ending.

"I need it faster," she whined, unable to help herself.

He had gained impeccable mastery over himself from centuries of practice, and she could tell he was holding back. His cock was already twitching hard inside her and leaking the beginnings of his suspended orgasm.

When he slid out of her she had to keep herself from screaming, missing him as he left.

"I told you to stop making demands," he said.

She brought herself up on her elbows and craned around to face him. "Perhaps you're just not up to the challenge." Her eyes flashed in daring, realising the fire she was stroking with her taunt. "It's all right, I won't hold it against you. I'd just hate for you to disappoint."

Darius scoffed in amusement, accepting the provocation with relish.

He wrapped a hand around her throat to bring them both up on their knees with her against his chest.

Laila had not even a moment to prepare before he was inside her again, sinking deeper due to their position.

"How fast do you want it?" he asked, his voice husky in her ear. He increased the tempo gradually, trying to keep himself from losing control from the sounds she was making.

"L-like that," she stammered out as he found a speed that worked for her. She gave herself over to the raw power of his thrusts, the pleasurable shockwaves pulsing through her body until she was overcome. "Darius—"

"This is what you asked for, princess."

She realised how much he'd been holding back and cried out as he ground his hips into her, one hand cupping over her breast as he traced his thumb over her nipple.

This vigour. This intensity. It was almost too much for her to bear. And Darius knew how to angle himself with enough precision to drive her to the edge of climax and keep her hovering over it, taunting her with the denial of release. She knew he could keep this going for as long as he wanted. Longer than even her own body could last before giving out from exhaustion.

"Kiss me," he ordered, pulling her head towards him to claim her lips.

Laila smothered a loud moan into the kiss. His hips were going at such a pace she could barely even recover for the next stroke. "Don't stop, don't stop—" she gasped as he began to slow down.

Darius groaned into her shoulder as he picked up the pace again, his hand gliding between her breasts and along her stomach, sliding between her thighs to stroke her clit.

She climaxed as soon as he touched her, losing all sense of her bearings, conscious of nothing but the pure sensation of white heat gushing through her. Still he kept going with his hand clamped around her neck, his laboured noises of exertion hot and heavy in her ear as he worked his way to his own release and scraped his fangs against her shoulder.

He embedded his teeth into the side of her neck as he came, and once the orgasm started, it didn't stop, continuing to seep down her thighs as her body went limp with the insertion of his venom. Had he not been holding onto her so tightly at that moment, she would've entirely crumbled.

By the time they were through he'd made her come so hard on his cock she was almost faint from it. The experience had left her mind and body shattered, and her legs so numb that she fell onto the mattress in a sweat-soaked heap once his grip on her loosened. It took a long time for her breathing to settle and the feeling to return to her legs.

Darius curled himself alongside her, pulling back her hair to nestle into the crook of her shoulder.

She sighed heavily as she angled herself towards him. "You should go."

"Don't." He slipped an arm possessively around her, nuzzling his mouth into her shoulder. "Let me stay."

The latter was spoken so softly that Laila knew any resolve she had was bound to fragment. He pulled her towards him into another kiss, his hand sliding over hers to interlock their fingers.

XV

WHEN DARIUS AWOKE IN THE MIDDLE OF THE NIGHT alone, he started to wonder if the events of the evening had been a dream. This was soothed by the discovery that he was still in Laila's bed with her scent thick around him. The only thing missing was the solarite herself.

Darius arose with a feline stretch, heavy-lidded eyes blinking as he scanned the room and found it empty. "Laila?"

Had she stolen away in his satiated stupor to avoid confronting what they'd done? He'd recalled having fallen asleep with the pliant warmth of her body against him, one leg snaked around his own. He'd been so thoroughly comforted by the mould of her flesh pressed to his that he wouldn't have noticed her slip away when he languished to slumber, too blissed for words.

He had hoped to keep her until morning, luxuriate in her radiant heat and her soft, quiet breaths against his chest before awakening caused her to shun him for propriety. Now it seemed she had abandoned him without even a gentle letdown. He ignored the tightening in his chest, having ultimately expected no different. He was about to begin the hunt for his clothing when he saw it had been neatly compiled into tight bundles on a chaise lounge—his shirt conspicuously absent.

To his surprise, Laila emerged from her bathroom wearing said shirt, humming to herself as she approached her bedside table.

She received his look of utter bewilderment with a scintillating smile. "Ah, you're awake." She lifted the stopper to a decanter of orange brandy decades older than her and poured herself a glass.

"Thought you'd left," he admitted, rubbing his eyes as though he could still hardly believe his sight. Here she was in front of him, wearing his clothing, acting as if she had not a care in the world.

"I had to receive a mirror transmission from Soleterea and I didn't want to disturb you," she said, taking a swig from her glass. It was only half-true; she also meant to conceal her bedroom guest. But he needn't know that. She set down her glass with a satisfied sigh and gestured towards the decanter. "Would you like one?"

He couldn't contain it for long. He lunged from the alcove to seize her wrist, tugging her into his lap. Laila barely had a moment to release a soft yelp of surprise before his lips covered hers. She smothered a small noise as he framed the side of her face and kissed her, fervently, before slowly pulling back with a peck to her bottom lip.

"Good morning," he murmured against her lips with a smile, stroking her chin with his thumb.

She bit back a laugh, nudging her nose against his. "Good morning." She tried to glance for a window. "Is it morning?"

"Near enough, I'd gather," he said, caring not as he brushed her curls aside to kiss her neck and nip her shoulder.

She closed her eyes, head reclining in contentment. "You should probably return to your chambers before full daylight."

"I will certainly not be doing that."

"Darius." She tugged him back by his hair to look at her. "Do you want the servants to talk?"

"What I want"—he began loosening the buttons to his shirt—"is to take my shirt back from you and never let you leave this bed."

She watched with her lip between her teeth as he loosened the last button. "One last time." She held up a finger. "Then you have to go."

She stifled a laugh as he wasted no hesitation pinning her to the bed. Then they were locked in an embrace, Darius gazing down at her with his eyes so full of something she was too fearful to name.

"God," he said, and it sounded so weary, like he'd been shouldering the burden of confession for so long and could no longer carry it. "I've missed you."

Laila reached out to push a few strands of hair from his eyes and cup his face in her palm, unable to deny the truth of it to herself any longer. "I've missed you, too," she said, guiding him down to kiss her. Whatever veneer of inhibition she had left soon melted as she arched her body into his. Her fingers slid along the nape of his neck to the muscular ridges of his back, gripping him tightly to shift her body onto its side and hook her leg around his waist.

She slid her other leg around his and brought his thigh to her until it was slightly bent against her slick heat. The ripple of his lean muscles pressed against her was enough to clutch him tighter and slowly bring herself to orgasm.

Darius rediscovered all the landscapes of her body that made her shiver most. The slope of her neck, the valley of her sternum, the hillside of her breast. He marked each spot with a seeding of bites that bloomed into red welts on her skin. Before he had been taunting; this time he was tender and exploratory, like he was too overwhelmed by her and wanted to touch her any way he could.

A ravenous hunger burgeoned until he'd hardened against her to the point of desperation. Enough so that he clasped his hand underneath her knee and pushed inside her with no preamble. A noise escaped him as he brought her knee to her chest to slide deeper until she made a sharp, high-pitched sound in response. Then he paused to check if he was going too intense.

"I'm still sore from last night," she told him and smiled in reassurance. "Be gentle."

He nodded, keeping his strokes careful and precise so that the next time she exclaimed it was followed by her arching towards him.

Tears sprang in her eyes from the overflow of how good he felt, and she wondered how she ever went so long without succumbing to this, if she could ever learn to do without it again. "Please..." A frail protest. She didn't want him to stop, but she knew if she let herself get whisked away by this she'd never get him to leave. "You need to finish..."

He stopped to wipe away her fallen tears. "Are you all right?"

It was like she was trying to stop an ocean with just her hand. She tried to hold it at bay but she was powerless to stop it. This was everything she'd been warned against, everything she'd feared would happen if she let herself get entangled with him again. The sensations he made her body feel awakened all the emotions in her she'd been trying to kill. Unable to speak, she managed to muster a soft whimper.

"I know," he said, and then he cradled her to his chest.

After a while she started to move on him again, and he responded with a few more languorous thrusts before he finally let himself come with a powerful surge, the forceful pumps of his orgasm making her walls quiver in arousal.

When he went soft he didn't withdraw. Instead he leaned over to kiss her one more time and trace his tongue along the edge of her own.

"That was the last time," she whispered, but she didn't try hard to extract him as he held her.

∞

Darius arrived into his drawing room scrubbed clean and buffed with the usual polish. He had poured himself into the tight confines of a pale silk tunic and midnight blue kaftan embroidered with moonlight silver thread. Even his hair exhibited a moistened gloss with a fine lacquer of pomade.

"And where in oblivion did *you* get off to last night?" Delanus asked, squeezing half a lemon into his tea before stirring it with a spoon. "I had to make apologies on your behalf."

Darius dropped onto the divan with one leg crossed over the other, gesturing for a servant to bring him his tea. "Nothing you couldn't handle, I'm sure." He received the porcelain cup and sipped liberally.

Delanus helped himself to a sour cherry dumpling. "Well, in any case, a fine line-up of occasselle have made their desire for a bridal pageant more than known. I'm thinking we could go over a selection one afternoon."

"Of course," Darius replied in a blithesome tone, picking up a lemon cake from the tray.

"That's it?" Delanus's eyes narrowed in scepticism. "No resistance? No arguments? No dramatic speech on your nefarious intentions to sever your bloodline?"

Darius chewed his cake in placid silence. His opinions had not altered on the matter in the least. An heir would only ever be a nuisance at best and competition at worst. Though it might take a matter of decades or even centuries before a son was ever ready to usurp him, the threat of challenge would forever linger. And he had no intention of facing death or dethronement any time soon.

"You are suspiciously cheerful," Delanus observed, eyeing him warily. "Who have you harmed?"

"No one yet." Darius took a pointed sip from his teacup. "Speaking of, how is our dear Sergius doing?" He'd left the prisoner rotting after extracting what little he could of his confession to trafficking, but Amira's demand for justice still loomed.

"He seems no closer to cracking now than he did before." Delanus bit into his cherry dumpling, squelching juice. "I have no idea what human he could possibly be so desperate to shield."

Neither could Darius. And it was a question he grew increasingly anxious to see answered. He could sense Laila arriving into the vicinity with a pattering of light footsteps and straightened in anticipation.

"Good morning, Darius Rex." She entered with a merry air, nodding to them both. "Prime Delanus."

"Princess," Delanus acknowledged stiffly.

"Please sit," Darius encouraged, gesturing to one of the many tufted velvet seats in the room. Then he ordered a servant to serve her milk with honey in a reeded glass.

Laila took an armchair between the occassi, hands primly arranged on her lap. Darius noticed that she'd chosen to wear a high-necked frock in filet lace, likely to disguise the bitemarks he'd left on her neck that had yet to fade.

"Actually, princess, it's good you're here." Darius set his cup down on the saucer and laced his fingers. "We were hoping to broach a topic with you."

Delanus gibbered in dissent. "Your Majesty! Please. I wouldn't sully the lady's ears with such vulgar business…"

"What's it regarding?" Laila lifted her glass of milk to her lips.

"Your impératrice had me put to the task of rooting out a notorious trafficker of chaotic magic wares to your continent. We've managed to locate him, but, well, he hasn't been particularly forthcoming with his insight." Darius cocked his head to one side. "I know your kind happen to be adept at *illuminating* the truth, in these matters. I was hoping I might call upon your aid."

"You want me to…" Laila hesitated, putting down her glass. Illumination was not something she took on heedlessly, nor the various other cerebral light tricks at her disposal. Should this be urgent, however… "Just how essential is this information you seek?"

"I'd consider it to be immensely high-stakes. You of all people ought to know that chaos magic should not be dabbled in by mortals. Should there be an individual or organisation with a vested interest in attaining it… Well, I should think we all ought to be privy to that."

Laila pressed her lips together, uncertain.

Darius readied himself to desist. "If it's too much to ask…"

"No, not at all." She couldn't argue his logic, in spite of her misgivings. "As a matter of fact, I may have an idea."

Delanus huffed in impatience. "Such as?"

"I assume that you have been… interrogating the fellow in question?" Laila kept her tone impartial.

"Indeed." Delanus smirked in response. "Quite vigorously."

"Then might I suggest something of a gentler approach? Flatter him, place him in a comfortable cell, cater to his needs, and he may yet feel comfortable to open up."

Delanus scoffed. "Is that truly how you conduct yourself with degenerates where you're from?"

Even Darius wasn't quick to support this. Though his previous exposure to solarite hospitality told him her intentions might not be so benign.

"I suppose it wouldn't hurt to consider."

"Your Majesty!" Delanus blustered. "You cannot possibly entertain the notion of... pampering him into confession?"

"Allow the princess to work her magic, Delanus." Darius drummed his fingers along the arm of his chair. "We'll see who emerges the victor in this debate. And if it doesn't work, then, well, we can always resume where we left off."

His implication was clear and the nonchalance with which he spoke made Laila tremble. Now that she knew the methodical way he could take her apart from pleasure, she could only fathom what he might be like when he employed that same focus to making someone submit to him through violence. She'd have to make it work, she realised, for that poor prisoner's sake.

It had taken much persuasion of both Darius and Delanus to eventually transfer their prisoner to a more comfortable abode and to cease the barbarous methods they used to obtain information from him. Such a virtuous display of rescue on her part was an easily exploitable entrance that Laila leveraged to make herself seem a friend to Sergius in a place where he had very little.

Predictably, he swallowed every morsel of kindness she was willing to toss his way, and she gradually introduced small luxuries to break the monotony of his routine. Whether it be a board game, or book, or a sneaky cigar, Laila was more than happy to oblige whatever whims he had until she had made it so that he came to view her arrival as his only point of enjoyment. Though in the interest of obtaining her goal, she kept her visits to the brutish business owner sparse by deliberation. She wanted the opportunity for him to miss her, after all.

Her current offering was handpicked from his own distillery—a frail glass bottle of his infamous spirit, stoppered with a cork that dampened the cacophony of loud wails and wispy pleas swarming within the contents of the liquor, scrabbling for release.

"Hush," she murmured and disoriented the spirit with a noisy shake to dilute the chorale of discordance. She stepped into the ornate mesh wiring and cast-iron deathtrap that was the Citadel's steam-powered lift, and it creakily lowered her down the gullet of the shaft and into the prison entryway.

There, she came to find two guards standing vigilant, their faces secreted away behind iron masks in the shape of hawk skulls.

"Who goes there?" called the one on the right as he took a provocative step forward.

Laila did not budge even as the bottle began to hiss again. "I arrive upon orders from the rex himself to visit Sergius Severis."

Had she the ability to recognise the sentries, she might have taken a chance to appeal to their familiarity with her visits. But these two stoics were giving little away, she'd have better luck trying to pilfer crumbs from crows. With a sigh, she lifted a scroll and offered it for them to see the royal crest visible in oily wax: the sextuple-headed eagle.

Upon the sight of it, the one on the left instantly became more amenable. He slipped a spider statuette from the chain of his belt into the concave of the prison door. The door was large, burnished bronze, ensnared with many bolts manifesting in the shape of a spider's web. Once the spider latched itself into place, all the bolts engulfing the door retracted and the door pulled open with a wheeze.

"Thank you."

Laila descended the steep stone steps, easing her way into the rising blanket of heat the prison provided. She passed the enchanted bars of the cells and the denizens they kept enclosed. Many of them had been reduced to a twitching animal awareness from extended imprisonment, barely lifting themselves up from a state of pure catatonia.

Beneath this floor, there were several hidden chambers where the sole purpose was to render harm in a manner both spiritual and somatic. Such punishments, Laila had been assured, befitted the crimes they committed. But fortunately for Sergius, she had managed to spare him of that particular fate.

She found him uncharacteristically docile in his cell when she approached the bars, the lurid glow of his orange eyes considerably dimmed in tiredness. Though when he saw her, the flame rekindled like the flip of a lighter and he revealed his teeth in a leer.

"What's that you've brought there for me?" he grunted, for his throat was ragged through dehydration.

Laila raised the bottle for him to see—it was his logo and matte-black glass. The content was so dire it dulled all the shine out of it. "A bottle of your finest spirit."

"Aw, you shouldn't have. For me?" He touched his chest. "You almost have me thinking you've a soft spot for me, little finch."

That engendered a little flicker of a smile from her. "I hope that Darius Rex was feeling generous enough to return your liver to you. And your stomach."

She popped the cork, and the bottle screeched with such yowl of anguish that one could feel it nudge at all the sensitive parts empathetic to another's plight.

Sergius closed his eyes and exhaled as though the sound alone was enough to quench him. "Ah, listen to that. Music to my ears, that is."

From the warmth cloying his tone Laila almost believed the bottle was dear to him, but then she figured he probably felt pride towards most of his handiwork.

She took out a little shot glass along with the bottle and filled it to the brim. "I was hoping we might chat a little more over a drink, like last time."

"You like to hear me chat, do you, little finch?" he asked, accepting the offering with a tipped salute in her direction. When he drank, a flood of vitality inflated his haggard cheeks to the point of youthful vivacity.

"Certainly," she said, a fluctuation of light blinking across her face.

Glamouring was a delicate art and seldom performed due to its notoriety. One could only influence, never control, and it was easier to gain a foothold if the recipient already felt favourable towards a solarite. Should they cotton on, the enchantment was easy to fragment, and the lack of trust made it difficult to repeat.

"Last time you were telling me about how you came to grow your clientele at The Memory Palace." Her face shimmered with radiant allure. "A fascinating tale, if I may say so. You must have shaken hands with a great many individuals of importance."

He bared his teeth in a grin. "Oh yes, indeed. Right up to the rex himself."

"How interesting," Laila said, head tilting like the bird he called her. "And what about overseas?"

"Well, now," he deflected this one with a chuckle. "I'm not one who is prone to kiss and tell when it comes to buyers. Tends to break the bond of trust, you see."

"You can tell me, can't you?" Laila reached out to touch the black furry pelt along his arm. She leaned forward with a whisper. "I can keep a secret."

Sergius glanced around in caution before leaning in. "All right then, little finch. But only because I like you so much. I have two main clients in your fine continent who pay me a rather handsome fee for my wares."

"And who are they?"

Sergius handed out his empty glass for Laila to top him off so that he might continue. "One's a big scientific organisation based in Odaka. The other... well. Some mortal lad with aims of being much larger than he is. Goes by the name of Sadik Yilan."

Laila withdrew with triumph. "Now isn't that something? Thank you for sharing that with me, Sergius."

"It's my pleasure."

She left the bottle on the table as a gesture of goodwill as she turned to leave, a wave of nausea overcoming her the moment she exited the dungeons.

XVI

Sadik continued to keep Dominus confined to the grounds of his beach house on the fringes of civilisation.

Dominus occupied most of his days with drawing and hunting—his beard either crusted with blood from his freshest kill or dusted with charcoal powder. It reminded him of his time in the rainforest, though the comforts of Sadik's extravagant home far surpassed his tiny shack.

His mind became begrimed with this monotony of eating, sleeping, drawing, and hunting, each moment becoming less distinguishable than the last. He couldn't tell you where his unfinished sketches kept appearing from, though every day he woke to another, and a miasma had started to waft from a growing pile of fly-swarmed carcasses.

One night he sought a brief reprieve from his hebetude by picking up the evening newspaper. What he had not anticipated was meeting the fiendishly smiling visage of a familiar face on the front page.

Him.

His mind registered the animated picture of Darius shaking hands with a group of Thal botanists. The headline spoke merrily of a new prosperous partnership in research and industry. It grew near impossible for him to breathe.

Dominus seized the edges of the table he had bent over for support, chips of wood fragmenting beneath the clench of his tightening knuckles. His skin shuddered, the muscles beneath rippling like storm-beaten waves.

What had become of him?

When he'd envisaged laying eyes on his brother again, he'd pictured *his* bones crumbling like sediment beneath Dominus's fingertips, rather than the furniture. *Him* arched over in agony. While the thundering in Dominus's chest would be one of a warrior's exhilaration in the midst of a brawl. It had certainly not been with this in mind—being bowed over in nausea as that traitor remained untouched behind a barrier of enchanted ink.

His ears twitched when the engines of Sadik's aeromobile sputtered outside the house. Dominus could only pitifully force himself to breathe as Sadik's footsteps grew louder and the mogul appeared through the door with a smile.

"Figured I would—" His genial mood flickered out. "Monster?"

It took everything in Dominus not to choke on his pride at being caught in this state, unable to prevent the frailty he felt in his body from touching his voice. "What's happening to me?" he asked—*demanded,* more like—as his chest inflated and flattened in rapid succession. "Am I dying?"

Sadik motioned towards him in careful steps, keeping his hands upfront and visible. He meticulously checked him over for physical symptoms and applied the leftover knowledge he'd absorbed from Elina's trade. "I think you are having a panic attack."

"A... what?" Dominus could barely comprehend the gravity of that. Far worse than any illness the body could inflict, it was his mind that had so grievously betrayed him when met with the image of his brother after close to two decades. Darius had weakened him. Again.

"I'm going to need you to breathe, all right?" Sadik gestured with his hand. "Deep breaths. Slow breaths."

Dominus followed the directives until his pulse settled to the sluggish pace he was accustomed to. He retracted his hands from the table.

"There now." Sadik glanced at him softly. "You feel better?"

Dominus grunted, scratching behind his ear. "Sanguine." He picked up the newspaper and tore it in two. Once, twice, thrice. Then watched it feather to the ground in pieces.

Sadik observed this with a wary crease in his forehead. "I'd ask what the paper did to inspire your rage but having read it already I think I can guess."

Dominus stared at the shreds of paper on the floor. A burn had spread behind his eyes. "He looks happy." His throat rolled with a swallow. "I used to think the guilt would have eaten away at him. Over time. That it would show in his face. That when I returned to him he'd be a shadow ravaged by the haunting of his sins." His watery eyes wobbled and he slapped a hand over his face. "I was d— I was gone all those years and he—"

"Hey." Sadik mimed a hand on his shoulder. "I think you could use a night out. Come and get cleaned up. I'll be entertaining my family for dinner this evening, and I need you looking sharp."

Dominus's black beetle-brows crept together. "Dinner?"

"Yes." Sadik smoothed out his embroidered sherwani. "They come to my penthouse to eat every so often as a family event, and for once we'll even have a whole set." He gestured for them to leave the house, and Dominus followed him out to the area where his aeromobile was kept.

"Why do you live away from your wife?" Dominus asked, curious about the foreign arrangements of the families here.

"Well, Elina hasn't been my beloved for some time. Though it's not uncommon for lovers to live apart from each other. Especially if they lead separate professional lives and when there are children involved. Elina lives with her sister and mother, and they all raise Yasmin together. Her mother and Aunty Anandi run the family farm."

"I don't understand," Dominus said. "I always thought it was a father's lot in life to rule his family to provide them with protection and a strong sense of leadership."

They stopped before the vehicle as the chauffeur opened the door for them.

Sadik clutched the frame with a wry smile. "I think you'll find that Elina rules herself. You've met her—she's a gentle soul but firm when she needs to be. Now her sister Maithra is the real wildcat, so you'd best be warned. She won't go easy on you."

He ducked his head into the vehicle and Dominus shrunk himself to a reasonable size to huddle after him.

The drive was smooth and sparse of chatter. Dominus made no attempts to resolve this. Sadik kept bringing up a compact mirror and alternating between several languages in his fluid manner of speaking. Some languages Dominus recognised, like Thal, but others were unfamiliar to him. He could see, just by the ease of his speech, how so many had become bewitched by Sadik over the years. His tongue was an inlet wearing away at the stone of their scepticism until they granted him entry to the ocean of their wealth.

Outside the window, a pastel-painted blur of residential buildings hemmed a wide and open street, and the crowds had dwindled to become more selective in fashion.

The chauffeur slowed to a crawl before the ritziest of all the buildings—a soft white block of flats bordered in lemon yellow with circular windows of sprite-blown glass.

"Welcome to my humble abode," Sadik said as they exited the carriage and entered the building.

They passed the grandeur of the lobby's medallion-emblazoned floors and its hanging chandeliers. Dominus's head swivelled open-mouthed at the auspicious decor. It had been so long since he had been properly exposed to luxury that he had forgotten how much awe it was capable of inspiring.

Sadik slid his hand into the gilded maw of the lion-shaped lift button, and they stepped inside, ascending directly into the entryway of his penthouse. The hall greeted them with warm strokes of lacquered oakwood panels veneered with tropical marquetry and brass figurines of serpents and elephants.

"Make yourself at home," he said as a Malakian manservant materialised from around the corner to greet him. "Cebrián, please show our guest here to the bathroom. And set some clothes out for him also."

Cebrián examined the dishevelled visage of Dominus with his blood-crusted beard, dismissing him at once with a snort and ushering him towards the bathroom.

The suite was a quaint, soft-toned beige with a cavernous sunken tub. Dominus disrobed and sank into the vat of fragrant neroli and sandalwood oils, taking care to ensure his head was kept well above the surface. He soaked until all that was weary and battle-worn seeped from his body and left him, for once, void of all that burdened him.

Dominus wondered if this was what it was to know true death, that one mortal assurance. To know eventually mortals would be able to lay down their arms in a ceasefire from this eternal strife called living. He did sometimes think of it, of once more slipping into the kind of rest that could never again be roused by his battering ram heart.

He had left the battlefield and yet the battlefield had never left him. The battle was in him, every breath and blink he took an endless conflict.

A servant washed his head and kneaded his scalp into a dense foam that he rinsed through with a porcelain bathing cup. His beard was trimmed next after being slathered in a conditioner that teased his nostrils with powerful notes of argan and oud. It took a concerted amount of effort to allow someone so close to his throat with a blade and not extend his claws in turn.

He was escorted after to a spare bedroom to dress in the garb arranged in neat rows for his use. He secured the silk trousers at his waist, slipped his arms through the sleeves of the midnight blue sherwani, and fastened the brass buttons. Then he tamed his hair into a tight bun tied with a ribbon.

Content he was presentable, he stepped out to join the muted drone of chatter that enlivened the halls—and found himself intruding upon the vivid tableau of an intimate family affair.

Elina was the first to detach herself from the foreground of the landscape, gathering her young daughter and holding her close.

"Why's he here?" Her head swivelled to Sadik in reproach.

"Elina," Sadik said.

"He shouldn't be here."

Her accusation roused something tight and irritable inside Dominus.

"Elina," Sadik repeated. "Please, he is my honoured guest."

"You're always picking up strays." Elina's chest seized in defiance as she tightly wound the spring of her temper. "Keep him away from

Yasmin." She put her hands on her daughter's shoulders and took her into the dining room.

Another witch, some years younger than her counterpart, tilted her head of cropped curls in contemplation.

"So, this is what the fuss is all about," she declared. "Well, he certainly is a lot bigger than I 'spected." She said this with some measure of disappointment, as though she had been hoping for a more manageable size.

Dominus eyed her with faint amusement. "My name is Doma."

"I know who you are," she responded. "It's been some years since I've had Elina all hot and bothered over a man, so I admit I was looking to give you a licking." She paused. "I still might."

"Maithra," Sadik admonished.

Her impish face only creased with mirth. "I'm just joking." She held out her hand to shake. It was rugged and firm as the rest of her but still slight in Dominus's bearish palm. "Welcome. You gotta tell me what it is they have you eating over the water that has you grown so big."

As they approached the dining area, Dominus informed Maithra of the creatures he had devoured, both great and small. He flipped through the memories of his youth, picking out notable anecdotes of the rigorous training regime and the battles that he had toiled through when he was still slim in the shoulders.

There was something oddly affirming at having someone so wide-eyed in infantile curiosity about his culture. Who did not shrink in shame and disgust about the brutality in which he had baptised himself.

"You wrestled a tiger?" Maithra asked as he'd begun his foray into his trials in the Abbakon mountains during the First Rite. "I'd like to see that." Then she turned to Yasmin. "Why don't you tell Baba to buy a tiger for the occasso to wrestle? Would you like that?"

Sadik clutched the bridge of his nose. "Maithra, he is not our circus exhibit."

"But Baba, I wanna see!" Yasmin piped up.

"Behave yourself," he said, and cast a secretive smile and a wink towards Dominus. "And pass the jasmine rice."

She did so and Sadik piled the steaming, fragrant grains onto his plate next to the thin roti and daylily curry.

Dominus tried a bit of everything from each bowl.

The courses were woefully devoid of meat, and that left his carnivorous belly wanting, but he didn't protest. Never before had he been exposed to the genial warmth of such unguarded familial affection, shared so lavishly in ways he had never thought to expect from his own kin. There was none of the strained, taut silence of words unspoken, nor the oppressive sovereignty of his father's voice over the terms and subject of the conversation. Sadik and his family spoke in equal measures, splitting shared anecdotes and interior humour and asking about one's day with genuine intrigue in their gaze.

"Shame your mother couldn't make it tonight," Sadik said, sipping from his glass of palm wine. "How is she?"

"Up to her eyeballs in blueprints," Maithra replied. "We barely get a glimpse of her either, to be fair."

"Well, you tell her she's welcome any time." Sadik chuckled, and then his eyes drift towards Elina. "The food all right, Ela? You're not eating."

Elina's plate remained untouched, her food arranged into impeccably neat piles from where she had nudged it with her hands. "It's fine," she said brusquely. "Sadik, I thought I'd made myself clear during our last discussion—"

"Ela, please." Sadik's exuberant glee diffused. "Not right now."

"But, you—"

"I made you a promise and I intend to keep it." Sadik raised his hand in surrender. "However, that doesn't mean I am going to prevent others from having the option should they choose."

Elina couldn't believe her ears. Her lips parted for an extended pause, trying to summon words. "Sadik, you can't be thinking—" She gesticulated wildly and, in her exasperation, accidentally sent one of the wine glasses careening to the floor.

The resulting smash reverberated through the tunnel of Dominus's memory. To his mother's body hitting portrait glass. How she pleaded with Lanius to spare her son as he clenched her by the throat. Then he punctured her chest with his fist, leaving an angry black hole where her heart should be. Dominus could remember how he held on for so long just to soak in her warmth, ichor dribbling past the edges of her lips and smearing her chin until her face wilted to protruding veins and mummified skin.

He leaped back with a start to find that the apparition had vanished and he remained in the dining area. He'd thought he'd banished that ghoul to the far reaches of his mind, never to return again.

"Excuse me." He scrambled from the table in a noisy clatter to escape onto the patio.

Fear pulsed through him and, with that, an unfathomable anger. Suddenly he wanted to tear the innocuous patio chair to shreds just to prove that, even if his own mind would remain incapable of being corralled under his control, he was still capable of exerting his will over *something*.

The door slid open, and he caught the vibrant dispersion of grapefruit and bergamot in the air. Then Elina stood beside him with a ripple of pale silk clutched about her shoulders. "Sadik wanted me to go check on you."

"Why?" he asked. "You loathe me."

She did not deny this was true. "How often do they occur, these…
episodes?"

"I know not what you refer to."

She tucked a springy coil behind her ear. "I can get you help. But
you have to be honest with me."

"There is nothing wrong with me!" he roared loud enough to
shudder a building, taking a menacing step forward. If it was monstrosity
she was determined to see in him, then he would give it. He would be
relentless, primordial blackness. The thing skittering uneasily across
one's spine urging you to *run*.

But she was still as morning in its gentle, soft peach hour. "You think
if you inspire fear in me then it will end the fear that plagues you. You
are wrong. You could beat me to death right here if you willed, and there
would be little I could do to stop you, but it won't make you whole. It
won't make you less afraid."

She stepped forward, and he receded from her proximity with a
pitiful quiver. His large bear paws clutched his temples with anguish.
What is wrong with me? What is wrong with me?

"It's okay," Elina soothed.

He responded by displaying his back to her, not being able to bear
looking at her in this state. Not being able to bear being looked at.

"I'm here to help."

Yet there was something instinctive in him that sensed this dove-
white placation for the falsity it was. An ancestral chant in his psyche
that urged him to turn and turn *now*.

He pivoted, and within Elina's grip was a crude wooden stake raised
to strike.

He snapped her frail wrist in his manacle grip and incarcerated her
with ease against the wall between the iron bars of his body.

"What a tender bedside manner you have," he sneered, his lips foaming with raucous laughter. "I'd almost say you have experience with this."

She did not scream or writhe or plead. Rather she submitted herself with solemn grace to her fate and fixed him with an expression of uncapped seething. "It's a physician's duty to end the suffering of those in our care. Sometimes that requires healing and in other times putting people out of their misery."

Is that what she saw in him? Misery and suffering? Many might consider those things his genetic predisposition and yet he could not revel in it, her ire.

"Do you wish you'd let me die that day, Elina? Do you believe that would absolve you of your guilt? If you'd simply turned and walked away and allowed my heart to eventually expire? Is that it? You think it would make you less of a monster, killing me?"

There was no clemency in her face as she said, "One is still less than the dozens of bodies you've dropped."

He curled his lip, snarling in defence. "The solarites *murdered my mother*! They took everything from me! Why should they live happily and in peace, fattening themselves on the well of my grief? Where is your *mercy—*"

"You don't deserve my mercy!" she hissed. "You are a plague. An abomination."

His mouth opened and snapped shut. He could prove her exactly right if he wanted, open her delicate little head against the wall with one jerk of his hand. And yet what would it do but affirm himself to be just as big and bad as she already considered him? A malevolent god that no one would worship.

He edged ever closer until Elina shifted back, but he'd left her nowhere further to go than the wall. She stood there before him with her sheer paper skin, the frail stem of her spine rigid as he leaned in.

"Well, go on then, Elina." The sweltering smog of his breath pummelled her cheek. He yanked her wrist forward and pressed the stake against the drumming pulse in his chest. "If you think I'm just a monster, that my life has no purpose but to bring doom and malignancy, put me out of my misery."

He stepped closer to the stake and its tapered point. His skin became defenceless to the proximity of it, languishing to its earthly power where he was once impenetrable. It grazed his chest as he moved nearer, causing his skin to peel back and offer up a small cabochon of ichor. It was red in its blackest shade—the most rotten and polluted wine of the underworld.

He watched her moon-glinted eyes flood with a deluge of unshed tears. But she did not lower the stake, and that emboldened him to take a step further until the wood was embedded in the spongy barrier of his muscle. His flesh withered at this bone-dry intrusion, draining all the waters of his life.

Elina's chest gave a little rabbit hitch, but she did not step back, her fingers compulsively twitching at the thick stump of the stake.

"Elina—"

The sound of Sadik's voice entering the patio came sharp and swift as an arrow, but not before Elina plunged the stake into Dominus's chest.

He bent to the penetration immediately. His body burned with anguish. And yet, it was not a deadly strike through the heart she inflicted upon him. He did not feel the life ebb away from him as he expected—

"You missed," he hissed out in derision with a light chuckle. He tugged the stake from his chest with a faint 'pop' and let it clatter to the ground with a faint, skeletal rattle.

"No, I didn't," she said.

Then she turned and she *fled* with all the disgruntled grace of a doe from the leer of a detected predator. One wouldn't think that she had been inches away from having ended him.

Sadik took Dominus back to the beach house. They never spoke again of what transpired, humiliation and anger stoking a burning temper in Dominus that kept him tight-lipped and morose.

Sadik's movements were careful in the days following, as he knew the Iron Clan was watching him as a person of interest. His encounters with Dominus were thus minimal; he didn't want to give them any reason to be on alert.

He spread the word that he was looking for a group of volunteers through his underground networks, and it was not long before a steady stream of men arrived, eager to take him up on the offer. He ended up choosing six as a testing batch.

On the night of the ceremony, Sadik descended into the basement where, among the disorganised rabble of old furniture, Tatiana was tinkering with Elina's old chemistry set. She used candlelight rather than ætherald, as they needed the room to be cleansed of aether, and she drew the symbol of Calante in unicorn blood on every apparatus.

Sadik cringed as he observed the freshly dead unicorn sprawled across the floor, bones mangled from torture and intestines spilling out from where Tatiana had slit him open. "Was that truly necessary?"

"All great acts of chaos magic require empowerment," she replied, attention still rooted on her task. "Preferably the pain and suffering of an innocent soul. Or someone beloved. His perishing will be the power source I use to channel." She turned to the occasso seated beside the table. "Now we just need your blood."

Dominus dipped his head in acquiescence.

"I want to thank you once again for doing this." Sadik's voice softened with earnestness as he looked upon him. "You're providing me with an exemplary gift. I can feel it. I couldn't ask for better."

Dominus almost couldn't fathom praise being given so freely without the annulling critique to follow. *You must do better* would be his father's afterword following any remark on his accomplishments. "I am grateful to have provided you decent service, Mr Yilan."

"You've done more than that, son," he said. "You've reinvigorated my business entirely. Should we get this venture working? We'll be sure to change the world."

Tatiana approached the small medical kit arranged for her on the counter and wrapped a tourniquet around his arm, taking up the needle and vial. He accepted the pricking in silence and let his blackberry blood fill the syringe.

"Perhaps you might even... consider staying here after, huh? Be of more help to me? I know you miss your home, but what can I say?" A wry laugh sounded. "I've grown a little fond of having you around."

An unwelcome feeling tightened in Dominus's gut, coiling further the more praise was lavished upon him. "Mr Yilan, I—" He swallowed. "I appreciate it. Truly." He glanced over at the cauldron burbling on a chaotic fire oscillating from blue to green. "Are you sure that you want this? This sort of magic. It will have consequences."

"I'm aware." He waved it off.

Dominus retained his scepticism but said nothing more. He didn't understand why he was warning him. This was what he was meant for, wasn't it? This was what Calante had designed them to do—spread the corruption of chaos among the world until he had gained enough of a foothold to claw it under his rule. He should want Sadik's undoing. And yet, in spite of his god-given nature, reluctance squirmed inside of him.

Smoke writhed in anguish from the cauldron as Tatiana added all the ingredients required. Nothing could hide the stench of this abhorrent act as one by one the offerings were poured in: the unicorn entrails, the glowing mushrooms, the strange-smelling herbs of unknown origin, and, finally, the ichor, crude and viscous as oil slick.

Sadik covered his nose against the odour as the potion wailed its birthing cry, followed by an ejaculation of asphyxiating smog. It grated down his throat, bringing tears to his eyes.

He wheezed through smoke-damaged vocals. "Is it done?"

"It's done," Tatiana confirmed. She poured the frothing concoction into six ornate goblets.

Sadik wiped his eyes dry with a sleeve before he picked up the goblets arranged on a cushion and brought them up to where his volunteers awaited.

The moon was new that night, the skies emptied of stars. He had told the men to fast in preparation for the elixir, for Calante would demand them empty. No lights but open flame were to be used.

They waited for him in the dining room, where everything was placed backwards—even chairs at the table.

"You all have been chosen for a very special honour," Sadik declared to the crowd of gathered men. "Before you now rest the keys to your deliverance from a lifetime of deprivation and denial, I present to you an opportunity for empowerment. For real magic. A chance to assert ourselves against those who have held us down for so long."

"How do you know it will work?" asked a more hesitant participant, eyeing with suspicion the brass goblet filled to the brim with the mystical elixir.

"It is an old Mortesian legend that imbibing the flesh and blood of the eldritch will bestow upon you some of its power," Sadik recited, having lifted it from the grimoire he had pilfered. He raised the tome of *Calante's Volume of Vices* as proof. "That is what I offer to you now, within these goblets. An opportunity to fight back against the forces that would have you cowed and downtrodden."

"How do we know it will do as described?" asked Naveen, another doubter. "These creatures—they seem more likely to harm than help."

"I can't promise I know how the potion will affect you, Naveen, but I am asking for your trust here," Sadik said, ever the pragmatist. "At the end of it all, I cannot do more than call upon you to seize this opportunity with both hands. For I cannot guarantee another."

The whispers from the crowd grew deeper in their agreement as their hands clasped the goblets and lifted them to their lips. They engulfed the sludge that Tatiana had toiled at her cauldron to make, downing every last drop. For a moment, nothing happened besides a collective black stain on their mouths, but then a spark ignited at their fingertips, charring their skin as it travelled relentlessly up to their knuckles.

Gasps of pain ensued as they dropped all their goblets. Their skin was blackening into porous carbon, the spark advancing over every line of vein and capillary. When they opened their mouths to scream, only smoke, suffocating and toxic, came surging out.

"What's happening?" Sadik asked, his voice uncertain as though he dared not affirm what was taking place before his eyes. A cacophony of hacks and wheezes was all he received in response as plumes of smoke curtained the transforming silhouettes of the men.

"What's *happening*?" he cried out, louder and more firm as he ran towards the nearest body he could reach.

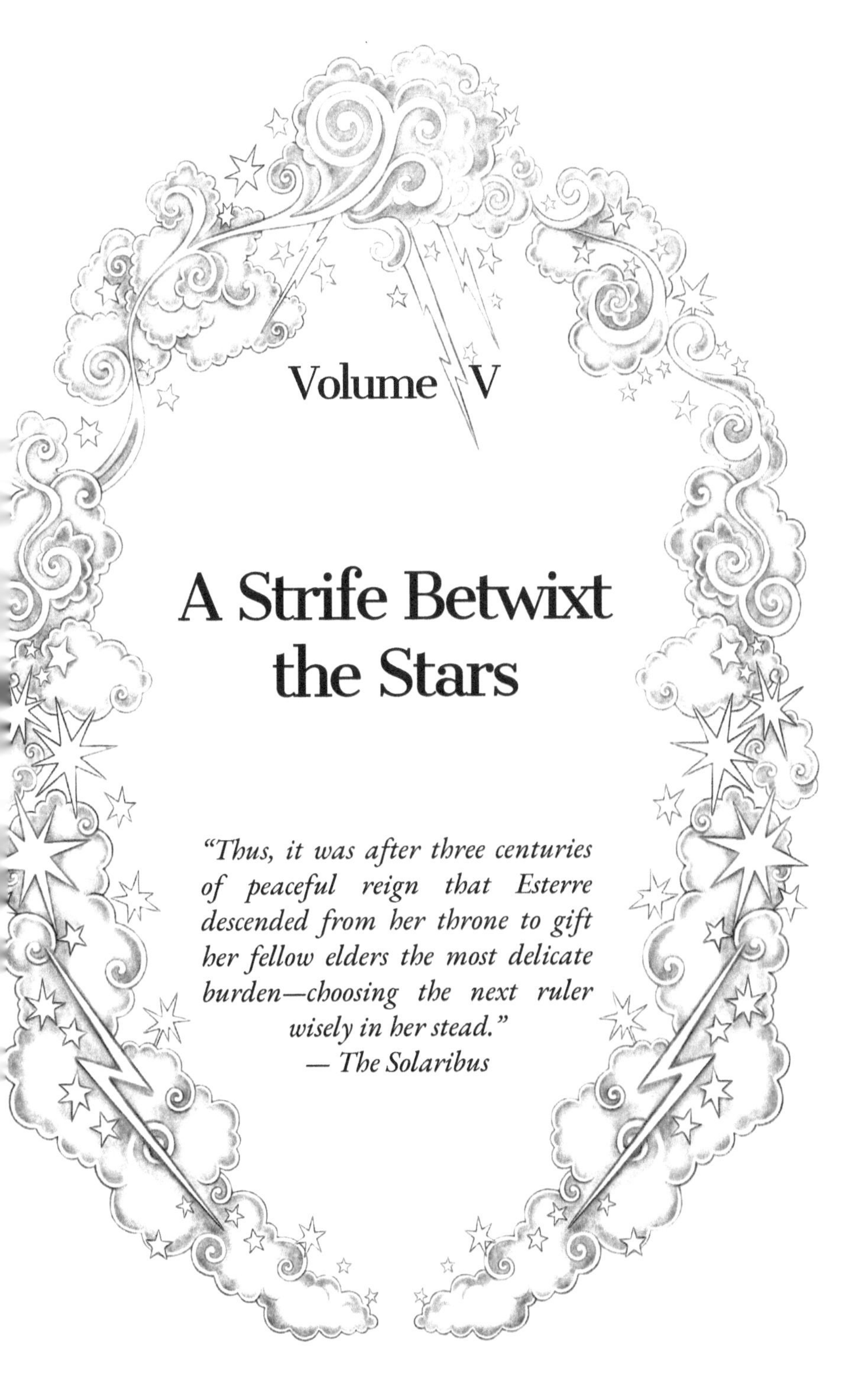

Volume V

A Strife Betwixt the Stars

"Thus, it was after three centuries of peaceful reign that Esterre descended from her throne to gift her fellow elders the most delicate burden—choosing the next ruler wisely in her stead."
— *The Solaribus*

XVII

WHEN LAILA BARGED HER WAY THROUGH INTO Darius's chambers it was without so much as a knock, and she found the occasso mid-repose with his riding boots propped up on his desk.

"Laila," he acknowledged with a smile. He was in full hunting attire and his fitted buckskin leathers shamelessly exhibited the powerful musculature of his thighs. The garments were spotless, however, as he hadn't yet left.

She closed the door behind her. "What would you say if I told you I'd discovered Sergius Severis had been exchanging memory boxes with Sadik Yilan?"

Darius's face migrated through a series of emotions before settling on acceptance. "Well, first of all, I would have to acquiesce to your methods and wish you a job well done. Second, I would have to say: Fucking oblivion." A roguish look settled on his features. "I didn't think you'd have it in you—using mind-altering enchantments to get what you want."

She squirmed under the pride he showed her, that there was a part of her soul that matched his. "I just didn't want you to torment him any longer. If using a glamour spares him the ordeal, then..."

"Of course." Darius fidgeted with his signet ring and lowered his legs from his desk. "Yes... I suppose there are ways of extracting information without roughing someone up a bit."

Laila made her way towards his desk and perched herself atop it. "Well?"

"Sadik Yilan has been a thorn in my side for the better part of a decade now. Seems he's found himself an alternate supplier of what he wants in my stead."

"And what does he want?"

"Power." Darius spread his arms out. "Particularly chaos magic, as it can be imbued in objects for the ease of use in mundane mortals. Though, as you can imagine, I doubt that will work out for him long-term..."

Laila's brow furrowed. "What is it?"

Darius closed his eyes, pinching the bridge of his nose. "I am going to tell you something I perhaps should have a long time ago."

"Darius, what?" Laila took his hand in both her own. "What is it?"

"It's Dominus," he revealed after a swallow. "He's alive."

Laila drew a breath. "But you—" Her body recoiled with fierceness before she managed to ask. "How... How long have you known?"

"Since before you came here."

Laila nodded in understanding. "And have you told anyone else?"

"No." He stroked his thumb over her backhand. "I wanted to tell

226

you this because I didn't want to keep this from you anymore. Because I think you deserve to know."

"So what happens now?"

Darius drooped his head. "I have to admit I don't know. I'm trying to craft a chimera to capture him, but after..."

After having killed Dominus the once, he didn't know if he had it in him to put him down again. But the threat he posed to his rule was prominent, and he couldn't afford to take risks.

"We'll approach that when the time comes." Laila nudged her way into his lap, resting her arm on his shoulder. "Do you know where he is?"

"Thalistan."

"Well, that's the largest country on the continent." Laila breathed a wry laugh. Then she remembered something. "Wait, Lyra, she..." Her sudden mission in Thalistan and her caginess therein grew clear. She'd always been an abysmal liar—avoidance was her key.

Darius searched her face for insight. "What?"

"My mother must know." As always, she was hurt but not remotely taken aback by Amira's deception. "She sent Lyra to Thalistan of all places. The coincidence would be too great."

"Then we'll have to find him first," Darius told her at once. "The trouble is... if Dominus somehow happens to cross paths with Sadik Yilan... Our blood has been purported to have special properties due to our direct descendancy from Calante. If Sadik gets ahold of him, he could do a lot of damage."

"How soon can you get your chimera prepared?"

"It'll take some time, but I'll get it done." He reached to tuck her hair behind her ear. "We'll get through this. I promise."

Laila closed her eyes as he traced his finger down her cheek, gripping his wrist to hold it there. It was inadvisable to let herself become accustomed to his touch again, but she couldn't keep herself from kissing his knuckles, one by one.

Darius let his hand linger before he took it away. "I think we've both earned ourselves a stiff drink."

Laila managed a soft chuckle and shook her head. "I'm not sure that's wise."

"Oh, come now, I don't see the harm in a little night indulgence." He grinned roguishly at her and gestured to a silver tray with a decanter filled with warm gold wine. "Graviji wine." He lifted the crystal topper and poured two glasses. "Traditionally it is meant to be served in times of sweetness and the presence of victory, so I think it appropriate."

He handed her a glass and clinked it against his with a smile.

She inhaled the perfumed bouquet and let it lightly fog her senses before she took a sip. The beverage soothed her palate with its saccharine composition. It was certainly no nectar wine, but she liked it all the same. "It's very sweet."

"Yes, it is made from a particular form of grape affected by a fungus known as noble rot, which enhances its flavour."

She sniffed in amusement. "Is there anything you Mortesians consume that isn't rotten in some form?"

"When you come to live in a land like ours, you either risk starvation or you start to become inventive with your culinary skills," Darius retorted before taking his own modest sip and closing his eyes to relish it. "And rot has its uses. It is how I managed to resolve some of our more finicky crop yields."

"Oh?" This caused her to straighten in interest.

"Without my father's egregious caps on funding, I was able to expand my intellectual investigations to agriculture. I started looking into ways to utilise poisons to eliminate pests and rodents. To transfer waste and excrement into compost to improve soil health. I even started looking into blood meals due to the relative power a faction called the Vidua Nocte attained through similar sorcery to keep their lands evergreen—"

"I think I heard about this," Laila said. "Dominus took me to their lands once."

"Ah, did he now?" His lips quirked as though he wasn't sure whether to be amused or not. "In any case... what I discovered was a pale imitation of what the sorceresses were able to generate, but I do believe with some progress I can bolster yields by quite a large margin."

"Ah... is that why you refused my mother's ætherglass initiative?"

"Not exactly. Food production has been a tug-of-war between landmasters and the Vidua Nocte for generations." Darius took a long sip from his glass. "Where the Vidua Nocte comes in is that they've exploited that to control the flow of crops, hiking up prices during famine. If your ætherglass plan is effective, then they'll likely be antagonised by it. Sabotage is sure to follow."

"Can we not reason with them?" Laila asked.

"They would sooner let this country fall to ruin than to give up any shred of power or influence over it."

"Can they really not be stopped?"

"It's complicated. They have the magic on their side. Blood magic amplifies, but it cannot do it alone. You've seen what occassi can do. Imagine one of us draining the power of an entire burial ground. To fight her is to go up against ten warriors at once. I saw the way the Vidua Nocte strong-armed my father during his reign, and it always ended with him on the losing end. I feared the same fate. However, that was before I had the chimeras. Now"—he smiled at her—"I think we could negotiate."

"You've accomplished a lot over the years." Laila traced the rim of her glass. "You've flourished."

"I have you to thank for that." His eyes lifted to her face in an unyielding smoulder. He was drinking in every inch of her lithe form, savouring her presence with the same thoroughness as he did the sip of wine.

Immediately, Laila could feel a heat seeping up her spine, spreading along her chest and rising up to her cheeks. She didn't know how he managed to do it. Make her flushed and breathless like she was an innocent starlet again. "Well, I think I did very little in the grand scheme."

"You undersell yourself immeasurably," Darius said, his voice low and softened in a way that felt unspeakably intimate. "I wouldn't be seated where I am today, accomplishing all I have, if it weren't you. Even now, twenty years later, you are still opening my eyes to new perspectives. Still challenging me."

She couldn't keep the swell of pride from blooming across her lips in a smile. "If I'm the only one to do that in all this time, then it seems you shall be in woeful need once I am in Soleterea again."

"I'll drink to that." He smirked into his glass as he took an even longer sip, his eyes never once leaving her.

Laila moistened her lips before joining him, and regretted it immediately for how the wine made her head swarm. The air between them had gone charged, crackling. She could feel it in the way the tension danced along her skin, making her throat tickle. "Perhaps you'll find someone else to do that for you. In time."

"Oh, that I doubt."

She flinched in bewilderment. "Surely you—"

"Laila." It was just that. Just her name. But the gravity with which he spoke it was enough to make her stammer into silence. "I already know there won't be someone else, because whoever it is will not be you."

Laila sucked in a breath, lips parting to speak.

He lifted a hand to halt her. "Please, don't take this as a heartfelt declaration of my affections. Though certainly I've done that enough times by now. And don't take this as a ploy to stir you into confessing the same. I just need you to know there will be no 'someone else' after you, Laila. For me, you're where it ends. This is true for me regardless of whether you reciprocate."

Laila's throat thickened. No matter how many times he expressed it, she would never be able to brace herself for how relentless his devotion was, without any rhyme or reason as to why. Her gaze dropped to the sculpted shape of his mouth, and without thinking she leaned in to press her lips against his. For a moment she rested there to feel him against her, to refamiliarise herself with the impression of his mouth as though it might be the last time she would ever experience it.

She drew back to find Darius chasing the trajectory of her lips before he brought her in to kiss her more forcefully. She renounced her better judgement, embracing the intensity with which he coaxed open her mouth and followed it with the skilful glide of his tongue. The kiss was a strenuous one, full of heavy breaths and drawn out sighs, both of them eager and ravenous to claw at each other however they could.

Laila was the one to pull back, take a sober breath, and rest her forehead against his. "We shouldn't do this here."

"I know," he said, preparing himself from the worst when she did not immediately leap from his lap. He'd been anticipating this. The gentle letdown. He stroked her hair one last time, just to get the chance to do so.

Laila looked down at him, eyes clouded with desire. "I want you again," she said, surprising them both. "I haven't thought of anything else."

The words made him throb with longing, and for a moment he debated whether he was in a dream. "You have me."

Laila smiled sadly, cupping his cheek in her palm. "For how long?"

"However long you want me." Darius kissed the tip of her nose. "I know you'll be going back to Soleterea. But, in the meantime, there's no reason why we simply can't enjoy each other's company while we have it."

She shook her head, rueful. "You won't content yourself with that. I know you, Darius. You'll always want more."

"I will," he replied, "but now that I've experienced what it is to have you in my arms again, we can't go back to how it was before. I'm going to come to you. I won't be able to stop myself."

Laila's pulse quickened. "And what if I don't let you in?"

"Oh, you'll let me in."

She couldn't deny that, no matter how much she may want to. "So what happens now?"

"I'm going to keep giving you very persuasive reasons why I think you should stay here and be with me... and perhaps one day you'll decide that's what you want too."

The research institution of Darkwater Towers rested on a broken chip of land off the coast of Mortos. Forebodingly named the Isle of Death, it gained infamy as a breeding ground for deep-sea monstrosities. Such creatures had sent many a wayward vessel to a watery grave and left ravaged skeletons strewn across the shore.

It was partially this air of danger and superstition that caused the ruling monarch of the time to seek out the land for construction. There, he created an impenetrable fortress that would later host the conclaves of his secret organisation. This order would concern themselves less with matters of brutal warfare and instead focus more on the cerebral and supernatural. All the mad, experimental acts of chaotic magic that were usually left to the realm of the feminine.

Darius travelled by hippogriff across the treacherous terrain, knowing it would be better to fly than to hazard his survival on the sea. He watched the lapping white waves, pale as milk, thrashing against rugged shoreline and rattling a few decaying remains as they descended onto the footpath leading to the gates of the tower. It was guarded by two imposing stone watchers that were quick to come to life and attack any suspected intruders.

Darius approached the enchanted barrier that had been cursed to only recognise a visitor by a spoken phrase, lest the stone guardians be roused from slumber.

"*From knowledge comes deliverance*," he recited, and the doors retracted with a shuddering rumble. He rode through to the stone pavilion and dismounted, handing off the reins to a stableboy who arrived to receive him. Then he ascended the steps into the foyer, where the hall was flanked by a procession of bronze busts depicting past patrons of the establishment. A gold plaque detailed the names, dates, and notable quotations of all individuals. He stopped to admire his own likeness as Faustus, head scholar of the institute, descended the steps to greet him.

"Ah, Your Majesty," the occasso greeted, cloaked in the deep plum velvet representative of the order. Around his shoulders jingled a livery collar fitted with the medallions of all the topics he had mastered. "You've been expected."

"Haven't been missing me too long, I hope?" Darius asked with a slight quirk of his lips.

"Somehow I manage to distract myself. There is still much to learn within these walls and many books to read."

"Well, at least I may soothe myself in knowing there is a productive outcome of me keeping you up at night," Darius retorted, his laugh a low tiger rumble.

Faustus had been a colleague and then travelling companion during the many expeditions Darius took touring the country uncovering ancient relics and cataloguing creatures of myth and legend.

Darius hadn't thought about him intimately in centuries, but he still derived pleasure from their toothless flirtation. "I received word that the chimera is ready."

"She is indeed. Come, I shall guide you to the fruits of your labour." Faustus ushered him towards the stairway that led up to the laboratories. He snatched the handle of a gas lamp along the way.

They ascended the humid gullet of the tower to the experimental chambers, where several alchemists and artificers swept the floors with their long velvet robes. They drifted in and out of rooms with scrolls and tomes in hand, murmuring academic chatter.

Each floor was dedicated to a specific branch of research—from the weaponization of black magic to the synthesis of toxic plants to pharmaceuticals. Most restricted of all was Darius's chimera creation, which he'd first put to use under his father and further expanded during his rule.

In the past, he had combined many creatures in the hopes he might create at least one that survived the process. Yet they had only degraded into amorphous masses of flesh with leech-like mouths, fused together with many limbs and teeth and tentacles.

Upon seeing each of these abominations, Darius had demanded the bodies disintegrated, and then he started over. He could still remember the agonised cries of horror as the flesh corroded, begging for escape, made even more harrowing by the fact that the pleas were multiplied by its many mouths.

The cries had stained his mind for years as he devoured his way through book after book, desperate to understand what it was he had missed, where he had gone wrong. That was when Dr Emica Hariken had stumbled into his lap, filled with chaos magic. It seemed that somehow her soul had become bonded to chaos magic, and it'd caused her to become torn between two opposing forces—a chimerical abomination of aether and chaos. If Darius were to guess, it was a combination of long-term exposure and dabbling with some powers that had been better left alone.

The results had taken some time to hone, with unexpected developments here and there, but he was more than happy with the outcome he had been given.

He entered a room emitting a black smog with writhing, curling tendrils. Held inside was none other than Emica herself, suspended within the swathe of black threads weaving in and out of her.

"Hello, Emica," Darius said.

She wouldn't respond, but she could still hear him. She'd lost whatever attachment she had to the material world years after her mutated form had collapsed under the strain of transformation. At first Darius had feared her dead and, in his desperation, injected her heart with a toxin to speed it back to life. The sudden dose of pain and adrenaline had caused a dark substance to spurt from her vulva, squealing a newborn cry. That was when he opened her up to find her uterus had crystallised with clusters of tiny black pearls, like caviar.

After that, he realised her potential had only magnified.

"I'm going to need you to make something new for me today." Darius made a gesture for one of the qarnun assistants to turn on the contraption Emica's body was wired to.

Once signalled, the device injected Emica with needles in her ovaries to induce painful uterine contractions, and she unleashed an echoic wail of pain.

From her cry came the ejection of a black ooze down her thighs. The materialisation of a shadow. Though this shadow was something richer and more animated than the vacant monotone of shape rendered by most bodies. It was a figment of primordial blackness, a deviously intelligent force that acted of its own will.

Darius regarded the monstrosity with paternal pride as it solidified into being—a reptilian huntress with the large leathery wings of a bat.

"Oh, well done, Emica," Darius whispered in awe. He reached out to the squawking creature and ran a hand along its scales, so cold they seared. "How soon before we deploy to Thalistan?" He asked Faustus.

"She should be ready within the next few days, sire."

"Good." He had no doubt she would be more than a match for Dominus's strength and speed, along with being impervious to his magic. "I know from a source that he is slumming it somewhere in Thalistan. Give her something to seek any sources of my blood in the near vicinity. I am certain that he will not remain in hiding for long."

The thought of his brother's apprehension did not bring him the relief he thought it would, but rather a sort of numbing. After killing Dominus he had been ready to face true solitude, to rid himself of his last familial shackle. Now, he was uncertain of what he wanted. To think, when he was young he would've done anything to fracture the prized family portrait that was the trueborn family of Mortos. The united triad of father, mother, and beloved son with him cast off to the side, one corner too many, an odd fit to this perfect equilateral.

He'd gotten his wish in the end, but the act had left him hollow.

Darius swallowed, feeling strangely cold, but he soon dispensed with it as he looked towards Faustus. "Well, I say this calls for a celebratory drink. I do hope you've been keeping up with that distillery in the basement. I must say I've tasted no whisky finer than whatever wizardry you've added during the process."

Laila drummed her fingers on her vanity before deciding to lift her mirror. She'd been avoiding this confrontation for too long and thought it best to get it over with.

"Lyra de Lis."

She waited for an answer with her heart in her throat. Even now she wasn't sure how to approach this, what she could say. She was given little chance to dither on it before the sprite answered.

"Laila!" Lyra beamed brightly at her. "You were in my thoughts. It's been a while, and I'd thought of reaching out."

Laila plastered a smile on her lips. "Thalistan keeping you busy, I suppose?"

"Ugh, you have no idea." Lyra rolled her eyes. "I'll have to tell you all about it when we meet at your bal masqué."

Laila had almost forgotten about the event, and that she'd extended her an invitation. "I can't wait to see you." Her chest flared with nerves for what she would say next. "I realised I never asked properly what my mother has you doing all the way out there."

"Oh, well. I wouldn't want to bore you with that." Lyra snorted, her face had turned a conspicuous shade of cranberry red. "It's just some blunder with the Iron Clan your mother desired to have overseen personally by a Lightshield. Nothing of note."

"I see." Laila ignored the pang in her chest. "You would tell me if it was more than that, wouldn't you? If she had you doing something dangerous. I mean, we've never had secrets, you and I. We've always been honest."

Lyra grew cautious, her expression guarded.

"Because I'd be hurt, Lyra, if I discovered you'd seen it fit to collude with my mother in keeping something important from me. A second time."

Here was where realisation dawned, causing Lyra to drop the act.

"You know, don't you?" she said quietly, shifting her jaw to one side. "How did you find out?"

"Darius told me." Laila exhaled, pressing her fist to her lips. "It seems odd that he, of all people, would be the only one who cares to be honest with me as of late."

"Well, it's easy enough for him to play the gallant knight when he's hoping to lead you into bed with him again." The venom in her tone was palpable, causing Laila to flinch. Lyra was quick to pick up on it. "Are you?"

"Am I what?"

"Getting into bed with him again," Lyra clarified with impatience, "since we're being honest and not keeping secrets and all. I figured I'd at least ask that."

Laila clenched her fist. "Don't change the subject."

"You are, aren't you?" Lyra's eyes lit in understanding. "Now it all makes sense."

"This is not about Darius!" Laila shivered in fury. "This is about you and my mother lying to me and treating me like a child."

"This is everything to do with Darius. Can't you see what he's doing? He's trying to turn us against each other, to make it so you trust only him."

"I wouldn't have had to trust him if you'd simply been honest with me in the first place!" Laila's voice had risen against her efforts. She inhaled sharply to smother her temper.

"I hadn't meant to lie to you, Laila. I was trying to protect you. Just like we—I always have." Lyra sighed as she glanced away. "I see now that it was no use."

"What are you talking about?"

"We're never going to be done with this, are we? This occassi problem. We won't be done with it because you *refuse* to be done with it. To be done with them. Seems ultimately I'd sent my uncle off to die for nothing."

Laila gasped, tears clouding her vision. She set her quivering jaw firm. "I am done with this discussion." She ceased the transmission and sent the mirror hurtling towards the wall. Then she clutched her face in her hands as her body rippled with sobs.

Darius found Laila in the underground spa.

She was trembling beneath the ice-cold rainfall pouring from its numerous nozzles, her head bent and arms huddled around her. Her golden hair had grown dim from the water and formed a shroud about her face.

He approached her unclothed, wrapping his arms around her and pushing her hair to one side to kiss the nape of her neck. She whimpered meekly in response.

He let his lips drift up to the top of her head as she interlaced her fingers with his. "What happened?"

"I've discovered," she began, her voice a mere wisp, "that I cannot trust anyone."

It was a feeling he understood all too well, though it pained him to see that sort of pessimism in her. He realised he had wanted her to retain her light, her youthful ebullience. He had not considered that time might slowly rob her of her glow ember by ember and leave her extinguished, dark and smouldering like her mother.

"You can trust me," he vowed, turning her to face him with her cheek in his hand. "Do you trust me?"

She gazed up into his crystal blue eyes and found them calm, steady. An undisturbed sea. It made her feel tranquil. She cupped her hand over his. "I do."

He leaned down to kiss her, his hand gliding gently down her spine.

Laila shut her eyes, muting a moan into his mouth, and let herself enjoy it. She was tired of trying to abstain, trying to be virtuous. She wanted to stand here in the dark with him and let him embrace her. It felt safe, the darkness, the way it coddled her with distant hands. It was silent. It did not judge. It did not make demands of her as so many others did.

She slung her arm around Darius's neck to draw her body closer to his, deepening the kiss. Then she dropped her lips to his neck, littering it with kisses and nips in all the places she knew he liked—underneath his jaw, the pulsing vein in his neck, the pressure point on his collarbone.

"Laila." He spoke her name in a cross between a whisper and a prayer.

"Why are you... always so kind to me?" She looked up at him with wide, sparkling eyes.

"Because at a time when I needed kindness you never failed to give it. Even in moments when I might not have deserved it. It's the least I could do to return the favour."

Laila's eyes brimmed with tears until they spilled down her cheeks.

"Hey..." Darius cupped her face to wipe them away. "It's all right. Don't cry."

"You shouldn't." She shook her head. "You shouldn't be kind to me. All I ever do is disappoint you, and hurt you, and..."

"You don't."

"I do!" she protested. "It's all I ever do to anyone, and that's why..."

"You stop that. Right now." He took her arms firmly in his own hands. "I don't want to hear you talk about yourself like that because it's not true. And if this is because of your mother, well, she is a deeply unpleasant person who projects her faults upon you because she cannot see past her own. It's nothing to do with you."

Laila sniffled softly.

"As for myself? Who am I to pass judgement? Even if you were the most selfish, rotten, petulant creature in the world it wouldn't leave a dent in how I feel because..."

"What?" Her breathing slowed.

"Because I embrace all of you. As you are. There's not a thing about you I would seek to change."

Laila's chest swelled. Something heavy and deeply rooted was taking sprout within her sternum and rapidly gaining growth. She couldn't stop it. Oh, how could she even want to prevent such a wondrous feeling as she was having now with his words in her ear? "Darius, I..."

"What?"

"I don't want to be alone tonight," she whispered, stroking her fingers through his hair. "Take me to bed with you. I want you to hold me."

His kiss was all the answer she needed. It was long and laborious, full of desperate moans, and he poured everything of himself into it. His longing, his loneliness, his need and adoration of her, hoping if he expressed it enough physically he could transmit it through touch.

Her hands were just as eager, and they roved over his chest before her arms encircled his neck. She pressed herself between his legs to bring their bodies closer, hooking her leg over his hip for more leverage.

Darius made a stifled noise. Against the icy downpour drenching their bodies, her warmth was an irresistible enticement. He lifted her into his arms, securing her legs around him, pausing to let out a weak, shuddery, overwhelmed breath.

"It's all right." She cradled his face and shushed him gently, tightening her legs around his waist before she kissed him again. It coaxed a muted sound from him, thick with emotion, and he carried her to the stone wall to press her against it.

XVIII

EAMS OF THE SETTING SUN LEAKED THROUGH THE LEAVES of a blooming lemon tree, casting prismatic patterns against the edge of Elina's crystal glass. She sipped the rum and coconut water tentatively and let the alcohol intermingle with the sensual rhythms of Malakian music playing in their yard. Its continuous ebb and flow coerced her hips into moving in fluid sync with its rumbling bassline and mellow guitar, and soon she was dancing, with the grass like warm silk beneath the lively pad of her bare feet.

She could hear Maithra's cheer as she danced, and that drew a smile from her. For though she was a Thal by her mother, there were parts of her that only came alive in the presence of this music with the taste of the rum on her tongue, causing her father's dormant Malakian blood to awaken.

"You're in a good mood," Maithra said as she came to join her sister in dancing.

But why wouldn't she be? This was her mother's land and her mother's before her. With the sunflower fields and the fruit trees she had climbed for years until her feet were sore and aching. This was a land of mango and lemon fruit, with the little creek downstream that she would sneak away to at night to swim nude beneath the moonlight.

Elina slung her arm around her sister's neck as they danced, her tongue tripping clumsily over the Malakian lyrics before stumbling into a giggle. Eventually, they stopped dancing and moved to sit on the wooden bench shaded beneath the leaves of the lemon tree.

Maithra picked up a glass of coconut rum and downed it. "We should take a trip down south one day. Reconnect with our roots."

"That sounds like a lovely idea," Elina said, warming herself beneath the sun.

In the corner of her eye, she saw their mother arrive with a white dish holding carved slices of banana, mango, and pineapple, all cut in whimsical shapes. Vidya set it down on the table before them.

"Thank you, Mama," they chorused in appreciation.

Their mother smiled enough to show the age lines and crow's feet that would form the template for what Elina would become in the coming decades. She had always taken after her mother not only in looks, but in spirit. They had the same instinct to invent, the same need to infuse creativity into the most mundane of habits.

Vidya wiped her hands on the edge of her apron and sat down on the bench. "So, tell me, what have my girls been up to as of late?"

"Honestly, not much," Maithra declared with a shrug.

"Really, Maithra?" Elina nudged her teasingly. "No new lover on the horizon?"

"If it happens it happens, but I'm certainly not on the lookout for it." Maithra took a star-shaped piece of pineapple. "I'm only twenty-one. I'm far too young to settle."

"I met Sadik when I was your age," Elina pointed out. "And him eighteen."

"You know I'm not like you, Elina. I'm a sailor at heart. Settling down in a nice house with children, it's not for me. Perhaps when I'm old and dusty I'll consider settling down by the seaside, but not before."

"Whatever makes you happy, Maithra. You have always pursued your joy." Vidya helped herself to a glass of rum and water. "How about you, Elina?"

"I'm worried about Sadik." Elina sighed. "He has become *obsessed* with dabbling in illegal magic, and I fear he may come to harm."

"Oh, love." Vidya drank from her glass in thought. "Truth be told, I am not sure what to tell you. I've encountered this from time to time with your father. Men can be delicate creatures, emotionally. They crave purpose, to feel useful. Siring children can often give them that use, but once they grow up..."

"I see." Elina's lips sagged in disappointment. "He has gotten it into his mind that being mundane makes him lesser."

"Now, that's just silly." Vidya rolled her eyes. "The part men have to play in society is essential. Supporting their lovers and children, nurturing them, caring for them... it's an entirely respectable role. One their mundanity designates them perfectly for. Would you still have been a healer of your calibre without your connection to the earth? Or Maithra a sailor without her connection to water? I cannot deny that my ability to meld wood has benefited me greatly when building houses. It's just as nature designed."

"Then how do we stop him?" Elina asked. "All of this is why I stopped associating with him in the first place. I keep thinking perhaps I should call the clan…"

"If you do that, how would you ever explain it to Yasmin?" Vidya put her hand over hers. "And you need to think about what's best for her, after all."

"Yasmin is *all* I think about."

"Then you might have to prepare her for a very difficult conversation."

Elina sighed before nodding. She picked up a slice of banana and tried to put the matter out of her mind.

Later that night, Elina prepared herself some chai before bed to dilute the effects of the alcohol. Her brewing was disturbed by a knock on the door, and Elina turned down the fire to answer it.

She was not prepared for who was on the other end.

"Naveen?" Her eyes widened in surprise at the sight of Sadik's old mentee. She hadn't seen him since he was at most fourteen, when he had been picked up by one of the many charitable programmes Sadik had run for troubled and deprived male youths. "My goodness, it's been years! Come inside, I've just put on some tea."

Naveen closed the door behind him, allowing Elina to lead him by the hand into the kitchen.

"It's good to see you again, Elina." Naveen said this bashfully, scratching behind his ear. "You're looking lovely as ever."

"Oh, stop." She smiled and brought out her porcelain jar of cookies. "What brings you here tonight?"

"I'm looking for Sadik," Naveen said, fidgeting absently with his fingers. "Have you seen him?"

"Not recently. He ain't been here at least."

"Are you certain?"

"'Fraid so." Elina tilted her head to one side. "What's this about?"

Naveen glanced out of the window at the growing moon with a gulp and began pacing. "I just... I need to see him, all right? Do you think you could contact him? Get him to come here?"

"Naveen, what is it? Talk to me." Elina reached to touch his arm and discovered with alarm that he was searing hot even through his clothing. "Naveen, you're boiling—"

He grunted, turning away from her. Rage flared in him, and he could feel it burning up his fingertips. He raised his hands and, in a panic, saw they were beginning to char.

"If you're running a fever, I should have a remedy on hand. Let me examine you." When he didn't answer, she marched forward to grab his shoulder. "Naveen, please, I—"

She stifled a scream when she saw him.

His veins had blackened across his features, his eyes igniting with an orange fire.

"Your face..."

"Elina." Naveen's skin had hardened to coal. When he lifted a hand, it was long and gnarled with the length of claws. "You have to go." Then he lost whatever increment of control he was maintaining over his body. "I'm so sorry..." he whispered. He seized her by the throat and drew her near, inhaling her aether through his mouth in a stream of gold dust.

Elina recoiled in horror as the energy slowly drained from her body. She tried to pull away as her muscles slackened, her pulse growing weak. With the last vestiges of her energy, she cast an enchantment to tear a hole in the ground and bury Naveen up to his neck.

The stream severed between them the moment he lost grip. Elina collapsed to the floor in a heap.

◦⧜◦

Lyra paced around the Iron Clan office.

She'd been tense and irritable ever since her argument with Laila. It had been her last intent to voice something so hurtful, but the mere image she had conjured of Laila in Darius's arms again had caused rage to churn in the pit of her belly. She couldn't keep herself from exhausting it as spite.

Rage prickled along every hair on her skin as her relative lack of success in her mission continued. Having Sadik Yilan followed garnered little progress, and the impératrice grew more impatient with her every day.

With a harrumph, she pulled up a chair and sat on it backwards. Strewn across the corkboard were all the dead ends she'd encountered thus far. Since then, all sightings of Dominus had ceased. He was almost too quiet.

Meanwhile, a crisis of a different sort had the clan knights in a stir. They'd been receiving reports of creatures with coal for skin leaving behind trails of corpses that had been completely fossilised—as though they had been forcibly drained of all life.

The case had perked Lyra's interest as chaos magic was undoubtedly the cause, but she'd pilfered scant details of the creatures since she first heard of them. The attacks were mainly happening at night, with no trace of the creatures after dawn broke. The running theory was they were nocturnal, susceptible to harm during daylight.

Tonight had brought another case to their attention, for it seemed that a creature had struck inside a residence this time. A valiant witch had managed to trap it, and so, finally, the clan knights would see their elusive nighttime killer in the flesh.

When word reached Lyra's ears, she was unable to resist the urge to pry. Stealthily, she made her way downstairs to the main lobby to catch a mere morsel of insight. She was surprised to be intercepted on the way there.

"Ser Lyra?" A clan squire hurried up towards her. "You're needed by the commander. It's urgent."

That certainly had her interest. She swiftly abandoned scavenging for irrelevant crumbs and pivoted towards Commander Clairmont, who was awaiting her outside.

"I believe I was summoned?" Lyra asked.

"Indeed," Clairmont said. "It seems this is your lucky day, ser. We've caught Yilan red-handed. The unfortunate thing is that his beloved was caught in the crossfire."

Lyra's brow wrinkled in confusion. "How do you mean?"

"The call we've received is from the Panja Household. It seems that poor Elina Panja was attacked tonight by one of the nightwalkers."

"By Asemani...." Lyra rubbed her temple.

"That's not all," Clairmont said. "They know where you can find Dominus Calantis."

Sadik shoved open the door to his beach house so violently it nearly rattled off its hinges. "Monster? Where are you?!"

He barged through all the rooms of the lower floor before retreating back where he started.

Tatiana slinked in behind him, leaning against the foyer wall. She took out a cigarette from a pack in her pocket and pointedly did not offer him one. Igniting the stick on her lighter, she took a contemplative drag.

"I hear him upstairs." She exhaled a current of smoke with each word.

Dominus came thudding down the steps not long after, pausing on the last one. "What's the commotion?"

"Please." Sadik rushed towards him to grab his shirt. Desperation had filled him to overflowing and pushed all sense of self-preservation to the fringes. "You have to help me. Whatever we did during that ritual it was—it was a mistake. We have to undo it." He started to shake him, but Dominus didn't budge an inch. "*You have to help me undo it!*"

Dominus glanced down upon him with the weariness of an ancient. "It cannot be undone. You knew the risks when you called upon my help."

Sadik reared back at this. "So—so that's it? You're not going to do *anything?*" He gaped at the silent graveyard calm of this creature, regarding him with new eyes. "You really are an evil scrote, you know that?"

Dominus took the insult with the recoil of being slapped before stiffening back into indifference. "And *you* have outlived your usefulness to me." He took a step down and loomed above the mogul. "So I would choose your next words carefully."

Sadik's throat bobbled but he kept his stance firm. "Was this your plan all along? To toy with me?"

"I kept my word to the very end." Dominus's voice was thunderous and booming, a natural calamity. "It is not my fault that you saw fit to trifle with forces beyond your comprehension. I needed two things from you. Money and connections." He lifted up his pouch full of corona. The coins sounded plentiful and tinkled like music. "Here's my money." He nodded towards Tatiana. "There's my connection."

Tatiana took another long inhale from her cigarette.

Sadik swivelled round to her. "You made a deal with him?"

Tatiana exhaled a veil of smoke, tapping ashes onto the rug. "So long as he pays me and stays far out of my way, I couldn't care less about your mortal concerns."

"So, what now?" Sadik arched his neck towards Dominus in daring. "You about to kill me? Is that it? Am I your loose end?"

His accusation roused something feral in Dominus's features before he relaxed into simple annoyance.

"I have no desire to kill you, Mr Yilan. Regardless of what you may think of me, your generosity has served me well. This is no personal slight. This is about my survival." He held out his wrists to him. "You may remove these shackles, and I'll be on my way."

Sadik wanted nothing more than to refuse but thought better of it. He unfastened the cosmic metal cuffs from Dominus's wrist and then the collar from his neck.

Dominus rubbed at his newly freed appendages. "Pleasure treating with you, mortal."

"Where will you go?" Sadik demanded.

Dominus breezed past him, halting before the door. "I don't believe that to be any of your concern." He paused, turning on his heel. "For the sake of your beloved and daughter, I would suggest against trying to notify the authorities about me. There is no reason for them to suffer more for your errors of judgement."

With that, Dominus stepped out into the night air and exhaled. His next agenda would be to reverse the damage made to his body by the solarites. Then he would deliver retaliation as he saw fit—and their much adored debutante season would provide the perfect moment to strike.

XIX

TATIANA WITHDREW HER CEREMONIAL BONE dagger from its sheath and cut a long incision down Dominus's bound wrists and ankles. His skin parted to release an oily spillage of blood into crystal vessels. Afterwards, she nailed crude spikes made from wood into his wounds to halt his body from healing.

Dominus grunted in pain but maintained his stillness. "How long will this take?"

Tatiana paced a neat circle around the table she'd pinned him to, her face drawn. "Whatever those solarites have done to you to bring you back to life, it seems to have completely corrupted your body and blood. You will, therefore, require a near total exsanguination. After which we will try a cleanse using the acidic waters of the Occassus River."

He thought of the red-orange stretch of water near the sacred mountain Calante resided in. The river was rich in sulphur and iron, long thought to have been cursed its hue by Calante's own hand.

A sheen of sweat moistened his nude body as he listened to his blood draining in a soft trickle. Tatiana had drawn a white sheet over his genitals to preserve his dignity, and he found himself grateful for the warmth as his temperature waned. As long as he retained enough of a pulse, however faint, recovery would be sure.

Tatiana picked up a bronze chalice and brought it to his lips. "Drink. It's mistletoe. It will aid what comes next."

Dominus swallowed several gulps from the chalice, trying not to choke on it.

She withdrew the chalice and placed it back on her altar. Then she dusted her hands with crushed mint and myrtle from her mortar and unsheathed her claws.

Dominus roared in pain as Tatiana embedded her claws into his chest, murmuring a rage curse to greatly accelerate his pulse. The blood flowed much faster then, ejecting from him in lively spurts as his skin shrivelled and veins protruded.

She observed this with a light tsk. "Never thought I'd see bloodshed like this again after I left Mortos."

Tatiana had lit several candles around the table. They cast shadows across her northern features—gaunt and spectral for the heralds of death that the occassi were. There would be no escape from it. This was to be their fate, shackled to their ankles like a malignant little imp spreading misfortune wherever they went. For they were true chaos, the root of all destruction and decomposition—the drought that shrivelled the wheat fields, the cancer that rotted the brains of healthy cerebral tissue until it degenerated into maddening porosity.

"We tried keeping you away from the worst of it," Dominus said, his voice slurred from sleepiness.

Tatiana cackled, her face shifting in the light of the flames to resemble something fiendish. "And who do you think was left guarding the homefront while you were off on the slaughter? We saw plenty of war, believe me, and that's not even mentioning those of you who brought the battle back into the home with you when it was meant to be times of peace."

"Is that why you left?" he asked, curious now why she would choose to abandon the haven that was built for her, imperfect as it may have been. "Delanus beat you?"

She retracted her claws from him, wiping them dry with a cloth. "No, he wouldn't dare. But there are worse things, as he soon showed me. Mostly, I didn't care to be his broodmare any longer."

"I'm sure you were compensated heavily for your service."

"My service?" She exhaled her disbelief in a laugh. "My body is not a service."

"We both had our roles to play in society to ensure our survival." Dominus gritted his teeth in annoyance. "Do you think any of us liked being warriors?"

"Yes, I do. I think you liked it very much. The power and the glory and the prestige. The accolades and riches. You liked being the ones in control, dividing us up like spoils to claim. Otherwise you wouldn't be fighting so hard to ensure that nothing of our circumstances changed for centuries. Don't play a victim. Had our positions had the chance to be reversed? I doubt any of you would choose to be us."

On that he could say nothing, though he longed to argue with her still. He wanted to tell her about the nights he'd been led barefoot and naked through the snow as a young boy to improve his hardiness to low temperature. The months he was starved of food and deprived of sleep, having to fight his brothers-in-arms for every morsel of nutrition. The forced viewings to executions and the pilgrimages through threatening terrains in the dead of night shadowed by monsters. But he knew she would not hear any of it, would only counter with her own horrors she was forced to endure, and so he elected to be silent.

"You should rest now, Dominus Regulus," Tatiana advised, tossing her cloth onto the altar. "Desiccation is a painful process, and will only get worse after the cleanse. You will need your strength."

She turned towards the stairs and ascended, closing and locking the door behind her.

∞

Lyra opened the doors to her armoury and perused its contents.

She withdrew her padded silk Lightshield armour first in the uniform celestial blue and slid it on over her clothes. Then she armed herself with bone throwing knives, a unicorn horn dagger (for it was the bane to all things monstrous), her lightning sword, and her sunbeam pistol.

After testimony from the Panja family, it had been easy enough to hunt down and detain Sadik Yilan for further questioning. He wasn't going to be allowed to wiggle away like a worm off of a hook this time. Thankfully, having learned a harsh lesson on the perils of chaos magic, he was rather forthcoming with his insights on where Dominus had been seen last and where he might be.

He was now held under arrest on charges of harbouring a fugitive and illegally practising chaotic magic. Lyra had her doubts on how much either would stick, but in Sadik's case, she was eager to see justice prevail.

Now she had authorised a monster hunt for Dominus Calantis and Tatiana Levitia. In the latter case, she had requisitioned the blood donation required of all occassi to register for chaotic magic licensing. Thus, it wouldn't take much to track her down with a bloodstone amulet. With any luck, Lyra could have this wrapped up in time for debutante season and be a part of the ensuing festivities.

Lyra opened the vial of Tatiana's blood and added a drop to the clear stone, watching it burn black with a fierce pulsating glow. She slid the amulet around her neck before turning to leave.

⸎

Dominus howled in anguish as the surge of sulphuric water filled his fiendish veins and inflated them full to bursting. The current of Calante's essence gushed through the dehydrated rivers of his empty canyon.

He could feel the war raging inside him until aether and chaos finally reached a stalemate. And then, a conclusion. Everything that had been split apart in him had now been repaired.

Tatiana removed the intravenous needles and looked him over. "How are you feeling?"

"Pure," Dominus rasped in relief. He'd never again hoped to feel this wholeness, this unity between body and soul.

Tatiana freed him from his binds and cleared her equipment. "It will take some time for you to stabilise, so I wouldn't overdo things for now."

Dominus rose to rub at his sore wrists, now healing as swiftly and flawlessly as he expected them to. He glanced towards the occassella in gratitude. "I can't thank you enough for what you've done."

"You can repay me in full by dropping that pouch of corona over there and never speaking to me again." She gestured towards her altar and continued to arrange her apparatus.

Dominus frowned at her before glancing at the pile of clothes left for him on a chair. These were the items Sadik had had tailormade for him, and he couldn't help but regard them with a brief pang of remorse. His actions regarding the mortal had been callous, he would admit it, but he must continue.

"You really ought to return to Mortos," he said to Tatiana as he redressed. "It's there you belong. Not here."

Tatiana stifled a laugh as she turned to him. "You simply cannot fathom that I would never return there, can you? That I have built a life for myself in this country."

"This life, as you so call it, is but a ruse, Tatiana. It is a farce." Dominus tugged his kurta over his head sharply. "You are deluding yourself if you think these mortals will ever truly accept creatures like us living amongst them without conflict."

"Maybe so," she conceded, "but I'd no sooner be welcomed home in my current state." She lifted her shirt to reveal a crude black cicatrice left from surgery along her abdomen.

"What is that?" Dominus peered closer.

Tatiana lowered her shirt. "The final piece of me I bartered before I left Delanus. He didn't put up much of a fight after that. It was all he valued." She finished sorting the rest of her things, added the contaminated objects to a basin, and lifted it. "You may see yourself out, Dominus Regulus. I am afraid I have other things to tend to instead of subjecting myself to your droning. I have clients to see. A business to run. I can do that now, you see. You have your fun back in the motherland."

With that, she climbed back up the stairs and left him.

Dominus regarded her parting words with a scowl. There were still things he had yet to accomplish in this accursed continent before he left it. All the same, he should think it a reward to be back home again. He thought of the snow-covered tracks where he'd played in as a youth, the cold clinging to his face before he returned home to the Citadel to drink hot sbiten by the fireplace. Vasilisa would be somewhere making sure they had enough firewood stocked to last them through the more perilous snowstorms, while Lanius would be secreted away in his office doing kingly things of undisclosed importance.

Ah, but Darius. Darius was the one he would find with his head enveloped between the leatherbound lips of some heavy tome. Dominus would often make a sport of hunting him, trying to wrestle him free from this idle hobby that still seemed so boring and incomprehensible even at the age he was now. Each time, he would watch Darius become seemingly engrossed by the contents of the page before he pounced, knocking them both to the floor in a clatter, and the look of rage and disgruntlement his brother would give him always had his stomach in comical knots, even though he knew it was coming...

Dominus sniffed in derision at the fading vestige of memory. Times seemed so much simpler when they were just boys who hadn't yet learned to immunise themselves from war and a father's violence. Perhaps if he hadn't suffered either, he might have been able to distinguish himself as a person apart from the enslavement of having to kill. Perhaps there never was anything to him but that.

He put on his shoes and ascended the steps from Tatiana's hidden basement, pausing when he heard the muffled sound of voices from above.

"Tatiana?" He made his way upstairs on a careful foot, trying his best not to creak the wood when he reached the upper floor. Tatiana stood before him in the sitting room but there was a wild panic in her eyes. "Tatiana?"

"*Run,*" was the final word she said before a pistol struck the back of her neck. Her body dropped to reveal a spritemaid standing behind her, her foot perched atop Tatiana's back.

"Remember me?" Lyra asked.

Dominus let his fangs scrape the edge of his bottom lip in warning. Then he lengthened his claws to strike. However, more sprites were sprouting ups, encircling him with pistols raised to shoot.

After making a quick calculation he dashed towards the window, using his speed to dodge the line of shots coming his way before he burst through the glass and rolled onto the street.

"After him!" Lyra blurred towards the window to launch herself out of it and landed gracefully in a shoulder roll.

Dominus grunted in surprise as he turned back to see her pursuing him. He made a sharp pivot into the bazaar and grabbed several crates full of food, hauling them Lyra's way with mammoth strength and ignoring the cry of indignation from the stall keeper.

Lyra dodged the shattered wooden crates and flying edible debris with agile feats, using one bouncing crate to propel herself upwards onto the tented roofs of the stalls.

Below her, Dominus was still sprinting ahead but not swiftly enough to prevent her from gaining on him.

Calante's wrath, she's too quick. His teeth gritted in determination. He knew this could only end in a skirmish. And with him weakened, he couldn't guarantee a victory. Sure enough, that was precisely what happened when Lyra flung herself onto his back and sent them both tumbling as frantic pedestrians scattered to safety.

Witches and men alike screamed as the ground cracked from the impact of their combined weight, but both immortals were deafened to it as they readied for a fight.

Dominus took the first punch, which Lyra avoided with a flexible recline of her back. She returned it by aiming low and ramming herself into his middle.

Dominus growled and staggered backwards, swinging again and

again, knowing one blow would be enough to shatter her lithe body. However, Lyra was taking advantage of his size and his relentless onslaught to tire him out by dodging. Once he was worn and panting, she used it as an opportunity to scale his torso and smash him down to the floor with a knee to the face.

Skull and stone crackled from the impact and caused his vision to blur. He could only just glimpse the hazy figure of Lyra as she paced around him before kicking him in the stomach. He snarled louder, this time from pain.

Lyra breathed heavily as she looked down upon him, wanting to hurt him more. But she knew she didn't have long before he got up. "Cuff him."

Dominus's gaze distorted, and he realised other sprites had gained on them during their fight.

A sprite stepped forward to fasten the shackles on his recently freed wrists and place a muzzle over his face. He was too winded to struggle as they lifted him out of the store and tossed him into the back of the carrier wagon.

"We've been searching for you for a long time, Dominus Regulus," sneered one of the clan knights on the bench across from him. "You are long overdue a visit to the reaper."

Dominus's eyes narrowed in loathing at the sanctimonious curve of a smirk on her pretty pink lips, and he decided that the moment he found an opportunity, this one would die slowly. If they intended to kill him again, he would not be giving up without a fight.

The wagon levitated silently above the streets, and he cursed the ill-luck that brought him to this predicament, deliberating alternate forms of escape. A memory flickered in his mind of a time he'd broken his thumb to free himself from shackles. Though he could not recall where it stemmed from. All he could recall was that he had not even made a whimper, just as his father had wanted from him.

The journey stretched long enough to turn him near-feral with rage, but he kept his temper. He would wait until they stopped before he tried to free himself. Then he would claw the nearest guard to ribbons. With this plan in motion, he allowed himself to recline in his seat.

Lyra watched his placidity with a wary gaze. She debated whether she should sedate him. Or at least pacify him enough so he couldn't try anything foolish. Where this journey would end was still something she had yet to confront, but she refused to let him slip away again after she'd worked so hard to catch him.

"Stick some ætherald in him."

"Yes, ser," answered the clan knight, and she brought out a large syringe and vial of solution and began to fill it.

Dominus narrowed his eyes at her, fully aware of how inconvenient this would be.

A smile twitched faintly on Lyra's lips as she propped her ankle on her knee.

The clan knight filled the syringe to the brim and squeezed out air, flicking the needle. But before she could inject, something slammed into the wagon and sent them spiralling.

Dominus smashed against the roof of the wagon hard enough to dent it, while the pale bodies of Lightshields were tossed limply from side to side with every roll of the vehicle until eventually it slowed to a stop.

A series of grunts and groans sounded as Lyra struggled to the top of the heap.

"What—?"

A heavy thud sounded on the side of the wagon, reverberating through it with a tremble. Then a clawed hand punctured through and spilled a stream of sunlight, prying apart the metal husk to reveal a reptilian face suffused with scales and broad leather bat wings spread.

Dominus's pulse quickened, breath stiffening in alarm as the behemoth extended her forked tongue in greeting. She withdrew her wings into her back and reached through to seize him by the kurta, tugging him out with swiftness.

"No," Lyra growled. She refused to let anyone take him. Blood was seeping down the side of her face in a bright cherry drizzle. She wiped it away and pushed herself up bit by bit, gritting her teeth against the pain of her mending wounds before she lifted herself out of the hole left by the assailant.

Outside, Dominus writhed and flopped against the iron grip of the huntress as she dragged him through the grass. The creature was nightmarishly large and could tug him by the collar with little strain, his binds making the motion far simpler.

With a quick jerk of his thumb he fractured bone and dragged it through his cuff, then he seized her by the wrist.

Sensing this, the huntress pummelled him down with her free hand and lifted him up by the throat, choking him relentlessly.

Dominus wheezed for breath, feeling a pain so egregious his vision bled red and his resolve slackened with it. The huntress clenched him tight enough to crack fissures into his spine. Then, in the corner of his mind, his father castigated, *Pain is only a mental bind, Dominus.* And that was enough to have him fighting again, digging his fangs into her wrist and chomping through muscle and bone in a bid to be free.

He spat out pieces of her as he became dislodged, the four-fingered hand still clutched around his throat. The huntress screeched in alarm but not before reforming her lost appendage.

Thankfully, Dominus was not the only opponent to the huntress's pursuit. And soon a loud whistle entered the fray as Lyra staggered forward, her sunbeam pistol aimed to shoot.

"Hey!" she called out in a guttural tone as she cocked her gun. "He's mine."

She lined up the shot and fired.

The mutant screamed and thrashed violently as the beam cooked her skin with a sibilant hiss. The wound flared an oscillating red, melting through several layers of flesh before it faded. She smacked Dominus away into the distance to retrieve for later. His body took flight through the boles of several trees, gaining enough momentum to roll over the edge of a cliffside and plummet into the waters below.

Then she charged at Lyra.

Lyra kept shooting at her as several sprites appeared to obstruct the mutant's path. They pelted her with a series of sunbeams that melted her flesh into a spray of ash and smouldering embers, staining the air with an aftertaste of char. But the creature was relentless and quick to regenerate. She barrelled her way through the troops, sending body parts dispersing through the air.

Lyra cursed under her breath, fear tightening her gut in the knowledge there was no chance she could fight this threat head on. Slowly, she lowered her gun, drew out her lightning sword, and ran towards the creature, gaining enough momentum to drop to her knees and slide forward, slicing off the creature's ankles.

The huntress squealed as she flopped over onto her belly, and Lyra didn't squander the opportunity to launch herself onto her back and hack and slash away at her until she was confident the creature would move no longer.

She turned in the direction of one of her spritemen who was still struggling his way out of the wagon.

"Hey!" she called, taking him by the hand and hauling him out. "Come on, we have to run. Are you all right?"

He nodded, still dazed. "Yes, I'm—" He stiffened. "Lyra, behind you!"

A shriek sounded as the huntress seized Lyra, ripping apart their entangled fingers. Lyra didn't have a chance to fathom how the creature could've regenerated so fast before the huntress crushed her ribcage in her hand and pounded her to the ground.

She could only make a weak, deflated sound from her perforated lungs as the huntress took off in pursuit of Dominus, having grown bored with her sprite prey.

Lyra could hear her companion speaking desperately. "Hold on..." Her eyes rolled closed. "Hold on..."

XX

Fanfare announced the arrival of Laila's masquerade ball. She'd spent the morning sifting through lace-edged envelopes of cards congratulating her on her fiftieth earthday. The day her mother inserted the star that gave her life. Then she made her way through the steady arrivals of flowers, gowns, jewels, and chocolate-covered fruit bouquets until she found Darius's gift at the bottom.

She picked up the rosewood music box, open-mouthed, observing the gilt roses inlaid on the lid. When she opened it, a ballerina sprang free and twirled to the tune of "My Radiant Warden." Her throat thickened at the sound as she recalled the many times Léandre had played the lyre for her during times of sorrow. When she needed someone to guide her as the twilight star did for the person in the song. Tears were already forming from the thoughtfulness alone, but when she uncovered the pile of love letters hidden in one of the compartments, her cheeks were saturated in them.

The letters had been tied together by pink ribbon and were dated for ease of reading. Missives Darius had penned to her but never had the bravery to send. On the top of the pile was a card which read: *In case you forget how adored you are when you return to Soleterea, here's a few reminders.*

She shut the box harshly, her chest trembling as she swallowed back a sob. She couldn't afford to lose herself now, so close to the event. Her mother would be there, along with many other solarites, and she would need to maintain a guise of lukewarm cordiality towards the rex. She let the tears fall liberally to free them before she had to go downstairs. She wondered if there would ever be a time she could have it not throw her completely off-guard—the depth of his feelings for her.

After drying her eyes at the vanity table she continued with her plans, issuing orders and arranging rooms and adding the small finishing touches until evening fell.

She returned to her vanity to prepare herself, twisting her curls and threading pearls into the strands. Her gown for the evening was in the style of seafoam—a pale silhouette of silk chiffon with coral ribbons tied around the sleeves. Her matching mask was embroidered with pearl-encrusted starfish, and she painted her lips with a translucent gloss in the same nubile shade of coral pink.

To ground herself from any emotional turmoil, she reached for her mother-of-pearl snuff box and took out a fever pill, crushing it into a spoon. Then she lifted the spoon and vacuumed the line of fever through her nostrils, receiving instant relief from the drowsiness at the sickly tingle it provided. She would need all the help she could get if she was to face her mother tonight.

After dabbing her nose with a tissue, she snuffled, feeling the warmth of a blush that could easily be mistaken for pigment tinting her naked cheeks. A quick inspection in the mirror had her declaring absolution from any suspicion before she made her way downstairs.

In keeping with the combined theme of the event, she'd had the staff allocate a series of rooms for six different forms of entertainment, each representing a trait Calante bestowed upon his occassi. The first room represented Austerity, and she had transformed it into a barren coral reef setting where a platform and podium was set to relay her announcements.

Laila took to the podium to deliver her opening speech to the cluster of guests. They had come from all corners of the continent to the land deemed too precarious to ever breach.

"Good evening. I would like to begin by thanking each and every one of you for coming. I appreciate that you've travelled a long way to be with me here tonight. It is my honour to welcome you to my Thirtieth Annual Bal Masqué, where we not only celebrate my earthday but also share the festivities of the Mortesian Hexacost. Before we begin, I would like to offer my personal gratitude to Darius Rex for being so kind as to open up his home to us to host this event. Malborg Citadel has a very long and storied history with many hidden treasures—treasures I hope to share with you tonight. Both figuratively and literally."

At this, the audience released a chortle.

"All proceeds from these treasures will help fund my initiative to bring ætherglass houses to Mortos. With your help, we can make this impenetrable soil bloom." Her eyes found Amira in the crowd, who gave a barely visible nod of approval. Tonight would be the night to sway the electoral's votes. "Now, I have invested my time into creating something I hope will be a bewitching experience. So please eat, drink, and be ready to loosen those purse strings. It is sure to be a magical evening."

When she finished her speech she cast an incantation, and at once each of the imposing statues of three great whales spouted a jet of fine beverages. From one came a pale lager, from another a sweet wine, and from the last a euphoric nectar. The guests rushed to fill their cups.

Laila grabbed a glass to fill it with wine when she noticed Darius approaching her through a sea of bodies. He had spared no theatricality in his costuming, which consisted of a fitted grey suit with a dorsal fin and a red satin waistcoat with a ruffled cravat. Sewn into the lapels of his jacket were several rows of diamond-encrusted shark teeth, making him look as though he was in the midst of being engulfed.

"I hope that my speech was to your liking," she said, seeking his eyes behind the red satin mask he wore.

"You spoke beautifully," he commended and stepped forward to brush his lips against her ear. "I hope you enjoyed your gift."

There was something so indecent about the smoothness of his voice that she shivered involuntarily.

"The gift was lovely," she said, straining against infusing too much emotion in her tone. "Thank you, Darius Rex."

A smile ghosted on his lips in response. "I'm also never going to forgive myself if I don't mention how ravishing you look in that dress."

Laila laughed, grateful for the levity. "Yes, you'd better get your best compliments in now, Darius Rex. I have to make room for all the others, after all."

He chuckled. "I'm certain I can think of a few others."

"Well, I wouldn't want to steal you away from your date," Laila said, with simpering falseness. "I assume that you have one."

Darius stretched out his arm, and a crimson-haired occassella stepped into it. She was conservative in a deep violet and iridescent blue kaftan with tiers of billowing tulle. Her head was eclipsed by a large hat, which protruded with the writhing appendages of an octopus.

Laila's heart softened at the sight of her. "You look wonderful tonight, Domina Sabina."

"As do you, princess." She elbowed Darius's chest. "Come on, I want a chance to demolish you at the tarot tables."

Darius gave Laila a wry look before allowing Sabina to lead him away.

Now alone, Laila immersed herself within the crowd in the hope of attaining a familiar face. While she intended to put off approaching her mother for as long as possible, she had hoped to see Lyra present among the towheaded sprite guests. She concluded she and her friend must still be in conflict when she didn't see her emerge.

Laila was trying not to let that sag too deeply in her chest when an occassella came swaggering into view with a brazen swinging of her wide hips. She cut an imposing figure in a dark green seaweed dress. Faced with her viciously rouged lips, her hair so black and unruly it slithered like tendrils past her shoulders, Laila felt suddenly pale and insubstantial.

"Well then, you must be the crown princess everyone has spoken so much about!" she exclaimed, her eyes of pure copper cast a scrutinising gaze from head to toe.

"Why yes," Laila said, all southern charm with her cherry-sweet voice. "And you are?"

"Well, I go by many names. But I suppose officially I am known as Serafina Blackwood, High Sorceress of the Vidua Nocte." Serafina curtseyed with flourish. "Though others may grudgingly refer to me as the rex's mother."

Laila recoiled. "You're—you're Darius's mother?"

"Guilty," she confirmed in an affectedly humble manner. "Are you all right, dear? You appear to be a bit red in the cheeks."

Laila resisted the urge to put a hand to her cheek, knowing the fever was still singing in her veins. "I— Forgive me, I'm just surprised. I must say I never thought I'd see the day that I met you. Darius doesn't talk much about you at all."

"I can't imagine he does. It would make for quite poor political discussion," Serafina responded with a dry chuckle. "That is after all why you're here, isn't it? To discuss politics?"

Laila matched the laugh with something frail and thin before quenching her nerves with a long drink of wine. "I'm afraid you'll have to excuse me, I have so many other guests to attend to."

She turned on her heel with the intent to evaporate into the crowd, wanting nothing more than to escape this current predicament and the shame and embarrassment she felt at being caught so unaware.

Not long after, however, Darius managed to apprehend her. He'd observed the interaction from afar with a growing sense of dread and sought to end it when he realised what occurred.

Laila rounded on him instantly, her tone low and accusatory. "I thought you told me your mother was dead."

"Not in so many words—"

She emitted a disgruntled sound in response and pivoted away from him only for him to pull her back.

"Wait," he insisted. "I'm sorry, that isn't how I wanted for you two to meet."

"From the looks of it, you never intended for us to meet at all," she said, trying to swallow the lump emerging in her throat. She squeezed her eyes shut. She could not lose it here. She refused.

"You're right, I didn't," he admitted, before sighing and massaging his temple. "Laila, you have to understand that things are complicated between my mother and me—"

"No, Darius, I cannot do this with you right now. I am in the middle of a party. Whatever excuses you have can wait." She punctuated this with a petulant stamp of her foot. "Let me go."

He released on instinct, and she disappeared once more into the crowd.

Exhaling, he turned back to where his mother was last seen.

"Well now," Serafina crooned. In her excitement, her lips had curved upwards into a feral grin. Pearlescent fangs hung low over her painted lips. "There's my precious boy."

His legs grew heavy at the sight of her. He fought against it. He fought against the shadow of his boyhood and the slow encroachment of memories he had long discarded, tossing them away like purposeless parts—spare cogs, rusted springs, anything that bogged down the efficiency of his internal machinery. He had repurposed himself into something sleek and mechanical, well-oiled clockwork, that ceaseless *tick, tick, tick* that always ran and never stopped.

But when Serafina stepped closer, something jammed him to a sudden halt. He grabbed her harshly by the arm to drag her near.

"What are you doing here?" he snarled at her under his breath.

"Open invite." Serafina cocked her head playfully. "Thought I'd dress up and join."

He could kill her. He could wrench her heart from her chest at this very moment.

"Leave," he ordered calmly.

"Now, Darius, don't be a spoilsport," Serafina sing-songed, tapping his cheek with a few condescending pats. "I'm already here, after all. And I don't think your lovely star princess would appreciate a scene on her big day."

He could feel his fangs aching at his gums and resisted. His mother was right. He couldn't afford to make a scene, and Serafina Blackwood was certainly not one to leave quietly.

"So." Serafina held out her arm with the blade of a smile. "Let's go and eat, shall we?"

An underwater landscape eclipsed every surface of the Vigour room from the walls to the tables, providing the sense of having sunk to the bottom of the ocean floor. Mermaids serenaded inside the plump interior of a large oyster shell, surrounded by kaleidoscopic swarms of fish and dancing dolphins.

Laila couldn't help but smile seeing it all come together like this, basking in the vocalised awe and admiration of her skilled work as an illusionist. She was so often unable to generate her own joy that only in the tangible emissions of others' praise and adoration of her was she capable of feeling it. She collected brief moments of intimacy among her audience, watching as they stared incredulously at the rollicking dolphins. As though they might burst through the barrier of her illusion and submerge the hall.

Tables had been set in accordance with relationship and national status, and the table of honour sat on a raised platform, consisting mainly of the ruling class as well as their companions.

Laila took a seat by her mother, who was resplendent in a gown of seawater pearls—thousands upon thousands of the iridescent baubles threaded into one gauzy netting that chattered like summer rain when she moved.

It felt like an age had passed since she had last been in her presence, but Laila settled quickly into the reticent obedience her mother had coached her from birth to attain. Had their relationship been of a different configuration, Laila might have felt comfortable enough to take her aside and unleash her sorrows upon her breast in return for comfort. Instead, she mourned her heartache alone and drowned her anguish in copious amounts of nectar.

The dishes began with blini topped with sour cream and gold

caviar, followed by several other delicacies offered by Mortesian waters: gleaming platters of oysters, mussels, and blood cockles; a phantom shrimp cocktail served in a thin-stemmed glass; miniature squids marinated in basil; and a rich, velvety soup of lobster claws. Even their more outlandish offerings made an arrival in the form of braised whale tongue and seal tenderloin dipped in cranberry sauce.

Laila had purchased it all from lupari fishermen for a fair price, for she wanted to familiarise herself with the local businesses and knew how much Darius favoured seafood over any other cuisine.

The chefs plucked live fish from the walls of her illusion with a steadied calm and deposited them squirming onto the chopping board, inserting spikes into their hindbrains. Laila watched the fish writhe anxiously against the inevitability of their fate before succumbing to limpness.

"Oh, how intriguing," Amira declared as the chef sliced and layered the pieces of fish in an attractive array of raw pinks, dipped in sauce and garnished with grated herbs. "This is not unlike the Odakan demonstrations I've observed before. Though I suppose you'd have plenty of opportunities to become inspired by them with how many of their ships must have wrecked at your shores."

She wrapped her pearl-encrusted lips around her glass of nectar with a subtle titter of amusement. Laila could already tell her earlier anxieties were not unfounded. Mortos' brutal isolationism leading to several mass shipwrecks was still a topic of sore discussion.

"You've reminded me that I shall have to take a visit to that fine country one day," Darius responded, unperturbed by Amira's commentary.

"I'd advise you to avoid some of the more devoutly religious areas." Amira smiled, sharp and scintillating as glass. "They don't take kindly to creatures of chaos."

"Duly noted."

Laila ate a bite of salmon topped with caviar and followed it with a sip of wine.

The thin pupils of Serafina's eyes watched her with interest the entire time they had been seated. Darius had insisted room be made at the table for her so he could keep her under his supervision.

"My, you're like a little bird the way you eat," Serafina commented. Her mouth was blackened from the ink of a squid as her teeth popped the skin of the caviar.

Laila suddenly felt self-conscious of her delicate, bite-sized portions. The way they matched the meticulous cuttings on her mother's plate. Yet she would be dignified, as she was in all things. Her neck muscles would always tense with the phantom weight of a crown.

"I beg your pardon?"

"Don't mind me, Your Radiance. I've just never managed to meet a creature that makes such a pleasant show out of eating the way you solarites do. So delicate. So refined. Flitting around from place to place with your little pretty chirpings. Like birds."

"Mother," Darius censured. Even now his tongue shrivelled at the word, at the unspoken entitlement she would always have to his origin. But he couldn't afford to be resentful, to feel *abandoned*, or anything less than pragmatic. Emotions like these were toxins in his bloodstream, something to be sterilised at once.

"Not to worry, Darius Rex, we little birds aren't so immune to receiving compliments," Laila assured him with a cutting smile directed towards Serafina. "I savour my meals, as I do all the little things that contribute to my overall existence. It gets easy to let things blur after a few decades, to forget the charm of seeing a sunset or letting a raindrop touch your cheek. I try not to forget what a joy it is to simply live, not even forever, but each blessed day."

She looked into Serafina's eyes and found them aflame with something indistinct.

"What a charming philosophy," Serafina said as she took a sip from her glass.

The servers arrived with dessert shortly after—a frothy delight of coconut cream and sand-biscuit pastry with concealed chunks of pineapple and mango. A Malakian delicacy as a brief reprieve from the Mortesian menu.

Laila scooped a gooey layer of cream and pastry with her spoon and took an immaculate bite. As she reached for her drink, her hand nudged against Serafina's sharp talons, her skin shredding easily against the edge of them.

Laila gasped out, snatching her hand back as a line of ichor rushed to the surface and dried against her skin.

"Oh, do forgive me, Your Radiance!" Serafina cried out in contrition as she retracted her fingers away into a fist. "I was trying to reach for the sushi platter."

"Of course," Laila said, still pitifully cradling her hand though the wound had already healed. She saw the faint glimmer of her golden blood encrusted on Serafina's nails and was faintly disquieted by the sight.

After dessert, the guests dispersed to explore the rest of the rooms and the delights awaiting them there. For many the room of Supremacy beckoned, which cultivated a mood of intimacy with the soft-toned glow of bioluminescence. Each transition of colour unearthed a new note of emotion that planted an implicit urge to generate merriment through a ritual of dance and drink.

The sight of it kindled the memory of the first night Laila had spent here, when Darius had presented the crystal formations in his room. Determined not to linger on it, she transferred to Tenacity, where partygoers gambled their souls and fortunes away at card tables resting upon a transparent floor of shark-infested waters. As cards were a popular activity in Mortesian events, she found most of the occassi had proceeded here, drawn in by the chaotic element of chance that a good gamble provided.

Next was the Cunning room where the occupants sat cosy in their tentacled seats, beguiled by sleights of hand and circus tricks from Mortos's finest magicians. Laila departed as a member of the audience was cajoled into being used as a target for knife-tossing, and she ended her journey in Ferocity, where many observed the theatrical showmanship of sparring occassi as they clashed swords and sorcery in carefully orchestrated routines.

During all of this, Laila took to the free-flowing nectar carried around by servers like a fish to water. The drink lulled her into a dreamy mood and softened the edges of her mind until the time soon came for her to return to the Austerity room to give another speech to commence the charity auction.

She ascended to a standing ovation as she took to the stage and dismissed the applause with a gesture. "Once again, I would like to thank you all for coming." Laila's voice was clear and sweet as a morning bird chirrup, gently coaxing the late-evening lethargy into awakening once more. "And I do hope that you have been having as enchanting a time as I have, seeing and experiencing all the unusual beauty the Citadel has to offer. To round it off for the evening, I would like to auction a series of offerings from the country's finest artists and artisans. So, ready your purses, folks, as we are about to present our first prize."

The applause ricocheted like thunder as a servant arrived with the first prize nestled on a tufted velvet pillow with gold tassels.

Then something shifted in the audience. Their faces lengthened to snouts with saliva-slickened teeth and their hollers of excitement rang out as the desperate howls of wolves.

Laila blinked once, then several times, in the hopes that her eyes would swipe away this madness and transport her back to reality. Yet the ravenous, black-furred predators remained where the partygoers had once been, and they were now starting to advance upon her with bloodlust in their glowing gazes...

She slipped out of the hallucination with a sudden jolt to find her body returned to its original state. With a quick cursory glance, she realised she was still onstage before the waiting eyes of an audience. The wolves were gone and in their place were the demons and celestials she was far more accustomed to. She rushed to whisper into the ear of the auctioneer that she would let him take over from this point.

Laila had never liked walking the Citadel halls, even accompanied, so she took care to stay in the path of the sconces and let the candlelight ease the way through the passage emptied of bodies besides the discordant creaks of age. She couldn't stifle her relief when she reached the staircase towards the Regina Wing and took the first step before a sharp twinge in her back made her gasp out in pain.

She fell to the floor with a cry, the stone cool and unwelcoming to her body. A sensation prickled along every inch of her body, and that was when she saw it. Fur. Soft and light and sprouting like the heads of dandelions. She could *feel* it tickling against the exposed skin of her neck as her bones twisted and mangled themselves into a rabbit's legs.

She tried to flee, making use of the small white paws she had no memory of having but that her mind suddenly registered, and got caught in the vice of a mouth enclosing its jaws around her, squeezing until her bones cracked. She opened her mouth to scream, and her vocal cords trembled with an animal screech as deep within the interior of her mind, she heard a voice, low and mocking. *Hold still, little rabbit.*

Laila released a vulnerable sound as fear and anguish paralysed her limbs. Still, she forced herself to move. She *must* move. *Please, stop. I don't want this.*

The wolf lapped its tongue over her trembling fur and exhaled its hot yearning in her ear. *Of course you do... It's what you long for. To be ravished by me, devoured by me. Why do you deny yourself what you most desire?*

Laila whimpered as its fangs sank into the nape of her neck. Her body arched to its hunger, wanting to be consumed. *No. We cannot do this. We mustn't.*

Mustn't. A mocking croon. *People only say this when they know what they want but are secretly ashamed to want it. Why are you ashamed of this, Laila?*

Because you make me question my own heart. What's righteous and true. You do so many things I can't understand and could never condone. And what's worse, you make it all cease to matter.

Perhaps you know the root of your unease is that despite the disparities in our nature, I am not wholly wicked. I am not the bloodthirsty wolf from the stories menacing you from under your bed.

No, you're the wolf I invite inside it to comfort me from menace.

The revelation made the sconces gasp their flames out all at once. For a moment, she saw only darkness around her and above her, but it was a living sort of gloom—one that throbbed and pulsated around her body.

Laila thrashed violently, but no matter how hard she flapped the darkness was more persistent, more greedy, expanding with each black pulse until she was engulfed by it. It forced its fingers inside her throat when she attempted to screech and reached deep within her core where her star rested. It pinched around its glowing heat—

There you are.

She forced her way free from the hallucination, shivering on the floor in darkness. By now she had the awareness to recognise illusory magic when it was being used against her. Solarite magic. *Her* magic. But she couldn't understand why one of her kinsfolk would want to torment her so.

The sconces lit with a whoosh, but instead of a servant or a kindly stray guest, she saw it was an occassella who stared down upon her with a taut composure. That startled her more than the darkness, being helplessly confronted with the menacing glow of preying eyes and the animal tilt of her head until, through the balmy glow of candlelight, she managed to make out the impression of Serafina's features.

"My, do you fight hard," she commended, scooping up the trembling solarite into her arms. "It took more effort to wear you down than I thought. No matter. I'll have plenty of time to become acquainted with your inner workings."

She carried her off down the hall.

Darius sighed as he leaned over the balcony, the cool wisp of midnight air a welcome balm to the nape of his neck.

A star shot through the sky above him. He let his hand follow its trajectory, looping his fingers around the white streak of its tail and clenched it like he would a rope until his fingers turned numb. If only he clenched enough he could hold its power in his hands and wish away his troubles.

That's what stars were for, after all, weren't they? Didn't they always say they were for wishing?

Defeated, his hand gripped the alabaster rail until it crunched into dust under his fists. His nerves felt exposed, stripped back like a wire without cover. Anger and loathing coursed through him from the unexpected arrival of his mother.

He felt the urge to cry, but nothing came. The emotion was trapped behind a panel of glass, keeping the rest of him chilled and numb. But all that pressure, it had to go somewhere; one couldn't just let something build and build and dissipate into nothing.

So he strained for the release of his tears, even mimicking the dry, heaving sobs he wanted to provoke. But it was to no avail. It only left him with a hoarse throat and rattling breath and a growing frustration.

"Your Majesty."

He shot up at the sound of his address, carnivorous instincts twitching in alertness.

Poking her head through the parting of drapes was Sabina, a cigar perched between her fingers. "Fancy some company?"

Darius huffed a laugh at the sight of her. "Be my guest."

Sabina rested her back against the banister. "My sincere apologies for your mother. I have no idea how she got in."

"Well, she has her ways."

"I could throw her out, if you wanted."

A corner of Darius's mouth twitched upwards. "As satisfying as that would be, it wouldn't be worth the fuss."

"Between you and your star princess." Sabina took a long drag and exhaled. "Right?"

Darius straightened. "How long have you known? About Laila and me. How long have you known? When did you see it?"

"When you sent me personally to escort her, if that matters. I knew she had to be precious to you for that." Sabina smiled wryly. "You always send me when it's something important to you. Though anyone with eyes would be able to see the way you look at her." She turned to look at him. "Are you in love, Your Majesty?"

"I hardly think these matters are appropriate for us to discuss."

"Come on, you know all my deepest, darkest secrets." Sabina gave him a knowing look.

Darius knew she was referring to her first kill. Not a monster, but one of the enforcers who'd tried to muscle his way into her bed during induction. A murder he'd been happy to pardon.

"So?"

Even though Darius did not admit to it, he did not deny it. He couldn't have even if he tried. To deny the truth of his love for Laila would be akin to refusing his own name.

"Well, if you require counsel," Sabina said, "here it is: I think she's very pretty, but you should find someplace far less inconvenient to dip your wick."

"Whatever I feel for her is irrelevant, as Princess Laila has no intention to return it. She'll be on her way home to Soleterea soon and all will be as normal."

"And what's normal? You brooding after her, continuing to turn down proposals and exasperating my father?" Sabina snorted. "You know he always wanted me to marry you. Part of me thinks it's because it was as close as he was ever going to get to being by your side. Glad it didn't work out, after seeing you with her. That would've been tragic."

"Indeed," he agreed. "You deserve far better. You deserve someone who will love you to the point they'd pry their heart in two and use it to shelter yours."

Sabina chuckled puffs of smoke at the old Mortesian saying. "Always hated that rot."

"You will until you find the one to whom it applies." Darius gave her one last smile before retreating back down to the party.

The auction was still deep in progress, but he couldn't see Laila onstage.

He approached Amira in confusion. "Have you seen the princess?"

"Hm?" Amira glanced at him. "Laila left the stage a while ago. I haven't seen her since."

Darius took a quick sweep about the room. "And my m—Serafina Blackwood. Have you seen her?"

"Not since dinner."

His nape prickled with a distinct sense of wrongness. Though he couldn't say why. Turning away from Amira, he sought Laila's scent in the crowd and followed it out into the hallway towards the staircase to the Regina's Wing. His mother's lingered alongside it.

Something cold seized his stomach. The food and drink he'd consumed roiled within. He had to find them, now. No matter the cost. He continued pursuing their intermingled scents relentlessly as they led him further and further down familiar territory.

He hadn't been this low in the Citadel since he'd become rex, since he'd left his old quarters. Where he once was the ill-begotten child of an unwilling mother and pitiless father, destined to know the victory of the firstborn in name only while his younger brother superseded him in the race for all things.

He still thought about that sometimes. How mother had cast him into the snow and how father had stomped his face into it, and yet he'd still picked himself up, twitching and determined, desirous of everything he knew he ought not to be.

Darius tiptoed down the staircase to the level above the servants. His old rooms were dust-clouded and cob-webbed, white sheets thrown over everything he hadn't yet moved. Darius knew what he'd see there but didn't want to confront it—the slim thread of candlelight lurking behind a bookcase, leading to his laboratory.

Instinct had him throwing off all caution as he blurred past the rugged staircase and through the tunnels to step into light once more inside that cavernous space.

Serafina was arranging medical utensils, picking up various scalpels and inspecting them for sharpness. Laila was stretched out unconscious on the table in front of her, head slumped, her breathing faint but present.

Sensing her son was near, Serafina put down her scalpel. "Come to join the fun, have you?"

Darius was used to keeping himself tightly wound. His shirts were buttoned right up to the collar, sleeves clasped with antique cufflinks, belts bound into constricting knots. It was through only this that he maintained his calm before his mother as he asked, "What are you doing in my laboratory?"

Serafina gave him a pitiful look. "My dear boy, do you really think your father would've gone to all the trouble to make *you* a secret lab? Oh, don't flatter yourself. This was mine long before it was yours." She hummed lightly to herself as she picked up a syringe and pierced it through Laila's wrist.

The solarite murmured faintly but did not rouse.

"What have you given her?" he asked, surprised at the evenness in his tone.

"Just something to keep her calm." Serafina cupped Laila's face, stroking it gently. "I've always been fascinated by these little star girls, myself. Did you know they have living *stars* in the core of them? It's quite fascinating. Legend has it that if you rip the thing out, you'll be granted immense power."

"Really? How intriguing."

Serafina eyed him sceptically. "Well, come now, don't play the fool. You know *precisely* what I'm talking about. Besides, this one is special, you see. Katerina has told me all about your little infatuation with her. I find it rather darling."

"So what is this, then?" Darius gestured towards her. "You're taking my toys away in a strop because I haven't answered your letters, is that it?"

"You know, I was hurt by that. You ignoring me in such a brazen manner. I thought perhaps if I sent Katerina to ask you nicely... but, well, I underestimated how little you'd care about such a thing, didn't I?" Serafina smoothed her hand through Laila's hair. "But this... you care about very much, don't you? I can see it in your eyes. It would hurt you to lose her, wouldn't it?"

He knew this was another test. Serafina had infiltrated his Citadel under the guise of civility to try and hurt him again, to exert dominance. How well-paired his parents were. Shame they never tore each other to pieces before they procreated.

"She's a valuable trinket, nothing more," Darius replied. "I could just as easily replace her with another."

"You're lying to me, Darius." Her tone flattened in reproach. "You forget I know how you function. I am your mother, after all. I made you."

"Believe what you will," Darius said. "However, I would caution against doing something too reckless. Her impératrice mother is right upstairs. Do you want to start a war?"

Serafina barked in laughter. "Seeing this country fall to ruin? Sometimes I think nothing would please me more. But no. That isn't quite what I have in mind here. See, I was fascinated by the power she could exert over the mind, and I wondered how far I could take it. I wouldn't get to kill her, but I could make you all but dead to her."

Darius suppressed the urge to flinch. His fury simmered.

"I thought perhaps I would simply erase her memories of you. Every touch. Every smile. Every embrace. That would please Katerina immensely. Then I realised that's not far enough... I should make her *hate* you. Make it so she can't even stand in your presence without being filled with a deep-seated loathing. That might be even worse than me killing her, wouldn't it?"

Darius fought against the embers of rage sparking to life in his chest, scorching a trail up his insides. "What do you *want*, Mother?"

"Now see, *that's* better." Serafina smiled wide enough to show her dimples. A trait they shared. "A little hospitality from you is all I desired. Now we can negotiate." She stabbed down her scalpel beside Laila's head. "I want my former position as the court sorceress restored."

His expression migrated through a variety of emotions, most of them negative. "Why?"

"I want to be close to you. Advise you. As a dutiful mother should."

Here, he flinched but disguised his visceral reaction with a chilled laugh. "Is that truly all you wanted? Well, why didn't you say so?"

"I might have if only you'd answered my letters." Serafina shrugged. "Do we have a deal, then?"

There was nothing he loathed more than this, to be once more strong-armed into a corner. While the urge to refuse wormed onto his tongue a quick glance at Laila was all it took to defuse it. He couldn't lose her. She was the one thing he couldn't do without.

"As you wish." His tongue stroked over the syllables like he would a cat, a tender croon of concession from the monster.

"Hm, perfect!" Serafina started to remove Laila's bindings. "Now I'll just untie her, and you are free to whisk her away to wherever—"

The moment she turned away from him, he struck. Seizing her by the back of the head, he rammed her face against the counter. Once, twice, thrice. Then let her slump to the ground in an unconscious heap. He fixed her with a gaze of pure repugnance before turning all his attention to Laila.

He injected her with another syringe to counter the effects of the former, unfastening her binds to take her into his arms. He tilted her head so that it rested easily into the crook of his neck before he carried her away.

∽

Laila awoke on Darius's divan in his antechamber with her mind still hazy and thick. She touched her fingers to her forehead, groaning sleepily.

"What is happening to me?" she asked, haughty and demanding but frightened still.

"It was my mother," Darius explained, his voice strained. "She used blood magic on you."

"Blood magic." She remembered the scratch of Serafina's talons as her fingers disappeared inside her fist. "Why?"

"She was trying to access your star. To siphon your aether power."

Laila shivered as she thought back to the intensity of her pain and the feel of being excavated. "Can I stop her?" Her teeth worried her bottom lip. Having Serafina use her own power against her had been the worst possible invasion. She could not have it happen again.

Darius tinkered about his room with a few mutters under his breath. He rummaged through the numerous cabinets until he eventually found what he sought and lifted a phial of amber liquid with strips of bark floating in the solution.

"What is that?"

"Bark and sap from our sacred white birch tree. It has some religious significance in our mythology—" Darius dismissed the need for the lengthy explanation with a shake of his hand. "A long story. But if I anoint you with this it should nullify the effects of her blood rune."

She did not protest against his hypothesis as he approached her and wet the tips of his fingers with the tincture. He traced a symbol reverently with his thumb on her forehead, her sternum and the space between her shoulder blades, the touch so light was practically hallucinatory.

"Well?"

The nudging had ceased, as well as the prickling itch behind her back from the burrowing. She breathed a little less frantically as she let herself go limp against the divan.

"I think it's stopped." She exhaled in relief and, without thinking, launched herself into his arms in gratitude. "Thank you."

"It's all right now, you're safe," Darius soothed, though the words were more for his assurance than hers. "You're safe."

She leaned her nose against his shoulder and inhaled the sharp, clean musk of his cologne. "I can see now why you didn't want us to meet."

His chest rumbled with a wry chuckle. "As it turns out, it was Katerina who was responsible. They're... close. You could think of her as a protégée to my mother."

"She loathes me that much?" Laila asked, though she found she couldn't be surprised. Darius Calantis was not someone one simply overcame. Being the object of his fixation was like sailing a tidal wave of extremes—euphoric, comforting, uplifting, terrifying. It had given her something she'd never before thought possible. The safety of an affection that endured through her faults, rather than in spite of them. Of there being no distance she could throw him that he wouldn't return from. She'd known him only a fraction of the time Katerina had and still suffered the white-hot flares of nonsensical rage at the mere thought of him being withdrawn.

Perhaps if she'd had him longer she would've acted with the same malice.

"Try not to take it too personally, princess. You're not a politician in Mortos without at least one serious threat to your life."

"Spare me your wit, Darius."

He slumped down next to her on the divan. "And how are you feeling?"

"I've been better," she admitted. "I'll feel even better when I understand just who your mother is exactly."

She watched the mirth drain from his face as his expression stiffened. "That's a story for another time."

"No, Darius, no," Laila said. Her nerves were too frazzled, too haywire, to be satisfied by such a vague promise. "You tell me what's going on, now."

She stared firmly at him until he sighed in relent.

He closed his eyes, breathing deeply. "Laila, my mother... it's more complicated than you can ever imagine."

"You think that I would not understand the complexity of the relationship one has with a mother?" She sounded affronted. "I could have already uncovered that with how you all but implied she was dead."

"I didn't mean to be dishonest with you, it's just—" His words faltered and he pinched the bridge of his nose. "I don't want her to be anywhere near anything that could be considered good in my life. And now you can see why."

"But *why* were you so intent on hiding her from me? If she is truly so dangerous, why did you never think to warn me about her before? Why did you leave me so unprepared?"

He looked away. Then he clenched down so hard on his teeth that his jaw twitched.

"Please just—just *talk* to me."

"All right, princess, if you really want to know: I was a bastard child between a king and a blood sorceress. The biggest scandal of our time. My father wanted to marry the problem away, but my mother was unwilling to give up her position. Unfortunately, Vidua Nocte custom states there are no males allowed on their land. So my mother had a few choices. She could leave the faction and forfeit her power or she could—" His voice seized before he continued. "She could get rid of the problem. She chose the latter and decided she would offer me as a ritual sacrifice to her goddess. Only, my father uncovered my existence and threatened her life if she didn't hand me over. She complied."

Laila felt something wet on her cheeks and realised she was crying. She wiped the tears away.

Darius averted his eyes from her. "The reason I never told you is that I try to forget every day who I am and where I came from. That I was a mistake. That I was unwanted. I didn't want you to ever look at me the way you are now. As though I'm some sad, troubled thing worthy of your pity."

"You think pity is the only thing I feel for you?" she asked as a quiver of lightning flashed outside the window, dancing across the soft glimmer on her skin. She climbed into his lap and took his face in her hands. "Because it isn't. Far from it."

Darius closed his eyes, resting his forehead against hers. "You don't have to comfort me, Laila. It's you who's been through an ordeal."

"I'm not saying this because I'm trying to comfort you, Darius." She moistened her lips, the words catching in her throat. "I'm saying this because... because I—" Her heart fluttered in apprehension. "Because I'm in love with you, Darius. And I so tire of trying to deny it or disguise it or make it disappear..."

Outside the storm roared with anguish, and the rain pelted the windows like a volley of arrows. Yet there was no moment more silent than this, with her hand on his cheek and her breath still warm with a declaration she couldn't bring herself to rescind.

"What did you say?" he asked, his voice a frail whisper.

"I said that I'm in love with you, Darius," Laila repeated, bolder now. Amazing how much easier it grew each time she said. "Darius, I love you—"

His mouth collided with hers urgently, swallowing the words from her lips. He kissed her with a yearning she didn't realise he'd been suppressing, and, gods, but she never truly realised before now just what it was she did to him. The taste of the sweet wine from his mouth stained hers before he had his hands in her hair.

"Say that again," he murmured against her lips.

"I love you," she whispered back.

He pushed her down onto the divan, pressing their bodies bruisingly close. He released a brief moan into her mouth as she coaxed his lips open to trace the edge of his tongue with hers.

"Again," he commanded.

"I love you."

She hooked her legs around him to deepen the kiss to the point where she could feel the graze of his fang against her lip. She pulled back to look into his blackened monster eyes, and she sucked the ichor from the wound left by his fang. Then he had his lips against her neck, her jawline, gliding down further as he murmured her name and followed it with gentle nips with his fangs before yanking down her dress.

They stripped each other with eagerness and clumsy gestures, desperate to meet each other bare, to remove any barrier. Laila ran her hands over the smooth muscled planes of his torso, the broadness in the shoulders, the firmness in the arms. He kept so much of himself tucked away beneath these layers, and she wanted to explore all of it.

He switched their positions and hooked her knees over his shoulders, gliding his tongue along her thigh before he kissed her clit. Her lips parted as he pressed the flat of his tongue against her, and she released a moan that expanded against the walls of the room.

"Try to keep quiet, or I might have to stop," he warned, sucking her clit into his mouth until she was trembling. Until all conscious thought was supplanted by a series of colours. Her hips ghosted the movement of his tongue as he brought her to a pinnacle of pleasure she didn't think was possible—and then he stopped.

Laila whined as he moved her down to rest on his hips, brow arched in expectancy.

"Keep going like that and you'll have the guards think I'm killing you."

She snorted in response, positioning herself to align her clit to the underside of his cock. Then it was his turn to quiet the throaty sounds from his lips as she ground herself against him.

Darius cursed as his fingers dug bruisingly into her thighs, head thrown back, crying out shakily. "Laila, please!"

She knew what he wanted but she wouldn't give it. She wanted to show him that she wouldn't be bested, to elicit the same fervour of driving him over the edge without taking him inside her. She leaned in to kiss him as her hips continued their frenzied gyrations until he was caught up in the erratic tide of her movements, drowning in the waves of ecstasy.

They were so immersed in each other they didn't hear the door creak to reveal Delanus, standing in gaping awe of the passionate embrace before him. He'd been on the search for Darius after his mysterious disappearance from yet another event. Little did he imagine the compromising position he would find his rex in. With the solarite princess no less. And it was with a slightly gaping mouth that he desisted, having the good grace to excuse himself.

Once they'd both finished, Laila slumped against Darius's chest before leaning up to kiss him, trailing her finger along his chest. "You know, I've never imagined I could ever feel this…"

"What?" he asked.

"Blissful." She nuzzled against him. "I was so afraid to be with you because I feared it would cause nothing but pain and suffering. But this… this is completely the opposite."

He kissed the top of her head, whispering words of Mortesian she couldn't decipher.

"What does that mean?" she asked, glancing up at him in confusion.

"It means you have devoured my heart." He brushed a twist behind her ear, bringing up her wrist to kiss it.

She breathed a laugh, shaking her head at the morbidity before she allowed herself to lean into his touch.

"I can't tell you how long I've wanted this," he murmured, his hand sinking within the depths of her abundant curls. "I used to think about it all the time, you coming here to Mortos. Choosing to be with me, finally, after so many decades. And I almost ruined it."

She met his gaze and found it soft with regret. Then she cupped his face in her palm, tracing his stubble with her thumb. "I almost ruined it too." She sighed with lament. "I didn't mean to make you wait so long, I was just… afraid. Of how much you wanted me and how much I wanted you and taking a risk on that. Even now, I… I can't say where we're even meant to go from here."

"Wherever we want," he replied, so unshakably firm. "I want us to start by officially offering you access to my quarters to come and go as you wish. I want you to treat it as your own home. And I hope you come to think of the Citadel that way, eventually."

She thought of this crumbling edifice and its shadowed hallways, its labyrinthine structures and impenetrable walls of ivy. She didn't think it would ever be hers, that she would ever belong to it in the same way he did. But she accepted his attempts to share it with her all the same.

"Won't that cause a fuss with your prefects?"

He chuckled, and it was a light vibration against her cheek. "Let them fuss. If any of them have an issue with it, they can take it up with me... and briskly find themselves cast out."

"I love you," she said. The phrase was still an acquired taste on her tongue, but she found she was quickly gaining a predilection for it. "I think part of me always knew, ever since you left after the coup, and all I did was wish for you to come back."

He kissed the tip of her nose before brushing his own against it. "I think I knew, ever since you tried and failed to break into my room to snoop through my journals, that you were the one for me." He smiled, warm with humour and undertoned with something she could scarcely find words for. "There's been no one else since."

"Do you think something like this could ever last?" Laila struggled to meet his eyes as she asked.

"Yes."

"How can you be sure?"

"Because I'll destroy anyone and anything that gets between us."

He meant it. She could see it in his eyes. The sheer animal intensity of them pierced her right through the marrow. It stopped her breath how ferocious he could be in his certainty of her. He sealed his promise with a kiss so impassioned it went all the way down to her weakening legs, and it was all she could do to let herself swoon into it as he wrapped his arms around her.

XXI

LINA HAD BEEN BEDRIDDEN SINCE HER ENCOUNTER with Naveen. No matter what salves were concocted or tinctures were mixed, the black webbing continued to spider along her collarbone until her vibrant brown hue had withered to the sickly grey of peeling snakeskin.

"It keeps getting worse," Vidya grunted as she slammed shut yet another medical journal and tossed it to the ground. "I went through all her journals. Everything. There has to be something else!"

"Mama." Maithra arrived behind her to put her hand on her mother's shoulder. "Some people have arrived. They say there are places that specialise in treating those sick by chaotic magic. They can take Elina there, if we allow them."

Vidya swallowed the impulse to reject, knowing it was selfish to keep Elina close at hand where she could feel with animal certainty her presence and make sure that she was alive. The thought of her having crossed the border into another territory where she might breathe her last—

"Send them up..." Elina moaned weakly, eyes fluttering open and shut. Her breaths were hollowed-out reverberations in a darkened cave.

"All right," Vidya relented, and blinked back tears as she did so. "I'll tell them."

Elina smiled in thanks, but it was an ephemeral flicker. She looked near death, the rise and ebb of her chest a faded motion beneath the sheets.

Is this what loving you has brought me to, Sadik?

It felt silly of her to think of him now. Much less to long for him to come to her. Being on one's deathbed tended to drive a heart to foolish sentiment. For all she knew, he was imprisoned or, worse yet, dead himself. Perhaps he'd be there in the netherworld waiting to welcome her into his arms.

She watched her mother leave down the stairs and suppressed a weak cough. She couldn't die in this bed. Not while Yasmin still needed her. All she needed was a little more time.

Footsteps sounded into her room and she discovered that they belonged to an Odakan witch. She was small and pale with lustrous dark hair neatly tamed into a strict, unyielding bun. When she saw Elina, she smiled in a way that sapped the air of its warmth.

"You must be Elina Panja?" she said. Her uniform was a starch white with no logo. "I hope it is all right for me to sit?"

Elina glanced her over, wary, before nodding towards her favourite armchair. "I can see you know my name, but I don't know yours."

"My name is Dr Akira Isuka. I represent a small organisation known as the Mountain that investigates complex cases of chaotic magic usage."

Dr Isuka put down her teacup on her saucer and folded her hands together. "With your permission, we would like to take you into custody to study your condition and hopefully treat it."

"Will I... will I be all right?"

"I am afraid it is difficult to say for certain." Dr Isuka frowned. "Having had experience with chaotic magic when it gets into the veins of a mortal, well... I suppose you could say it works like a virus slowly eating away at the cells. It bonds to its host, always shifting and camouflaging itself until it is too late to stop it."

Elina's hands trembled. "So I... I'm doomed?"

Dr Isuka regarded her wide brown eyes and the deep concern in them. She couldn't look at her for too long before it reminded her of another pair. "I can't promise you a miracle, but I can say you are far from doomed. Come with us, and we can sustain your life until a cure can be crafted." Dr Isuka's lips flexed with sympathy. "I lost someone I held dear to chaos magic a long time ago. Since then, I have dedicated my life to ensuring others are spared the same fate. I'll give you a little time to think about it before I contact you again. Here is my mirror frequency." She produced a card between her fingers and set it down on the table. "I'm afraid I must depart now."

"Of course." Elina picked up the card and held it like a lifeline. "Thank you... so much, Dr Isuka."

Dr Isuka nodded at her briefly before turning to leave.

The Mielette Spa was a private wellness retreat tucked inside the blue-grey mountains of highland Soleterea. Patients of grievous magic-related injury or illness would be treated to a strict regime of rest and respite, their every need catered to by solarites. Much went into crafting this rejuvenating stay, from the catering of gourmet meals to the deluxe array of facilities. But the most important treatment of all was by far the solarites' best kept secret—their very own ichor.

For centuries the celestials had been synthesising their blood to craft a hidden elixir of youth that (should the individual not already be too far gone) was capable of restoring a patient to perfect health. Such a cure had understandably been kept concealed from the masses, both to protect the solarites and to prevent acts of foolish hubris on the part of humans.

Here Lyra de Lis slowly healed after her catastrophic battle with the huntress left her clinging to the knife's edge of survival. Her injuries had been numerous—consisting mainly of swollen, jagged lumps of fragmented bone where the huntress had nearly pummelled her senseless.

The fight had been a test of humility for Lyra, if nothing else. Never before had she been rendered to such childlike feebleness. If not for her sheer indomitable will to survive, it was doubtful Lyra would have lived to tell the tale.

The solarites had wasted little time applying their elixir to her through an intravenous drip. Thus, Lyra awoke to discover her bones smoothed straight as though ironed—not a single fissure remaining. She glanced with interest at the gold-flecked fluid entering her bloodstream via the drip.

"Well, I certainly don't know what you are, but we ought to have you bottled," she weakly quipped to the elixir, glancing about at her surroundings. What she found instead at her bedside was a table with a drawer, and on the drawer a note that read: *Open me.*

Lyra's brow furrowed in interest at this, and she found a blue velvet box inside. She opened the box next to reveal a solid gold rose with a diamond stud in the centre. The sight of it took her aback, and she glanced around the ward again for any sign of the person who put it there.

Lyra picked up the rose, studying it. The first thing she noticed was that the petals were all perfect. She ran her fingers along the length of one, its smooth, cool surface, and something wound tight in her, like the crank of a music box slowly playing inside her memory. The rose garden at Rosâtre with the pavilion in the centre and its delicately curling white iron. How Laila used to run for hours, gathering and kicking up petals until her skin became a patchwork of them.

The ones Lyra remembered best were the pure gold roses that skirted around the pavilion with their opulent lustre, commanding sight but refusing touch (they were much like stars that way). That same bloom had adorned Soleterea's national flag for generations, symbolic of the beauty and prosperity of their rule.

Lyra observed the figurine in her hand with its bejewelled centre, taunting her intrepid curiosity until eventually she relented. She vacated her bed and padded down the ward on quicksilver footsteps until she found a bathroom. Locking herself in one of the cubicles, she sat down on the toilet lid and twisted the bud.

The jewel ignited with a thin ray of light beaming so suddenly into existence that Lyra was unprepared. It burrowed right through her eyes and into her cerebral tissue, nearly causing her to drop it. She realised the transmission was hypnotic when her eyes grew heavy and slow with tiredness. It was a common method used by solarites to coax others into the Astral Realm during meetings they wanted to keep clandestine.

Now Lyra was even more curious, and her desire to uncover the truth overruled whatever hesitation she might hold towards the owner of such trickery. So she made herself comfortable once more and let her spirit drift away with the soft oscillations of shallow consciousness.

She awoke in a villa made of marble. The windows were arched cavities in the walls with no glass or lattice, streaming with undiluted sunlight. There was no angle Lyra could walk to escape or weaken it, no shadow to seek refuge behind. She could only walk forward through the passage until she reached a large fresco wall coated in gilt, glistening with the smoothness of honey.

She followed the iridescent animations as they unfurled. First, the star that shuttled down from the sky and burst in a swirl of splintering cinders. Then, the roses that yawned and stretched from the rolling hills of apple-green. Then, the silver shears that severed the green umbilical cord of the bush. And finally, the rose that ascended untethered and became the sun.

Lyra found the sun-rose by stairs made of marble veined with gold. They wound up for miles like the body of a vine, taking her past multiple floors each quaking with their own beckons of laughter and conversation.

She felt a magnetic drag towards each of the doors, with their ornately carved knobs in gold or crystal. Some even wafted scents of sweet wine and honey. But she knew she must ascend to the final tier, to the doors of carved alabaster awaiting her.

The doors withdrew with a gasp the moment she touched them, and a gush of light consumed her.

When Lyra blinked again she was seated at a large round silver disc of a table, polished like a mirror. Her feet settled on the pliant moisture of a cloud. Above her, leering with a lustful intensity, was a sun so unlike the golden orb of her own world that sprinkled magnanimously the coins of its wealth upon every tree, flower, and bush.

This sun was a vulgar red, pulsing like the heart of a giant. It erased all it surrounded, sucking all stars and space and then expanding three sizes too large.

Lyra regarded it with revulsion and fascination in equal measure, the foul hunger of it, throbbing and rubescent.

"Welcome, Ser Lyra," came a voice, several voices, united as one and yet fragmented as wishes spoken into a well.

Lyra's head darted every which way to the vague figures seated around her, outlined only by floating stars.

"Is this magician's farce truly necessary?" she asked, her voice thin and bladed with irritation.

"We act the same to all in the first meeting," the choral voice replied. "When you prove yourself worthy, we will reveal ourselves."

"And who are you?"

A large, fat petal sailed in front of her face, followed by another, and she could see that the sun before them had opened into the corolla of a rose.

"We are the Order of the Golden Rose."

The sun-rose transformed into the aureate hue she knew and loved.

"And what do you seek from me?"

A petal landed on the table's reflective glass and melted with a shuddering ripple into the face of the first impératrice.

"Our order was established by Impératrice Esterre Rose, the First Who Fell, who decreed that we be the ones to protect Vysteria, improve Vysteria, and eliminate all who pose a threat to its existence."

Lyra observed the visage of the famed solarite, matching her features to Laila's. She was all fawn and rose with hair whiter than starlight, and her eyes were a pale lilac. She'd not been seen since her abdication from the throne led to the power vacuum that kickstarted centuries of dynastic infighting. Legend had it she'd retreated into the Astral Realm for good to guard the source of all magic—the Holy Phoenix.

"What has this to do with me?"

The table shuddered, and Esterre was replaced with the arctic landscape of Mortos.

"There is a blight," they said, and the image of an occasso was rendered. "A great and ancient terror that threatens to destabilise all we mean to protect. We are seeking all possible candidates to aid us in eliminating it."

Lyra was startled by the knowledge that there were others working behind the scenes regarding Mortos.

"You were chosen for your moral fortitude and martial strength. Both things we will need. Before we would have thought to recruit your uncle, but sadly he has passed."

Lyra swallowed at this. "What sort of threat are we discussing?"

"The occassi are but mere footsoldiers. Their creator is a deposed god who wishes to rule through them and drag us into an age of blood and chaos. Only when the occassi scourge is sterilised will we be safe."

"Sterilised?" Lyra grimaced as though the word were something sour. They spoke of it as though it was something innocuous, something mild.

"We intend to cleanse the world of chaos magic and all its pernicious effects. That means extracting it from all creatures whom it has affected. In particular, Calante's direct bloodline."

An image formed of the Calantis family.

"So that's why you desired Dominus," Lyra said.

"The occasso has provided us much needed insight on how to purge chaos. But much work still requires doing. You allowed him once to slip from your grasp—"

Lyra laughed at this. "Yes, do forgive me for being beaten within an inch of my life."

"—but this can be rectified. Provided you are willing."

There was nothing Lyra would like to see more than the end of chaos. Though she knew well Laila might have conflicting views on that matter. Should she accept this mission, it might well mean the ruin of their friendship. Could she sacrifice a bond she once considered so essential?

"What must I do?"

An image fluctuated across the table and formed Dominus's face.

"Find Dominus. Detain him. And deliver him to us alive. You will be contacted by an agent when you awaken. Do not fail."

Lyra stammered to ask more questions, but her words were stifled by another deluge of light.

She awoke with a startled spasm, her muscles clenched as though she had been falling and was braced for a very harsh landing. With a quick glance around her, she found herself within the toilet cubicle. She looked down at the rose in her palm and clenched it. Her mission was clear: She must find Dominus.

Wind rustled along Dr Isuka's woollen coat as she approached her airship. A gleam of evening sun oscillated across the aluminium husk of the *Hariken*, ramp descended to make way for the levitating aerochair lifting Elina Panja onto the flight.

Once she had boarded, the scholar ensured her patient was made comfortable with offerings of green tea and cherry blossom rice cakes as they took to the skies towards Odaka.

"The flight shouldn't take more than a couple of hours at most, which gives us plenty of time to become acquainted," Dr. Isuka said, taking a sip of her tea. "So, do tell me, what questions do you have?"

"I don't even know where to begin..." Elina snuffled. "How did this all start?"

"The Mountain was established twenty years ago by a solarite benefactor. A reaction to the discovery of Mortos." Dr Isuka munched on a rice cake. "When we first encountered the country, we became aware of just how little we knew about chaos: its power, its weaknesses, how to counter and safeguard against it. Thus, a small group of scholars came together to form our organisation, and we've been working steadily ever since."

"And... who is this benefactor?"

"She prefers anonymity," Dr Isuka said, "but sometimes she visits, so you may see her."

Elina didn't think she'd ever seen a solarite in the flesh before, and the thought electrified her. "This facility... I hope I should be perfectly safe there?"

"Of course!" Dr Isuka said. "We have no ill intentions towards you whatsoever, I can assure you of that. You are a mere unfortunate victim of circumstance. We all know how reckless men can be. Hence we step in."

Elina nodded, glancing out of the window to watch the landscape transform to the altitudinous region of Odaka, hoary with mist. Growing out from the craggy mountain slopes were the spires of a city joined by swaying rope bridges, the glistening silver thread of a river seeping between.

"That's our capital," Dr Isuka told her as they flew by. "I will have to show you around for a visit one day. Once you're well again. Our destination, however, is a little further north."

"All the way into the mountains?" Elina asked, seeing nothing but slate-blue ranges beyond the city boundaries.

"Our work requires that we have a little more privacy than would be afforded when operating within city limits," Dr Isuka explained as they approached one particular mountain with a gushing waterfall.

Elina was astonished when it split apart to allow them entrance.

The airship flew inside the cave mouth and landed in its impenetrable blackness. As the engine quieted, the area was flooded with fluorescent lights igniting along the walls of the caves.

"Come along, mata." Dr Isuka ushered Elina out of the ship and into the cave, smiling at her wary disbelief. "You haven't seen anything yet."

Elina followed her into the hollow of the cave towards two large metal doors, which opened into a chamber. Dr Isuka stepped inside and placed her open palm against a glowing hand imprint and, just like that, the chamber began to move.

A lift, Elina realised as the doors sealed shut.

They descended into the bowels of the cave, receiving only darkness, but soon the chasm opened once more into a laboratory of several floors all enclosed within a circular structure.

Elina could scarcely believe her eyes when she looked upon it, for never before had she seen a facility so grand dedicated for the sole purposes of learning. Polished oak bookcases inlaid with porcelain plaques soared even taller than sycamores. False windows of verre églomisé nearly tricked the mind with idyllic woodland sceneries. Though the surfaces were so polished Elina could see how unwell she had grown in them.

"I can see you've found this place to be to your liking." Dr Isuka smiled as she gestured at her labs. "Welcome to the Mountain."

They passed various floors of the facility where the scholars did their work. Most of them were Odakans, though there were some Thals and Serajis among them too.

At the end of it, Isuka took her to the patient ward, where she was settled in a bed of sturdy mahogany with silk so plush Elina felt she'd been floated away on a cloud.

"We'll just need to take a sample of your blood for examination and then we can begin treatment," Dr Isuka said. She snapped her fingers and gestured for the orderlies to get started.

"Thank you again for all you're doing, Dr Isuka," Elina replied. "I can't thank you enough."

"Of course. Remember the person I told you I'd lost to chaos magic? Well, she died long before I was able to save her. Long before I knew I could do anything about it. It's been twenty years now, and still I..." She trailed off with a hitch in her chest. "I would do anything if it meant I could spare her such an awful fate. Which is why I feel an obligation to you, mata. I won't say this work will be easy and light, but it *will* save you."

"I put my life in your hands."

Dr Isuka smiled one last time before she left the ward and travelled even further down into the subterranean floors where she performed most of her experiments.

She placed her hand into another imprint, and the door opened into a room flanked with observation cells on either side. The Bestiary.

Rows upon rows of cells housed creatures of all variations. Some she knew of beforehand, others were entirely alien. But where her knowledge failed, the labels were more than happy to inform. *Subject: Griffin. Subject: Mermaid. Subject: Siren.*

On and on Isuka walked as the sleepy eyes of her captives stalked her. Most were barely mobile and only had the energy to cling helplessly to her with their gaze before their vigour was once more snuffed. Subject: Firedrake. Subject: Arassas. *Subject: Hippogriff. Subject: Unknown Mutation—*

Her steps halted as she looked inside the cell. A strange reptilian creature with retracted bat wings was crumpled in a heap of limbs. Capturing one of Darius's chimeras was an unexpected prize, one that would be most useful.

She continued on, seeing names labelled on cells she'd been studying recently. All from Mortos. *Lupari. Qarnun. Melltith. Bilken.* The subjects looked dazed. In order to study the effects of chaos magic, she knew she needed to see how it functioned in those who were born with it. Should she be successful extracting chaos from them, it shouldn't be too far-fetched to remove it from mortals. And finally, after so long, she would have freed everyone from this evil.

Dr Isuka exhaled, glancing at the cells. "Let's get started, then."

XXII

WRAPPED TIGHT IN THE RED SILK SHEETS OF THE rex's bed, Laila slumbered. It was a most unguarded sleep, peaceful as a babe's, with tender sounds expelled between restless shifts across the mattress. She looked so delicate, so *serene*, a pristine porcelain beauty you purchased to place on your most visible shelf.

Only the blackest of hearts would have wanted to disturb it. Unfortunately for Laila, that was just the sort of creature whose shadow now fell across her sleeping form, silver filigreed claws at the ready to peel away the cocoon of silk and lay bare the pale negligee covering what she sought.

Serafina traced a claw across the flimsy gauze shielding Laila's core. Her star sat insulated from external harm, all that power compressed in one tiny ball of flame just waiting to be snatched. On the bedside, a bottle of white birch sap remained open with the dried cork rolled slightly to one side. Serafina picked it up, examining it, sniffing at the contents with the critical refinement of a wine connoisseur. Then she began to laugh and laugh low, which was enough to startle the sleeping princess awake.

"What are you doing here?" Laila asked, her eyes soft and heavy-lidded, but her body glowed with an infinite amount of heat and light that threatened to erase all in its path.

Serafina only smiled and brandished the bottle towards her with faint amusement. "You didn't think you'd gotten rid of me that easily, did you?" She lashed out with armoured talons, embedding them in Laila's stomach.

Laila let out a scream as her skin was shredded with the ease of tearing tissue paper, leaving behind four newly dug trenches of her golden blood.

She awoke gasping, stomach damp with sweat, her negligee untarnished upon inspection. Her chest fluttered in relief, the claws of her nightmare slowly retracting as her senses burned through the fogginess of half-sleep.

Beside her, the bottle of tree sap sat uncapped, and she anointed herself three times with the same symbols Darius used before. At the thought of him, her hand slid across the mattress and found it disappointingly empty of his warmth. She clutched the sheets to her now exposed body, cold without the furnace-heat of his arms, which she had fallen asleep in.

Since the night of the masquerade, Darius had flaunted their relationship openly—an action that had not gone unnoticed or unremarked upon at court. But in his absence, she'd been unable to adjust to the funereal surroundings, the sense that she was sitting in the mouth of an old tomb.

Even his bed was like a sepulchre—built into an alcove and dressed with heavy drapes of velvet, bordered with dark polished wood and grotesques hacked into the frame. Permeating the room was a heavy incense that smelled subtly of myrrh and the residue left on your hands from touching autumn leaves.

A creak at the door stopped her pulse, and she turned with a whirlwind of curls to find that, instead of Serafina, the infiltrator slinking into bed was Darius himself.

"Hey now," he said, wrapping his arms around her and pressing a kiss to her shoulder. "What's gotten you so alert?"

Laila relaxed into his embrace and leaned her head on his chest. She didn't realise how much she longed for his presence to feel secure. "Nothing. Where did you go?"

He pressed another kiss to the corner of her neck. "To speak with my mother."

Laila grimaced. "I don't like that you're keeping her here."

"We struck an agreement that you would no longer be harmed by her. And I'll ensure she'll respect it."

"Still..."

"Laila, trust me," Darius said. "She claims she desires to be closer to me out of some... maternal obligation. I don't believe it for a moment, but sometimes it's better to keep a dangerous opponent right under your nose. Your safety will always be of the utmost priority. I promise."

Laila huffed in response, uneasy, but his words provided a soothing balm.

Sensing her disgruntlement, he attempted to counter it. "I want to take you somewhere today. Somewhere nice."

"Where?" Laila eyed him in suspicion.

"It's a secret." He smirked against her neck as his lips trailed up the long column of it.

She didn't trust that look on his face no matter how nice his kisses felt. She brought him up to look at her, palming his cheek. "Don't I deserve a little hint?"

His smile only grew more sly.

"Well now you're making me alarmed."

He chuckled, leaning in to kiss her. "It's nothing wicked, I promise. Just wait for it. It'll be worth the suspense."

The morning bestowed her with a rejuvenated purpose as a maid arrived to deliver her mail. Laila sat at her rosewood writing desk and broke the wax seal to find mostly positive correspondence in response to her ball. Then she checked the total sums received from the auction.

"What is it, madame?" Marta asked as she caught sight of Laila's stunned face.

"Well, we received a number of generous donations during the auction, my mother included. I'm certain we can consider this a roaring success!" Laila said as she sorted her letters into a pile. "Were there any other messages?"

"Delanus Levitis wishes to schedule a meeting," Marta said. "I can get him to come by this afternoon if you'd like."

"Make it a brunch appointment. I'd rather get that out of the way." Laila sighed, feeling a twitch of dread in her stomach. "I shall have to wear something... decorous. My blue silk dress should do. The one with the blonde lace."

Marta assisted her in picking out the appropriate frock and sent a servant to relay the message to Delanus, as well as to the kitchen to prepare a menu of her choosing. Laila opted to leave her hair loose in wheat-gold spirals, half pinned back by the ivory hair comb Darius gifted to her during her stay.

"Well, how do I look?" she asks, doing a slow turn to ensure she got the best of each view.

"Like a princess," Marta replied.

"That's the idea." Laila smiled in amusement, always seeking her reflection in the mirror of others' sensory acknowledgement of her. Every detail of her appearance was meticulous in choice, so that through every look of desire and scowl of jealousy, she could combat the feeling she was not quite real.

Hearing a knock at the door, she pivoted quickly before turning back. "Wish me luck."

She bid the knocker enter, and a servant escorted Delanus Levitis into her quarters.

"Thank you for agreeing to see me, Your Radiance," he said while unclipping the brooch securing his cloak at the shoulders. The engraving of his family crest glinted in her field of vision, some form of sea monster with a long pit of a mouth.

"It is not a problem at all, Prime Delanus," Laila said, bright and peppy, with buoyancy in her step. "Please make yourself comfortable. We have plenty of lunch for two."

Delanus paused with his cloak neatly slung and smoothed over his forearm. "That wasn't necessary."

"Nonsense," she admonished, but her tone was whimsical, paired with a swish of her hand. "You don't think I'd let you talk on an empty stomach, do you?"

Delanus remained cautious and uncertain, not losing his harried expression until a servant came and had to practically wrestle his outerwear away. "I didn't mean for this to be more than a quick visit."

"Oh, come now," Laila insisted. "You'll make me feel simply rotten eating alone. It's about time we talk since the... incident."

She could see this has the intended effect, as he shifted even more uncomfortably and his chest deflated. "I suppose it wouldn't hurt."

Her smile beamed bright enough to scald.

"Excellent," she said, pirouetting into the room, where the table had already been set for two. White bobbin lace shawled the mahogany, with a fragrant rose runner reclining across the middle, tumbling petals across the ornate rug. She had used her own gold-rimmed porcelain with a scalloped edge and a chiselled frieze of plump-cheeked starlets set in the lip.

"Please sit," she said, drawing out a seat for him.

Suspended beneath glass domes was the first course: a strawberry gazpacho garnished with cornflowers, served with fresh steaming flatbread garnished with rosemary. Sliced bread was folded neatly in a handwoven basket with a small bowl of olive oil for dip.

Delanus did as she said and reached for the folded napkin, fanning it out and tucking it within his collar.

"Well, I don't know about you, but I am starving." Laila slid into her seat and spread her napkin across her lap. "Can I offer you something to drink? I have rose cordial at hand, but I do know how you occassi like that fancy wine from rotted grapes so I have plenty of it stocked up, if that's what your palate desires."

He piped up a little too eagerly. "I'll take the graviji wine, if you'd please."

She turned to the servants applying the finishing touches to the table. "You heard the fellow, and it'll be cordial for me, thank you."

She took a demure sip of soup as the sweet cordial tinkled into her glass.

"So if we might return, Your Radiance, to why I am here," Delanus said, setting his glass of wine at the table.

She picked up a slice of warm bread and dipped it in olive oil. "By all means."

"Let us not mince our words," Delanus said, then took a spoonful of soup—for politeness or courage, she could not yet tell. "I'd like to ask that you stop bedding the rex."

Her piece of bread paused before its journey's end, and she let herself take a bite to stall for thought. She hadn't expected him to be so direct, but she could see this was simply the way of the country. "I'm afraid what I do with my spare time isn't any of your business, Prime Delanus."

"Now on that, you are incorrect." He sounded irritable as he pinched the bridge of his nose and took a long drink. "If what you are doing in your spare time puts my country at risk, then it happens to be very much my business."

The suggestion within those words sent a ripple of dread through her. Several unwanted scenarios flashed through her mind about how he was willing to enforce this request, instead she decided to settle for pridefulness.

"With all due respect, Prime Delanus, if me sleeping with the rex is enough to destabilise your nation, then I fear it may have far greater issues to contend with."

"And Darius Rex is in the midst of sorting them. Hence he can't afford any diversions from his goals. He is the most logical person I have ever known, and yet when it comes to you, he appears to cease on that. Now he is all but cohabiting with a solarite. You cannot imagine how this looks."

Her fingers bristled with static. She suppressed it by clutching the handle of her spoon and soothing the swell in her throat with soup. "I don't see what this has to do with me."

"It has everything to do with you. Before you, Darius was somewhat sensible about how to maintain his position here, which has been a delicate thing since his father was overthrown. He needs to secure his line and produce an heir for the nation. A full-blooded occasso. You can offer him neither of these things."

She dropped her spoon. "I may not be a fitting candidate for the much-desired role of broodmare, but it appears that hasn't stopped him from desiring me."

Delanus's expression settled into one of cautious resignation. "No, it hasn't. Hence the problem."

Now she was furious and insulted. A surge of power sparked at her fingertips. She closed her hands into fists. "And suppose I reject your request? What then?"

He shifted a little in his seat, crossing his legs, curling his fingers. She wondered how much effort it was taking him not to reveal his fangs, to succumb to his ancestral plea to dominate and threaten. Such was the nature of the beast, the master of the food chain.

"Your Radiance." Delanus exhaled with an exasperated chuckle as the capillaries in his eyes began to blacken. He ran a hand down to his chin. "I was hoping you wouldn't make this difficult."

But she was numb and impassive, a carved glass figurine. Delanus found himself wanting to seize her and shake her—put a scuff on that perfect composure.

"Perhaps you and I can come to some other arrangement." A lecherous scrawl of a smirk came as Delanus reached for her knee. "Darius always seemed idiotically happy after a night in your presence. You ought to let me have a dip between your thighs and see if I'll become a fool too."

Laila primly clipped her knees together and secreted her disgust behind a smile, unwilling to let him get a rise out of her like he intended. "I think the rex might have some objections."

"Well, you wouldn't be the first lover we've shared."

That had given her pause, a weakness he was quick to scent.

"Ah, you didn't know about that, did you? Our history? Yes, I've had quite a bit of him myself in the past. It's how he lures you. Keeps you enthralled. I'm afraid you're just another in a long line of pretty butterflies he's seduced into his net." His sneer grew pronounced, a drop of pure venom clinging to the edge of his words. "You think you're special? I can assure you, you're not. He'll have you believe you're the sole subject of his fascination for a time—he always does. But once the novelty has passed and he finds another whose utility surpasses your own... well. Then you'll be pinned to a mount and shoved in a drawer with the rest of us."

His words shook her confidence, but she refused to let on how much, choosing instead to steer the direction of the conversation to something more her speed. "We're not on opposing sides, you and I, Delanus. I am probably one of the only true allies that you have in Soleterea. I have invested a lot of my time and energy to keep you all in the good graces of my mother and advocate on your behalf. Brokering treaties, speaking up on your immigration grievances, sending you aid throughout your harshest winters. Part of that is out of fondness for Darius, I'll admit, but also out of affection to your land despite how it feels about me in turn. It'd be a shame to squander such a mutually beneficial arrangement."

She lifted another spoonful of soup to her mouth and sipped daintily at the edge, her lashes sweeping low. An innocent display for one not quite so altruistic as she might seem.

"Are you making a threat?" he asked. And there it was, the fine point of a canine poised to descend. Not that she could blame him too much.

After all, she knew what came of backing a feral animal into a corner, but she didn't arrive without an arsenal.

"Not a threat, no," she said, and she polished it with a smile. "Just a... polite suggestion."

He leaned back in his chair. "You know, for a moment I thought the rumours about you were true and you were nothing more than a feather-headed socialite," he said. "It appears I was wrong."

"Stay for the entree, won't you?" Her chilled veneer unsheathed as the roseate warmth returned to her voice. If he was going to challenge her, let it be under full illumination of what he was taking on.

He grunted, a beast humbled, and took up his soup spoon. "Of course."

They dined on doves in hibiscus sauce, presented on a bed of couscous and toasted pistachios. For dessert, there was a sweet pastry of candied raspberries, white chocolate, and flakes of gold leaf filled with rosewater mousse.

A light summer meal for the one who emitted the season—who would thaw through the ancient permafrost of tradition with her scorching equatorial heart.

From the shores of his black sand beach, Laila and Darius took a boat out onto the pale waters, bringing with them cherry wine and midsummer fruit dipped in white chocolate, which they took turns feeding each other as Darius rowed.

Laila leaned back against the myriad of cushions, a bouncing cascade of ribbon curls against her shoulders. The ocean air was smooth and saline, the glum sky cotton-soft with overcast until streaks of pure sunlight bled through the gauze of clouds and struck her glittering skin. She was radiant as always; she had never not been.

When he had rowed them out far enough, Darius paused and helped himself to a drink of wine. "We should hear back from my chimera soon and learn if she was successful in her mission."

Laila deliberated on this as she stuck out her hand and let her fingers skate across the water. "Let's hope it's good news." She moved forward and framed the hollow crevice of his cheek with a hand, and then sought the other. "How are you feeling?"

"Resolute, mostly. To be perfectly honest, I just want this over with." He took her by her hips and pulled her to lie on his chest. "And you?"

"I don't know how I feel about seeing him again but... I don't think Dominus should die. I didn't then, and I don't now. Like you, I want this to be over with. No more violence. No more conflict. No more death."

Her sweet perfume intermingled with the warmth of her body, and Darius could think of no place he'd rather expire than this one.

"Death is for lesser creatures, Laila, not for us," he assured her, sealing it with a kiss pressed to her forehead. "What else is troubling you? You've been quiet on the entire journey here."

She withdrew from him and moved to sit back on the other end of the boat. "I was paid a visit by Delanus today. He seemed to be under the impression he could threaten me to stay away from you."

He exhaled in irritation and traced his fingers down the bridge of his nose. "I'm sorry he did that."

"You should be. It was *humiliating*. Not to mention ineffective. Tell me, just how many of your old lovers will attempt to intimidate me?"

"He will not do something like that again, you have my word," he said, taking a buoyant curl from her abundant mane and tracing his thumb over the soft, feathered texture. "I can kill him if you want me to."

She knew he would do it if she asked it of him. He would be the hunter with the bloody maw dragging his fresh catch between his teeth. He would be the woodcutter with the rusted axe ready to fell forests to feed her fire.

There was a little self-satisfied twitch in her lips she was quick to mask as she gave an inquisitive tilt of her head. "Wouldn't that be an awful inconvenience?"

"Delanus is replaceable," he said with a shrug. "It is not a contest as to which of you I value more, Laila."

She gave him a look soft-edged with intimacy before she shook her head. "No, I think Delanus and I have come to an understanding. The last thing I need in this country is more enemies."

"As you wish," he granted, lowering his hand to her shoulder. "But he will still require punishment. I can't have anyone else in the ranks thinking they can treat you with anything but the respect you deserve."

Her spine prickled in remembrance of his earlier words when he had promised her that he would destroy anyone who got between them. It didn't scare her or disgust her the way she felt it should. The relentless torch of his affections and the monstrous devotion that inflamed it. She'd be dead in this country several times over without it. Perhaps that made her something of a monster too.

Singing beckoned in the distance, the eerie and enigmatic vocals of a siren. It snuck upon Darius's shoulders with insidious allure and evoked a chill on his neck that seeped down to his spine. "It's started."

Laila sat up so suddenly that the boat swerved.

He steadied it with ease, a rise of laughter warming his chest as he watched her, eyes shining with intrigue when the first cluster of sirens swooped near them.

They circulated in elegant formation, their wings and scales bioluminescent with fluctuations of colour, unified in a harmony that was as devastatingly beautiful as it was cruel. For this was their mating call, the song they sang to lure the travel-wearied sailor to his early grave. Even now Darius could feel the inescapable tug of it, surpassed only by his fixation on Laila's unearthly joy.

"Oh, it's beautiful," she sighed with longing, head coming to rest against her arms on the edge of the boat.

"There's nothing quite like it," he said, saluting to her with his wine glass. "I'm glad I was able to show it to you before the season's end."

He watched the sunlight filter through the clouds, ordaining her with its halo, and something stirred in him, more refined than carnal hunger: true *aspiration*.

An ideal to reach for.

He saw in her a freedom he couldn't embody. So close to him he could almost grasp it. The freedom to be benevolent, gentle, *incorruptible*. How thirstily he scuttled to the sweetness of this newborn blossom at the cusp of spring. For if he could have no absolution, never feel the cleansing waters of redemption purify him of the centuries of blood caked beneath his fingernails, then at least he could have this—a guiding light in the sunless forest of his depraved mind.

"I want you to marry me."

How quickly her smile froze on her lips in surprise. "What?"

He realised the severity of his words once he'd said them, but he couldn't bring himself to pull back. "I once offered you a country and a crown. That offer still holds if you'd take it."

She paused, but there was a small glint of a challenge in her eyes. "Regina is a large step down from impératrice."

"Then why stop there? Let us be insatiable gluttons who will unite a realm in our vision. Together we could be unconquerable. If you choose to be by my side now, I cannot promise that it will be without trial or dissent. Only that I will love you as much as it is possible for something like me to love, that I will shelter and support you, that I will fight and kill for you. Always and everlasting." He took her hands and bowed his head, as though it were the most natural position he could take. Let him be the first of the land she conquered. Let her pitch her flag on the arch of his spine. "Do you accept?"

She thought of every trial they'd faced together thus far and knew, whatever path she took, there was not a single one she'd want to walk without his constancy at her side. As long as he was near, nothing seemed insurmountable. Not even the doubts plaguing her heart. "I accept."

He united their mouths as behind them the sun was consumed by a cloud, leaving them cross-hatched in light and shadow.

"We shall have to tell my mother, someday," Laila mentioned as they travelled back towards his quarters through the Portrait Hall. She had her arm slung through his elbow, and as they walked, he stole a glance at the empty space across from his likeness, the place where her own portrait would soon hang.

"Don't suppose you might... soften her up before the news?"

Laila slowed to a pause. "You're not afraid of my mother, are you, Darius?"

"Afraid? No," he said with a soft chuckle. "Petrified? Only a little bit."

She laughed before leaning in to kiss him. "Don't worry, we'll just tell her she'll be the impératrice of six realms rather than five. That ought to soften the blow of our marriage."

"Well now, isn't that something?" came Katerina's soft, mocking croon as she obstructed the doorway to his quarters. "I suppose congratulations are in order." She moved forward, the shadow she cast long and relentless.

"You," Laila seethed.

"Stay away from her," Darius said, a snarl in his voice and venom on his fangs. "Your presence is not wanted."

Katerina tutted in disapproval. "Now, now, I'm just here on behalf of your mother. She's been missed back at the Widowlands."

"By all means, take her," Laila retorted.

"Laila." Darius stepped in front of her as if to shield the delicacy of her light. "If you don't mind, I would like to speak with Katerina alone." He could see that her face was set for arguing so he was quick to add, "We'll talk later, I promise."

Laila huffed angrily, but she nodded as she looked to Katerina with a simmering rage.

"As you wish." She leaned in to seize his lips for an extended kiss before she looked at Katerina, the possession infused in the gesture clear. Then she clicked away in her court heels and closed the door with a whiny groan behind her.

Darius blurred towards Katerina too fast for her to comprehend, slamming her body against the wall with a crack. "Give me one good reason," he taunted as he gripped her chin, "why I shouldn't slay you where you stand?"

"Aw," Katerina pouted. "Don't tell me you're still harbouring a grudge? Just think, if it weren't for me, you two might have continued dancing around each other for a century!"

Darius snarled as he wrestled the urge to rip her heart out. If only to prove she had one.

Katerina arched towards him with a croon of appreciation, egging him to go further. "I guess it's true what they say. Occassi will tell you they aren't the marrying sort for decades and then snap up a bride in under six months."

"Please." Darius rolled his eyes. "You never wanted to be regina."

"Perhaps not." Katerina pushed herself further to ghost her lips against his. "I did rather like our arrangement. Still, it would've been nice to be offered."

Darius tugged away from her. "What's this about, Katerina?"

"We had a *deal*, Darius. And you're letting her ruin everything. Do whatever you wish with the kingdom, but allow the Vidua Nocte to remain untouched. This ætherglass? You know what will happen if blood magic loses its hold. The moment that shield slips, the landmasters will hunt us for sport." Katerina lifted a hand to strike him, but Darius caught her wrist.

"Raise your hand to me again, and I'll break it." His eyes smouldered in warning. "If you do what I ask, then I will make the Vidua Nocte a protected class, enshrined into law. There will be no hunt. No mass slaughter. But I'm going to need something from you."

Katerina's shoulders sagged from the departure of her pride, and she kept her eyes downcast to avoid facing him and the defeat she'd suffered, wondering when the scales had tipped to her needing approval from *him*. "Such as?"

"Perform the heartless ritual."

"That's Serafina's spell and you know it. And you knew better than to ask *her*."

"Perhaps I will, then." Darius cast her a cold smile as he heard footsteps approach. "Hello, Mother."

Serafina prowled into the room and propped a hand on her hip. "I can see I've been summoned."

"Serafina..." Katerina's entire body sagged with relief. "Thank Calante, you're safe. We worried he was—"

"Harming me?" Serafina's lips lifted in one corner. "And you thought you'd come to plead on my behalf? You never beg an occasso for mercy. I taught you better than that." Her attention turned to Darius. "I heard about your betrothal through the wall. Congratulations. Though not my first choice for a daughter-in-law."

It shouldn't have struck him so hard that she might comment on his choice of bride, as though she had any right to. "I'd prefer if you'd refrain from making comments where my betrothed is concerned."

"Why? Are you concerned I might offer you advice that you might actually listen to?"

"I have no interest in your advice. I'm not my father."

"Well clearly against all odds you are, Darius. I won't lie—you are in many respects his better, but you have his same hubris and the same utterly aggravating habit of being led astray by the whims of your cockhead." Serafina narrowed her eyes at him. "Choosing not to marry an occassella, as much as I may despise the institution, is inadvisable, and walking out in public with a solarite on your arm is all but advertising to your country where your priorities lie. And that it is not with them."

"You *dare* lecture me about priorities when you saw fit to walk out on yours on a mere whim? Where were your feelings of duty when you cast me aside, when you tried to murder me for the sake of appeasing your mistresses in the Vidua Nocte? When you turned your back to my father when he asked for your hand?" Darius had to balk at her audacity, pacing from side to side. "Marriage and queenship were never good enough for you, but you'd still wish for me to bind myself to someone I do not care for and sire sons from her."

"I do not pretend to like the system, but unless you intend to change it or cheat it then this is simply what it is, Darius. And if the alternative is allowing Soleterea greater gains over controlling us, then I cannot in all honesty say I approve of that. I do not trust those creatures, nor that their intentions are honest and true. For all they claim to represent the light, they had no trouble going under the cloak of darkness to rid themselves of your father."

"Then I will learn from my father, by taking his tactics and making them better." Darius put his hand absently over the dark drum in his chest and felt the steady rhythm of all his frailty. He heard the leer of his father's mockery in his ear telling him he couldn't have it all. Not the foreign bride and the peace of his kingdom both at once. The demand for a Calantis heir would make it so he would need to shoulder the survival of his line alone. For that, he would need to be better than strong. He would need to be invulnerable. "You did the ritual once before to make him heartless so that he might be shielded eternally from true death. Do the same for me, and I will not make the mistake that he did. Heartless, I will be unstoppable by both the kingdom *and* Soleterea."

Serafina's jaw twitched in disapproval. "You don't even see that you are already making a mistake. Completing that ritual for him was the worst thing I ever did. It was completely reckless. You were too young to understand what losing his heart did to your father, Darius, how it ruined him irreparably. I cannot do the same to you. I refuse to."

His back tightened at the challenge. "I could *make* you."

She held the intensity of his gaze and the threat therein with ease. "What more could you do to me that hasn't been done already? Many rexes before you have tried to triumph over us and failed."

His upper lip peeled back into a snarl as he turned his back. "Then you all can rot."

"Darius—" Katerina lunged for him before being halted by Serafina's hand.

"Don't." Serafina took her hand and laced their fingers together to lead her away. "This discussion is not over, Darius. I hope you know that."

Darius suppressed the pang of envy as he observed their tenderness. "You know, you were wrong before. You ripped my father's heart out long before you completed the ritual, and he never stopped punishing me for it."

325

XXIII

PEALS OF LAILA'S LAUGHTER CAME SOFT AND BEGUILING to Dominus's ears, before his vision refocused to see the glint of her hair beneath the moonlight.

"Come on, don't tell me that the big bad occasso is afraid of a little water," she teased, releasing another peal of laughter that echoed against the face of the cliffs surrounding them.

"I'm not afraid," Dominus said vehemently. "I'm just—not fond."

She quirked a brow in that way she often did when she was daring you to live up to her expectations. Then she stood and began, unabashedly, to shed her clothes—piles of filmy silk and gossamer undergarments sailing through the humid air until she was bare beneath the pearl sheen of moonlight.

He watched her run towards the ocean, her golden brown body

vanishing between swathes of black velvet. He could still see the puddle of her sunlit glow in the sea.

"Come on in! A little water isn't going to kill you," she urged once resurfaced, head cocked in invitation. She was an ethereal blur of watercolour: hair plastered down to her neck, skin iridescent with saltwater. She looked like she belonged to the sea.

Dominus recalled times at the Citadel as a boy, in the last moments he was allowed to be. Before his innocence was shredded away from him like skin before a lupari's claws. He remembered morning swimming drills by the river, where the cubs would run fast as their older counterparts scrambled to catch them, throwing them headfirst into the deepest water and waiting to see who resurfaced.

Among the runners, he'd been one of the best, like he'd been among the best at everything. As though he could allow himself to be anything less. But even he was caught and tossed, plunged into the deep pit of the water.

He'd done nothing to struggle for several seconds, allowing his muscles and mind to go still. Pinned beneath the high pressure of the river water, all manner of thought leaked through his ears, leaving him just aware enough of the rushing current and the immediacy of his own breathing. Strangely, it was the last time he could ever recall feeling truly at peace.

He kicked off his boots, sliding his cloak down the steep slant of his mountainous shoulders. Then he shed his clothes, arranging them in neat piles against the discarded trail of Laila's clothes, and stalked towards the ocean unhurried, making large treads in the water until the crown of his head was completely submerged. He stood for what seemed like an age with his eyes wired shut, his mind swiped blank of anything but the trail of air bubbles he released through his nostrils.

He remained for the duration of his exhale before allowing his slow rise to the surface.

When he inhaled again it was followed by a spurt of water from his lungs which he emptied onto the ground. He could tell instantly he was in Soleterea from the mere scent of the wildflowers, the mystical blue-green hue of pellucid lake water. This became further reinforced by the feverish heat and the musical composition of cicadas.

He hauled himself onto the plush blanket of grass and closed his eyes with a groan. Against all odds, he had finally made it where he needed to be. His mission could continue. He dislocated his hand bones to free himself from his shackles before using his claws to saw off his muzzle.

Peering up at the sky, he let the sun burn through the thin layer of his eyelids and send his mind spiralling back into the overheated confines of a laboratory. There, the floors glistened with glass confetti, the disembodied pages of books fluttered like the dying corpses of butterflies, and a hand with streaked fingers was printed in blood against a gurgling glass tank.

Dominus's fangs were brandished in the reflection of the glass as he lunged for the solarite with pearl-blonde corkscrew curls, her serenely smiling face aglow with mirth. He could not remember her name now. But her face still filled him with the same blood-curdling odium as before. That was what he knew he had to focus on. The hatred. It eroded him inside out, numbing the nerve endings to any other emotion that might take its place.

He used that apathy to cast off the mental anchor of his pain and peel himself up from the grass. The solarites had taken so much from him now. Too much. He would see them pay for it. Even if it was the last action he ever took.

Oh, how Amira loathed these events!

Her lips stretched taut as she lounged beneath her parasol, watching newly blossomed starlet debutantes toddle their first steps into solaritehood. The debutante season always required Amira to make an appearance at—and even host—several social events, where dynasties paraded their daughters before le beau monde to foster alliances, learn the political landscape, or ingratiate themselves to academy representatives to further broaden their girl's horizons.

That Amira found it so migraine-inducing was likely half the reason why she'd limited herself to only one daughter. Usually it would be Laila whom she would assign to these activities on her behalf. Alas, since she'd all but banished her daughter to the far reaches of the north, Amira now had to contend with her duties catching up to her.

She took a light sip of rose lemonade as she glanced about her surroundings. The Annual Summer Picnic in Aurea Park had seen lovely weather this year at least, and having their food and drink delivered to them via miniature hot air balloons was rather convenient.

Amira summoned one such balloon with her aether to help herself to a cherry pie as her kin braided their hair with wildflowers, drank rose lemonade on their gingham blankets, and picked from the fairy-floss trees.

Everything was idyllic. Everything was utterly tedious!

What Amira wouldn't give for a touch of excitement to this event. Unfortunately for her, the thought came too soon. Sliding underneath her parasol to join her was none other than Lucrèce Mielette, a glass of nectar wine fizzling with fairy-floss in her hand.

"Why, Lucrèce!" Amira exclaimed in astonishment. "This *is* a surprise. For what do we owe the honour of you gracing us mere Soletereans with your presence?"

Lucrèce smirked into her glass, her pearl-white braids tinkled with gold bells. "Odaka is charming, but its charm can wear thin after a time.

I'm here to see little Luna make her grand debut." She jutted her chin towards her starlet granddaughter, who was schmoozing along with Hélène. "Speaking of family, how is our princess? I couldn't make it to this year's bal masqué, but I hear it was a roaring success."

"Yes, indeed," Amira asserted in pride. "Everyone keeps telling me what a wondrous time they had. Oh, you really should've been there."

"I'm surprised those occassi beasts composed themselves well enough, but it seems the event went off without a hitch. Our Laila seems to be having quite the positive influence already..."

"Certainly I've had my doubts, but the most recent rex installed, Darius Calantis, has been much more amenable to reason and debate than his predecessor." Amira concealed her triumphant smile as she drank her lemonade. "I am certain we'll see a turn in public opinion when it comes to them. Oh, there'll be setbacks—there always are—but the path to progress is clear, and with the Rose dynasty remaining at the helm we'll see more from them yet."

Lucrèce clicked her tongue. "Positioning your dynasty as the only ones capable of reining the beasts in... Well played, Amira. I must commend you. Truly. That might be *almost* as effective as what I have up my sleeve."

Amira bristled in annoyance. "And what is that?"

"Ah, now that would be telling, Your Luminosity." Lucrèce's cerulean eyes sparkled with mischief. "I must excuse myself, I believe I hear my family calling for me. Wonderful to chat with you, madame."

With that, the solarite blurred her way towards her relatives and left Amira with her lips pursed in vexation. She smothered her flare of temper with another drink, savouring the residue on her lips. Madhali, her magistress of defence, had still not been able to uncover what it was Lucrèce had been planning, and with Dominus remaining on the loose she knew she shouldn't declare her victories too soon. If only she could know where Dominus was...

⤬

Dominus trudged through the streets of Le Creissant as the sights long buried in his subconscious flitted ephemerally into view: the storefronts infested with wisteria and honeysuckle, the scent of fresh bread, the picturesque pediments and animated friezes, the mesmerising newspaper stands with their moving images.

He passed all this and more, oozing from shadow to shadow, relentlessly stalking the scent on his nostrils until he encountered what he sought. The aroma of a solarite would never leave his nose—that charged, faintly metallic impression, warm and electrifying like the scent of air before a storm. Even a mere whiff left a tingle in his fingertips.

A most tuneful melody floated through his ears when he turned the corner. Laughter and chatter interspersed with the squeal of running starlets as they clutched their straw hats and a fistful of skirts. The scene caused his jaw to clench as he sank deeper into the black miasma of hate surrounding him. He allowed the hate to fuel him, flow through him, fill him up to bursting.

It wasn't often that occassi would use their own negative emotion to invigorate themselves, as it caused one's chaos to self-cannibalise to allow the emotion to enlarge. The results were incomparable, but it was akin to forging an explosive of oneself.

However, Dominus was too far gone to be able to reason with such dire consequences. For with each breath he inhaled, sheer spite was exuding out to such an extent that the flowers around him wilted and the birds took flight in a panic. These radiant emissions were so forceful that they soon caught the notice of a few patrolling sprites as Dominus marched forward, uncaring to disguise himself further.

Upon seeing the notorious target, they wasted little time rushing forward to apprehend him.

"Halt! Occasso! I demand you halt!"

Their demands went unheard as Dominus continued walking forward, merely offering a look of searing disdain.

"*Choke*," he commanded in an ancient, forbidden tongue.

The sprites retched on their words, hands enclosing around their throats as they wheezed for air. Their veins blackened and protruded in calligraphic figures before they yielded to the lack of oxygen and collapsed onto the street.

Dominus stepped over the flimsy mass of doll limbs and crossed the threshold into the park. The commotion was now noticeable enough that even a few solarites halted in their cosy nooks beneath their parasols, the starlets freezing mid-chase, as all consciousness in the area found a new body to orbit.

He saw himself in the reflection of their vision: the blacked-out eyes and their demoniacal green glow. His dark clothes now soaked through with the tar of his loathing, saturating him to abyssal black.

He didn't give them a moment to wield aether in defence before he unlatched his jaw and released a spew of noxious black smog that flooded the park in an oppressive surge.

"Come on! Come on! *Move it*," Lyra huffed under her breath as she poked her head out of the window.

The aeromobiles surrounding her own chauffeured vehicle had been unmoving for what seemed like hours now, and she had little time to waste. She couldn't fathom how much had been lost in the search for Dominus, and knowing they'd crossed into Soleterea shortly before losing him, she feared for the safety of her sovereign.

"Ugh! Forget it. I'll walk," Lyra snarled, opening the door to the aeromobile and dropping onto the street. She reached above her head to shut it after her before she started walking, then pacing, then running.

While she had never paid much mind to the social calendar, she was at least aware of it enough to know today was the Annual Picnic. She took a shortcut through an alleyway towards Aurea Park, thinking of the time she and Laila had gotten drunk and stumbled through the streets in moonlit laughter.

She dispensed with her thoughts as soon as she saw the plumes of smoke trailing upwards in the distance. Her heart seized.

"No," she whispered.

She pushed past the crowd gathering around the park with grunted orders until she uncovered the cause. The park was buried beneath a tenebrous woollen cloud. She could hear blood roaring in her ears as she staggered forward and fell to her knees, too stunned for words or sobs.

She was too late. She had *failed*. Chaos had vanquished her that day.

XXIV

SINCE THE BAL MASQUÉ, THE ENFORCERS HAD BEEN whispering about Serafina Blackwood's arrival. There was no refuge or reprieve anyone could seek from it. It rippled to all corners, eclipsing the rex's inner circle of trusted advisers to even reach the more talkative of courtiers.

The repetitive subject intrigued Sabina, especially when she had never been in the presence of a blood sorceress before. Hence, when a servant arrived to inform her that the rex had requested she join him and his mother for breakfast, she couldn't quicken her pace enough.

She made her way through the enigmatic passage to the royal apartments, where she was greeted by a servant opening the double oak doors of the upper chambers.

Serafina Blackwood and Darius sat on opposing ends of the table.

They looked so imposing together it relaxed the joints in one's knees through sheer terror alone.

The table wedged in between them was set with tea, nettle bread, water infused with dandelions, and silver trays stacked full of little tarts filled with butter and preserves.

Sabina neared an empty seat at the table and bowed her head. "Good morning, Your Majesty."

"Good morning, Sabina," Darius replied.

"So this is she, then, I'm assuming?" Serafina asked. Her voice was low and dulcet like the sweet honey spread she smoothed onto her slice of black bread. "My keeper?"

"Mother, this is Sabina Vernostia Levitia." Darius gestured towards his enforcer. "Sabina, this is my mother, Serafina Blackwood."

"It is an honour, Serafina Blackwood."

"An *honour*," Serafina exclaimed as her oxblood lips arranged themselves into a smile that pronounced her dimples. Such an endearing feature for a face otherwise ferocious in its beauty. "It's been a long time since anyone has ever considered me in such high regard."

"Sabina is who I shall entrust to keep watch of you while you're in the Citadel." Darius took a sip of tea. "Make sure you stay out of trouble."

Serafina hummed in interest, glancing Sabina up and down. "You don't often see an occassella prove herself to reach the ranks of an officer. You'll have to tell me all about the First Rite someday. I'm ever so curious."

"Tell you what." Sabina lounged lazily in her chair. "I'll tell you everything you want to know if you spill your secrets about blood magic."

Serafina cackled. "It's doubtless you've heard many tales about us, what we do."

Such tales were wide and varied, depending upon the source. To matriarchs, they were little more than bloodthirsty harridans who brainwashed the feeble minds of occasselle youth. Forcing them to abandon the true and proper course of marriage and motherhood to sacrifice the unborn under the waxing moon and bathe in their bloodshed.

To the church, they were runaway brides and exiled daughters who, in their banishment, came to be stewards of the only ever-fertile sliver of land in the country. Through dutiful ritual, they deposited fresh crops and animal products to the markets daily. In both cases, they were seen as a nuisance, a dangerously corruptive force to the established order and shunned by many as a result.

"Only that you kill occassi males," Sabina said, drinking from a glass of dandelion water. "Do you kill occassi males?"

Serafina's face degraded into something perfectly wicked before she glanced at Darius, as though almost seeking approval.

"She gave it her best to be rid of me," he revealed, and his own cheekbones sharpened like the points of daggers when he smiled. "Guess I'm a stubborn old thing."

"And look at you now," Serafina said, something of a simulated maternal pride in her voice.

"Before I send you both off"—Darius set down a cup of tea—"if I might have a word, Mother."

Sabina took the initiative and made herself scarce, clasping the brass knob to close the door all but for a tiny fragment of an inch.

It was Serafina who spoke next. "I must ask: You're not still serious about what we earlier discussed?" The treacly drawl of her voice was unmistakable.

"I am."

"Darius—"

"Since you've been so desperate to trick your way past the Citadel gates again, you could at least be of use to me."

"You are stubborn, Darius." Serafina's chair legs scraped and cutlery rustled as she reached over the table for her son. "I must ask you to reconsider—"

He massaged his temples with a grunt. "I still don't see why we can't just go forth and do it."

"It has consequences, Darius. It always has. And I will not risk putting myself in jeopardy again by repeating it."

He tensed in aggravation, dragging a hand down his face. "There has to be some way for you to perform the ritual without me having to sacrifice my sanity and my ability to feel—"

"You mean your ability to love her?" Serafina interjected, her smile mocking.

His throat clenched in response. No elaboration was necessary.

"I only ever performed the ritual once. It's possible that it could do with some refining. However, I am unable to do much without having someone I might examine the effects on first—"

"You mean if I had test subjects?"

She furrowed her brow in response. Her expression was an impartial mask of contemplation being slowly nibbled away by unease. "What are you thinking, Darius? Yes, it would certainly help, but I can't imagine many people willingly signing up for this."

He responded with a smile nothing short of ferocious. "Who said anything about being willing?"

For a while they stared at each other, bodies tensed at this revelation.

"And if I refuse?"

"Then I suppose you won't mind if I leave the Vidua Nocte twisting in the wind."

"Careful, Darius. You're forgetting I could make things quite unpleasant for you and your new bride." Serafina glanced around the vicinity. "Where is she, by the by? I can't imagine she approves of your foolish venture?"

"Listen to me very closely." Darius's tone was steely composure but his eyes blazed a fiery blue. "Let this be the last time you imply anything untoward about Laila in my presence. If you so much as glance menacingly in her direction, I won't be the only one who's heartless. Do you understand?"

"You really do love her, don't you?" The revelation caused her to beam in his direction. "You should not have let me know that. Because now I know as long as she exists there is something of you I can touch."

Darius clenched his jaw, unable to refute her words.

A silence stretched thin before Serafina rose from the table, her boots scrunching softly on the antique rug as she made her way towards the door.

Sabina was quick to shuffle out of earshot before Serafina exited into the hallway, her sinuous coils bouncing with wild carnality beneath the cloak of her veil.

"Shall we go?" She gestured for Sabina to lead the way and then followed her through the vaulted passageways to her new dwellings.

"This is to be your room." Sabina twisted the knob to show Serafina into Darius's old quarters.

She snorted at the irony. "Oh, he does think he's funny, my son."

Sabina closed the door behind her. "What were you discussing earlier?"

Serafina approached the bookcases and lifted one of the leatherbound tomes, flicking through it. "If that was something he wanted you to know he would've allowed you to stay in the room."

"Hence I'm asking you."

Serafina closed the book with an audible snap. "A secret for another time, perhaps."

"He mentioned a ritual," Sabina continued. "I kept going over it in my head until I thought... How did the past rex become heartless? It was you, wasn't it?"

Serafina slid her book back onto the shelf. "You are exceedingly, frightfully sharp. I see why my son has taken you under his wing. It pains me that I never reached you first."

"To become a sorceress?"

"I really think you might have taken to it."

Sabina considered that, unsure of whether to be flattered. "How do you do it?"

Serafina strolled over to sit upon the chaise lounge with one knee slung across the other. She snapped her fingers and her athame materialised, landing on her palm with a light slap. The blade was smooth obsidian with an iridescent sheen that glided in vibrant fluctuations of colour when she moved it. "To perform blood magic, one must draw life from where it already exists. This symbol makes a link between my life force and another's, and in completing the ritual I am able to access their power, use it, and sometimes drain it completely from them. It's how we become widows. It's where our name originates from."

Sabina had heard the stories. The widows who trailed away into the night, leaving behind a decaying household, a severed bloodline. They were the worst kind of occasselle, the ones who took life instead of giving it, the ones who decided that their selves superseded society.

"You killed your husband?"

"No." Serafina shook her head. "Fortunately, I managed to avoid the shackles of marriage. Though it cost me. But a father is as much an owner as a husband is. He brands you first, breaks you in, and then hands you off to your new master. I'm sure you understand."

"I do." Perhaps more than she would like to. "What made you decide? To become a widow?"

She took some time to ruminate on the answer. "Do you remember the old wives' tale they used to tell you about barren occasselle? About how they'd tie balls and chains around their ankles and leave them to drown until they became river wraiths? It was always one of my favourites. But what interested me most is what would happen after. See, these creatures wouldn't spend eternity wallowing in the pit of their own neglect and abandonment. They would rise up with vengeance, grabbing any male that dared venture out into the waters and drag them down into oblivion. Well, it's the same principle here. I chose to take the violence inflicted upon me and absorb it, transform myself into an even bigger monstrosity than the one that came before me."

She smiled, and it was a deceptively tender thing.

Darius sat before a chequerboard filled with silver pieces and moved them about in solo play. Chess had always been a favourite game of his father's, and later his too. He had tried to teach Dominus to play several times, but his brother had never had the patience. Through every trying attempt, he would always give up after an hour or so and scatter the board, demanding to go boxing. Once he had even swallowed one of the pieces. His father had given Darius a good hiding that day, one he'd never forgotten, and after that Darius stopped trying.

He picked up his final and favourite piece, the hippogriff, its chiselled beak attentively painted in gold, and ran his thumb over it.

"What are you playing at, Darius?" Delanus burst into the room with golden eyes aglow. "Giving over my daughter to that harlot you call your mother?"

"Calm yourself, Delanus." Darius returned the piece to the board. "Every move I make has its rationale, I assure you."

"Well I certainly would've appreciated being consulted before this!"

"I could return the sentiment, seeing as you saw fit to issue threats to the crown princess."

Delanus tensed in irritation. "I hope you don't expect me to get down on my knees and ask for forgiveness, Darius. I've had concerns about your behaviour for some time now, but I decided to keep it to myself and offer you my guidance, which you've refused. Repeatedly. And now look where we are, with you moving your solarite lover into your rooms as though she is of importance."

Darius responded with a chuckle as he redid a button on his kaftan to keep from the impulse to throttle Delanus. "Yes, I suppose it would be too much to ask for you to concede to your misconduct and admit, for once, you do not know best. But the fact of the matter is Laila is the bride I chose, and you will respect my actions as your leader and lay your personal opinions to one side."

The word *bride* caused Delanus's face to harden. "You know, I waited patiently for you to get yourself back on track, Darius. *This* is where I have to draw the line." He forcefully stabbed his finger towards the floor. "Oh, it's not that I don't understand why you might be drawn to her, Darius. When you've sampled enough of what our country has to offer, it makes sense that you'd develop a taste for something a little more exotic. To have a dalliance is something I am happy to turn a blind eye to, but to *marry* her? To make her your regina? That is inexcusable... and I cannot make sense of it from what I've seen of your actions so far."

Darius turned his head to hide what was undoubtedly the blackening of his eyes. His fangs itched to descend from his gums and sink and sink and sink into Delanus's throat until his sanctimonious mouth could say no more. "Listen to me. Whoever brought Dominus back from the dead is certain to have more motive than pure altruism. What this means is there is a very high chance they are tampering with forces that could threaten us. And there is only one faction who conceivably could have access to that amount of power. Now, isolationism hasn't worked. The world knows of us, and there is no putting that creature back in the bottle. We need a new path forward. My chimeras provide one layer of defence, and I may yet have an idea for another. But our biggest asset is Laila. With her hand, I can join our countries and attempt to normalise us."

"You really believe that's going to work?"

"What choice do we have to prevent more hostility? Further conflict? We cannot continue to exclude ourselves, Delanus. We must bridge the gap."

A knock at the door gave him a new pinpoint on which to focus.

"Come in, Kirill," Darius said.

The servant entered with a silver tray holding a decanter of graviji wine and two brass goblets, which he set neatly on the table.

"Have a drink, Delanus." Darius slid another piece across the board. "I'd like us to toast to my betrothal."

Kirill lifted the stopper and filled two goblets with a noisy gurgle. He held out the glass to Delanus.

Delanus accepted it with a sneer. "I cannot believe this..." He shook his head in scorn. "I thought after your father, it could only go upwards but look what we got in turn, hm? An imbecile who will fling the keys of the kingdom to foreigners so he can continue to stick his cock into one of them. Your father would never have done that. He would've sooner died. Calante willing, he would die again from shame if he saw you now. I had so many reservations when you came into power but I thought... I thought perhaps you just needed some coaxing in the right direction.

But now I see clearly. You're an embarrassment to him and his name! You're an embarrassment to this country!"

"That's it, get it all out." Darius took a lethargic drink of wine. "I'm sure you've been withholding that for decades. It must've been tiresome, toiling under the weight of your martyrdom for so long."

"Someone has to do something to save the drowning wreck that is this country!" Delanus cracked, spilling the yolk of his truth. "Calante only knows that with you at the helm of this ship you'll steer us right into ruin. One might almost think that is your goal. *Poor Darius*, conceived in misfortune and birthed in shame, a creature so unlovable your own mother would rather smother you in childbed than see you nurse at her breast—"

Darius stood suddenly, breathing hard, the chair behind him springing back on its hind legs with a loud clatter.

In his first century, he dug up the grave of a philosopher and cast a black enchantment that would summon his ghost for a lengthy discourse. The philosopher had been prolific in his writings, penning extensive debates on the nature of evil. Darius could still remember the moments when he'd been at the mercy of fickle candlelight in his deerskin hammock at sea, tracing with careful restraint those delicate leaf pages and inhaling words of black-glossed ink, breathless and bewildered.

Something in him broke its seal that night, opening into a voracious hunger for a conclusion he could not hope to seek within the contents of the calfskin tome. Nature versus nurture, that eternal bind—which came first, and was it truly possible for a beast to turn against his own instincts, his own hereditary burden, or was it simply vanity that led them to think they could battle against such cardinal forces and emerge victorious?

He found his answer from the eroded lips of Antonius Volgis, and for a while he wandered, defeated and tormented, left with the knowledge that it was a theory he could only deduce from his own judgement.

Now Darius stood before his second-in-command, who hurled towards him such *vitriol*, and Laila, she would want him to forgive, she would want him to show *clemency*, when everything in him ached to shred the flimsy tissue of Delanus's heart muscle as he begged and gurgled for release.

He pressed forward with all his unfathomable speed, plunged his fist inside the warm viscera of Delanus's chest, and squeezed down on his heart. "You think you know war? You think you know strength? You think you know *survival*? I weathered centuries of domestic warfare with my very own father from the tender age of eleven. I was beaten, maimed, and tortured. And you know what I realised, throughout it all? It's that causing pain, hurting others, that's all easy. Do you want to know what is difficult? *Peace* is difficult. *Mercy* is difficult. Such a tenuous thing it is. Peace. It requires such patience and precision, such a delicacy in the handling of it because every so often little upstarts like you want to disturb it for the sake of satisfying your own narrow-ended means."

Delanus's throat kept making a hollow burbling sound as he lifted his hands and attempted to seal around this artificial orifice, his mouth seeping with black discharge.

"You know, my father, whom you *idolise* so much, never would have shown you the leniency I have. He would've ended your miserable life and then turned his attention towards your wife and your pretty little daughters. But I'll be *fairer* to you, since that's my way, after all. So in the interest of showing mercy, I've decided that I shall put your worthless, mewling existence to use in helping me accomplish what my father could not. Heartlessness with no defect." He withdrew his hand and deposited Delanus to the floor, coughing and wheezing. He took out a folded handkerchief and fluffed it out to wipe his bloodied hand, and then, after dashing it towards him, turned away. "Clean yourself up."

⌒∞⌒

Laila filled the marble pool in Darius's balneum, testing the water to find it pleasantly warm. As the water surged she added a few droplets of her chosen oils: lavender, lemongrass, and marjoram—each chosen for their calming effect on the muscles. After a lingering admiration of her work, she sprinkled in a sachet of dried rose petals, and then she went back into the bedroom.

"Hm, let's see, let's see," Laila said, tapping her lips absently as she checked the vicinity for anything out of place. The oppressive velvet drapes to his room had been drawn and she had carefully orchestrated the scene for a romantic ambience, complete with scented candlelight, heated massage oils, and a bouquet of chocolate-covered strawberries.

She resisted the urge to pluck one of the berries while she waited and climbed onto the bed to tuck her legs beneath her, knees positioned outward, demurely arranging her hands in her lap. Her garment for the evening—or lack thereof—was sheer tulle in pale pink with intricate gold-threaded flower detailing. The rounded collar and ruched capped sleeves were edged with lace frills, and a row of gold buttons descended down the front.

Laila could recall her unbridled delight as she unravelled the silk bow of the pastel pink box and peeled back the layers of tissue paper after days of waiting. Now she waited again, only this time to share her new frock with her chosen recipient. A gift from her to him. She twirled a ringlet of her hair around one finger in impatience before she heard Darius's footsteps in the corridor outside the antechamber, and she quickly rearranged her hands in anticipation.

The footsteps grew as loud as her pulse, and he finally entered the bedroom and found her awaiting him on his bed. His breath caught as his eyes leisurely travelled up her form to meet hers. His cold blue stare was so intense it crystallised her on the spot.

She swallowed thickly, breaking her pose to descend from the bed. "About time you got here, I was beginning to get bored."

He seemed to remember himself as she spoke, and he closed the door behind him. He slid his hands into his pockets, scuffing the floor with his boot.

"What's all this?" he asked, giving a quick glance about the room.

"For you." She gripped the parted folds of his kaftan to bring him close. "I recognise you've been labouring under a lot of pressure. You've been doing so much for me, and I feel I haven't done enough to return the favour. So I wanted to do something nice for you. To help you relax."

It was enough to catch in his throat. How rare it was to be offered such consideration from another. That someone would seek to soothe his ills and unburden him of his troubles was a luxury of love he'd sorely lacked. He didn't know what it meant to have someone want to take care of him.

"Well," he said, smirking to disguise how much the gesture had affected him, "aren't I fortunate?"

She smiled softly as she lifted her hands to his collar and pulled him closer. "First order of business is for you to slip out of those clothes and get into the nice hot bath I've run for you."

Darius seized her hips. "Hm, I think I'd rather you join me."

"Not yet," she laughed, moving his hands away. "Good things come to those who wait."

She slipped his kaftan off from his shoulders and unbuttoned his shirt, gradually peeling him free of every layer.

Darius watched her intently as she did this, making no gesture to move, though his body simmered with desire for it. She left his drawers for last, hooking her thumbs into them when he finally reacted.

"Isn't it enough you've been teasing me without doing this?" he asked, sounding almost pained as she took his drawers off and discovered him already aroused.

"Bath first, then a massage," she said as she pecked him on the lips, her imperious gaze unflinching. "And we'll go from there."

He did as she asked, albeit not without stealing a slightly longer kiss from her first. She couldn't help but swoon a little into him, against herself, before she sent him off with a shove.

She helped herself to a strawberry as she waited for him to finish bathing, dipping the fruit periodically into her glass of sparkling nectar.

He emerged from the balneum in a haze of steam, his russet skin moistened and diamond-studded with droplets. His hair had gone tousled as it dried, revealing the natural bounce of his waves.

"Come here," she said, bringing him over to the bed to push him on top of it. She picked up one of the bottles of massage oil and tested the temperature on her backhand. "Turn over onto your front."

He obeyed and she sat astride his waist, rubbing her oiled hands together before she started on his back. She heard his moan become muted into the pillow as she kneaded him.

"You're so tense," Laila observed with a frown as her hands attempted to loosen the stiffness in his shoulders.

"It's been... a demanding few decades to say the least," he grunted. "Who would've thought such a heavy burden would mount up so much tension beneath it?"

She could feel a smile forming at the wry tone in his voice. "You know the burden doesn't have to be so heavy if you'd share it."

"And who do you suggest I entrust with such responsibility?" He chuckled. "Delanus?"

Laila slid her hands up and down his back. "I don't understand why you made him prime prefect if you respect him so little."

"Delanus has the merit of being a traditionalist, a perspective I lack. Keeping him near allowed me to understand how that faction of the country functions. Besides, my father had the right of it... Delanus lacks spine but he's desperate to stay relevant. That makes him exploitable."

Laila digested this in silence. "Is there no one you keep near to you out of reliance for their abilities?"

"This is Mortos, Laila. Reliance on others is an excellent way to get yourself killed." He stifled a noise when she touched a particularly tender spot. "Each member of my Eyrie was subjected to rigorous exams and testing to ensure their utility, I can guarantee you that. But do I *trust* them? No more than a tiger in its cage."

"Sounds lonely." Laila frowned, pressing deeper into the stubborn knot along his spine. "I didn't realise you'd been lonely for so long."

"No one has ever... been interested like that before."

"Well, I am," she declared boldly. "I'm interested in every part of you, Darius. You don't have to hide anything from me."

"I have a feeling you're going to regret saying that."

She peeled away the towel to reveal his lower half and cupped her hands around his buttocks. She marvelled at the rounded firmness of them, muscles taut as a drum, and almost broke her resolve.

"Try to stay focused, Laila," Darius taunted her with a smirk in his voice. "I can feel you drooling on me already. Or is that meant to be oil?"

"Is it so wrong of me to admire how pretty you are?" she teased lightly in his ear before moving back, striking him suddenly on the rear. She watched him flinch in surprise with a laugh before she mounted his buttocks.

Darius muffled another moan into the pillow as she firmly kneaded his back.

Laila bit her lip, feeling herself growing more agitated and distracted with him between her legs. She could feel the strength of him beneath her palms, his skin supple and violet-veined. She kissed a trail along the nape of his neck, nipping at his pointed ear.

"Does that feel nice?"

Darius hummed in response before their eyes met.

"What about this?" She kissed his shoulder as her palms dug into his sides, moving in circular motions.

Darius went languid beneath her, all that winter-hardened tension in him turning to spring melt.

"Laila." Her name came hoarse and strangled from him as she wandered down to his thighs, caressing the delicate inner skin. "Lightly, lightly."

She did as he asked, moving her palm along him in a long, slow glide as he shuddered. His muscles clenched against her hand, and she could tell he was trying hard not to lose control. She pulled back to focus more attention on the back of his leg, rubbing her thumbs into it.

"I want to try something," Laila asked, then bashfully she hovered her hand above his back and caused a small static to prickle along his skin, light and feather-soft. "I perform it on myself sometimes. Though it can be a little... intense. Is that all right?"

Darius nodded, though his eyes were wary.

"You can stop me any time you like." Laila let the static dance along his skin in anticipation to prepare him. She used a low charge at first, letting him adjust to the feel of it, before her hand slid along the nape of his neck.

She kneaded between his shoulder blades with her other hand, her fingertips maddening in their softness, but that was always how it had been when they were together. As someone whose body had been the site of indescribable acts of violence—shattered and pieced together and shattered again—he relished the way the golden lacquer of her touch seemed to be smoothing over his fault lines, seemed to be sealing him whole.

Darius's hips arched instantly in reaction to her touch as she applied a stronger current to his spine, disentangling centuries of aches and pains he wasn't even aware his body held.

Laila had never heard him so loud nor so vulnerable, but his noises enticed her, and before long she was increasing speed aside pressure, coaxing his hips to writhe more vigorously until he went rigid.

His climax was potent and full-bodied, rippling through him in overpowering waves as his muscles spasmed with a shudder. He looked over his shoulder at her in a state of near-terror she had not seen in him before as he grabbed a moist towel to wipe the trickle he'd exuded, a fine layer of sheen dampening his forehead.

"Are you all right?" Laila asked in a cross between amusement and concern. She slid down from his back to cup his face in her hands when he didn't answer her. "Darius?"

"That was... overwhelming."

Laila couldn't help but chuckle at his disbelief as she nuzzled the crook of his neck. She could tell he wasn't used to being caught so off-guard during intimacy, and she felt a swell of triumph at having accomplished the unthinkable. "Is that a good sort of overwhelming, or...?"

"I just... I need a moment," he said, wrapping his hands around her waist to bring them both down to the mattress. He rested his face on her breast, curving his whole body against hers, and she in turn wrapped her legs around his waist and cradled him to her.

They remained clasped like this for some time before he spoke again.

"Your devious plot worked, by the way."

"Hm?"

"This is the most thoroughly relaxed I've felt in a long while."

She smiled as she nuzzled into him. She was all set to swoon into a sleep when a flash in the corner of her eye drew her attention.

"Is that my mirror...?" She rose from the bed to investigate, but stopped when Darius encircled his arms around her waist.

"Let it pass," he pleaded, clinging to her.

"Release me, you brute!" Laila swatted him. She turned and drew him in by the chin to kiss him. "I'll be right back."

He pouted at her and she pecked his bottom lip before vacating the bed. He watched her adjust her hair and clothing before she picked up her mirror and went into the antechamber. He propped up his elbow and rested his cheek on his fist, finding it hard to suppress the elation he felt. In all his centuries he never imagined he'd be gifted the love and power he craved, let alone both at once. Yet when he looked into Laila's eyes he saw she was as foolishly doomed as he was the moment he met her.

Darius helped himself to a glass of wine as he waited for Laila to return to him. He was about to take to a strawberry when a scream sounded and had him jolting upright in alarm.

"Laila?" he called out, speeding to dress himself to see whatever threat had come to his betrothed.

"No, no, no, no..."

"Laila!"

Darius rushed into the other room.

XXV

Vacancy had replaced the usual bustle of energy Laila was used to in the city streets. She missed the squealing starlets who would flock among the doves. The faint yet familiar burble of chatter from her fellow solarites beneath their brightly feathered hats as their shoes clopped along the pavement.

They passed by several Lightshields in her aero-limousine on the way to the château. Laila gave them courteous nods of acknowledgement. Already, their presence made her feel somewhat safer, though that sense of safety all but disappeared once the château came into view.

Laila inhaled sharply, her back going blade-straight. She knew her mother was alive; that much was clear. Had she not been, then this visit would have been entirely more urgent, and she'd have been called to take the throne in the interim of another election as all crown princesses were summoned to do.

Beside her, Darius shifted in his seat and debated whether to take her hand. They'd scarcely touched—or even spoken a word—to each other since Lyra had contacted her through the mirror.

"If you want, I don't have to come in with you," he said, when the desperation to say something could no longer be withheld. "I could just as easily have the driver escort me to the embassy."

"No." She seized his hand forcefully and interlocked their fingers. "I want you here with me."

Having it confirmed lifted his chest, but the nearing of the gates made him waver. It had not gone unnoticed how the sprite driver had looked upon him with accusation in his eyes, as though he too were culpable for Dominus's atrocity. Perhaps he was.

"Are you certain you can say the same for others?" he asked.

Laila nibbled on her bottom lip. "Just don't think about it right now. All anyone needs to know is that you're here for me."

Lyra was awaiting them at the bottom of the steps when the aero-limousine touched down in the courtyard. She found herself straightening in anticipation, inflating her chest to seem firmer. A part of her still floundered in uncertainty on how she was to face Laila—to seek forgiveness from the purifying light of absolution. Yet the moment the door opened she did not linger, moving fiercely towards her friend to gather her into her arms.

"Oh, Laila." Lyra rested her head into the crook of her shoulder. "I'm so sorry. I'm so sorry."

"Don't, please." Laila shushed her as she stroked her hand along the back of her head. "It wasn't your fault."

"I should've stopped him." Lyra squeezed back the tears that threatened to fall as she thought of the mass grave of withered black-veined bodies when the fog had cleared. She nuzzled her face into Laila's shoulder, grateful to not count hers among them.

Laila slowly drew back to frame her cheeks in her palms. "My mother?"

"In her chambers," Lyra explained. "They have the entire wing completely sealed. No one goes in or out without express approval."

Laila nodded and smoothed the skirt of her lavender tulle gown. "I want to see her."

"Of course, just follow me..." Lyra's voice trailed when she noticed Darius slip out of the carriage. Her eyes grew hard. "What is he doing here?"

"Lyra, not now," Laila pleaded with a sigh.

However, nothing could calm Lyra from the ferity that overcame her upon seeing Darius. She launched herself at him, fingers aiming to claw out his eyes.

"Lyra!" Laila steadied her friend in her grip. "What are you doing?!"

"He has some nerve to show his face around here!" Her voice had degraded into something raw and guttural, spiny with malice. "After everything he did. His brother. His entire accursed *family*. They should all *perish*—"

"Lyra, stop it!" Laila could hardly fathom the rage in her friend. She took Lyra's face in her hands. "He's here for me. Please, let him be."

Lyra huffed in incredulity, but it worked in nullifying the fury she felt, if only for a moment. "Follow me."

She turned towards the steps to lead Laila inside.

Darius swallowed, contrition softening the annoyance he might have otherwise felt at this reception. "I wanted to say how sorry am I for—"

"You know what?" Lyra exploded immediately as she turned on her heel, pointing at him with ire. "You shut your mouth. Open it again and I promise you the next thing in it will be my blade—"

"Stop!" Laila ordered, sharp as a spindle. She tugged Lyra by the wrist up the steps. "You, with me. Now." She glanced apologetically at Darius over her shoulder before turning to see her mother.

Amira lay outstretched on her canopy bed, wrapped in sheets of white satin. Chaos had polluted her veins and made them black and stiff, protruding outwards into skeletal branches along her skin. Her vibrant brown hue had bleached to blanched greyness; her cheeks were sunken pits. Her once unblemished face now resembled flaccid ruched silk and sagged limply from her eye sockets.

She had, unsurprisingly, it would seem, been one of the few to escape the initial exposure. She had erected force shields with a few others and fled from the smog, but the encounter had still left them weak. To consider herself a lucky survivor would be as far as she would recount her experience. She might well have, in her darkest moment, embraced the reaper's scythe if it could grant her reprieve from this seemingly endless torment—where even to talk and eat and yawn was an excruciating practice.

She allowed herself to be seen by only the most trusted servants in her retinue. They kept her on a steady diet of morning dew and liquid starlight, and left sunlamps trained on her to bathe her in twilight. In many respects, she had been reverted to the infantile state of a starlet, left helpless to the whims of her guardians who kept her sunned and watered like a plant.

Laila entered her boudoir unprepared for the sight that would befall her, having been desperate to confirm with her own eyes her mother's continued presence among the living. Though the moment she saw the figure she had elevated to divinity reduced to this hollowed-out cask of a being, she couldn't keep herself from violently flinching and stepping back. It was as though all the pillars of worship in her mind had been demolished, a believer confronted with a false god.

"Maman—" Laila's hand flew up to her mouth to stifle her weep. She collapsed to her knees and clasped her mother's emaciated hand. "Oh, Maman."

"Aurore…" Amira's lips could barely part from the rigidity in her features.

Laila pressed her face into her mother's sheets as she sobbed, inhaling her moist earth scent.

Amira curved her hand over the back of her daughter's head, stroking her curls. "I'm glad you came."

Laila sniffled a few times to compose herself, drying her eyes. "He did this to us." Her lips stiffened as fury burned in her gaze. "Where is he?"

"Sun room…"

This surprised her, for she would have expected the House of Corrections. Yet when she thought of schism forming between themselves and the Mielettes, the sun room made more sense.

"Do we know how many—" She couldn't force herself to complete the question. As a people the solarites had never been numerous, and the opportunities for more of them sparse. It hurt too much to think how many had been lost. "It's all right. Don't speak." She smoothed her hand over Amira's and kissed her forehead. "I'll see to this. As I should've done twenty years ago."

With that, she rose up to make her way down to the sun room.

The cell was located on a floor made entirely of glass; all fixtures in the room were similarly made of glass or metal. The result being an accommodation that offered little comfort or reprieve from the elements—particularly the relentless pierce of Soleterean sunshine that elevated the temperature until all was hot to the touch.

Each step Laila took towards the transparent prison infused her with more resolve. By the time she reached Lyra at the entrance, she was marching.

Lyra absorbed the waves of fury emanating from her with a calm onceover. "I can see you've made your mind up, so I won't try to dissuade you. But I'll be honest—I don't think you should see him."

"Let me pass, Lyra." Laila's tone did not betray the depths of her current emotion. She conducted herself with a poised pleasantry, as though to refuse her entry would be the height of irrationality. "This confrontation has been a long time coming."

Lyra shifted her jaw, refusal lingering on the edge of her tongue. "Want me to join you?"

"That won't be necessary," Laila said, wielding a smile as a shield. "I'll be fine. I assure you."

Lyra nodded in uncertainty, but she stepped aside to let her through all the same. She was meant to keep watch over Dominus until the Order contacted her with a means of secreting him away. But she knew Laila needed to face this particular demon, and she wasn't feeling partial towards safeguarding his wellbeing.

Laila's court heels clacked along the corridor as sheer veils of sunlight bled through the windows, bathing her in its heavenly halo. She was incandescent with rage when she faced Dominus, who lay on a glass bed as little more than a silhouette of the grand beast she had once feared.

The use of his own hatred had cost him dearly indeed, whittling down his broad oak body to a mere toothpick. Forget a strong gust of wind—the lightest touch of a seaside breeze would be enough to cause him destruction. As with her mother, the sight took her aback, but he had never been a deity that she had knelt towards.

"You," she seethed, her hands clenched around the metal rail around the cell.

Dominus drew up his head towards her, clearly an arduous task. "Well, well. Aren't you a sight for sore eyes?"

Laila choked down her anger. She didn't want to electrify the metal. "The state of you."

"Yes, well." Dominus spread his arms to encompass his wretched form. "I can't say it wasn't worth it in the end. If only to see the look on your face now." A smirk crawled across his lips. "Tell me, Laila. Do you feel that rage eating away at you in the pit of your stomach? Exhilarating, isn't it? It's a shame you can't put it to use in the way I did."

"You mean when you *massacred* dozens of innocents?" Laila hissed at him through gritted teeth. "How could you?"

"How could I?" That had him sitting upright. "How could *I*? Let us not forget who is the wronged party, Laila. You went behind my back and endangered my mother and enthralled my brother to your whims when I wouldn't do your bidding. She *died* as a result of your carelessness. I only sought to return the favour."

Laila burst out laughing. "Goodness. How long have you been clinging onto that particular misfortune? You are pitiful." Before she could default to reason, she had opened the door to his cell and entered it, pacing towards him. "You want to know whose fault it was that your mother died, Dominus?"

"Don't you dare say another word—"

"*Yours*," Laila snarled as she bared down upon him in a way she had never been able to before. "Through your irresponsibility, *your* ineptitude, your *sheer* inaction. You left me with no choice. Your father was a loose cannon and he needed to be stopped." Tears were streaming down her cheeks. She didn't halt them. "And because you refused to, you let your mother die. And countless others."

"Stop *talking!*" he bellowed, his nostrils flaring. He clenched his fists as he squared up his trembling twig arms, and oh, if only he had use of his claws and fangs still, what a mess he would make of her pretty throat.

"So yes, I went to Darius." Laila daintily smudged the tears on her cheeks. "I'm not going to apologise for that."

"Of course you aren't, because you're just like him. Selfish and self-interested. You two deserve each other." Dominus wheezed a frail chuckle. "I bet you fucked him too for the added motivation."

"You *cut* into me with your claws and you *bit* me and you want to talk about *deserve*, Dominus?" Laila shook her head at him in exasperation. "I could've done a lot worse after what you did. Asemani only knows I should have. But you're right. I fucked your brother. Repeatedly. And I had myself a good time doing it. We were at it all night the first time we were together—"

Dominus seized her by the throat and dragged her to him, his breaths coming heavy.

"What? What are you going to do, Dominus? What *can* you do?" Laila smirked at him as she peeled off his fingers with little effort. "You are *pitiful*."

Dominus quivered, his lip peering back in a sneer. "And you're poison. God, I feel sorry for Darius. He doesn't even know what he's invited into his bed. But he's not like me. He will soon. And when he does... I hope he leaves you in ruins."

"Well, if he does... you certainly won't be around to see it." She grabbed him by the throat before he could react, imbuing him with pure light. The light spilled through his veins, disintegrating the lining of his vessels and liquefying his entrails.

Dominus made a sound in agony as his organs ruptured, too low for a scream. It was a strangled, almost gurgling baritone. A seismic boom.

Laila didn't loosen her hold on him even as he steamed in her grip, until his face crackled and he crumbled into dust at her fingertips. She unclenched her fingers with a tremulous gasp, almost fearful of what she'd done. She'd never acted in so vicious a manner as to take a life before. Let alone so barbarously.

Nausea rippled through her stomach as she glanced at the ashes of who Dominus once was. He would never hurt anyone again. Surely that benefit outweighed her cruelty. Yet she couldn't extract his frailty from her mind. He'd been of no harm to anyone when she'd purged him from this realm. This was not a just kill ruled by law; she had crushed him in her palm like a spider. She hadn't even let Darius have a chance to talk to him. That thought caused the bile to rise up in a scorch along her throat. She stifled it.

Oh gods, what am I going to tell Darius? She slid the offending hand down her dress as though that would be enough to erase the crime, and she fiddled with her fingers in a panic. She knew that she had to think and think fast. Her mother was the only one who knew she intended to come here. Lyra would be a simple enough fix. And Dominus was already weak, frail. It was only a matter of time before he succumbed.

Nodding to herself in affirmation, Laila made her way back to Lyra at the door.

"Y-you should call someone, tell them that Dominus perished due to frailty." Laila gulped, tracing the words on her tongue. Perhaps if she said them enough she might eventually believe it.

Lyra looked at her for a long time, a mixture of disbelief, disappointment, and eventual resigned acceptance cycling through her. Laila knew she didn't believe a word of it, and yet there was nothing but acquiescence in her tone when she spoke.

"As you wish." A thin smile spread across her lips. "And good riddance."

⚮

Darius sat down on Laila's bed as he waited for her to arrive. He brought out the black velvet box he had been meaning to offer her, having never found the right time. Inside was the betrothal carcanet he knew she wouldn't want to wear until the news was broken to her mother.

He'd had it modelled in the style of a sun encircled by the golden roses frequently seen in her family heraldry. One large rose-cut canary diamond was accented by a diamond aureole setting, paired with smaller yellow diamonds embedded in diamond floral designs to articulate her ethereal origins in contrast to the country into which she would wed.

He traced a finger along the carcanet affectionately, hoping she would wear it, to find it a small joy in all this moroseness. He heard her approaching up the hall and snapped the box shut, hiding it under her pillow.

She entered looking wan and shaken, causing any slim impression of a smile he had to fade.

"Laila?" He was up and at her side in moments, cupping her face. "What is it? Is it your mother?"

Laila breathed in and exhaled in a weep.

"Oh, princess, what's wrong?" Darius brought her into his arms, pressing her face to his chest as she wept and shivered.

"I—I did—" Her voice retched on the words. "I did something terrible."

"What is it?" He pulled back to look into her tear-stained face, wiping beneath her eye with his thumb. "You can tell me."

She shook her head frantically at him. "I can't."

"Yes, you can. Laila look at me." He steadied her face in his grip. "There is nothing you could do that I wouldn't forgive."

Her breath hitched at the words, the unspoken promise in them. Who else but he would be so persistent and unflinching in his affection towards her?

She couldn't meet his eyes for long before she broke away, stepping out of his reach.

"Laila—"

"Dominus is dead." She cradled her arms around herself, rocking back and forth. "I'm sorry."

Darius's chest deflated, a minute flicker of upset grazing within before he snuffed it. "That's not your fault."

"It *is* my fault." Laila slid her hands through her curls and tugged them as though she meant to tear them out in chunks. "I just—I just wanted to talk to him, is all. But he was so... *cruel*. And I was so angry, and... I couldn't let him get away with it. Not after everything I let him do. I had to make it right."

Realisation sunk into Darius's features. His throat bobbled in speechlessness.

Laila took his silence to its worst conclusion. "Please..." She stepped forward to reach for him.

Was this it, then? Was this the moment she made herself unlovable to the only one who always swore he would never turn from her, never look at her with the shine dulled from his eyes and find her lacking as so many others did?

"Please say something."

Darius paused for a moment. A single, calculating moment as Laila laced her fingers into his shirt before he looked down at her. "Well my first question is... Did anyone see you? Who else knows?"

Laila blinked in confusion before the words had time to process.

"M-my mother knew I was visiting him, but there was only Lyra. She'll say nothing."

"Good. That's good." Darius thought a moment longer, realising after the initial shock he'd been left with one singular emotion. Relief. "Well, he foolishly made himself into an explosive to accomplish a killing of such a large degree. I am surprised he didn't perish immediately after doing it. Stubbornness... a Calantis family trait, it seems."

She couldn't fathom his levity, nor the cold logic he used to reason with her murder of his brother. "But you didn't even get to say goodbye to him..."

"Laila." Darius took his hands in hers and caressed them, a thanks for her taking up the executing sword he'd been reluctant to bear. "I've had twenty years to make peace with Dominus being dead. That he was alive again— It was... it was a simple error that has been corrected now. We might never know how or why it occurred but... as far as my feelings for you are concerned, this changes nothing."

Only now did Laila contemplate that her impulsivity had lost her the opportunity to discover more insight into Dominus's miraculous resurrection. She could curse herself for it.

"Let me show you something." Darius made his way over to the bed to take the box out from beneath the pillow. He opened it up to reveal the carcanet.

Laila's lips parted in amazement.

"It's a custom in our land to give your betrothed a carcanet as a display of fondness." His head bowed sheepishly. "I was hoping you might wear it, if... you wouldn't mind, of course."

Laila touched her neck. "But I didn't get anything for you."

"That's all right." Darius took the necklace out. "Though if you want you can certainly get me a matching ring."

She laughed at him as she turned, allowing him to fasten it to her neck. She stroked her hands along the diamonds. "I haven't been able to tell my mother..."

"Don't worry about that." He rested his hands on her shoulders and spun her around to face him. "No time like the present, is there?"

He tilted her head up towards him and leaned in to press his lips against hers.

XXVI

AMIRA SLURPED QUIETLY FROM HER CANISTER OF liquid starlight, waiting for Laila to return to her after her visit with Dominus. Much had happened in the immediate aftermath of the attack, and she needed her daughter to remain on top of things if they were to escape from the breadth of this tragedy unscathed.

The numbers of the dead had yet to be confirmed. The number of injured, herself included, would inflate the figure more so. Anti-occassi sentiment couldn't be more pervasive thanks to the devastating scope of just one. Now, more than ever before, she and Laila would need to distance themselves largely from any semblance of sympathy towards these creatures.

It couldn't have taken her more aback to see her daughter arrive on the arm of one, his jewels clasped around her throat, as they exchanged anxious looks in unison.

Amira strained in anguish to sit up on the bed. "What... is he...?"

"Maman, don't strain yourself!" Laila chastised, speeding to her side to still her. The stress induced by the movement caused Amira's skin to begin oozing blackness. Laila picked up a towel to wipe her clean, discarding it with a grimace. "He's here with me."

"If this is about trying to make amends for the atrocity *his brother* committed—"

"No, Maman!" Laila took her gently by the shoulders. "It's not that at all. It's. Well..." She gradually inched her way back until she was in Darius's arms again.

Her carcanet twinkled, catching Amira's eye. "You'd best not... be preparing to tell me something immensely foolish..."

"Darius and I are to be married," Laila asserted before her mother could finish and cause her to lose her nerve.

Amira sighed, rubbing at her temples. "Please excuse us, Darius Rex."

Darius hesitated behind Laila before she turned to nod at him over her shoulder.

"I'll be right outside," he vowed, then made his brisk exit from the room.

Laila sucked in a breath, preparing for the worst.

"What do you think you are doing?" Amira's eyes narrowed. "I would have thought you would've had enough sense in that... thick little skull of yours... to withhold from doing something so... impetuous. Today of all days."

"Maman, I recognise a marriage between us might not be the best course of action at the moment. But there is no rush. Darius and I, we can wait..."

"Long enough past the election?" Amira's lips curved in mockery. "That long? How is your occasso beau going to feel after you've spent that much time denouncing his kind as the abominations of nature that they are?"

Laila pressed her lips together. After everything she'd set in place with the peace-making, the ætherglass, the qarna, how could she abandon it all? "Can't we—"

"*No*, Laila." The discomfort of speaking lessened the more she did it, and so she continued. "I am afraid your dear Dominus has forced our hand. We cannot afford to show even an *inkling* of positivity towards occassi or Mortos. Now or in the future. The deaths are too numerous and the grief too great. There will be no marriage here. Darius Rex can consider it a fortune I do not think to declare war."

"Maman…" Laila could feel her voice shrinking further and further.

"You are to return to Soleterea permanently. At once." Amira paused for thought. "In fact, do not even think of leaving now. I shall arrange for your belongings to be fetched. There is much work that needs doing. Events you must attend. Speeches you must make."

Laila could feel tears clouding her vision but held them back. She touched her carcanet. "I understand."

Amira glanced her over upon noticing her distress. "Aurore, it's for the best. How was it even to work? A marriage between you two? You were bound to be parted by sea sooner or later. And what? You think that supposed fondness won't strain under distance when you are both out of sight? A barrage of far more eligible companions ripe for the choosing right in front of you… oh, don't make me laugh."

Laila nodded faintly. "You are right, Maman."

"Come here, my girl." Amira raised her hand until Laila went to take it. "I do feel part of this is my doing. I have been too… lenient with you, in hindsight. I should have allowed myself to nip this occassi menace in the bud long ago. Well. No time like the present, as they say, hm? You will tell Darius Rex you will no longer be accepting his proposal. And return that gaudy trinket to him." Amira rubbed at her eyelid. "It hurts my eyes."

Laila strained a smile for her mother. "As you wish, Maman. You do know what's best."

⤬

In the end she discovered him not outside like he'd promised, but in the rose garden. Laila couldn't help but find irony in that as she spotted his rigid silhouette beneath the pavilion of ornate iron.

Her footfalls were soft on the path, but she knew he'd be able to hear her coming all the same. He separated a rose from one of the bushes and twirled the golden petals around to glimpse the opulent lustre of them in the moonlight.

"I see the roses are in fine form this summer," he said, but she knew better than to be netted into idle chatter.

"Darius," she began.

"It's all right, princess." He looked at the rose again, perhaps to avoid having to look at her. There was a nervous bobble in his throat as he swallowed, and he parted his lips as though the air might have the words that eluded him. "I'm afraid I must admit to eavesdropping. Though I did try hard not to."

She blinked and swallowed, a rush of heat that she immediately tried to obstruct puddling behind her eyes. "Darius—"

He abandoned the flower by the bench, cupping her face to shush her. He slid his thumb down the incline of her high-boned cheek where her tears had shed. "Don't cry for me, princess. It's nothing personal, it's just politics." His eyes lowered to the carcanet. "At least I got to see how it looked on you. Just once."

The sheer tenderness in his voice was enough to make her cry again. She cupped his hand against her face and nuzzled into it with a laugh. "Gods, you always make this so difficult..."

Darius laughed with her, tears staining his vision. "Well, it's an old habit by now." He inhaled shakily, tears sliding down his cheeks to match hers. "I'm assuming you'll... be wanting to give me that carcanet back?"

She interlocked their fingers. "That's what I keep trying to tell you. It's..." She bit down on her lip. "What I'm trying to say is that..."

Darius paused, his breath suspending.

"I've decided that I might... keep it. And you." A pause. "If that's all right?"

He moved in quickly to kiss her, causing any words she might have uttered next to become stuck in her throat. Laila made a soft whimper as she wrapped her arms around his neck, pulling him that much closer.

He drew back to rest his forehead against hers. "Are you sure?"

"No," she admitted, laughing nervously. "But it helps when you kiss me."

He smothered her lips with his again, the message clearly received. Laila let herself yield to it. Yield to the desire she'd kept hidden to take his hand and wander blissfully into the unknown, accepting all the judgement and condemnation such a decision would surely reap.

Darius parted their lips to kiss her neck, and she shivered at how attentive he was with his mouth even as she felt the scrape of his canines descending. It was when his lips reached a particularly delicate spot beneath her jaw that she finally put a stop to it.

"Darius," she breathed, feeble yet forceful as she gathered enough strength to push him away from her. Behind him, Lyra was lurking, having watched the scene unfold with a stiffened jaw. "Give us a moment."

Laila disentangled herself from him as she fiddled with her fingers, knowing this was the part she'd been dreading most.

"Heard the news." Lyra jutted out her chin. "Still hoping it's part of a sleepwalk, though."

"Lyra." Laila inhaled, unable to begin knowing what to say.

"Tell me I misheard." Lyra took a step forward with desperation in her gaze. "Tell me you're not this *foolish*."

"I *love* him, Lyra."

For what else was there to possibly say than this?

Lyra flexed her jaw in disdain. "Laila, think about this. Think about everything you've worked towards. Everything you're giving up. The election. The country... Me. Look me in the eye and tell me that he's worth all of that."

Laila parted her lips, wordless. Then she met her gaze. "I gave him up for that before. I... I can't do it again. I can't."

"That's... so very disappointing." Lyra squeezed her eyes shut and sucked in a breath. "Well don't ask me to watch you do this. Because I won't, Laila. If you want to muck up your life that's your business, but I will not be a part of it."

"That's regretful," Laila said, eyes lowering to the floor. "But I understand."

Lyra's chin wobbled before she hardened it. She refused to waste her tears on this. She instead directed one last look of sheer loathing towards Darius before she turned on her heel and disappeared into the night.

Watching her leave was enough to make Laila's legs unsteady. She felt flat and empty and weak, like nectar when all the fizzle ran out. Darius rushed towards her, catching her before she could fall completely.

He held her close in his arms. "Not too late to change your mind."

Laila shook her head, resting against his chest. If she just lay here for a while she knew the vigour would return to her soon and she could muster the resolve she needed to face the world again. "No. I've made my decision. She's made hers."

Darius kissed the top of her head. "We'll make this right again, I promise. We have all the time in the world to unravel this mess. And we will. Together."

She twisted round in his arms to cup his face and bring his forehead to hers. "Let's go home."

EPILOGUE

MUSIC AND MERRIMENT SHUDDERED ALONG THE marble steps of the Aureate Theatre as Dr Isuka made her way upwards. Within these gilt-lacquered walls, a formation of sprite ballerinas danced as if they were marionettes pulled by the strings of the orchestra, their bodies glitter-smeared and shimmering under the spotlight. They pranced en pointe as if reaching towards the stars, flaring skirts of petals, feathers, and butterfly wings bouncing in immaculate precision to their movements.

The scientist didn't spare a moment to become entranced by the show, too focused on completing her objective—reaching the velvet-padded booth of the solarite she intended to see. She reached the top of the endless stairs as the current dance finished, and the theatre roared with an ovation as the curtains fell for an interlude. It was a perfectly timed arrival. Almost certainly planned. But such was the meticulous attention to detail Dr Isuka had come to expect of her enigmatic partner.

Inside the booth, Dr Mielette clasped her hands in delight and brought them with a wistful sigh to her chest. Upon noticing her guest, her star-flecked visage twinkled in greeting as she patted the empty seat beside her.

"You're as punctual as always, Dr Isuka," Dr Mielette commended, and she lifted a bottle of red wine from its holder. "Can I interest you in a drink?"

The bottle popped open to release the sound of an ocean wave inside a shell. As Dr Mielette filled the glasses, the flow of liquid came laced with a mermaid's melisma.

"Thank you." Dr Isuka took a sip, finding it to be a sweet, sharp white that tasted of citrus peel and peach. "I came as soon as I could, following your instructions down to the letter."

"Yes, I am most pleased." Dr Mielette beamed in response. "We have a lot to discuss, you and I. I thought it best to do so in an area where we can have both discretion and privacy."

"You're looking well," Dr Isuka said, unable to help noticing how untouched she looked in comparison to the other victims of the occasso assault.

"I had a narrow escape from the atrocity. Others... were not so fortunate." Dr Mielette's glow dimmed. "What is even more unfortunate is that we were unable to retrieve Dominus Calantis from Rosâtre before his untimely passing."

"He's dead?" Dr Isuka stifled the flare of rage that overcame her. "What a nuisance."

"I had feared someone would do away with him in the château walls, but his loss will come as a great inconvenience to our work. Especially since we can't regenerate him again."

Dr Isuka exhaled in defeat before perking up again. "Fortunately, he is not the only occasso of Calantis blood still living."

"Accessing Darius Rex will prove troublesome considering how well-protected he is." Dr Mielette swirled her wine in her glass. "If only it were possible to move on him without risking a devastating backlash. Ah, something to invest in for the future, I suppose."

"In the meantime, our work continues with the victims of Sadik Yilan's hubris," Dr Isuka said. "Hopefully, the presence of Dominus's blood in their system will be enough to give us what we need. Total eradication of chaos from the body."

"*Without* being able to recover it," Dr Mielette added with emphasis. "Dominus was able to counter the effects that the Pit had on him and regain his abilities. That won't serve. And that's why we still needed him." She huffed, massaging her temples. "I have Sadik Yilan remanded in the House of Corrections. After all the trouble he wrought, I have means to keep him there for the remainder of his lifespan. But he is being cooperative and accommodating. I think he believes that if he does enough to aid us he'll be allowed to see Elina."

"And *will* you allow him?"

"I'll consider it. He has at least returned the grimoire to solarite possession."

"Good." Dr Isuka pressed her lips together in thought. "Now that we have it back we should be able to divine more on chaos. Particularly, these chimeras Darius Rex has been producing." She had made the last one she caught a subject of obsession. The creature was unlike anything she'd witnessed of monsters in the past. "As for Yilan... have the nightmares started?"

"Not quite yet, it seems. I am, however, keeping a close eye on him and will expect them to start soon now he's used the grimoire to call upon Calante directly. How soon was it for Dr Hariken?"

"I don't…" Dr Isuka looked away from her, swallowing, for the answer shamed her too much to share. "I don't recall, exactly."

"That's fine," Dr Mielette soothed. "We can use Yilan to divine what we did not do with her."

"And…" Dr Isuka cleared her throat. "Ser de Lis?"

"She has reported that Princess Laila has absconded with the rex." Dr Mielette let out a cackle. "Oh, Amira must be furious. How poetic. Two bloodlines built to destroy each other uniting in love. A weed that sprouted entirely against nature's design."

"Do you think we could use that?"

"Oh, most *certainly*. However, such a thing will require some careful planning on our end. Ser de Lis will be useful. She seems adrift, which is perfect for our aims. Keep an eye on her."

"As you wish," Dr Isuka said.

The blare of music cut the conversation short as Dr Mielette wiggled in her seat.

"The show returns!" she exclaimed with glee, turning towards her companion. "Do stay for the rest of it, Dr Isuka. It's like nothing you've ever seen before."

Dr Isuka nodded and settled into her seat as the lights dimmed for the opening of the curtains.

Once her decision to return to Mortos had passed and the gravity of its repercussions cemented, a deep melancholy swept over Laila and left her too physically and emotionally drained to do anything but curl in Darius's bed. Her bed. *Their* bed. This was all hers now. This had been what she'd traded her summer-blessed country for.

Laila nestled within a mass of sanguine silk, overwatched by the gargoyles looming from the ceiling of the ironwood canopy. Her eyes drifted over to the window, where the unconquerable forest of Mortos reigned eternal, ever poised to invade.

Tears fogged her vision as she wondered how long it would take before she stopped expecting to see the view from her old window—the astronomical clock tower's stained glass face, how the sun always caught the chameleon flecks of seagreen, blue and gold in perfect sequence as it rose.

Perhaps she deserved the world that she'd chosen. Tainted as she was by murder, she couldn't bear to face the innocent glow of rising starlets looking up to her in awe and knowing how much her own shine had dimmed. How far she'd fallen.

"What are you thinking about?" Darius wrapped his arms around her from behind and kissed the side of her head.

She fiddled with her carcanet and twisted the answer on her tongue. "You." She turned to nuzzle him. "Being with you. How much I'll have to grow acclimated to... all of this."

"It'll take some time," he said, "and as for Lyra..."

"I don't want to talk about her." Hearing her name still pierced Laila's chest. She had not expected happiness, much less acceptance, but the venom that trickled off her former friend's tongue still blistered.

"I think you should."

"No." She burrowed her face in the crook of his neck. "She made her feelings clear. There is nothing more to say about it. You're all I have, now."

Darius grew silent upon the soft whisper of this confession. "I will always be here when you need me." He stroked a hand down her hair. "But I shouldn't be all that you have."

"I know. But you are the choice that I made. I thought about what would've been... if I'd made the good choice. The right choice. If I'd stayed at my mother's side like the dutiful princess I was raised to be and refused you. I did it before. I stand by that choice. But all I can remember from those years is the niggling 'what if...' that wouldn't leave me be. The imagined future of if I'd said yes to you. It would soothe me during those failures when I was attempting to live up to expectations. And I knew if I refused you again I would forever be plagued by that ghost." A lump formed in her throat. "I've never said that to anyone before."

"I didn't realise you'd thought about it so much."

"Well, you were shockingly difficult to forget." Laila breathed an embarrassed laugh. "I had spent every waking moment having a life anyone could dream of... yet the moment I closed my eyes, I longed for you."

He leaned in to seal their mouths together and drew from her a slight muffled breath. "I know I don't deserve to have you. You ought to be with an honourable, gallant knight. Someone who walks your righteous path. That's something I can't ever be... but you've granted me the freedom to pretend to be something other than a monster. And I needed that."

"Don't speak so poorly of yourself. I've been loved before by the gallant and the righteous—neither has devoted themselves to me with quite the ferocity that you've shown. You need a bit of monstrousness for that, I think." Laila's hands rested lightly against his kaftan, melding her body as much as she could to his to chase his lips again. His kisses always served to anchor her when she felt adrift in her sorrow, giving her a core of stillness she couldn't help but soak herself in.

"Remember what I promised you?" he murmured against her lips, nose stroking against hers.

She gazed into his eyes and nodded. "We have all the time in the world to make this right."

"And we will." He traced his thumb along her cheek. "Just trust me."

"I do."

Laila kissed him, hungrier this time, entwining her arms around his neck to crush their bodies together. "I don't want us to ever be apart again." She unbuttoned his shirt and kissed along his collarbone down to his chest.

"We won't be," he vowed.

"I want you to wrap your arms around me so tightly they'd never pry us free." She was already beginning to unbutton his trousers. "They'd have to chisel away at us like stone." She'd barely gotten them down to his ankles before he seized her by the waist.

There couldn't have been a worse time for the door to knock.

"Your Majesty?"

Darius huffed in impatience. "What is it, Kirill?"

"My apologies for the disturbance, but your presence is required urgently."

Darius suppressed a long sigh and then muttered a word underneath his breath, clearly agitated. "Can it not wait?"

"It's regarding the matter of the prime prefect."

That seemed to be enough for him to know he couldn't let the matter lie. "Apologies, princess." Darius reached for his trousers and pulled them up his legs. "I have to see to this."

"Don't go," she pouted at him, hoping to make herself seem too pitiful to abandon. "Aren't I more important?"

He tugged on the rest of his clothes while giving her a look of exasperated fondness. "Night's still young and we have many ahead of us yet." He brought her into his arms and kissed the tip of her nose. "Wait for me." He dropped his mouth to hers next long enough for her to try and grab hold of him. Then he bolted from the room before she could catch a grip.

"Hmph," Laila sniffed, chest flaring with resentment. Well. She hardly needed him to find release. Flopping back on her stomach, she resumed where she was before and caressed along her breasts, squeezing and kneading, gliding her fingers along her thighs to build anticipation until finally she was touching herself again.

It felt good to relieve frustration, somewhat, but it didn't help that all the while she kept fantasising Darius's presence. His voice crooning in her ear to encourage her. The weight of him pressed atop her body. His breaths. His lips leaving a trail along her neck and shoulders...

Her orgasm came quick but left her unsated, and she loathed herself for the fact. Grunting, she slithered off of the bed and sought for any trace of him she could find, but the only thing she could lay hands on was the cloak he'd abandoned in his hurry to dress.

She brought the dark mass of velvet to her nose, breathed in deep, and wrapped it around her shoulders. The fabric rippled along the curves of her body, heavy, but not quite heavy enough to pretend they were his arms around her. It was no use. She had to be with him.

Under the hushed gloom of dwindling candlelight, Darius took an audience with his prefects to discuss a number of topics. Delanus. His mother's presence at court. The uncertainty of relations with Soleterea after the recent disaster, and how to proceed.

"I understand your concern, what with the prime prefect being... indisposed at this time." Darius was reclined on his bone throne with a leisurely grace, one knee tucked over the other, his temple pressed against his thumb and forefinger. "But I have hand chosen a replacement to appoint in his absence." With this, he made a gesture to beckon her forward. "Sabina Levitia."

Prefect Augustus snorted in disbelief. "Surely, you jest."

"It is customary for an heir to take up her predecessor's mantle in the event he is impaired, is it not? As Prime Levitis has been imprisoned, his eldest child is the most eligible candidate."

"She'd be an heir if she were—" Augustus snuffed his off-colour joke when met with Darius's baleful stare. "As you command, Your Majesty."

"Then it's settled." Darius steepled his fingers. "You are all dismissed but Prime Levitia."

Sabina resisted her instinct to wither at the envy-driven looks they gave her before filing out of the room. Once she was sure they were sufficiently alone she turned towards Darius. "You cannot be serious."

"I confess to not seeing the levity. Whilst your father serves his punishment, I shall need a replacement. And you're exactly what I'm looking for. Strong, intelligent, adaptable. What's more is that you are a choice that might end up appeasing all factions."

Sabina straightened in her seat, lowering her ankle from her knee and her elbow from the top of the divan. "I'm listening."

"You are an occassella from a distinguished clan. You have passed the trials of the First Rite, so no occasso can claim you have no idea of what burdens him. Being an occassella on the fringes means the Vidua Nocte are likely to take to you, too."

"I see." Sabina realised he'd given this thought, much more than she anticipated. "Even so, this"—she gestured around them—"is all a farce, is it not? You don't honestly mean to unseat my father."

"Not yet," Darius said. "However, there may be something more vital I require him for, so he may be absent for some time. Upon that event, I'd want to entrust the kingdom into someone's hands. It could be yours, if you're willing. We'd make a good partnership, you and I, and

I'd ensure anyone who contests your rule on the premise of sex would be swiftly dealt with."

Sabina's eyes narrowed in thought.

"What say you, Sabina? Are you ready to take your father's seat?"

The offer had appeal. How could it not? Who in her position wouldn't think of herself slouched at the rex's right hand side, lauding it all above those who once mocked and shunned her?

"Prime Levitia..." She rolled it along her tongue. It had the carnal savour of rare meat, enough to make her fangs lengthen and scrap against her lip. "It has a nice ring to it."

"That it does."

"And I suppose it helps that I already know your secrets." Sabina's lips broadened in an empty smile. "How do you do it?"

"Do what?"

"Lie to everyone all the time." Sabina glanced towards the door. "How do you do it?"

"I never lie, Sabina," Darius said. "I only offer a version of the truth they require to know."

"And Laila? Don't you think she deserves to know the truth?"

"What I think Laila deserves, more than anything, is to be happy." Darius's voice softened upon the mention of her. There was not even a hint of artifice in his weary downward glance, the faint tremor on Laila's name. "After everything she's been through, I want that for her. Burdening her with all of this... It comes at a cost. If her ignorance spares her pain, then am I truly so cruel to indulge it?"

Watching him speak stripped away one impermeable layer of his armour from Sabina. He *believed* what he'd uttered. Enough to make it difficult for her to remain unmoved by his plea. His most potent lies, she discovered, must be the ones first spoken to himself.

Laila clenched Darius's cloak tight around her body as she made her way to the audience room. The oppressive length of velvet made a useful shield against the draft of the Citadel halls, its lingering scent of him comforting her.

Along her journey, she could already decipher the reservedly elegant notes of oakmoss and rose, followed by the rare expense of ambergris. The heady fragrance brought a warmth to her skin from remembrance of where she'd experienced it last—a further protective layer against the hallway's penetrative chill.

When she reached the audience room, she slipped in silently to observe its occupants. Upon entering she noticed the slight shift in Darius's demeanour. Though he did not look directly at her, she knew he sensed her presence all the same. She often felt it too. It was a recognition of each other that transcended anything physical.

Laila took a seat on one of the benches, watching him. She had to admit she'd never much had a liking for that dour throne, built from the skeletal remains of fallen enemies. Yet something about the way Darius took command of it enticed her. She couldn't keep her eyes off of him— his effortlessly regal posture as he dismissed Sabina from the room.

"No further visitors," he told Sabina before she both bowed and took her leave. Once she was gone, his eyes fell upon Laila. "Just when I was starting to wonder where I mislaid my cloak."

"I quite like it," Laila said, with a mischievous curl to her lips. "It's warm."

Darius hummed in agreement. "Suits you well. However, I shall be wanting it back."

"Well." Laila blushed and clutched it to her. "Not just yet. I'll be needing it a little longer."

Darius arched his brow. "Why?"

"It's a surprise."

"Then let's hear it." He crooked two fingers to beckon her forth. "Come over here and show me."

She got up from her seat and travelled up the few steps towards his throne before him. Her head cocked to one side, playfully coquettish. "Perhaps I'm not ready to show you."

"Laila." Her name was spoken with the utmost affection, but there was a hint of reproach encroaching beneath. "Take off the cloak."

Laila bit her lip as their eyes met, a shock of energy going through her that set her nerves alight. She could tell he was growing agitated, and yet she made no move to do as he asked. However, his stare was unceasing, and the longer she held it the harder it grew.

"Take it off," he repeated. Once. Only once, she knew, before he got up to take matters into his own hands.

She decided she'd taunted him long enough and withdrew the cloak from her shoulders, allowing it to crumple into a heap on the floor. What lay beneath was nothing but bare skin and the luminous twinkle of the betrothal carcanet he'd gifted her.

Darius stiffened immediately. A feral hunger had darkened his gaze, enlarging his pupils until they nearly eclipsed his blue irises. His larynx rolled as he swallowed and moistened his lips. "Well, I can see why you looked so pleased with yourself."

Laila's smile outshone even the brightest of her diamonds.

"Couldn't wait for me, then?"

"Don't flatter yourself. I was able to finish what you started quite swiftly in your absence."

"And yet here you stand." He seized her by the hips and tugged her to sit on his lap. "Let me look at you properly." He brushed her hair away from her neck and sucked in a sharp breath. "You travelled all the way here like that?"

"No one saw me," she assured him. "This is meant for your eyes only."

"Good." His voice had roughened to a husky rasp. "You're exquisite."

His heartfelt whisper sent a shiver down her spine. She leaned in to kiss him, gently coasting her mouth along his as she unbuttoned his kaftan.

Darius released a thick sound as he let her undress him, stripping off the layers of his kaftan and shirt before she unbuttoned his trousers. They parted briefly to manoeuvre the pieces of clothing off along with his drawers. Once he too was sufficiently naked, Darius dragged her back into a kiss, crushing their bodies fervently together so she could feel how stiff he was with arousal.

Laila clutched his shoulders, rolling her hips into him.

He soon put a stop to it by grabbing her and holding her firm, migrating his lips down her neck and over the tops of her breasts. "I can't tell you how many times I've thought of this."

Laila tipped back her neck with a sigh as he lavished her with kisses. "Thought of what?"

"Taking you." His words were muffled through his mouth's eager smacks along her skin. "Right here on this throne."

Her chest lurched from the thrill of it. Their shared desire. "How would you do it?"

"Like this." He picked her up and pivoted her so her back was now pressed against him. He cupped her breast in his large hand, the other now stroking between her thighs to fondle her clit.

Laila gave a frail whimper, her head lolling as he nibbled her neck. There was a perverse sort of excitement she got from being placed on display like this, taking his lap for a throne while he pleasured her with relish. She squirmed as he made skilful work of her with his fingers and left her skin prickling and oversensitive, her breaths growing shallow.

Her half-lidded eyes swept over the expanse of the room in the realisation this would be hers someday. Theirs. To rule over side by side.

She couldn't take much more in the way of teasing. Her thighs were already slick with want of him and she was, once more, throbbing with a deeply rooted ache that needed to be soothed. She pushed her hips back against him until she was met with his tip and hoped that would be enough to demonstrate her point.

"That's what you came all this way for, isn't it?" His voice took on a mocking edge. "I never knew you could be so desperate."

"I-I'm... not..." She hated how shaky she sounded in comparison to his calmness.

"No?" He aligned his cock against her until the tip was barely inside.

She couldn't help herself then. "Darius," she whined. Her words were little more than short, desperate pants. "Please."

"As you wish."

Laila gripped the arms of the throne to brace as he entered her. She started to writhe in his lap before Darius placed a hand on her stomach to keep her still. That only added to the pressure, as the bulge from his cock struck against the weight of his palm.

"Uh uh," he scolded. "We're staying like this."

"For how long?" she complained.

"As long as I want us to."

That wouldn't do for her, and he knew it. She refused to be obedient, flexing her muscles around him to get some of the pulsations she required.

"*God*," he moaned helplessly into her shoulder. "You truly are desperate." He bit into her shoulder, leaving a mark. "Couldn't help yourself even for a moment."

He knew he'd caught her when her rebellious nature sought both to refute his claim as well as defy his wishes. The only move left was to get off of him entirely, but she wouldn't do that. Instead, she'd prove the mutuality of their passion.

"Are you saying you're any better?" she taunted, coaxing him to action with another powerful flex.

There was a rumble deep in the back of his throat. "I think you already know what you do to me."

"Why don't you show me?" Laila said, once more making circular motions with her hips and drawing an anguished sound from him. "Show me what I do to you."

Darius could no longer keep himself from pushing up into her. "Laila—"

That was all the provocation she needed to start bouncing in his lap, their hips rocking on each other in a seesawing motion. She clenched around him until he was finally spent, wilting beneath her with a shudder.

"You're going to murder me one day."

Laila regarded him with a smirk.

Darius caught a glance at her expression and resisted rolling his eyes. "Knew I shouldn't have said that."

Her smirk intensified as she swivelled to pull him into a kiss. "I love you." Her thumb eased over his cheek. "I never thought I could feel this way. This... hopeful and excited about our future. I really think you and I could make something good here. Something great."

"We can," he said, hands on her thighs. "We can do anything we want."

How far they'd come from her first refusal in the garden. Now she bore his carcanet with pride, dutiful to his kingdom and his heart.

THANK YOU FOR READING!
WHAT'S NEXT?

A great big thank you for reaching the end of my novel!

Please do remember to leave a review on your website of choice if you'd like to support me further. Every little helps, even just a rating or sentence.

Feel free to drop me a line at contact@aninkwellofnectar.com if you'd like to chat with me—I love hearing from readers!

Go to www.aninkwellofnectar.com for exclusive content, snippets, and release updates for all future novels.

I can also be found on Instagram, Facebook, Tiktok and Tumblr under **@aninkwellofnectar.**

ACKNOWLEDGEMENTS

This was a book that very nearly didn't happen, due to a number of factors, so I'd like to take a moment to thank the writing community at large for rallying around me during a difficult time in my life. Thank you especially to my ko-fi members: Lau, Tyler, Nix, Han, Valmont, DC and Mia whose financial contributions go a long way towards helping me stay afloat.

I also want to give a thank you to those who beta-read the book: Valmont (again), Lau (again), Tyler (again), Timi, and Rose. Your feedback was immensely encouraging and what kept me from giving up on this series entirely.

Thank you once again to Eeva Nikunen for lending your incomparable artistic skill to this series. When the Stars Alight would not have made it nearly as far without you and I cannot sing your praises enough to all who become enamoured with your work on these covers. My condolences to the loss of your studio assistant, Willow, whose mischievous pencil-stealing ways I will dearly miss seeing on Instagram.

Thank you to Molly Rookwood for your enduring enthusiasm to work with me on this series. As an author, it means a lot to me to have an editor on board who loves and cherishes this story and these characters, and to work with someone who respects my vision. Knowing how committed you are to collaborating with me on this really helped to lift my spirits last year and I'm looking forward to finishing off this narrative with you.

Finally, thank you to the readers who have decided to return for the second instalment of this series. It means a lot to me to have your loyalty and to know there are people out there who are eager to read more about Laila, Darius, and their journey together as characters. You're the ones extending this series' lifespan and know that I cherish every kind word, message, fanwork, and am keeping an increasingly large folder of screenshots to turn back to when my moods are low.

ABOUT THE AUTHOR

Camilla Andrew lives in a leafy English town that sounds remarkably like a fairytale setting with talking animals in suits. She spends her days writing, reading, drinking tea and working diligently at her (remote) office job. Her works also feature in Cloaked Press and midnight & indigo.

www.aninkwellofnectar.com

www.ingramcontent.com/pod-product-compliance
Lightning Source LLC
Chambersburg PA
CBHW050609170726
48283CB00001B/174